Cemetery Club

By
JG Faherty

JournalStone
San Francisco

JournalStone books may be ordered through booksellers or by contacting:

JournalStone
199 State Street
San Mateo, CA 94401
www.journalstone.com

The views expressed in this work are solely those of the authors and do not necessarily reflect the views of the publisher, and the publisher hereby disclaims any responsibility for them.

ISBN: 978-1-936564-23-1   (sc)
ISBN: 978-1-936564-24-8   (ebook)

Library of Congress Control Number: 2011943919

Printed in the United States of America
JournalStone rev. date: March 16, 2012

Cover Design: Denise Daniel
Cover Art: Philip Renne

Edited By: Elizabeth Reuter

Endorsements

CEMETERY CLUB is like a plastic pumpkin bucket filled to the top with all of your favorite candies. Loads of gory fun!" --Jeff Strand, author of PRESSURE and DWELLER.

"JG Faherty nails the whole small town horror concept with a King-like flair. I definitely identified with the main characters, both past and present. All in all, I thought it was excellent." - Michael McBride, author of PREDATORY INSTINCT and QUIET, KEEPS TO HIMSELF.

"With plenty of new twists on some old favorites, Faherty's latest novel provides readers with as much fun in a graveyard as the law will allow. Ancient legends, demonic shadow-creatures and ravenous zombies--what more could you ask for?" -Hank Schwaeble, Bram Stoker Award-winning author of DAMNABLE and DIABOLICAL.

"JG Faherty seizes his readers by the throat and drags them straight towards the grave with CEMETERY CLUB, a nail biter in the tradition of the best scare-'em-ups from the 80s. Faherty's strong characterizations and gripping suspense will leave readers hungry for more." --Gregory Lamberson, author of COSMIC FORCES and THE FRENZY WAY.

"I've known JG Faherty since he was an up-and-comer. Now he's arrived. Start reading him now - as in TODAY - so you won't have to play catch-up later." - F. Paul Wilson, author of the bestselling Repairman Jack series.

Check out these titles from JournalStone:

That Which Should Not Be
Brett J. Talley

The Traiteur's Ring
Jeffrey Wilson

Ghosts of Coronado Bay
JG Faherty

Jokers Club
Gregory Bastianelli

Women Scorned
Angela Alsaleem

Shaman's Blood
Anne C. Petty

The Pentacle Pendant
Stephen M. DeBock

Pazuzu's Girl
Rachel Coles

Available through your local and online bookseller or at
www.journalstone.com

Acknowledgements

I want to thank the people who are most important in my life: my wife Andrea, my parents, and my good friends, all of whom have supported me, knowingly it or not, during the writing of this book and as a writer in general. They might not like what being a writer means – the hours spent alone on the computer, the travel, etc. – but they are proud of what I do and they're supportive in the endeavor.

Special thanks as well to the people who made this book possible: Chris Payne and the staff at JournalStone, Michael McBride, F. Paul Wilson, Hank Schwaeble, Jeff Strand, Gregory Lamberson, Shaun Jeffrey, and Stephen Owen. Also thanks to Philip Renne for the great cover art.

Finally, I want to acknowledge the individuals that have suffered in understaffed, poorly-run, and downright dangerous mental institutions across the country. One of these is found in my hometown.

The terrible medical experiments carried out there in the early 1900s are what gave me the inspiration for this story.

I've spent countless hours roaming the abandoned grounds and exploring the crumbling buildings, both alone and with family/friends. I've read through patient files that described atrocities performed before and after a patient's institutionalization, set in dark rooms that once served as morgues, shock therapy stations and laboratories. I've examined medical and dental x-rays and seen the rooms where children were packed like sardines, patients were washed with hoses, and misunderstood people spent years alone, waiting for visitors who never came.

How could places like that *not* be haunted?

To urban explorers like me, spending an afternoon in a desolate, run-down hospital, castle or house will always be more invigorating than watching a ballgame on TV.

Thank you for reading.
JG Faherty, March, 2012

Check out these titles from JournalStone:

JournalStone's 2011 Warped Words: 90 Minutes to Live
Joel Kirkpatrick

JournalStone's 2010 Warped Words: For Twisted Minds
Christopher C. Payne

Duncan's Diary, Birth of a Serial Killer
Christopher C. Payne

The Donors
Jeffrey Wilson

The Void
Brett J. Talley

The Demon of Renaissance Drive
Elizabeth Reuter

Reign of the Nightmare Prince
Mike Phillips

Duncan's Diary, Birth of a Serial Killer
Christopher C. Payne

Available through your local and online bookseller or at
www.journalstone.com

Section I
Beginnings

Village of Rocky Pointe, 1779

"Sinners!"

The word rode through Martha's Tavern on a gust of warm, damp summer air that made candle flames dance and sent more than one man's hat spinning to the floor. The muggy breeze faded away as the door closed behind Nathaniel Randolph. Tall and thin, with an Adam's apple so large it looked like he'd swallowed a plum, Randolph glanced around the room, his perpetually wild eyes wide and full of righteous fury.

"Sinners!" he shouted again, lifting one hand to wave the aged Bible he habitually carried. "Ye shall all burn in Hell for your transgressions!"

"Shut your hole, Randolph," one of the men at the bar called out. His companions raised their mugs and laughed.

"Aye. Go preach someplace else and leave hard-working folk alone, will ye?" called out another.

One of Martha's ladies approached Nathaniel, her hair mussed from providing pleasure to trappers and tradesmen alike the past several hours. She shook her stained skirt and gave the town's self-appointed reverend a wink. "Say now, preacher man, if its sin you be worried about, allow me to demonstrate how the pleasures of my flesh might just be worth spending eternity with the Devil."

"Blasphemer!" Randolph held his Bible out like a shield.

More laughter rose from the bar and Martha herself let loose one of her braying honks.

"Suit yourself," the whore said. As she turned and walked away, she lifted the back of her dress and gave Randolph a quick flash of her pale buttocks.

Randolph scowled and thumped his hand on his Good Book. "Listen to me! Repent before it is too late!"

When no one paid any mind to him, he thrust his well-worn Bible into his pants pocket and left the pub, mumbling under his breath about the folly of sinners.

"Good riddance, ye arsehole!" someone shouted at his back.

Outside the building, Nathaniel took a moment to compose himself, and then went behind a nearby bush where he'd stored a large sack and an oil lantern before entering the tavern.

They had their chance and they chose the path of the Devil. So be it.

He opened the sack and removed an iron bar, which he slipped through the handles of the pub's doors. Then he took out two large jars of rum and splashed their contents liberally on each of the four walls. When he was finished, Nathaniel held up the lantern.

"Forgive me Lord, but what I do, I do for you."

Wicked flames burst into life as he broke the lantern against the rum-soaked wood.

And in doing so, he sealed the town's fate.

* * *

Rocky Point, NY, 1847

Flickering shadows danced against the trees as the residents of Rocky Point gathered outside the clinic. Nearly half the town stood ready, their torches lighting up the clearing until it seemed almost as bright as day.

Reverend Hollister Randolph, the only son of the long-deceased Nathanial Randolph, placed a frail hand on Percival Boyd's arm. "Is there no other way, Mayor?"

Boyd shook his head, his silver hair turned bronze by the flames. "I'm sorry. We cannot abide lepers near our town. We gave Doctor Charles fair warning; he chose to continue his misbegotten work. Now we have to think of ourselves."

Turning away from the elderly minister, Boyd raised his hand. "It is time! Burn the sickness from our town!"

At his words the angry mob cheered and stormed forward. Men and women cast burning torches through windows and onto the roof of Effram Charles' Medical Clinic. Within minutes the clinic was ablaze on all sides. Screams echoed from inside the building, growing louder as the fire spread from room to room and the roof timbers collapsed.

Two hours later, nothing remained of the clinic but smoking stone, burnt wood and charred flesh.

The following day, the men of Rocky Point began digging a burial pit.

* * *

Rocky Point, NY, 1922

Dr. Grover Lillian hurried through the maze of tunnels hidden beneath the buildings of Wood Hill Sanitarium, followed closely by Hilary White. The property covered more than forty acres and the tunnels - most used for heat and water pipe access, others built so people could move comfortably between buildings during the frigid New York winters - would have stretched for more than two miles if laid end to end.

"Hurry," Lillian urged his assistant, as he turned down a side passage that led to the burial area. "We can't let them find out."

White said nothing, focusing all her energy on keeping pace with the doctor while straining to retain her grip on the box of papers she carried. Lillian held a similar box, the last of the files pertaining to his small pox vaccine trials.

Trials. Lillian turned the word over in his mind as he jogged along the hard-packed dirt. It carried a foul taste and he wished he could just spit it out.

The very name implies a lack of perfection. And yet those short-sighted administrators refused to understand, bowed to public pressure. What did they expect? It's a new drug; there were bound to be deaths.

His last conversation with the sanitarium's Chief Administrator still echoed in his head.

"*Thirty-seven children?*" Wirth's voice had reeked of false outrage. "*That's more than half your volunteers! We can't allow this to go any further.*"

Lillian clenched his jaw as he relived being made the scapegoat for the medical system's inherent problems.

Volunteers. Hah! Another way for Wirth and his cronies to cover their involvement. Fifty children, ages twelve to eighteen, all of them suffering from serious mental incapacities. They couldn't volunteer for a walk in the park, let alone a scientific experiment. Wirth had given him the fifty files to begin with; all minors who had no families to miss them should anything go wrong.

Nothing would have gone wrong either, if it wasn't for that damn nurse! She'd been loitering in an off-limits stairwell, playing kissy-face with one of the orderlies, when they'd spotted Lillian carrying a body into the sub-basement for disposal. Instead of reporting it to Wirth, the tramp had suddenly found her morals and gone to the police.

And now...

Now they had only minutes to hide his research away before the police raided the building.

Lillian turned another corner and stopped so fast Hilary ran into him and dropped her box, spilling papers onto the dusty floor. She started to apologize but Lillian hushed her.

Up ahead, lights reflected off the cement walls, lights that bobbed and moved.

Someone had found the burial pit.

Pushing Hilary to the side, Lillian turned and started back the way they'd come.

More lights were heading towards them from that direction as well.

It didn't take him long to consider his options. Being caught with the files and the bodies would be an automatic death sentence.

Why give them the satisfaction?

He drew his pistol and shot Hillary White in the back of the head.

Hot metal burned his tongue as he placed the barrel in his mouth.

What a waste. All because people cared what happened to a bunch of drooling idiots. No wonder science never advances.

He pulled the trigger.

* * *

Rocky Point, NY, 20 years ago

"It has to be me," Todd Randolph said, clutching the bag to his skinny chest as the rain continued to drench the cemetery. Muddy streams cascaded alongside the blacktopped paths and cut miniature canyons between graves "I started it. I have to finish it."

Cory Miles shook his head. "We can do it together. We *should* do it together. All of us. The Cemetery Club."

John Boyd and Marisol Flores voiced their agreement. The four of them were huddled under the overhang of a mausoleum that was so old the date on the plaque couldn't even be read through the crust of dirt and corrosion. The door stood open, exposing cobweb-covered cement casket boxes to the dim light of the stormy afternoon. In the center of the floor, a ragged hole several feet wide showed black against the gray cement. A fetid odor rose up from the darkness, death, mold and wet soil all entwined into a palpable stench that seemed bent on forcing their stomachs to turn somersaults.

"No. I'm the only one who can stop it." Todd lowered himself into the pit, his rail-thin body disappearing from view almost immediately.

"What do we do?" Marisol asked. Her dark brown hair hung in long, dripping strands. Her bra was visible beneath the pink Duran Duran t-shirt that clung to the curves she'd started developing over the summer.

Cory knew that image of her would stay with him the rest of his life; just as he knew he was more in love with her now than he'd ever been. "I don't know." He took a step towards the hole and stopped.

John frowned. "We can't let him go down there by himself. The aliens..."

Cory shook his head, sending water droplets cascading in all directions. "John, they're not aliens. There's no such thing..."

"Fine. Aliens, demons, it doesn't matter. They're all fucking impossible. But we can't let Todd...not alone." I think it's Todd...not alone

"I know. But..."

"But what?"

"Maybe it's better if we split up. That way if anything...happens, there's still two of us to try something else."

"Like what?" said John. "Go to the police? They'll think we're crazy."

"Well, we can't just stand here. We--"

A terrible scream rose up from the hole, the high-pitched wail reverberating off the stone walls until it sounded like a thousand people were crying out in pain. As abruptly as it started, the cry of distress cut off, leaving nothing but a mental echo in everyone's head.

"Shit! We have to help him." John glanced from Marisol to Cory. Even in the near-dark, the pleading look in John's eyes was too powerful for Cory to ignore.

"Let's go." Cory walked to the hole and stepped into the black depths, which seemed to swallow his legs as they vanished into the darkness.

When Cory's head dipped below the edge it was as if someone had turned off all the lights in a room. He held out his hands to either side for balance and cold, damp earth met his palms. Rocks and old tree roots made the footing tricky, forcing him to walk with a shuffle-step motion so he wouldn't trip. Scuffling sounds behind him told him his two friends were doing the same thing.

"Cory? Can you see anything?"

Marisol's voice, a few feet back. Her words sounded strangely flat, as if the hard-packed dirt of the tunnel had drained all the life from them.

"No. Just keep walking slow."

Cory followed his own advice, advancing one deliberate step at a time as the tunnel gradually sloped downward at a gentle angle. The pounding of his heart grew worse, until it felt like it was inside his head instead of his chest. He found himself breathing in rapid, shallow bursts, and he tried to force his lungs to draw in slow, deep breaths. The fear built inside him until it was an almost physical being, a creature lodged in his guts, pressing against his stomach and bladder. Never in his life had he felt so scared, not even back in June when he'd ridden the Category Six roller coaster at the amusement park.

Something brushed against his foot and he stopped, praying it wasn't a hand - or a tentacle - ready to pull him down to Hell. Behind him, Marisol let out a short scream.

"It was a rat." John's voice, sounding close and far away at the same time, thanks to the impenetrable darkness that clouded all sense of distance.

Without warning, bright light exploded from further down the tunnel, so intense it blinded him as effectively as the darkness had. At the same time a terrible BANG echoed in his ears. Cory had time to yell "M80!" and then the ground started to shake and dance all around them.

"What's happening?" Marisol shouted, as the rumbling in the earth grew stronger.

"I don't know!" Dirt and stone cascaded down on them. "Hang on to something!" Cory dug his fingers into the tunnel wall, groping for a root or anything solid. Something wrapped around him and he let out a terrified shout until he realized it was only Marisol, clutching at him from behind. He felt her breasts pressing against his back and her hair falling on his neck like a wet mop.

The earth shifted again and Cory fell to his knees. Marisol landed on top of him and another body fell across them. He hoped it was John but his mind provided a different picture: a rotting corpse, its eyes glowing with putrid light, its mouth ready to sink decayed brown teeth into soft human flesh.

Cory opened his mouth to scream, and then the ceiling collapsed on them in a rain of dirt and stone.

Something hard struck his head and the world disappeared.

Section II

Returns and Regrets

Chapter 1

Rocky Point, present day

Todd Randolph looked at the door to his mother's house and sighed. The weight of the suitcase hanging from his bony hand was nothing compared the emotional baggage he carried inside him, a burden he knew he'd never be free of.

Even though he'd never been inside the home - there'd been a fire in the old place not long after his hospitalization and his parents had moved instead of rebuilding - there was a strong sense of familiarity to the modest structure, thanks to the pictures his mother had sent him over the years. The old house had sat behind the Rocky Point Episcopalian Church, overlooking the Gates of Heaven Cemetery like a sentinel straddling the line between life and death. Todd got the same feeling looking at the current house, as it occupied one of the streets that divided the upper middle class neighborhoods to the east and the problem areas to the west.

During the twenty years he'd been incarcerated in Wood Hill Sanitarium, he'd kept up with the events at home through his mother's sporadic letters. A new appliance for the kitchen. New wallpaper for their bedroom. Always with pictures, until she'd written of his father's passing four years ago. In that letter she'd mentioned how the few remaining friends and relatives had gathered in the living room and Uncle Ron had spilled coffee on the rug.

For some reason the mental image of that spot had occupied a great deal of Todd's thoughts, even after Uncle Ron had joined Father in the great beyond, leaving only a set of cousins on the West Coast as Todd's last living relatives.

Except for Mother of course. And according to the doctors she didn't have long to go either. Her emphysema required her to use an oxygen tank at all times and she spent a good portion of her day lying in bed because too much walking robbed her of her ability to breathe. Luckily, Father's insurance plan had been a good one, which paid for a private care nurse to come out each day and help Mother with her daily living tasks such as bathing, getting dressed and making breakfast and lunch. Todd's only contributions as the newest member of the household would be to clean, make dinner and do the shopping.

Seeing as how he was terminally unemployable, he figured he could handle those tasks. And it would leave him plenty of time to continue his research.

In a way, it wouldn't be all that different from his prolonged stay at the sanitarium, the only difference being he could actually take a crap in private.

He wondered what would happen to all the other patients of Wood Hill, especially the ones not eligible for release into the real world. The closing of the area's largest mental health facility was bound to have serious repercussions on the surrounding towns; ever since he'd found out about his impending release, he'd thanked the heavens the doctors hadn't decided to place him in one of the many group homes that would no doubt be springing up in Rocky Point.

A curtain moved in one of the front windows, a dark face peering out for just a moment before the gauzy material fell back in place. That would be Mrs. Clinton, the home health aide. She'd come to Wood Hill the previous day to introduce herself and give Todd a key.

She knows I'm here. Might as well go inside. He realized he'd been unconsciously putting off seeing his mother.

Your first face-to-face with her in almost seven years. Of course there's bound to be trepidation. The best thing to do is just get it over with and start down the road to renewing your relationship with her. Before it's too late. Doctor Sloan's advice, delivered in their last session.

He's right. Time to start my new life.

With a heavy sigh, Todd started up the steps.

* * *

Doctor Eli Sloan stared out the window of his office and wondered at the irony of it all. Past the perfectly-manicured back lawn of Wood Hill

Sanitarium lay the Gates of Heaven cemetery, the largest and oldest cemetery in Rocky Point. A strip of woods separated the sanitarium's property from the back of the graveyard, the section where the oldest graves - some dating back well over a hundred years - looked down a rolling hill at their younger neighbors.

All they had to do was spend a little money. The cemetery probably would have cut them a deal. But no. Instead, they'd buried their dead in secret and covered up the whole mess just like the administration before them.

The news was all over the papers. It was the reason the sanitarium was closing. **Gruesome discovery beneath insane asylum!**

Over a hundred bodies buried in the ground under one of the old hospital buildings, one that hadn't been used since the seventies. Patients without relatives or friends.

They should have cremated them. Then there'd have been no evidence.

Instead, the whole mess had been uncovered by two teenagers who'd snuck into the building and down into the basement with a digital camcorder, hoping to film a scene for a home-made horror movie they were making.

They'd gotten all the horror they imagined, and much more.

Sloan was fairly sure he couldn't be tied to the scandal, even though a good portion of the patients had been part of his special treatment group. He'd kept all his notes on the clinical trials at his home rather than in the office, just in case the sanitarium ever got audited. Running human trials without permission was a federal offense; he'd taken great care to make sure the nurses at the sanitarium never knew he'd been injecting certain patients with his various formulas for two decades. Most of his secret test subjects had responded surprisingly well.

Only a small percentage had suffered any side effects.

But those side effects had been pretty bad: convulsions, agonizing joint pain and death from seizure were the three most common. One out of twenty had responded adversely to the last version of the medication. Not nearly as bad as his first trial, twenty years earlier, but still bad enough that he knew he'd never get federal approval for human trials. So as far as anyone at the clinic knew his testing was still being done on rats and mice, which unfortunately, were showing similar side effect ratios.

The problem was rats and mice weren't humans. It was conceivable he could come up with a formula that didn't work in rodents but meshed well with human physiologies. Certainly the opposite was true when it came to clinical trials. And when you worked with compounds intended to affect psychological function rather than a disease state, well, the only true test was how the drug worked in people.

His thoughts returned to the irony of the situation. He'd caused more than sixty deaths since coming to Wood Hill but no one suspected his patients – many of whom suffered physical as well as mental ailments - had died from anything but natural causes. And yet he was still losing his job, because the state was shutting down the facility for illegal burial practices.

At least I can honestly say I had no idea what they were doing with the bodies after I signed the death certificates. He'd been as shocked as anyone when the news broke. He's assumed the corpses ended up in cheap wooden caskets at the ass end of the cemetery, a step up from a Potter's Field burial.

Assholes.

Sloan turned away from the window and finished packing his desk. He'd signed the release for his last patient yesterday, Todd Randolph. Now there was a true success story, one he could write about someday: *How I cured Rocky Point's Reverend of Death.*

The boy had come in at the age of sixteen, only a month after Sloan's near catastrophe with his first trial of his drug. Thirteen patients, thirteen dead. If he hadn't thought quick and set the wing on fire, making sure all the bodies were in one of the group therapy rooms, he'd have spent the last twenty years locked away, just like Todd Randolph.

Instead, he'd ended up as the psychiatrist in charge of one of the most sensational criminals in the town's history. The local preacher's son, accused of murdering dozens of people, found in his secret lair surrounded by the corpses of his victims and clutching a Bible, Holy water and a cross all stolen from his father's church.

In their first session together, Todd had admitted his guilt, claiming he'd "raised a demon" and the demon had killed everyone.

It had taken Sloan fourteen years to rid the Randolph boy of his delusions and another six to convince the state he was no danger to society. That decision had only come about when the closing of the sanitarium seemed imminent, leading Sloan to believe they'd finally agreed to release Todd because it was easier than relocating him to a new facility.

Sloan was confident Randolph would live out the rest of his life in relative normalcy. All his issues had stemmed from his relationship with his over-bearing, ultra-conservative religious father. Now that the dad was dead, there was nothing for the adult son to rebel against.

That would be a good theme for the book, he thought, as he closed his office door and headed for the exit. *Modern psychiatry, wiping away the sins of the past.*

* * *

Todd Randolph walked past the front desk of the Rocky Point Library, pretending he didn't notice the cold stares cast in his direction by the two old women behind the counter. Their animosity didn't surprise him. He'd received the same glares everywhere in town, from the post office to supermarket, and even at the Chinese takeout place. He'd only been home three days but he was already Number One on everyone's most-hated list.

Twenty years and no one's forgotten. Of course, he hadn't expected they would. People tended to remember mass murderers.

Let them stare. I have work to do.

Locating an unoccupied cubicle with a PC, he sat down and initiated his first Google search of the day.

"demons+underground"

A few minutes later, the feeling of being watched and judged went away as the library's patrons returned to their own tasks.

But Todd's guilt and self-loathing remained as strong as ever.

* * *

Pete Webster scooped another shovelful of dirt and tossed it into the wheelbarrow. The hot, muggy June day had evolved into an even hotter, muggier June evening. He felt like he'd sweated out a gallon of water from all the shoveling and planting he'd been doing.

What the hell does the cemetery need more plants for? he thought, pausing to wipe his arm across his forehead. The dirt and grime on his forearm were like sandpaper across his face. *Damn place has more bushes than hippie porn.*

Of course, these bushes were different. They were being planted around an old mausoleum in an effort to hide the cracked stone exterior. Someone in management had decided the whole damn cemetery needed sprucing up and it was a lot cheaper to have the groundskeepers plant flowers and shrubs than to actually fix the physical structures.

Next to him, Frank Adams, his shift partner for the past five years, leaned his shovel against the mausoleum and took his gloves off. "Christ, it's fuckin' hot as an oven. Why'd they pick summer to do this shit?"

Pete gave a sarcastic laugh that caused drops of sweat to fly off his face. "'Cause their brains are in their asses. But just think how good the beer'll taste later."

"Fuck later, I need something right now, before I pass out."

"There's still a couple of Cokes left," Pete said.

"Good. You want one?"

"Naw, I'm saving mine for when we're done."

"Suit yourself." Frank walked over to the cooler that sat next to the old green pickup truck and opened a can of soda.

Pete leaned on his shovel and tried to catch his breath, no easy task when there seemed to be as much moisture in the air as on his skin. As he inhaled, he caught a whiff of something nasty, a stink that reminded him of the beer bottles they'd sometimes find after kids partied in the cemetery. Every now and then a mouse would crawl inside of one and drown in the leftover beer, producing a sickly-sweet rotten smell.

Turning around, Pete sniffed at the air, trying to determine where the odor came from. Something that strong had to be bigger than a mouse. If there was a dead animal in the cemetery they'd have to get rid of it before morning. People preferred to visit graves without actually being reminded what death looked and smelled like.

The odor seemed strongest near the mausoleum. Pete grabbed his shovel and headed for the back of the building, intent on finding the woodchuck or cat that was stinking up the place. As he rounded the corner, a strange feeling enveloped him, icy fingers tickling his back while at the same time a giant centipede ran circles in his stomach. The last time he'd felt something similar was when the ice started crackling beneath him as he crossed Jensen Pond on a snowy winter afternoon. He'd been terrified the ice would give way and send him to his death in the frigid waters.

A dark figure rose up from behind a nearby headstone and Pete jumped. His first thought was that a child was playing a joke on him.

Then he saw the face.

Pete opened his mouth to scream but before any sounds came out, the *thing* shot through the air, its stubby arms outstretched as it raced towards him like a black cat. It latched onto his face with icy-cold hands. Pete tried to grab it but his fingers passed right through as if he was trying to catch smoke. It pressed itself against his flesh and forced its head into his mouth. He fell to the ground, clutching at his neck as it clawed its way down his throat.

Frank Adams put down his soda and headed back to the mausoleum. He'd seen Pete go around to the other side of the old building. "Hey, Pete? Whatcha doin'?"

When there was no answer, he walked around the corner. As he did, he noticed a rotten meat smell. He was about to call for Pete again when a flash of movement caught his eye. There was no time to raise his arms as he realized it was a shovel coming at his head. Cold metal struck him across his cheek and temple and his whole world turned into a jumbled kaleidoscope of images as he stumbled backwards. It took a moment for the pain to register, but when it did, it was like someone had lit his face on fire and then put it out by dropping cement blocks on it.

Frank staggered like a drunken man attempting a waltz and then tripped over one of the bushes waiting for planting. His vision tripled and he fought to focus as someone came into view.

The man's arms rose up, the shovel silhouetted against the afternoon sky for a moment before it started its downward arc. In that brief instant Frank's heart skipped a beat. He recognized his attacker.

The shovel came down, flattening Frank's nose and knocking out all his front teeth. Pain exploded in his face, a thousand times worse than the first blow. He tried to shout but only a raspy, choking cough came out, accompanied by a mouthful of blood and teeth. More blood streamed down from his ruined nose, mixing with the tears flowing from his eyes.

He never saw the shovel blade come down the third time but he felt its edge bite into his neck, cutting through skin and muscle and gristle until it scraped against bone.

The last thing he saw was a heavy work-boot hovering in the air over his ruined face.

Pete Webster watched Frank's head roll away, the stump of the man's fat neck still dribbling blood. He stared at his friend's corpse for a moment, his head tilted as if listening to a distant sound. Then he went to the truck and retrieved the heavy pickaxe, which he used to break the lock on the mausoleum door. Inside, he raised the pick and attacked an irregularly shaped patch of cement that was a different color than the rest of the floor. It took a dozen blows before a large section collapsed, exposing a night-black hole in the earth.

Pete tossed the pick aside and went back for Frank's body. He dragged it into the crypt and tore into it with his teeth, ripping mouthfuls of flesh and swallowing them whole. Only after he'd sated his dark hunger did he drop the remains of the corpse into the dark depths of the pit. Then he closed the door, wedged the pick against it and climbed into the hole.

Frank's head lay undisturbed for less than a minute before a crow landed near it. The bird approached carefully, ready to take flight at the first sign of movement. When the head remained still, the crow jumped onto Frank's face and drove its beak into a soft, juicy eye.

* * *

A hundred yards away, lying in the shade of a large elm tree, John Boyd shivered, whimpering as he chugged Old Granddad straight from the bottle. Although he'd witnessed Pete Webster attack Frank Adams with the shovel and then disappear into the old mausoleum, it wasn't the murder that had him terrified.

It was what he'd seen *before* Pete attacked Frank.

The thing that had entered Pete's body.

One of them. It was one of them!

Eyes squeezed shut, John took another mouthful, hoping the rotgut whiskey would erase his memories of the past ten minutes. Hoping it had only been a hallucination. It was possible. More than once since climbing off the sobriety wagon, he'd seen things that weren't really there.

But it had seemed so real! The grayish-black body, shorter than a man, more like a child's shadow against a wall. The egg-shaped head, with the round, black mouth that was like a hole in the fabric of reality.

And the eyes - ovals of red fire set at angles in the flat face, with elliptical black pupils in their centers.

It couldn't be one of them. We killed them all. Todd *killed them all.*

Didn't he?

In that instant John knew he had to get away before the grays got him too. He stood up, chugged the last few inches of bourbon and staggered down the path that led to the main gate on Hickory Street. From there it was only a few blocks to the shelter he'd been staying at lately.

"Not again, not again, not again," he mumbled as he stumbled down the cracked, broken sidewalks lining both sides of the once-prosperous street. "The Grays are back. The Grays are back."

Inside the shelter he let his body fall onto the first unoccupied bunk he found. By the time his face hit the stained pillow, his mind had already gone blank.

The next morning, the events of the cemetery were no more than a dim nightmare, no worse than any of the others he'd suffered for the past five years.

Chapter 2

Todd Randolph registered the howls of multiple police sirens just as the first squad car skidded around the corner at the end of the street. He paused in the act of getting the newspaper out of the mailbox to watch, curious as to what could be the cause of such a commotion at just after eight in the morning.

He was still standing by the sidewalk, paper in hand, when the police cars stopped in front of his house and a loud voice ordered him to lay on the ground with his hands behind his head.

"What?" Todd looked at the officers approaching him, their guns drawn, angry expressions on their faces.

"Get down, now!" one of them shouted.

"Me? What's going on?"

Something hard struck him between the shoulder and neck, driving him to his knees. Through the colored lights swirling in his vision, he saw a burly man with a mustache raise his baton for another blow.

Todd ducked as the baton came down and the hard plastic caught him across the back instead of on the head. He cried out and fell to the ground, the sting of stones and cement grit against his face, barely noticeable against the pounding agony in his neck and shoulders.

Someone screamed - *Mother? Is she watching this?* - but the words were lost to Todd as a foot pressed against the side of his head, covering one ear and crushing the other one into the concrete. For a moment he thought the cop might be getting ready to snap his neck. Then someone yanked his arms roughly behind his back and he felt something cut painfully into his skin, pressing his wrists together.

The foot disappeared and hands lifted him up, held him there as the world swam around and his knees buckled. He tried to speak but only succeeded in moaning. Sharp fragmented grains covered his tongue and lips. He spat some of it out. Someone grabbed his neck and shook his head, setting off new fireworks in his brain. This time there were answering flares in his stomach as the dizziness brought on a bout of nausea.

"Watch where you spit fuckface," a voice said near his ear. Todd opened his mouth again to defend himself. Before he could say anything, someone slapped the back of his head and his teeth closed against his tongue.

Immediately his mouth filled with the metallic tang of blood but he stopped himself from spitting it out, wary of the officer's warning. Instead, he let it dribble over his swelling lips.

A large black and white shape appeared in front of him and he realized the cops were leading him to a police car. He caught a glimpse of himself in a window before his escort opened the door for him. Smudges of dust and dirt stained his face, gunpowder dark against his pale skin. Thick, bloody strands of drool hung from his open mouth, lending him the appearance of a rabid dog.

It came to him then that they were arresting him and he had no idea why. He started to ask and someone - *probably the same piece of shit who slapped me* - grabbed his neck and shoved him down and forward towards the open back door of the cruiser.

"Better duck dipshit," someone said with a laugh.

Then his forehead struck the metal frame and the world went dark.

The first thing Todd noticed when he woke was the smell. A combination of stale body odor, piss and industrial cleaner, topped off with a healthy dose of alcohol and a hint of marijuana. The last two he remembered from high school. The other odors were just as familiar though, because they'd been staples at Wood Hill. Since the sanitarium was no longer in operation, there was only one place he could be.

Jail.

Opening his eyes, Todd found he'd guessed correctly. Someone had been kind enough to dump his body right next to the source of the piss odors: a lidless toilet with yellow and brown stains all over it. Apparently moving him another two feet and placing him on the cell's cot had been too much effort.

Turning his head produced spasms of pain in his neck and back, which in turn brought back the memory of being beaten in front of his house like a derelict on COPS. In front of his own mother for Christ's sake.

Mother!

Todd looked for his watch but it was gone; either stolen, lying broken in the street or confiscated. He had no idea how long he'd been unconscious but he knew his mother would be worried sick, no matter how long it had been. He had to let her know he was all right.

His muscles protested mightily as he pushed himself into a sitting position. The room tilted and his vision doubled for a sickening moment before everything returned to normal. With a groan, he hauled his aching body up to the cot. After several deep breaths and another rest, he was able to stand up.

The short walk to the cell's bars was an exercise in torture, each step sending jolts of pain up his back, into his head and then down again. He let the cold steel of the bars sooth his bruised forehead while he gathered the strength to speak.

"Hey." The word came out in a raspy whisper. Todd ran his tongue around the inside of his mouth, trying to work up some saliva to swallow. The resulting sting made him hiss as he sucked in air through clenched teeth. He tried again, this time being careful not to rub the bitten part against the roof of his mouth. It took several minutes before he was able to swallow enough moisture to lubricate his throat properly.

"Hey!" This time his shout was louder and it woke up a malicious part of his brain that started hammering the inside of his head. "Hey, I need to make a phone call."

Down the row of cells, another prisoner answered him. "It's lunchtime asshole. Ain't nobody gonna come down here for another hour."

Lunchtime? Assuming that meant noon, he'd been unconscious for almost four hours. Judging by the crusted blood and dirt on his face and hands, no one had bothered to give him any medical attention during all that time.

What if I'd had a concussion? Or a broken neck? Those fucking cops with their night sticks...

Wait a minute. I still don't know why they arrested me in the first place. If there was a mistake, a mix-up, Ma would have me out by now. That means...they think I did something. And for them to think I did it...

Fear rushed through Todd's body, momentarily washing away his pain on a wave of adrenaline.

Oh God, no. Don't tell me it's happening again.

Todd stumbled backwards until his legs hit the bunk and then he half-sat, half-fell onto the thin, hard mattress.

"What am I going to do?"

"Wake up, sleeping beauty." A series of metallic bangs accompanied the loud voice.

Todd opened his eyes. A scowling guard stood outside the cell.

"I need to make a phone call," he said to the burly officer.

"Well, la-de-da for you. You're lucky we don't throw you in the chair right now you fuckin' sicko."

"Whatever you think I did, I didn't do it." Todd shook his head. "There's been a mistake."

The guard glared at him. "Only mistake was ever lettin' you out in the first place. You shoulda been in Sing Sing or Rikers from day one, 'stead of takin' it easy in the nuthouse."

Todd didn't argue; he barely had enough strength to hold his head up. "I still have the right to a phone call."

His eyes narrowed with anger, the guard reluctantly agreed. "Yeah. All you assholes got rights. Turn around and back up to the bars, hands behind you. You ain't leavin' that cell without cuffs on."

Doing his best not to fall, Todd shuffled his way backwards across the cell until he felt the metal bars against his arms. The guard grabbed him by the wrists and snapped the handcuffs on, tightening them until Todd let out an involuntary moan.

"Step forward," the guard said.

Todd took three steps forward and waited while the guard opened the door.

"Turn around."

Todd did as he was told and then let the guard march him down the hall and up the stairs to a small interview room, complete with two-way mirror and stained table. The table had two chairs on one side and one on the other, facing the mirror. The only other object in the room was the wireless phone on the table.

Todd sat in the single chair and waited. The guard went to the other side of the table and picked up the phone. "What's the number?"

"I don't know. I want to call my lawyer. His number is in my wallet." Todd said a silent prayer of thanks that he'd kept up-to-date contact information for all the Cemetery Club members on a scrap of paper, in case he ever needed it.

"Oh, for the love of Christ." The guard took the phone and went to the door. "Don't even think about moving." Then he was gone.

Todd heard the sound of the door lock engaging. He didn't bother to move. Instead, he stared at his reflection in the mirror while he waited.

He'd watched himself grow older over the past twenty years but now, sitting under the flickering fluorescent light, his face swollen from his beating, he saw himself for the first time as a middle aged man. *Thirty-six isn't old,* he reminded himself, but that didn't change how he looked. The hair he'd once worn in shoulder-length defiance to an overbearing father was now cut military short and his hairline had receded almost to his ears. The sandy-brown color hid the scattering of gray well enough but time hadn't been kind to him and it showed in the bags under his eyes and the lines on his forehead.

I wonder how the others look. he thought. At that moment the guard returned with Todd's wallet in hand, interrupting his musings.

"What's the name?" he asked, after Todd told him where to find the scrap of paper.

"Cory Miles," Todd said, and then waited while the man dialed.

"Here." The guard placed the phone on Todd's shoulder and waited until Todd scrunched his neck, pinning the phone between ear and shoulder. Then he moved away, pretending the gap of four feet provided any privacy.

Someone picked up on the third ring. "Cory Miles, Attorney at Law. Can I help you?"

"Cory?" Todd didn't recognize the voice. But then who sounded the same at thirty-six as they did at sixteen?

"Yes, this is he. How can I help you?"

"Cory, it's... Todd Randolph. I need your help. I...think it's starting again."

* * *

Cory Miles stared at the phone.

It's starting again.

After a moment of stunned silence he'd taken Todd's information and promised to be there before six. Rocky Point was a two-hour car ride from Stamford and he'd need to make some phone calls before leaving, put cases on hold or pass them on to other attorneys.

It's starting again.

Three simple words but enough to assure Cory it was Todd Randolph on the other end, apparently freed from the sanitarium and now in jail for a murder he said he didn't commit.

Todd's innocence was something Cory didn't need convincing of. He was one of three people in the world who knew beyond a doubt Todd had never killed any of those people that summer, that he'd taken the blame out of guilt. A guilt they'd all shared. Cory felt a different kind of guilt now. Todd's call made him realize it had been almost three years since he'd thought of Rocky Point or the Cemetery Club.

The Cemetery Club. That's what we called ourselves. Todd, John Boyd, me, and Marisol.

Marisol Flores. Just thinking about her brought an image to life in his mind. Tall, dark-complexioned, with a skinny body just beginning to blossom into adulthood. Hair and eyes as dark as obsidian, courtesy of her half-Puerto Rican, half-West Indian heritage.

Cory wondered where Marisol was now, what she was doing. Did she still live in Rocky Point? He hadn't seen her since...since the events of their junior year. His family had moved right before senior year started, when his father got transferred to Connecticut. The only time he'd been back since was three years ago, for a golf outing at the Patriot Hills Golf Course, one town over from his old stomping grounds. Afterwards, he'd intended to drive through Rocky Point but at the last minute had changed his mind. He'd told himself he didn't have time, that there was nothing there he needed to see. But in his heart of hearts, that place where you have no choice but to be honest with yourself, he knew he'd steered away from the exit because just thinking about entering that small, innocuous section of suburbia sent a chill through his veins, a desire to be as far away from the Point's rocky bluffs and historical parks as possible.

And yet here I am, going back after all these years. To help a man who once was one of my best friends and who I never visited the entire twenty years he was in a mental institution, serving time so we wouldn't have to.

Cory opened his appointment book. A shiver ran up his spine that had nothing to do with the air conditioning.

It's starting again.

* * *

Marisol Flores.

Marisol stared at her signature for a moment before placing the log-in sheet back on the front desk.

Seeing her name - her original name - still felt strange. How long had it been since she'd signed her name like that? Seventeen years, her mind supplied the number. She'd married Jack the year after high school and finalized her divorce less than three weeks ago.

For the seventeen years in between, she'd been Mary Smith. Mary, because that's what Jack had always called her, as if giving her the nickname could erase the fact that she stood out among his lily-white, Protestant family like...well, like a black rose in a bouquet of lilies. And Smith because she'd married a Smith, a vanilla name for a vanilla family.

Seventeen years of being arm candy, window dressing and a conversation piece for her ex-swim captain, insurance-selling, deputy mayor of a husband. Getting the divorce had been more than just escaping a relationship that alternated between cold detachment and verbal abuse; it was as if she'd found herself again, become whole again, a real person rather than just someone's possession.

More than going back to school, earning her degree in forensic laboratory sciences and going to work at the ME's office, getting up the nerve to leave Jack had returned something to her she hadn't even realized she'd lost: her sense of self.

And no one's going to take it away again. It was her personal mantra.

Her ultimate goal had ultimately been to leave Jack and start her own life but she'd completed her education and worked for a year first because without Jack she'd never have been able to afford it.

Does that make me a user? she thought, as she walked down the gleaming white hallway of the County Medical Examiner's office. *Maybe it does. But Jack sure as hell can't complain, not after the way he used me for seventeen years.*

Although she hadn't realized it at the time, he'd been using her from the very beginning. First for sex and then for her very color. Marrying an obvious minority had allowed him to court the black and Hispanic votes when he'd run for deputy mayor at the tender age of twenty-five. He'd won that year, the same way he'd won every election since. Of course, there'd been no replacing Mayor Dawes, because he had something even a multi-racial campaign couldn't beat: ownership of the town's largest bank, along with nearly a quarter of the commercial properties on Main Street. No, Warner Dawes would remain Mayor until he died, retired or got exposed in a scandal not even the people in his pocket could overlook.

But then it would be Jack Smith's turn, as Jack had so often said.

He'll just have to do it without me.

Marisol pushed open the doors that led to the exam room. Frank Adams' torn-up body lay on Table One, a blood-stained green sheet concealing the corpse. She didn't need to lift thin covering to know how bad the damage was. She'd already taken blood, spinal fluid and stomach content samples.

Not that there was any doubt as to what had happened. Even a relative novice could see the multiple traumas to the head and face and the jagged marks where the shovel had cut through his neck.

But the absence of defensive wounds on the hands meant he'd either been caught by surprise or unable to defend himself properly. The presence of drugs, alcohol or poisons in his system would make a big difference in the case the DA was preparing against Todd Randolph, the difference between a drunken fight gone wrong and premeditated murder.

The previously prepared samples were already running in the other room; Marisol had returned to take fingernail scrapings. The hope was to get some DNA evidence linking Randolph to the murder victim. The fact that Pete Webster was still missing meant there was the ever-so-slight chance Pete wasn't a second victim, as everyone was already assuming but another suspect in the case.

Marisol finished bagging the scrapings and headed for the exit, eager to be back in her lab. Not that being around dead bodies bothered her all that much but she preferred working with the mass spectrometer and gas chromatograph to the rancid smell of decaying corpses and the cold feel of dead flesh.

Freddy Alou, Rocky Point's gregarious town clerk, was passing by as she opened the door. The Coroner's Office shared a building with the town offices and police department, it wasn't unusual to find Freddy wandering the halls, as he preferred to deliver and pick up paperwork by hand rather than using interoffice mail.

"Hey *chica*. How's things in the land of the dead?"

Marisol laughed. Freddy was sixty-four and happily married but it didn't stop him from flirting shamelessly with every woman in the building. "Quiet, thank god. Frank's our only case right now, which is good. The big brass is gonna want this one wrapped up double quick."

"I hear that." Freddy pursed his lips and shook his head. "Some crazy shit, huh? You think he did it?"

"The evidence is still being processed." Although Marisol hadn't had anything to do with Todd – or the other members of the Cemetery Club - since the summer before senior year, she always felt guilty if she didn't defend him whenever his name got brought up. After all, if it wasn't for him, who knew what would have ended up happening? He'd been her friend at one time and it wasn't his fault that had changed.

"Think about it, *chica*." Freddy's accent grew stronger in accordance to his emotions as he spoke. "He's back in town what, two, three days and somethin' like this happens? I'm not saying he did it but there's a connection, you bet your last dollar on it."

"A connection? What are you--"

"MARISOL SMITH, PHONE CALL LINE TWO." The receptionist's amplified voice echoed off the drab cement block walls. "MARISOL SMITH, PHONE CALL LINE TWO."

"Smith? I thought you was Flores again." Freddy raised an eyebrow at her.

"I am but some people are having a hard time getting used to the change. I'll see you later."

Freddy waved goodbye and continued down the hall as Marisol turned left into the laboratory, their conversation slipping from her mind as she picked up the phone and started reading preliminary results to the Medical Examiner. It would be several days before she remembered Freddy's words.

By then, it would already be too late.

Chapter 3

"Don't I know you?"

Cory looked up from signing in at the police station's front desk. A tall, lanky police officer with a weather-beaten face was eying him, his eyes narrowed to suspicious slits. The eyes alone would have been enough for Cory to recognize him, but the long, drooping mustache - which looked like he'd stolen it from a face on an Old West Wanted poster - was a dead giveaway.

Nick Travers. I can't believe he's still here.

"I'm Cory Miles. I used to live here, back in high school." Cory held out his hand.

"I knew you looked familiar." Travers ignored Cory's attempt at a handshake. "I busted you and your friends a bunch of times. What the hell brings you back to Rocky Point?"

"Pleasure to see you again too Officer." Cory allowed a hint of sarcasm to color his tone. The drive down from Connecticut had taken longer than he'd expected, thanks to an overturned tractor-trailer on I95. Sitting in traffic on a hot day was not how he enjoyed spending his afternoon.

"It's Chief Travers now Mister Miles. And I don't like it when troublemakers come back to my town. What's your business here?"

"I'm Todd Randolph's lawyer. I'm here to get him released."

Travers smiled, an unpleasant turning of his lips that narrowed his eyes even further. Cory remembered how he and his friends would always make fun of Officer Travers, calling him Clint Eastwood because of his squinting gaze and cowboy mustache. For his part, Travers had always been happy to catch them smoking behind the school or drinking beer in the cemetery. He'd take great pleasure in bringing them to the station so their parents would have to come pick them up.

"Randolph's lawyer? Figures you'd be representing that scumbag. Well, you're gonna have to cool your heels awhile. It's already after six." The Chief nodded at a nearby wall clock. "Ain't no judges around on a Friday to arrange bail. You're boy's stuck in there 'til Monday. And between you and me..." Travers leaned closer, his garlic breath filling the space between them, "...I doubt he's gonna get out then either."

"Why's that?" Cory tried to breathe shallow breaths.

"The man murdered one, maybe two people, out in that cemetery you kids used to party in. It's gonna be right back to the nut house for him on Monday. Do not pass Go, do not collect a hundred dollars."

"Two hundred," Cory said as he finished writing his name and address in the log book.

"What?" Travers' eyes closed even further as he frowned.

"Two hundred. You collect two hundred dollars when you pass Go."

"Still a smart ass, huh? Point is, you might as well go back to wherever you came from. Randolph's never gonna get out this time."

"Well, I think I'll stick around anyway, reminisce a little. Now, if you'll excuse me, I've got a client to see."

Cory followed the desk sergeant as the man led him towards the holding cells at the back of the jail. As he walked away, he heard Travers call out from behind him.

"I'm gonna have my eyes on you Miles."

Great. Welcome home, Cory. No wonder you never missed this town.

The sergeant unlocked the cell and slid the door open. "You got thirty minutes. No more than that, understand?"

"Got it," Cory said, stepping inside. He waited until the door clanged shut and the officer wandered down the hall before addressing the man seated on the single cot.

"Jesus, Todd. You look awful."

He'd expected Todd Randolph to look different; hell, it'd been twenty years since they'd last seen each other. He knew he'd changed over the years, filling out in the chest and gut, losing an inch of hairline, adding some wrinkles around the eyes. No one looked the same at thirty-six as they did at sixteen. So Todd's salt and pepper hair was no surprise. Nor was his skinny frame or the bags under his haunted eyes.

But the bruises and scrapes covering his face and arms weren't part of getting older.

Todd managed a small smile. "Nice to see you too, Cory."

"Sorry. But what the hell happened to you?"

"Apparently asking what I was being arrested for constitutes resisting arrest in this town, at least when you're the resident psycho. A few of the officers decided they needed to subdue me."

Cory gave a low whistle. "It looks like you went six rounds with Mike Tyson. Did you get the names of the officers?"

"Yes, I believe their names were billy club, fist and shoe. Does that help?" Todd leaned back against the wall with a moan and shook his head. "Sorry. I was too busy getting the shit beat out of me to check their badges."

"That's all right. The names of the arresting officers will be on the police report." Cory sat down on the bunk. "Are you hurt? Anything broken? Have they brought in a doctor to see you?"

"No, no, and no, but it's okay. Listen, I want to thank you for calling my mother and letting her know I'm all right. Goddamn cops did this right in front of her."

"No problem. Now I've only got about twenty minutes left before they kick me out, so fill me in on everything that happened today. And then I'll take some pictures of your face."

"Cory, I wasn't joking on the phone. It's happening again. The cemetery--"

"Wait." Cory held up his hand. "First things first. We'll talk about...that...after I get you out of here."

Todd nodded his head. "Okay." He took a deep breath. "I went out this morning to get the newspaper..."

Nick Travers looked up as his office door opened and Cory Miles walked in without so much as a courtesy knock.

"What the hell's your problem, Miles? I--"

"You'll shut up and sit down if you want to keep your job, Travers," the lawyer said.

"You better watch yourself sonny boy. I'll put your ass in a cell next to your friend."

Miles crossed his arms and smiled. "Go ahead. Then you'll have two unlawful arrests to deal with, not to mention a whole shitload of bad press."

"What're you jabbering about?" Travers asked, but he had a sinking feeling he knew exactly what Miles meant. He'd done a little research while Cory had been talking with Randolph. Apparently the man had made something of himself after leaving Rocky Point. He wasn't the small-time ambulance chaser Travers had figured him for; instead, he was a big-shot criminal attorney.

"Well for starters, there's police brutality. Three counts of it by my reckoning. Officers Foster, Harris and Cruz." Cory tapped his briefcase. "I've got the pictures here to prove it. And I'll bet I can find some witnesses who'll testify Todd did not resist arrest before he was beaten. This will make the Rodney King case look like pre-school. Then there's the fact that you denied him medical care. And to top it off, you delayed the paperwork just long enough to make sure he couldn't be arraigned until Monday. Now, are you ready to correct these incidents of gross misconduct by your staff or should I start filing charges and talking to the press?"

"Go ahead, talk to the press. You think your friend's gonna get a sympathetic ear in this town? I'm surprised people ain't lining up outside already to buy tickets to his execution."

"That's probably true. So just think how they'll feel when his case gets thrown out of court and he goes free, all because your department screwed up his arrest. This police department will be the laughing stock of the East Coast. And you've got an election coming up in November, don't you?"

Travers took a deep breath and silently counted to ten. The asshole was right; Mayor Dawes would have his head on a platter if Randolph went free on a technicality. Putting on his best professional smile, he leaned back in his chair. "So, what kind of 'corrections' were you thinking of?"

Miles ticked off the items on his fingers as he answered. "Todd Randolph is released on his own recognizance. The department pays any medical bills relating to the injuries sustained during his arrest. And you issue a statement that Mr. Randolph was simply brought in for questioning regarding the murders, that he has not been charged with anything."

Travers pretended to think about the offer. "I can take care of the last two but I can't let Randolph go." He held up his hand when Miles started to object. "It's out of my hands. There are no judges available until Saturday afternoon. You come back here tomorrow after twelve and I'll release your pal, on one condition."

"What's that?"

"You're responsible for him. He kills somebody or tries to run, and you're going to jail with him. Got it?"

"That's fine. Todd's not a flight risk and he's not a murderer. I'll be back tomorrow."

Miles left the office before Travers could say anything else. The Chief waited until he saw the lawyer walking across the parking lot and then he picked up the phone. "Doris? Tell Foster, Harris and Cruz to get their goddamned asses in here, pronto."

* * *

The Adams funeral on Saturday morning was a somber affair, made worse by the drenching showers that rolled in during the priest's graveside sermon. The dozens of black umbrellas that sprouted up like giant mushrooms were next to useless as the wind whipped around in powerful gusts. Father O'Malley brought the ceremony to a quick conclusion, skipping several paragraphs in his prepared speech as the unseasonably cold rain soaked the small gathering. One by one the mourners dropped roses on the casket and hurried through the deepening puddles to their waiting cars.

Lester Boone remained behind after the other mourners had hurried off. He'd told Aimee to meet him at the motel after the funeral but he could have sworn he'd caught a glimpse of her off in the distance as he walked from his car to the grave, a flash of black trench coat disappearing behind the very same mausoleum where they'd found Frank's remains only a few days earlier. It would be just like her to show up here, thinking that doing it at a crime scene – and in a graveyard no less - would add even more spice to their illicit rendezvous. As soon as he was sure they were alone, he sloshed up the hill to where she'd been playing hide and seek.

"Aimee! C'mon, don't play games. It's too fucking cold and wet. Let's just go to the motel like we planned."

More movement, a flash of black against the dark gray of the crypt. Christ, what was it with her and cemeteries? They'd done it in every half-assed collection of graves from here to Albany. "Aimee! I'm not fooling. Let's go."

When there was still no answer he walked over to the mausoleum, his feet soaked, his body shivering from the cold water running from his hair and down inside his collar.

He reached the stone structure and stopped, overcome with a sudden desire to do anything except take another step forward. A chill ran through him that had nothing to do with the cold falling rain. His heart pounded hard and fast. He rested one hand against the stone wall of the crypt to steady himself.

What the hell's going on? There's nothing here to be scared of. Lester took a deep breath. *Get a grip. You're acting like a little girl.* Purposely ignoring the voice inside his head that was begging him to turn around, he stepped forward and peered around the back of the building. "Aimee?"

It took a moment for him to recognize the shape on the ground as his mistress. Someone had pulled her black trench coat over her head, exposing her naked body to the elements. Only it no longer looked like a body; rainwater had filled in the giant hole extending from her chest to her pelvic region, turning it into a flesh bowl of cold, red soup.

Lester opened his mouth to scream just as the ghostly shadow emerged from the stone wall of the mausoleum. He recognized it instantly even though he'd never seen one before, unless you counted pictures on the Discovery Channel. *Aliens!* The roughly humanoid figure stood as tall as his waist, with an egg-shaped head framing two slanted eyes, eyes as red as if the fires of Mercury burned behind them. Instead of walking, it floated a few inches above the ground.

Lester had no time to react as the creature shot forward and entered his mouth in an icy wave. He gagged and clawed at his throat, fighting for air. Struggling to remain conscious, he fell to his knees next to Aimee's body.

Then he heard the voice. It spoke quietly but forcefully inside his head, telling him what he needed to do.

No longer aware of the falling rain, Lester stood up and lifted Aimee's corpse from the ground. He walked around to the front of the mausoleum. The door opened slowly and stiffly when he pushed on it, rusty metal hinges squealing like mechanical mice. Although only a hint of gray daylight entered through the doorway and the one small stained glass window, Lester had no trouble finding his way to the dark hole in the center of the floor.

Aimee's bloody carcass balanced on his shoulder, he entered the pit, his steps sure and steady as he descended into darkness.

* * *

The door to Gus's Bar and Grill opened up, letting in a quick gust of damp wind that sped through the room, lifting collars and cutting channels through musty air permanently tainted by decades of smoke, urine and cheap beer.

"Shut the damn door!" Gus Mellonis shouted from behind the bar. His voice echoed off the walls, easily overpowering the Rolling Stones ballad playing on the jukebox. It was after midnight and only six stools supported customers; another half hour and they'd be gone, too, which was just the way Gus liked it.

The door slammed shut and two figures emerged from the shadows of the front alcove into the bar. One of them wore a black suit so wet from the rain that rivulets of water ran from the jacket onto the floor, where they formed puddles as soon as he stopped walking. Fresh mud stains covered both his knees. The second figure was just as wet. Mud and grime coated his faded green shirt and Dickies.

"Holy shit!" Chuck Passella, a long-time regular at Gus's, slammed his hand on the bar. "Pete Webster? What the hell you doin' here? Half the town's lookin' for you and the other half thinks you're dead. Hey, you want a beer?"

Pete gave him a crooked smile, as if his mouth wasn't working quite right and nodded.

Chuck turned to Gus. "Pour him a beer, on me."

Gus poured the drink. As he set the mug down, he stared at the blotchy white marks on Pete's face. "Christ, Pete. You don't look good. What happened to you?"

Pete just stared at him.

When no explanation followed, Gus shrugged and turned to Pete's companion, who had similar markings on his cheeks. "How 'bout you, pal?"

The man shook his head but remained silent.

"Where the hell you been Pete?" asked Chuck. "And what happened to Frankie?"

Pete leaned on the bar and motioned for Chuck to lean closer. The other patrons slid their chairs over as well.

Without warning Pete smashed his beer mug against Chuck's head. As the old man's unconscious body toppled to the floor, Lester Boone vaulted over the bar and punched Gus in the nose, knocking him into the liquor bottles on the shelf next to the cash register. Gus grabbed a bottle and swung it at his attacker but Lester paid no mind as it bounced off his temple. Before Gus could swing again, Lester shoved his thumbs into Gus's eyes. The bartender screamed high and loud as blood and fluids spurted from his ruined orbs.

The remaining five men seated at the bar reacted quickly, despite their varying degrees of sobriety. Four of them ran towards Pete while the fifth climbed over the counter to help Gus.

Pete picked up a barstool and swung it by one leg, baseball style, catching two men and sending them stumbling backwards. Shards of wood flew in all directions as the stool splintered, leaving Pete with a two-foot section in his hands.

Nick Pacinino charged forward and swung his fist into Pete's face. The brittle crunch of bones breaking filled the bar and Nick howled in pain as his knuckles snapped. Then he had to step backwards when Pete, his jaw hanging to one side, swung the stool leg at him. Nick took another step and tripped on some debris. The pain of landing on his injured hand caused him to cry out again. A moment later, Pete stood over him, gripping the wooden leg with both hands.

"No, Pete, don't!" Nick raised his arms to ward off the blow he knew was coming.

Pete brought his arms down in a vicious arc, driving the broken end through Nick's throat. The older man managed a final gurgling, blood-filled gasp before his life pumped out in a red geyser.

"Fuckin' bastard!" Rory Calbert wrapped his arms around Pete's chest and brought him down to the floor, executing the tackle exactly the way his old football coach had taught him to do. Kneeling on the smaller man's chest, Rory raised his fist. "Say your prayers asshole," he shouted.

Before Rory could throw the punch, Pete grabbed his other arm with both hands and pulled it forward towards his mouth. Suddenly off balance, Rory could only watch as Pete bit a chunk of meat from his forearm.

"Aaah!" Rory screamed and fell to the side, cradling the torn fleshy hole. Pete got to his hands and knees, swallowed the piece of meat and dove forward, this time closing his teeth on the soft skin of Rory's throat.

Rory's cry for help turned into a gurgling, choking sound as the hole in his neck sprayed blood across Pete's face and the front of the bar.

Behind the bar, Lester pushed Benny Jurgen's face into the hot, soapy water of the glass washer. He held the man under until his screams stopped and then pulled him out. Jurgen vomited up beer and dishwater as he fell to the floor, his face red and blistered from the boiling liquid. Under the cash register, Gus howled and held his hands over his ruined eyes. Blood and other liquids painted jagged red and yellow trails through the gray stubble covering his cheeks. Lester ignored him as he delivered a series of violent kicks to Benny's head.

Bud Grant, his fighting days more than thirty years behind him, darted around Pete and ran for the door as fast as his arthritic legs would carry him, a single thought buzzing through his beer-addled brain.

Gotta get away. Gotta get away.

He was ten feet from the door when Pete tackled him. The last thing he saw was the grimy, black stained wooden floor approaching his eyes.

Lester picked up Benny Jurgen and placed him on his shoulder, much as he'd done earlier with Aimee's body. Pete hoisted the unconscious forms of Bud Grant and Chuck Passella and he and Lester carried their loads out of the bar.

On the jukebox the Rolling Stones song came to end. For several minutes, nothing moved, as if a magical force had turned the tavern into a 3D depiction of death. Then dark, smoky tendrils rose up from the two dead bodies on the floor. The grayish, insubstantial ropes wound themselves together over each corpse, growing vaguely humanoid in shape. As more ethereal matter emerged, the ghostly beings formed themselves into child-sized creatures. Circular mouths and burning red eyes appeared.

The two apparitions floated towards the ceiling and passed through it, leaving the bar empty except for the corpses and Gus Mellonis, who saw nothing as he clutched the remains of his eyeballs and shrieked to the heavens for someone to stop the pain.

Chapter 4

Cory Miles woke up just after ten, according to the digital clock radio next to his surprisingly comfortable king-size bed. The Holiday Inn on Route 9W hadn't been there the last time he'd been to town; the fact that Rocky Point had grown large enough to even rate a hotel, let alone a four-story Holiday Inn, had surprised him.

Usually an early riser, Cory had allowed himself the luxury of sleeping in because he'd been up until two in the morning. Every time he'd tried to close his eyes, Todd's words – *I think it's happening again* - came back to haunt him. Cory was pretty sure he knew what *it* was. If he'd had any doubts, Todd's mention of the cemetery had put them to rest, hard and painfully. A chorus of police and ambulance sirens just before midnight hadn't helped either.

It can't be happening again. Todd went down there, he ended it. No one died after that day.

Even after Cory had drifted off to sleep, dreams of strange creatures, black-skinned aliens with egg-shaped heads and glowing red eyes, tormented him through the night and into the morning, leaving him feeling as if he hadn't slept at all.

"What I need is coffee, lots of it, followed by a long, hot shower."

His plan for the morning was to grab breakfast from the Dunkin' Donuts next door, read the newspaper and then shower. Then he'd head back to the police station, hopefully to find a judge on duty who'd sign Todd's release.

Everything changed when, on his way through the lobby with his breakfast, he picked up a copy of the local paper from the rack by the front desk.

'Bloodbath shocks Rocky Point!'

Five minutes later he was on his way to the police station.

Cory squeezed between the photographers and reporters crammed shoulder-to-shoulder in front of the sergeant's desk, only to have a uniformed cop tell him he had to wait with the rest of the press.

"You don't understand. I'm here on official business," Cory said to the officer.

"Yeah, you and all these other jerks. Now move back."

As he tried to find a way around the human obstacle, he spotted Chief Travers entering through a side door at the back of the station.

"Travers! Travers, it's Cory Miles. Tell this guy to let me through."

Travers looked over and frowned. For a moment Cory thought the man was going to ignore him. Then the Chief came over and tapped the desk sergeant on the shoulder.

"Let him through," he said, raising his voice over the cries of "Chief! Chief! Give us a statement!" from the gathered press. "He's Randolph's attorney."

Cory smiled and stepped forward but his victory was short-lived as the crowd of reporters immediately turned on him and shouted a barrage of questions.

"What's Mr. Randolph's status?"

"Is it true he ate the bodies after he killed them?"

"What kind of defense are you preparing?"

A series of flashes momentarily blinded him and when he opened his eyes, a bouquet of microphones had blossomed in front of his face.

"Um, no comment. Please, I'll provide a statement later. Right now I have to see my client." He turned away and found Chief Travers grinning in a decidedly evil fashion.

"You did that on purpose," Cory said, as he and Travers entered the Chief's office.

"First time I've smiled all day." Travers shut the door and sat down behind his desk, motioning for Cory to take one of the other chairs. "Lemme guess. You're here to get Randolph released. Well, too bad. Judge Beckett ain't in yet."

Cory took the morning newspaper from his briefcase and slammed it on the desk so that the headline faced Travers.

"I don't have to wait for the judge anymore. According to this, you had five more murders last night. And unless one of your boys let my client out for a midnight stroll, he's got a rock-solid alibi. Between that and the eyewitnesses that place him at the library on the afternoon of the first murder, you don't have enough to hold my client another minute."

Travers' lips tightened until they almost disappeared. When he spoke, his tone carried a bitter edge. "It's bullshit and you know it counselor. The time of death could be wrong for Frank Adams. Your buddy Randolph could have somebody else working for him, one of his nut house buddies. God knows they let enough loonies out of that place when it closed. And Randolph's a convicted killer."

Cory leaned back and allowed himself his own malicious smile. "Not good enough and we both know it. Now let him go, and you can get to work finding the real killer."

"Fine." Travers stood up so fast his chair rolled back, banging into a file cabinet. "But he's still remanded into your custody Miles. One fuck-up and you're both back here faster than you can say *'habus corpus'*."

"Whatever you say, Chief. And if you don't mind, I'd like to take my client out the back, rather than face the press. He's been through enough."

"Don't push your luck, son."

"Gee, and I figured you wouldn't want Todd's face all over the newspapers, what with those cuts and bruises and all."

Travers glared at him and then called out to the desk sergeant. "Harris! Escort Mr. Miles to Randolph's cell."

"Thanks Chief." Cory headed down the hall and then stopped, turning back. "Hey Chief!"

Travers paused by his office door.

"It's *habeas corpus*. Not habus."

Travers slammed the door without responding but even from twenty feet away Cory heard the man cursing.

"Have a good day Chief," he said, as he turned back to follow Sergeant Harris.

"I just want to say thanks again Cory. I didn't expect to be home so soon." Todd Randolph stared at his house from inside Cory's car, as if afraid he'd get beaten again if he got out.

"Don't thank me," Cory said. "Travers had no choice."

"Anyway..." Todd's voice trailed off into an awkward pause.

Cory cringed inside, knowing what was coming but dreading the words. *Please don't say it...*

"Listen. About the murders. We need to talk."

Dammit!

"I know. But not today. You need to take a little time, let your mother know you're all right and get a good night's sleep. How 'bout if we grab lunch tomorrow? My treat."

Todd shook his head. "No, I've got some research to finish before we get together. Let's make it dinner. But come over here. I'll cook. I...well, I wasn't getting such a good reception in town before all this happened. I'd hate to have someone spit in your food just because you're eating with me."

"Okay. I'm staying at the Holiday Inn, Room 306. Call me."

"I will." Todd paused again and then slowly exited the car, his stiff movements and prematurely graying hair making him look like an old man. Cory waited until Todd entered the house before driving away.

Twenty years, Cory thought as he entered his hotel room. He tossed his key card on the desk and lay down on the bed. *All that time, locked up like a prisoner, just to protect us. God knows what it was like in there. I don't think I could have handled it without going crazy.*

Memories burst open inside Cory's head, like infected boils unable to take the pressure of the diseased fluids building under the skin.

Todd. Marisol. John.

The Cemetery Club.

* * *

Rocky Point High School, 20 years ago

"All right. Everyone shut up and sit down." Drexel Harrison slammed the door shut, officially beginning the day's detention period. Harrison doubled as truant officer and detention monitor for the junior class of Rocky Point High School, a job he considered more important than teaching history or science or math. "Anyone can teach," he liked to tell his friends and family. "But it takes someone with real dedication to make sure students obey the rules."

For Drexel Harrison, "obey" was the operative word when it came to the endless parade of delinquents he dealt with on a daily basis. At least once a day he wondered at the astounding number of mental rejects masquerading as parents. Parents who had no clue their children were drinking, smoking, even fucking when they were supposed to be in class.

And, of course, the children followed right in their parents' cognitively deficient footsteps.

The current day's crop was a perfect example. Two kids caught smoking behind the school, one boy who saw nothing wrong with wearing a t-shirt emblazoned with a giant marijuana leaf and three hoodlums who'd decided it would be fun to take some poor freshman and dunk his head into a toilet.

But the worst offender was, of all people, the son of the local minister. He'd been caught selling answers to a math test.

The man can preach to his flock every Sunday but can't even get his son to obey the Ten Commandments. Typical.

Harrison waited until all seven students were giving him their undivided attention, then he launched into his standard speech.

"Listen up and listen good. For the next forty-five minutes we'll be playing by *my* rules. That means no talking, no reading anything other than schoolwork and no sleeping. You want to screw around, do it on your own time. Anyone doesn't follow the rules, you get another day with me. Now, get started on your homework. If you don't have any, raise a hand and I'll give you something to do."

No one raised a hand. Harrison watched as they opened their schoolbooks. Unlike other detention monitors, he made it a point to remain at his desk and keep a watchful eye on his charges. He knew some teachers preferred to spend the time grading papers, catching up on reading or even standing out in the hall chatting with co-workers. But in his experience, that led to talking, passing notes and general fucking around.

None of which equated with his definition of "obey."

Instead, he sat statue-like behind the desk, his eyes only moving when he checked his watch.

He sat stone still and relished the silence.

Cory Miles jumped when the bell announced the end of detention. Next to him, the three seniors who'd been pretending to read their history texts slammed their books shut and bolted from the room the second Harrison opened the door.

As he packed his stuff into his backpack and smiled at Marisol Flores, Cory eyed the remaining two students. He knew their names; Rocky Point wasn't so large a school that you didn't know all the other students in your grade. But he'd never actually had a class with either of them.

"Let's exit this taco stand." Marisol slapped a hand on his arm as she went by. "I'm dying for a cigarette."

Knowing Harrison would be watching, they waited until they were across the street and officially off school grounds before lighting up. As he inhaled, Cory watched John Boyd and the preacher's kid walking towards them.

"Hey," John said. His sandy brown hair fell across his forehead in limp strands, as if strangled by the humid warmth of the early spring day. "You guys got an extra smoke?"

"Sure." Cory handed him his pack of Marlboro Lights and a lighter. Boyd took one and returned the pack. Cory held it out to the preacher's son – *Todd, Todd Randolph, that's his name.* "You want one?"

Todd smiled, a kind of sneaky grin that filled his eyes with happy mischief. "Naw. I got something better."

"Oh yeah?" Marisol's eyebrows went up. "What?"

"I stole a bottle of wine from my dad's cabinet last night and hid it in the cemetery. You guys wanna try some?"

Marisol, who Cory knew would look for any excuse not to go home, burst out laughing. "Hell yeah! Let's go."

The two-mile walk took them almost an hour. When they got to Gates of Heaven Cemetery, Todd led them past rows of graves and up the hill to the older section, where some of the headstones had dates going back to the seventeen hundreds. He stopped at a large mausoleum whose door hung open a few inches.

"I hid it in there."

Marisol's dark eyes narrowed. "This ain't some kind of trick, is it? I mean, you're not planning to lock us in there are you?"

Todd shook his head. "No, I hang out here all the time. My house is over that way." He pointed west, where they could see the top of the First Church of Christ sticking up over some trees. "I come out here at night when I need to get out of my house."

"Man, I hate being home too," Marisol said, "but isn't this place creepy at night?"

"Naw, it's kind of cool. It's quiet. You can just sit and think without anyone bothering you." The door screeched like metal against a blackboard as he pushed it open.

Cory looked at the others and shrugged. "What the hell." He

entered the crypt, an involuntary shudder passing through him as he crossed the line from sunny afternoon to cool, damp, twilight.

"Watch out for the floor." Todd indicated a small hole in the center of the stone room where the cement had collapsed.

A large concrete casket container took up a good portion of the available space but Todd had found enough room on the other side to lay out a sleeping bag. Next to it sat an over-sized flashlight, a couple of MAD magazines and a half gallon of Mogen David Chianti.

"Fuckin' shit. Don't tell me you sleep here?" John asked, pointing at the sleeping bag.

"No, but I don't like sitting on the cement. It gets real cold, especially in the winter."

Marisol hugged herself and shivered. "It's chilly now. Break open that wine so we can warm up."

Cory fought down a surge of jealousy as Marisol sat down next to Todd, close enough that their knees were almost touching. He'd been crazy about her for over a year, ever since he'd seen her entering his sophomore English class. Hell, he'd only started smoking 'cause she did; it gave him an excuse to spend time with her. That had led to eating lunch together and then hanging out after school.

The only thing he hadn't done was get up the nerve to actually ask her out on a date.

Not wanting Todd to get all of her attention, he took a seat on her other side. John sat between him and Todd, completing the circle.

"Like my dad always says, bottoms up!" Todd hefted the jug and took a big sip, then passed it to Marisol.

"Hey, that's not bad," she said after swallowing her mouthful.

Cory accepted the bottle from her and brought it to his lips. The smell was strong and acidic, like super-powered grape juice. He'd tasted alcohol before, when he'd snuck sips of his father's beer or his mother's Saturday night whiskey sour. But the deep red wine was something different. It burned its way down his throat and started a warm feeling in his stomach.

"Wow," he said, passing the wine to John, who took a long swig. "That's nothing like the wine they have in church."

"That's 'cause churches water the wine down." Todd took his turn and wiped his hand across his lips, which had already taken on a purple tint. "Wine's expensive. That's what my dad says."

"If people got to drink like this in church, maybe more people would go." Marisol laughed at her own joke, sending a spray of purple droplets onto the floor.

The bottle was beginning its fourth go-round when John, who'd been quiet up until then, reached into his pocket and pulled out a joint.

"You guys wanna try something better than wine?"

* * *

Rocky Point, Present Day

That was the defining moment, when John lit up that joint, Cory thought, rising from the bed and making his way to the bathroom. He felt more tired than when he'd laid down, his muscles stiff and his back aching. *We shared more than just a high.* Somehow, partying in that musty old crypt, four outcasts formed a bond. A bond Todd made official when they staggered out into the cemetery three hours later, drunk, stoned and laughing.

> *"We should do this again tomorrow," Marisol said.*
> *"We should do it every day," Todd replied. "Just the four of us."*
> *"Like a club," John said.*
> *"The Cemetery Club." Todd raised his hand, and everyone high-fived*
him.

"Christ." Cory splashed water on his face and looked into the mirror. If he stared hard enough, he could still see a ghostly image of his sixteen-year-old self hiding beneath his current features. "Maybe we were doomed from the moment he said it," he told his younger self.

Was that even possible? It sounded too much like fate - or a bad movie - to him, but the idea wouldn't go away, that they'd somehow attracted the notice of a supernatural entity with their foolish high school antics.

With sleep rendered an impossible goal, Cory decided to put his past on the back burner by focusing on work. Even with Todd loose and no longer a prime suspect, there was always the chance of the police arresting him again and a good lawyer had to be prepared.

"First stop, the morgue."

Chapter 5

Marisol recognized the man at the desk as Cory Miles before he even turned around to face her. Something about the way he stood, the shape of his nose and chin seen from a partial profile, instantly brought back memories of the boy who'd been her best friend in high school.

The boy she'd hoped to marry someday but he'd moved away, leaving her with no one but the assholes who only wanted to get into her pants.

"Cory?" She hadn't meant to say it out loud and had to fight the urge to duck into an office before he looked at her.

"Marisol?"

Holy shit, it really is him! She stood frozen as a broad smile bloomed on his face and he started towards her. *Cory Miles is here, right here.* Aware she must look totally disheveled after a ten-hour shift in the lab, her cheeks grew hot with embarrassment and the moisture magically evaporated from her tongue, leaving her with an acute case of cotton mouth.

Cory stopped a few feet away, his hands held partially out, as if he wasn't sure if he should hug her or shake her hand. The fact that he looked like a man imitating the classic Virgin Mary benediction pose made her want to laugh, which in turn broke the spell holding her immobile. She grasped his hands in hers and stepped forward to give him a quick kiss on the cheek.

"I can't believe you're here! What are you doing in town? Wait; what the hell are you doing in the morgue?"

"It's a long story," he said, still smiling and staring at her. "Can you grab a cup of coffee?

Marisol hated to divert her eyes away from him, as if doing so might reveal that his appearance was just a hallucination. But she chanced a quick look at her watch, realizing in the process they were still holding hands.

"My shift ends in fifteen minutes." She reluctantly relinquished her grip. Did it seem as if he was slow in letting go as well? "Meet me in the lobby and we'll go to the diner."

"Hogan's?"

"Of course."

"That sounds great."

He stood there smiling at her and she wondered if her own grin looked as goofy. She considered giving him another kiss but just then the lab door opened and Randy, another lab tech, stuck his head out.

"Hey Marisol, I can't find the sample vials for the micro centrifuge. Do you know where they are?"

Cory took a step backwards. "I'll let you get back to work. See you in fifteen."

Before she could say anything, he turned and walked down the hall towards the elevator.

"Marisol?"

She sighed. "I'm coming Randy. Hold your horses."

I still can't believe I'm sitting with Cory Miles again. The two of them had instinctively taken the same booth in the back corner that they'd always tried to get when they were in high school. *How many nights did we sit here, me desperate to avoid going home, Cory bored with life in general and just looking for something to do?*

In the bright lights of the diner she saw he hadn't changed all that much since high school. His hairline had receded a bit and he had a few lines around his dark brown eyes but he'd managed to stay in shape. He'd been tall when they were juniors, almost six feet, but it looked like he'd only added an inch or two since then.

As they regarded each other over their coffee cups, she wondered if his assessment of her was as favorable. She certainly didn't look the same as when he'd known her. A two-cup increase in her bra size and an almost overnight rounding of her ass had changed her figure from model-thin to Playboy curvy during senior year, one of the main reasons she'd become so popular with the boys after being virtually invisible the year before.

A strict diet, lots of exercise and an ex-husband who belittled her whenever she gained weight had helped her keep the pounds off in the years since high school, but it was still a never-ending struggle.

"I can't believe we're sitting here," Cory said, breaking the silence. He gestured at the booths and patrons around them. "Shit. I can't believe the diner's still here."

"You mean you can't believe *I'm* still here." Marisol sipped her coffee and smiled to let him know she wasn't insulted.

He nodded. "That too. You always hated this town. I figured you'd be gone before the ink on your diploma was dry."

She shrugged. "You know how it is. The classic story. Girl falls for wrong guy. Girl gets married. Guy abuses girl. Girl takes fifteen years to get her shit together and leave him." She stopped, aware of the bitterness creeping into her voice.

Am I mad at myself or at Cory for leaving me behind?

Cory looked down at his cup. "I'm sorry."

"It's not your fault. After you moved, I...well, I guess you could say I blossomed." She gave her boobs a quick pat and he laughed. "I started getting attention from all the guys. I was too stupid to realize they only wanted my body."

"Who was it?"

"Who *wasn't* it? People always thought of me as a poor spic from the Lowlands. By the middle of senior year I was the slutty poor spic from the Lowlands. Except, I didn't know it. I thought I was popular 'cause I had a date every weekend."

A blush crept up Cory's neck and cheeks. "I meant, who was it you married?"

Shit! Good one Marisol. Way to give too much information. "Jack Smith," she said, not able to meet Cory's eyes.

"Jack Smith? The swim team captain? Mister My-Shit-Don't-Stink?"

Marisol nodded. "Yeah. Classic, huh? I actually thought he loved me. It wasn't until after we were married that I found out he just wanted me 'cause of my looks. I was 'an exotic beauty,' as he put it, a toy he could show off at his business dinners. Oh, he didn't say that last part out loud, but then he didn't have to."

"Why not?"

"His parents told me. The day we came back from our honeymoon. I almost left him right there but Jack insisted they were wrong, he really loved me, and just because his parents had a problem with my background and skin color didn't mean he did."

Cory signaled the waitress to bring them more coffee and then turned back to Marisol. "So what happened then?"

"I got to star in my own private version of *My Fair Lady*. I had to act a certain way, dress a certain way, even talk a certain way, so I'd 'fit in' at the country club, the Rotary dinners or the fucking fund raisers we went to every weekend. And then I found out Jack liked to tell his friends what a firecracker I was in bed because I was Hispanic."

"That sucks." Cory looked like he was about to say something else but he closed his mouth and cast his eyes downward yet again.

"Yeah. But enough about me. What have you been up to since you moved away?"

Cory smiled, the same self-deprecating grin he'd always used in high school when he tried to make light of the honor roll status he'd maintained despite cutting classes and hardly studying. "Not much. We moved to Connecticut and I went to college in Boston."

"Harvard? Yale?" Marisol teased.

"No smart ass. Boston University. Then law school at University of Connecticut. After that, a few years bouncing around as a junior associate before starting my own practice. Criminal law, mostly."

"Criminal...wait. Is that why you're in town? Are you representing Todd?"

"Yep. He called me out of the blue. Said he needed my help. How could I say no? Not after what he went through because of us." Cory leaned forward, a serious look on his face. "He also said something else. That--"

A loud chime cut off his next words. "Hold that thought," Marisol said, lifting up her cell phone. "Crap. There's a problem at the lab. I have to go."

"Wait." Cory placed his hand on her arm. "What are you doing tomorrow night?"

"Why? Are you asking me on a date?" Marisol tried to keep her tone light but his words had her body in a tizzy, her stomach full of butterflies and her heart beating double-time.

"What? No, I...um...I'm having dinner with Todd and I think you should be there."

"Oh." A hole opened up in her gut and all her sudden hopes drained away. "I don't think so. I'm...busy."

"Please? It's really important. For all of us."

Something in his voice made her pause. It was the kind of tone the police used when they informed someone of a loved one's death. She started to say no again, thinking she was better off not getting involved, and then reconsidered. *It's better than sitting home watching reruns.*

"Okay. Here's my number." She handed him a business card. "I get off at two tomorrow."

"Thanks. And Marisol?"

"Yeah?"

"It was great seeing you." He smiled and for a moment she saw nothing except the sixteen-year-old boy she'd been secretly in love with.

"You too. I'll talk to you tomorrow." She hurried away before she said anything stupid.

But for the rest of the day, she couldn't get that smile out of her mind.

* * *

The setting sun splashed pastel reds and oranges across the decades-old tract houses and trailers that made up the Lowlands, providing a few minutes of picturesque color to a section of town where most of the residents considered 'lower middle-class' an unattainable financial goal. The standard for landscaping in this area was car parts and broken toys peeking through overgrown lawns. For that brief moment of time, something approaching beauty held sway over a neighborhood defined for decades by its ugliness.

Sitting between Gates of Heaven Cemetery and the factory district, the Lowlands was home to more than five hundred families, the majority of whom rented rather than owned. Most of the men worked in factories or as laborers. Some didn't work at all. The women who didn't stay home, smoking endless packs of cigarettes while they ironed clothes and watched Oprah, took whatever work they could get in order to supplement their husbands' earnings, a good portion of which went to beer and bowling. Children in the Lowlands made do with hand-me-downs for Christmas and Hamburger Helper for dinner and didn't complain, unless they wanted to feel the sting of a leather belt.

It was a place where spousal abuse, drunken revelry and shouting matches were as common as fine wine and roast duck in the restaurant district. Like most neighborhoods of its kind, it was a place where people minded their own business.

Which was unfortunate for Duffy Walters and his wife.

Just as the sun completed its descent, pulling the beauty from the Lowlands like a coroner lifting a sheet from a corpse, Pete Webster and Lester Boone had mounted the sagging steps of the Walters' single-level house and kicked in the front door, surprising Duffy and Patty as they sat in front of the TV, watching *Cops* and eating Hungry Man dinners.

Duffy had time to shout, "What the fuck!" and then Pete crashed into him, sending an explosion of meatloaf and peas into the air. Next to him, Patty never had a chance to raise her portly body out of her chair before Lester landed on her, his added weight sending the recliner reeling over backwards.

"Help! He--aack" Patty's scream ended in a wet, choking gasp as Lester wrapped his hands around her throat, just below her second chin. She beat her hands ineffectually against her attacker's shoulders as he leaned close and squeezed the soft flab of her neck. Lester's face remained expressionless while he choked her, and even as her consciousness faded, she still couldn't believe it was really happening.

Duffy Walters paid no attention to his wife's struggles. As his back hit the ground, he rolled to the side, his body still remembering its military training from Vietnam. But while his body knew what to do, his muscles, forty years older and wasted away from years of bad food and cheap booze, couldn't keep up with the orders being sent to them.

He was still on his stomach when Pete grabbed him by the shirt and pants, lifting him up and back, like a farmer preparing to toss a bale of hay.

"Nooo!" Duffy watched the TV moved away from him in slow motion and then come towards him again as Pete swung him forward. Duffy's next scream was silenced as his head crashed into the glass screen with a sound like firecrackers going off. White flashes of light detonated around him, accompanied by crackling sounds and a pounding in his skull.

Lost amid the noise and pain was the single, sharp sting of the jagged glass shard that sliced his throat open. His blood sizzled on exposed wires and electronic boards as it ran from his neck but Duffy never noticed, just as he never noticed when the darkness inside the television set blended into the darkness of death.

Pete dragged the old man's body out of the fragmented screen and dropped it on the floor. At the same time, Lester removed his hands from Patty's neck and stood up. They both stepped away from the bodies as a swirling cloud of grayish-black matter entered the room and rapidly coalesced into a twisted parody of a human form, like a skinny ghost caught in a miniature tornado. The red-eyed apparition dropped onto Patty's face and proceeded to drag itself into her mouth and down her throat.

Patty's eyes opened and she gasped for air, clutching at her throat. After a moment, her hands fell away and an emotionless expression came over her features, matching the ones worn by Pete and Lester. Patty sat up, her overweight form showing a grace of movement she'd never had while alive. Red marks in the shape of thin fingertips marred the pale color of her neck. She looked to the side, where Duffy's corpse was slowly staining the carpet dark crimson.

A thin string of saliva escaped from between her lips. Without hesitation, she bent over and attacked her husband's body with her mouth and hands.

Pete and Lester stood up and exited the house.

Patty ignored them as she continued to eat the man she'd been married to for almost fifty years.

Down the street, Pete and Lester kicked in another door, their night's work just beginning. Not long after, more cries for help echoed through the warm night air.

Sometime after midnight, five blood-soaked people followed Pete and Lester back to the Gates of Heaven Cemetery.

Not one of the neighbors thought to call the police.

In the Lowlands, people made it a habit not to get involved.

* * *

It was just before noon when John Boyd sat down at the farthest booth in the McDonald's dining area. He didn't need to see the looks the other patrons cast his way to know he wasn't welcome; he was well aware of his current state of repulsiveness. His clothes gave off the rancid cheese smell of weeks-old perspiration and layers of dirt had combined to stain everything he wore to the same dun-colored brown. Even the hot, greasy odors of grilling burgers, sizzling French fries and steaming buns couldn't overpower the acrid reek surrounding his body. It was one of the reasons he hadn't made a fuss when he'd been given a wide birth while waiting in line for his food.

Even now, sitting only a few feet from the bathrooms, his own stink seemed more than a match for the antiseptic pine scent and stale urine odor that drifted past him each time someone emerged.

Fuck 'em all, he thought with a mental smile as he tore a huge, dripping bite from his Big Mac. Sauce, lettuce and melted cheese dripped onto his thrift store sports jacket and he scooped it up with a filth-encrusted finger, ignoring the black specks that rested atop the spillage like cinnamon on rice pudding. *I got just as much right to eat here as they do.*

Besides, he was starving. It had taken him two days of collecting bottles and cans to make enough money for this meal. The shelter provided coffee all day but unless you got in line before seven a.m. you missed out on the free pastries. Thanks to booze and exhaustion, he rarely got up before nine. Of course, sleeping late was just one of many bad habits he'd developed since joining the unwashed masses.

In fact, when he really thought about it, the only things in life he could still be proud of were his ability to not shit himself the way some of his shelter-mates did and the fact that no matter how polluted he got, he never forgot Susie's or Kyle's birthdays.

Thinking about his ex-wife and child created a pain in his chest, a knife inside him that twisted and turned, digging a little deeper each time he thought about them. In response, John forced those thoughts back down to that deep place where the booze and years held them at bay, and focused on his burger. He knew he only had a limited amount of time to finish his food before the manager, a pimply-faced little jerk with a penguin nose and a Hitler attitude, did his supposed civic duty and chased him from the restaurant.

And while John had no problem eating his food outside, the chance to sit in an air conditioned room on a sweltering day was a pleasure almost as great as filling his stomach.

Another glob of sauce slid off his bun and onto his shirt. Using two fries, he scraped the dressing up and popped the fries into his mouth, then washed the whole mess down with a big sip of orange soda.

He was just unwrapping his second burger when Adolf Pimple-face served him with his eviction notice.

"I'm sorry, but you'll have to leave, sir. Your...odor is offending some of our other customers."

John stood up; at six-three he towered over the acne-cream poster child, who backed up two steps in response. John glanced around the dining area. Families and couples stared at their meals while surreptitiously watching him from the corners of their eyes. The idea of making a scene crossed his mind but then he'd probably end up arrested. Spending the night in the slammer was okay in the winter but in the summer the cells were hot as hell and stunk worse than his own ragged underwear. Besides, he didn't want his other burger taken away from him.

"Fine." He put his food back in the bag and made his way towards the door. Just before leaving, he spied the newspaper rack and grabbed a copy of the local rag. The penguin yelled something about the papers having to stay inside the building but John ignored him. Past experience had taught him that fast-food employees, even managers, wouldn't escalate a small issue, not when losing a fifty-cent paper meant getting rid of a stinking bum.

Across the street was one of Rocky Point's three town parks. John took his meal and paper to an empty bench under a shady tree. He planned on finishing his lunch and then catching a nap. The paper would protect his face from the sun and allow him to pretend no one was staring at him. Most of the time, the cops would let him sleep a few hours before rousting him.

His plans changed the minute he saw the front page.

'Police Clueless in Murders'

The image of Pete Webster wacking Frank Adams with a shovel wavered into existence in John's mind. *I only saw one person get killed. Who else did they get?*

He read further, catching up on the rash of murders and missing persons he'd been oblivious to over the past several days.

Conflicting thoughts fought each other in his brain.

It's just like twenty years ago.

*Don't think about…*them!

His lunch churned in his stomach, threatening to climb the ladder of his throat and make a messy escape. John swallowed back bile and special sauce, unwilling to part with his hard-earned food, wishing he had some Maalox or Rolaids. His stomach always bothered him when he thought about the Grays; many was the night when their images tortured him in his sleep as well. It was one of the reasons he preferred to drink himself to sleep. He was about to toss the paper away when something else caught his eye, something at the bottom of the article.

When questioned why they'd released their number one suspect, Chief Travers stated, "At this time we have insufficient evidence to hold Mr. Randolph and we've released him into the custody of his attorney, Mr. Cory Miles."

Randolph? Todd Randolph? And Cory Miles?

Too many coincidences. John knew he could no longer deny the truth. Just like twenty years ago, people were dying.

And for the first time since that fateful summer, the members of the Cemetery Club were all in town.

Chapter 6

Deputies Buck Foster and Mack Harris knelt on the ground where Frank Adams' head had been discovered. After Todd Randolph's release, Chief Travers had sent them back to the original crime scene to see if they could turn up anything the first team had missed. A similar investigation was going on at Gus's Bar and Grill.

"I don't know what the Chief expects us to find, not after that rain the other night." Foster stood up and wiped mud from his knees.

"Yeah, I know what you - wait, what's that?" Harris pointed towards the front of the nearby mausoleum, where a splash of red peeked out from beneath one of the bushes lining the entrance.

"Beats me." Foster crouched beside the brush. "I'll be damned. It's a woman's shoe. What the hell's it doing here?"

Harris came over with the digital camera and snapped two pictures. "More importantly, when did it get here? No way anyone could've missed this when they ran the scene the first time."

"You think maybe someone hid in the mausoleum and came back out after the scene was cleared?"

Harris opened his notepad and flipped through the pages. "According to the report, the mausoleum door was closed and padlocked."

Both men looked at the metal door. A gap of several inches showed between the edge and the frame.

Without speaking, Foster and Harris drew their guns and moved to either side of the opening. A dank, putrid smell wafted through the crack. Harris used his fingers to give a silent count to three and then pushed the door open with his foot. At the same time, Foster went down on one knee, gun aimed inside the crypt. After glancing in both directions, he stood and quickly stepped into the burial chamber, Harris right behind him.

Doing his best to breathe through his mouth, Foster motioned Harris to the right. They circled the small room and made sure the lid on the coffin box was too heavy for one person to lift. Only then did they speak again.

"Someone was here, I feel it," Harris whispered. In fact, he felt more than that; a sudden fear had sprouted inside him, causing his gun hand to quiver.

"They're not here now. You think it was kids screwin' around?"

"No. I recognize that stink. It's like when you drive past a dead deer on the road. That's rotten meat." He moved to the center of the crypt and stood over the wide hole in the cement floor. "And it's coming from down there."

Foster knelt down and wiped at the jagged edges of the opening. "Looks like tool marks. Somebody busted the cement and dug this hole."

A fresh wave of corrupt air wafted up and Foster backed away, gagging, wiping tears from his eyes. "Jesus, that's fuckin' rank. I...I think maybe we oughta get outta here and call for backup."

"Don't be a wuss. We can't just report a hole in the floor. Gimme your flashlight." Harris desperately wanted to leave too, but he wasn't about to admit it. Instead, he took the light and aimed it down the dark opening. "Looks like a tunnel. I can barely see...wait a second, what's that?" He took a deep breath and then lay down on his stomach, his arm and head in the hole.

"What is it?" Foster asked.

"Jesus Christ!" Harris scooted backwards, using his elbows and knees until he was far enough away from the hole to sit up. He took a deep breath. In the gray light inside the crypt, his face had gone winter pale.

"What the hell is it?" Foster had his gun out and aimed at the hole. A warm wetness ran down his leg, soaking his sock.

"There's...there's a body down there. Maybe more than one, I couldn't tell. It's all chewed up, like animals were eating it. But..."

"But what?"

"I don't think it was animals. Some of those bite marks looked awfully big."

Foster stared at his partner. "You think people did it? Like fucking cannibals?" His voice rose in pitch as he spoke.

Harris stood up and backed away from the hole. Dust motes

created psychedelic designs as they passed through the shaft of afternoon sunlight entering through the small stained glass window high on one wall. "I'll tell you what I think. I think we've got devil worshipers in town."

"Devil worshipers? Fuck that shit. C'mon, let's get out of here. It's - look out!" He stopped and pointed at the opening.

Harris turned around in time to see the creature rise up from the darkness like a ghost. Its devilish red eyes, almond-shaped and slanted down towards where the nose should have been, took up half the thing's face. The ovoid head was completely devoid of hair and smooth where the ears would normally have sat. A round, toothless opening served as a mouth.

The creature's gray skin was several shades darker than the inside walls of the crypt, enough so to make it look like a shadow in the gloom. It hovered at the top of the hole, its head the same height as a man's chest.

"Holy fuckin' shit, it's an alien," Foster whispered. He tried to aim his gun at the creature, gripping it with both hands to control his trembling. "Don't move another inch," he said to it, putting as much authority into his voice as he could.

Without a sound, the creature raised a hand towards Foster, who pulled the trigger three times in quick succession, filling the room with ear-shattering echoes and the metallic *zing* of ricocheting rounds.

Harris cried out, grabbing his arm, dropping the flashlight in the process. "Fuck! You shot me!"

Foster backed away, his hands shaking worse than before. "The bullets went right through it!"

As if unconcerned by Foster's gun, the apparition turned towards Harris, who was leaning against the cement coffin box, one hand gripping his wounded arm. Hot blood, dark in the poorly-lit crypt, ran down his shirt and stained his uniform sleeve.

"Get away!" Harris shouted at the approaching figure.

The alien floated towards its target, its feet several inches above the floor. Foster followed it with the gun but didn't dare pull the trigger, not even when the creature grasped Harris by the wrist of his injured arm and pressed its body against his. Harris screamed as the long fingers touched his skin and tightened like iron bands.

"Oh, God! Help me! It's cold! So cold!"

Harris tried to bat the creature away with his good arm but it was like fighting smoke; his hands passed through unimpeded.

The alien floated up until its face was even with Harris's and then it dove forward, twisting and shrinking as it entered Harris's mouth and disappeared down his throat. Harris choked and gagged, clawing at his neck with both hands. Only when the alien was completely inside him did he fall to the ground, his eyes open, bulging out.

"Harris?" Foster hurried to his partner, aware that he'd committed a cardinal sin in law enforcement. He'd frozen while his partner needed him. He knelt and grabbed his friend by the shoulders, started shaking him. "Harris! Say something!"

Faster than Foster's eyes could follow, Mack Harris grabbed the flashlight off the floor and smashed it against his partner's head.

Buck Foster fell onto his back, his gun forgotten as he tried to make sense of what was happening. Through the swirling colors obscuring his vision, he saw his best friend since high school crawl towards him, flashlight raised like a club.

"Mack--" The word came out in a gasping croak. He never had time to finish the sentence.

Harris brought the flashlight down, striking Foster's mouth and sending blood and teeth onto the floor. The next blow tore a flap of skin from Foster's forehead and created a broken windshield pattern in the white bone.

On the third swing, the flashlight smashed through Foster's skull, splattering his brains across the floor.

Harris continued to robotically swing the police-issue flashlight until Foster's head was reduced to a flattened, pulpy mess. Only then did he drag his kill to the hole and drop it into the darkness, where the rest of the Horde attacked it, the sounds of their gorging eerily reminiscent of a lion pride devouring a gazelle.

Lowering himself down, after the lifeless meal, he elbowed a fat housewife out of the way and used his teeth to tear off Foster's genitals, which he swallowed whole.

The feast continued until only a skeleton, its bones draped with a few ribbons of skin and muscle, remained.

* * *

At Angels of Mercy Hospital, Gus Mellonis woke from his nightmare and screamed at the darkness surrounding him. "Get away!

Get away!" He tried to reach for his face but his hands refused to move. Fire filled his head, radiating outward from his eyes.

"Help!"

"Calm down, Mr. Mellonis." Sue-Anne Davis, the shift nurse on duty, hurried to Gus's side and injected a dose of morphine into his IV. "I've given you something for the pain. You're in the hospital. You're safe."

Gus continued to thrash against the straps holding him down but his struggles gradually subsided as the morphine took effect. When he'd relaxed to the point where he lay still, Sue-Anne spoke to him again.

"Mr. Mellonis. Can you understand what I'm saying?"

Gus moaned and nodded his head.

"My name is Sue-Anne. I'm your nurse. I'm going to get Doctor Snyder."

"No, don't leave me!" Gus tried to reach for her. "They're going to kill me. Why can't I see anything? Why is everything so dark?"

Sue-Anne bit her lip. She knew she shouldn't say anything; it was up to Dr. Snyder to explain to Gus that his eyes had been damaged beyond repair. But she felt she had to give him some kind of answer, just to calm him down.

"You have bandages on your face Mr. Mellonis. Doctor Snyder will explain. Who's after you?"

"Them! The ones who did it, who killed everyone. Pete Webster and the other fellow. Oh God, my eyes!" His words trailed off into more moaning and Sue-Anne took the opportunity to leave. Snyder had left specific orders to be paged the minute Mellonis was conscious. As she hurried down the hall, she thought about what the old man had said.

Pete Webster? She knew the name from the papers. He was one of the missing men from the cemetery. Had he murdered those men in Gus's bar?

In her mind she was already preparing her phone call to the newspaper.

* * *

"Chief, I've got reports of shots fired at Gates of Heaven Cemetery."

Nick Travers approached the desk where Charlie Samuels, the evening shift desk sergeant, was entering the call into the system.

"What about Foster and Harris? They're supposed to be over there."

Samuels shrugged. "I tried them. No answer. Should I send over another car?"

The burning sensation in Travers' stomach grew stronger. He'd been popping antacids all day but eight cups of crappy police station coffee had beaten the medicine into submission, burying it in a deep grave. Having a serial killer running loose wasn't exactly good for the digestion.

"Yeah. Send Cruz and Sullivan. Can you get a position on Foster and Harris's car?" He said a silent prayer of thanks that the town hadn't overruled his request last year for GPS systems in all the cars.

"I've got them. The car's stationary. They're...shit. According to this, they're at the mall." Samuels looked up, his brow furrowed in confusion. "What are they doing there?"

"How the fuck should I know? Send Coleman to get them," Travers said, nodding towards the rookie who was currently typing a report. "And they better have a damn good explanation."

But as he returned to his office, he had a feeling he wasn't going to like what he heard.

Chapter 7

Todd smelled John Boyd before he saw him. Todd was returning to his cubicle, head down, eyes scanning the pages of the book he carried, when the stench of unwashed flesh and long-festering halitosis unexpectedly assaulted him. He looked up and saw a tall, skinny homeless man - what his mother used to call a soup-kitchen regular - standing in front of him, his bloodshot eyes wide with surprise.

"Todd Randolph?"

Todd felt his own eyebrows go up as he tried to figure out how a street denizen might know him and why the man's unshaven face was so familiar. His first thought was that the stranger was a past resident of Wood Hill Sanitarium. Had they shared a group session together? Dined at the same table? Played checkers or cards while banal game and talk shows played endlessly in the game room to the drug-induced zombies?

Then it came to him.

"Holy...John Boyd? Is that you?"

The man gave a sheepish smile, exposing yellowish-brown teeth. Bits of food tumbled to the ground from his unkempt beard and mustache, dislodged by the movement of his lips. Boyd shifted the books he carried to one arm and held out his hand. "It's me. Or what's left of me anyway."

Todd responded automatically to the gesture, grasping Boyd's dirt-encrusted hand. He immediately regretted it, as each movement of John's arm acted like a foul bellows, pumping more rancid odors into the air. Doing his best to take shallow breaths, Todd inched back two steps and said the first thing that came to his mind. "What brings you here?"

Something moved across John's face, self-acknowledgment of his sad state of personal affairs. It made Todd sorry that he'd been unable to ignore the man's hygienically-challenged situation. No one, not even the homeless, enjoyed being reminded that they didn't meet society's arbitrary expectations.

Then John spoke and all other thoughts disappeared from Todd's head.

"It's happening again."

Todd sat down at his mother's kitchen table, sipped from a can of soda, and then held the cold, damp metal against his forehead as he tried to get his thoughts in order. In the few days since he'd been released from Wood Hills, his life had turned into a maelstrom of chaos and confusion. He'd thought the rest of his life would be relatively quiet; other than the animosity of the townspeople, he'd anticipated nothing worse than helping his mother get through her twilight.

Instead, he was currently a suspect in multiple murders, murders that were eerily similar to the ones from his childhood. And that wasn't all. For the first time since that hot, steamy summer after junior year, all four members of the Cemetery Club were back in town. In fact, one of them was upstairs scrubbing years of accumulated filth and disease from his rancid body in the spare bath.

The other two were due for dinner in a few hours.

"Mister Todd?"

Todd opened his eyes to find Abigail Clinton, his mother's home health aide, standing in the entranceway. Her dark, West Indian eyes were full of concern.

"Yes?"

"The Missus is almost out of the medicine. Only a few more days. You want I should get?"

"No, that's all right. I'll take care of it." He held back a smile. Abigail was overcautious and prone to exaggeration. If she said it was going to storm, it meant they were going to get some showers. Two days ago she'd said her nephew was on his death bed and she might need to take time off; it turned out he had a stomach virus. So Todd knew that if she said his mother's medicine would run out in a few days there was probably close to two weeks of pills left in the bottle. Still, he made a mental note to check the next time he was upstairs.

"Okay then. I see you on Monday. I leave dinner in the refrigerator."

"Thanks Abigail. Have a good weekend."

Todd waited until she left and then opened the Tupperware bowl on the top shelf of the 'fridge. Soup of some kind; thick and full of a brown meat he assumed was beef, although with Abigail you could never be sure. He'd come home one day and found her boiling a big pot of pig's feet. From then on he'd never been entirely comfortable eating the meals she prepared. Luckily, his mother never complained.

She'd always been good at keeping her feelings hidden though. Maybe if she'd been different...

Todd sighed and pushed away unhappy childhood memories before they could take a firm grip on him. A metallic squeal from upstairs announced the shower faucets shutting off. His cue to get dinner started. He put the soup back and instead grabbed a package of ground beef from the freezer. He'd be feeding four adults tonight, so it had to be something fast but filling, and something he knew how to cook.

Which meant either hamburgers or meatloaf.

"Meatloaf it is," he said to the package of dead, minced frozen cow. "Nothing but the best for old friends." He placed it in the microwave and hit defrost. While the machine hummed and buzzed, Todd gathered the rest of the ingredients he'd need: breadcrumbs, eggs, an onion, salt, pepper and A1 Sauce. He allowed himself a little smile. Who'd have thought the hospital's kitchen training program would actually come in handy for entertaining?

He was browning the onion in olive oil when John's voice came from the entrance to the kitchen.

"Damn, that smells good. I don't suppose you've got something to hold me over until dinner? All I've had today is McDonalds."

"Sure. Grab a chair and I'll make us a couple of sandwiches." Todd turned away from the stove and had to pause; it took a moment for him to register that the man sitting down at the table was the same person he'd brought home.

Washed, shaved and wrapped in Todd's bathrobe, John Boyd looked a lot more like the friend Todd remembered, albeit with some changes. He'd been skinny in high school. Now he was practically emaciated. His limp, sandy hair had faded to mostly gray thanks to malnutrition, and a web of red capillaries created mystical patterns on a nose that leaned slightly to the left.

His nose was straight in high school, Todd thought. *He must have broken it after I got locked away.*

One thing hadn't changed: John's lips still avoided smiling the way a religious man avoided swearing. You could occasionally tease or surprise one out of him but more often than not he maintained a stoic expression that would make a poker player jealous.

"So." Todd opened the 'fridge and checked the meat compartment. "Bologna and American cheese okay?" He hoped so. It was either that or peanut butter and jelly.

One of John's eyebrow's went up, a typical Boyd expression of self-deprecating humor. "Hell. Half my meals come from dumpsters. Anything where you don't have to scrape the mold off is a treat."

Todd cringed internally. How easy it was to forget the man had been living on the street for years. He made two sandwiches for John and one for himself, opened two more cans of soda and set everything on the table. After giving the onions another stir, he turned the burner off and sat down.

"What happened, John?"

John took a big gulp of soda, washing his mouth clean of white bread and lunch meat, and let out a soft belch. "You mean at the cemetery or to me in general?"

"Both, but hold off on the cemetery story until the others get here."

"I guess that just leaves the rise and fall of John Boyd. You sure you want to hear it?"

Todd shrugged and took a bite of his sandwich. "I spent the last two decades in a mental institution. Any conversation with another sane person is welcome."

"I don't know how many people would classify me as sane, but okay. I'll do us both a favor and give you the summation. After high school, I did the college thing, got my degree in marketing. Opened an insurance business. Did well too. Got married. You remember Susie Mellick?"

Todd nodded. "Cute girl lived over on Balsam Street."

"That's her. We had a son, Kyle. A great kid."

"Sounds nice." Todd smiled but he was already regretting his insistence that John talk. Something bad had to be lurking in the shadows, waiting to pounce.

"It was. In the beginning. But then business started getting crazy. Meetings, conferences, training programs, wining and dining clients. The more money I made, the less I was home to enjoy it. To enjoy my family."

Oh shit. Here it comes.

John chugged more soda. "I started gambling to relieve the stress. It was easy. I didn't even have to go to Atlantic City or Connecticut. Maybe if I had...instead, I just hit the local OTB. Betting a few races on a Friday afternoon turned into four or five nights a week. I lost more than I won but I didn't care. The money was rolling in and I was only twenty-nine. And then..."

"Then what?" The words came out before Todd could stop them.

"I lost ten grand in one week. The same week Susie wrote some checks, big ones. New washing machine. Mortgage. The usual home owner shit. They bounced before I could transfer money from another account. That's how she caught me. We had a fight, I stormed out. I'd never been a big drinker but I went to Gus's and really tied one on. And on the way home, I fell asleep. Or maybe I passed out. I honestly don't remember and it doesn't make a difference anyhow. Next thing I knew I woke up in the hospital. I had a broken rib and a concussion."

"You were lucky."

"No, I wasn't. And neither was the kid I killed. Sixteen years old. Found out from the cops that I ran him over as he crossed the road."

"Oh Christ." *There it was. The turning point in John's life. Mine was getting locked away. Do all of us have one? Are they all just as bad?*

Was that the ultimate curse of the Cemetery Club?

"I did six months in jail. Would've been more but my lawyer pulled some strings and I called in all my favors. Plus, it turned out the kid had been just as drunk as I was. The judge lowered the charges to negligent homicide. Susie divorced me. Took Kyle and left town before I got out. When I did, I had nothing. No family, no money, no house. I threw myself into Lake Alcohol and I've been drowning my sorrows ever since."

John reached for his soda with a shaking hand. The trembling grew worse as he brought the drink to his mouth.

"Are you all right?" Todd asked, thinking his old friend overcome with emotion.

"I got the shakes, real bad." He held out his hands which were doing a good imitation of Parkinson's disease. "I haven't had a drink since yesterday afternoon."

"I don't have anything here," Todd said.

"Good." John's face hardened, his previously morose expression transforming into solid determination. "If the creatures really are back, I need to be sober."

Rather than get started on a track he wasn't ready for, Todd opted to avoid it completely. "Why don't you lie down and rest for a few hours? I have to get dinner finished and take care of my mother. You can use my room. Help yourself to clothes too. I'll wake you up in a couple hours."

The tiniest of smiles touched John's lips, a rare flower blossoming in a desolate landscape. "Thanks. I haven't slept on a real bed in...I don't know how long." Soda in hand, he headed for the stairs.

Todd watched him climb the steps like an old man, arms and legs quivering, planting each foot solidly before lifting the other.

Dear God. Twenty years and the curse I initiated is still hurting people.

Chapter 8

Nick Travers watched the tow truck lower the squad car to the ground. As soon as the winch unhooked, he motioned towards the waiting lab techs. "Hop to it. I want every inch of this car dusted, tested and photographed. And I want it done yesterday."

The forensic team moved in like jackals approaching a corpse. A blue glow filled the interior of the car as ultraviolet lights danced across the seats and console.

"What do you think Chief?" Lieutenant Bobby Mallory asked.

"I think the Mayor's gonna have my ass for having two cops go missing, that's what I think," Travers said, his voice rougher than usual. "I--"

"Chief!" One of the techs stood up. "I've got positive traces of blood."

"Here too," said the woman examining the inside of the trunk. "And fingerprints all over."

"Get 'em to the lab, quick. I don't care if they have to work overtime."

"Chief, do you think--"

"Shut up Mallory. Right now I don't feel like thinking."

"Marisol!" Denny Rankin burst into the lab just as Marisol Flores was unbuttoning her lab coat.

"What?"

"Priority samples. From the police car that belonged to the missing cops. Chief Travers wants the results ASAP."

"Give 'em to Carlson. My shift is over."

Rankin shook his head, his long hair flipping back and forth. "OT baby. Carlson's running fiber samples. Chief said no one goes home 'til the tests are run."

"Fuck." Marisol took the sample tray. "Are they all blood?"

"Yeah."

"Hmm. There's enough here for multiple tests. All right. Tell him I'll have the results in about...two and a half hours."

Rankin nodded and exited in the same frantic fashion as he'd entered, which had more to do with his four-can-a-day energy drink habit than the sudden emergency assignments. Marisol turned on the DNA analyzer and quickly prepared the samples, purposely doing two of each. Once the tests were running, she went to the phone and dialed Cory Miles' cell.

"Hello?"

"Cory? It's Marisol. Where are you?"

"County records room," came the tinny reply. "What's up?"

"I'm stuck here in the lab for at least three more hours. We're gonna have to skip lunch." She tried to keep the disappointment from her voice. They'd had plans to grab a late lunch and continue their 'catching up' before going to Todd's house for dinner.

"That's okay, I'm knee deep in files right now anyway. I'll swing by your house on my way to Todd's, how's that sound?"

"No, you go ahead without me. I'll meet you at Todd's."

"You sure?" He sounded concerned.

Or maybe worried I won't show? Is he that eager to see me?

"Crosses." The word came out unexpectedly; it was what they'd said back in high school, short for 'cross my heart.'

She thought he might make fun of her for using their old slang but Cory just laughed and said goodbye.

Marisol hung up the phone and glanced at the clock. Only four minutes had passed.

It's gonna be a long afternoon.

The soft beep of the DNA analyzer finishing its run startled Marisol from her crossword puzzle. She hurried to grab the report as it printed out.

One glance brought her completely awake.

"Hol-ly shit."

"You've got to be kidding me." Chief Travers looked from Marisol to Dr. Edwin Corish, the County Medical Examiner, who also doubled as

Rocky Point's coroner. "What kind of bullshit is this?"

Marisol clenched her jaw to keep an angry retort from slipping out. They were standing in the Chief's office. She'd expected him to question her results. After all, she was the new girl. It was the reason she'd run the samples twice. Of course she hadn't expected **these** particular results. She'd just wanted to be extra thorough. However, as soon as she'd seen them, she'd gone straight to her boss.

Corish hadn't believed her at first either. But at least he'd been diplomatic enough not to chew her out in front of other people. And after careful review of her work he was ready to back her up.

"There's no doubt Nick," Corish said. "Five different DNA donors. Foster and Harris, plus Pete Webster and two unidentified contributors."

"And the two unidentified samples came from inside the trunk?"

"According to the labels on the samples sir," Marisol answered the police chief. "Foster and Harris came from the front seat, Webster from the back and the other two from the trunk."

"You're sure you didn't screw up the order when you loaded them into the machine?"

"I didn't screw anything up. As long as they were labeled correctly..." She let the implication hang.

"My fucking guys didn't fuck this up!" Travers shouted. Then he took a deep breath before continuing in a more normal tone. "All right. So we've got something weird going on. We knew that already. At least now we know Foster and Harris drove out of the cemetery. Maybe...maybe Webster attacked them and they subdued him. They put him in the back seat, and--"

"And what?" a new voice interrupted.

Marisol and the others turned as Deputy Mayor Jack Smith entered the Chief's office. Marisol gave a silent groan. *Oh great. This day just keeps getting better.*

"The Mayor doesn't want maybes Chief. He wants answers. Now." Smith glanced at Marisol, his handsome face twisting into a sneer. "Hello, **Ms.** Flores. I should have guessed you'd be involved in this mess somehow."

Marisol felt her face flush. "This isn't the time Jack."

"Marisol performed the tests correctly Mr. Smith," Corish said.

Jack turned towards the Coroner. "Tell it to the Mayor Doctor. He wants to see you and Chief Travers right now."

"I'll go too," Marisol said. If someone was going to question her work, she wanted to be there to defend herself.

Jack gave her one of his oozing, fake smiles, the same one he used when schmoozing potential campaign contributors. It'd taken Marisol years to see the supercilious attitude hiding behind it. "I don't think that's necessary. If the M.E. vouches for your work, that's good enough for us. I believe the Mayor is more interested in discussing the...ramifications of your findings. Of course, if it turns out there were any problems with the tests, well...Wal-Mart is always hiring."

Her ex-husband turned and exited the office, putting his back to her before she could respond.

"Don't worry Marisol," Corish said. "We both know the data is correct. He's just being an ass. Go home and get some rest."

"If you want I can go back to the lab and--"

"Go home." Corish escorted her to the door. When he spoke again, his voice had dropped to a whisper. "This is a situation that calls for diplomacy Marisol. You're great in the lab. That's why I hired you. But when it comes to placating an irate mayor..."

Marisol sighed. "Yeah. I'd probably end up getting us both fired. Thanks Chief."

He nodded and went back inside Travers' office. As the door shut, she heard the police chief say, "I sure hope that techie of yours didn't fuck this up."

Asshole. She walked away, not wanting to hear any more. Each insult, each insinuation that her skills weren't up to par, was a knife in her stomach. She'd worked her ass off to be the best at what she did. In the short time she'd been at the M.E.'s office she'd already earned two promotions. But a life of being told she was worthless, first by her father and then by her shitbag of a husband, had succeeded in eroding her self-esteem until only a thin crust remained. A dangerously thin layer of ice over a seemingly bottomless lake of insecurity.

Fuck them all. She looked at her watch. She had an hour to get home, shower and drive over to Todd's house.

I'm going to forget about work and enjoy my night. Catch up with old friends, especially one in particular.

Then she remembered Cory's odd, serious tone when he'd asked her to join them.

I hope this doesn't turn out to be worse than staying at the lab.

Chapter 9

John Boyd tossed and turned on the bed in Todd's guest room. At one point, he cried out and opened his eyes, dimly aware of clanking pans downstairs and someone humming a gentle tune.

Then the nightmare took hold again, another variation on the same theme that had haunted him for twenty years.

They were hanging out inside that old crypt, like always. John, Cory and Marisol. And then Todd showed up...

With it.

Gates of Heaven Cemetery, 20 years ago

"You guys wanna smoke a doob while we wait?"

John pulled the joint from his shirt pocket and waved it in the air like a man offering his dog a treat.

"Nah, let's wait," Cory said. "Todd'll be here in a minute." Next to him, Marisol nodded her head, her dark hair brushing against Cory's shoulder. He seemed unaware of her proximity, his eyes focused on the copy of *Rolling Stone* he'd brought to the mausoleum with him.

How can he not know she likes him? John thought. It's obvious to everyone else. "I got plenty more where this one came from." He patted his pocket. "My brother has like, six ounces stashed in his closet. I snuck almost a whole dime bag out of it. He'll never know."

Before anyone could answer, a shadow appeared at the crypt's entrance. The door swung open with a grating squeal and Todd entered, a large cardboard box in his hands.

"Sorry I'm late." He set the box down. White speckles dotted his summer-tanned arms. "I had to help my father paint the church doors."

"Whatcha got?" Marisol asked, pointing at the box.

In the three weeks since school let out, they'd turned the dank mausoleum into their own private hideaway. Several sleeping bags and pillows made a makeshift sitting area, offering a soft seat and protection from the cold, damp floor. Cory had supplied two Coleman lanterns and two folding snack trays that served as end tables. Marisol had contributed a heavy-duty hasp and padlock so they could lock the door when they weren't there. When asked where she'd gotten it, she'd shrugged off the question, leading John to believe she'd stolen it from the hardware store. Not that he cared; Mr. Fleming, the man who owned the store, was kind of an asshole anyway, always yelling at kids to stay away from the spray paint or he'd call their parents.

For his part, John had pilfered an oversized flashlight, matches, two bottles of wine and a two-burner camp stove from his garage. He knew his parents would never miss the items. They hadn't gone camping in ten years and they had something like six cases of wine in the basement.

But it was Todd who'd done the lion's share of turning the dusty, creepy space into a totally cool hangout. Every day he showed up with something new: cards and poker chips, a portable radio, even a roll of heavy black material to hang on the inside of the window so the light from the lamps didn't give them away at night.

Best of all, he always managed to snag some food and soda from the canned goods, crackers and soft drinks his father collected each month as donations for the local soup kitchens and shelters.

"Don't you worry about getting caught?" Marisol had asked one day, as they'd unpacked several cans of Beef-A-Roni and a liter bottle of Coke.

Todd had shrugged. "Nah. There's cases of this shit down in the church basement. And it's not like we keep track. People bring it in and stack it themselves. Once a month my dad drives around delivering it. At least this way it's not going to feed some alky bum."

"Got that right," Cory had said, hefting a bottle of wine and taking a drink. Everyone had laughed.

So when Todd showed up with the cardboard carton, everyone had expected more of the same.

They'd been wrong.

"Check this out," Todd said, his voice full of excitement. He reached into the box and pulled out a smaller box, this one flat and long.

At first John thought it might be Monopoly or some other board game, then he saw the name.

"Ooji? What the fuck is ooji?"

Cory laughed. "It's Ouji, not ooji. *Wee-gee.* Where'd you get it?" he asked Todd.

"It was with the donations. Beats me why anyone would give it to a church."

"What is it?" John asked. "Some kind of board game?"

"It's supposed to be a way to communicate with ghosts. My cousin had one but we never got around to playing with it." Cory opened the box, revealing a board with fancy letters on it and a flat, heart-shaped object with a hole in the middle.

"Get the fuck out of here!" Marisol pushed her way between Todd and Cory to check out the game. "That's too cool!"

"I don't think it actually works," Cory said with a bemused smile.

"Only one way to find out." Todd placed the board on the blanket and motioned for them all to sit down around it. "Let's conjure ourselves a spirit!"

Just then, a loud CRACK! echoed through the crypt. Marisol screamed.

"Something's in here!"

* * *

John sat up, his heart pounding, his teeth clamped down on his own terrified shout. The banging sounded again, only this time it was just knuckles rapping on the bedroom door.

"John? Rise and shine buddy. Dinner's almost ready and the others will be here soon. I'll meet you downstairs in a minute; I just have to bring my mother her dinner."

"Okay." John rested his head against the wall and closed his eyes as Todd's footsteps receded down the hall. His heart was beating so violently it actually made his head vibrate against the cool plaster.

Christ, it felt so real, almost as if I time-traveled back into my own body. Even now he could smell the musty odors of the crypt beneath the tantalizing scents drifting up from downstairs.

His hands still shaking, he levered himself from the bed and pulled on the sweatpants and t-shirt he'd taken from Todd's closet. The sweats were kind of short on him but they'd do. He looked in the mirror, almost expecting to see the sixteen-year-old boy he'd been in his dream. Instead, the sunken, bloodshot eyes of his present day alcoholic self stared back at him, their clear blue color dimmed by too many bottles of cheap booze and too many nights of no sleep. He combed his longish, sleep-flattened hair back with his fingers and headed downstairs.

He'd just given the gravy a stir and snuck a fingerful of mashed potatoes when a knock on the back door made him jump. He replaced the lid on the potatoes, feeling foolishly guilty, as if he'd been caught stealing rather than tasting the food at a friend's house.

"C'mon in," he said, seeing Cory Miles's face through the window.

Cory entered, a wide smile on his face. John tried to return the man's enthusiastic greeting but instead of making him feel better, Cory's presence brought back the fear he'd felt during his recent trip down memory lane.

"John? John Boyd? Todd didn't tell me you'd be here. Man, it's good to see you. Jesus, you're as skinny as you were in high school." Cory patted the slight roll of his own midsection. "I haven't been so lucky. What's your secret?"

John backed up, putting the corner of the table between them. "Alcoholism and living on the streets."

Cory's face froze and then his expression slowly grew serious, as if someone held a match to a wax smile. "Oh shit. I didn't know. John, I'm sorry. If there's--"

"Forget it." John opened the 'fridge and pulled out two sodas, wishing he had the power to turn them into beer. "Todd can fill you in another time. Tonight he wants to talk about something else."

"What's happening in town." Cory opened his soda. "Todd thinks...he thinks it's like twenty years ago."

"It is." John sat down. "I've seen them. In the graveyard. The Grays."

"C'mon John. That alien shit didn't cut it in high school. You don't still believe it, do you?" Cory sat down across from him.

"Oh, so it's okay to believe in demons and ghosts but not aliens?"

"I didn't say I believed in them either. Just because something weird happens doesn't mean there's a supernatural cause. I'd rather focus on a rational explanation."

"Yeah? Like what?"

Cory frowned. "That's kind of why we're getting together tonight, to figure that out. But offhand, I could say toxic gasses, drugs, a cult of Satanists or even just some psycho serial killer."

"None of that explains what we saw in those tunnels."

"Christ John, we were sixteen and scared shitless. Even if there wasn't some kind of toxic waste down there, our imaginations could have conjured up anything and we'd have believed it."

"Then how come what Todd did...why did it work?"

"I don't know. But it does kind of disprove aliens, doesn't it? Maybe it was a mass psychosis."

"That kind of closed-minded thinking could get us killed. I--"

"Hey, calm down you two," Todd said as he entered the room. "We're gonna talk this all out tonight, in a calm, rational way. But first we're going to eat dinner." He opened the oven and pulled out a square cake pan covered in foil.

"Shouldn't we wait for Marisol?" Cory asked.

As if in response, someone knocked on the back door.

"Come in," Todd called out. He grinned at Cory and John "I saw her pull into the driveway just before I came downstairs."

John watched Cory's face as Marisol entered the kitchen. *Shit. He still hasn't gotten over her. And judging from the way she's staring at him, she's carrying a major torch too.*

Marisol greeted Cory with a hug and a kiss on the cheek. Something about the way the two of them said hello - the inflection of their words, the nonchalant way they touched - told John it wasn't the first time they'd seen each other recently. Her demeanor with Todd was different. She squealed like a little girl and wrapped her arms around him.

"Todd! It's so good to see you! I heard what happened. It was terrible but I'm so glad you called Cory to get you out."

"It's good to see you too," Todd said. He was obviously uncomfortable with her display of affection. After patting her once on the back, he gently escaped her bear hug and took a step backwards.

Marisol either didn't notice or chose not to comment; instead, she turned her vibrant energy in John's direction. "John? Oh, my, God! I can't believe you're here as well!"

She held out her arms but John backed away before she could reach him. He didn't even realize what he'd done until he saw the happy smile fade from her face, leaving a bewildered look in its place.

"Sorry," he said. "I'm not used to people wanting to get close to me."

"What?" She turned towards Cory, who shrugged.

Todd saved John the embarrassment of explaining. "Um, until recently, John was...staying in a shelter."

"A shelter?" She looked from Todd back to John.

"What Todd's trying to say is that I've been a homeless bum for awhile now. Today was my first shower in months. If you'd run across me this morning you wouldn't have wanted to be within ten feet of me."

"Oh."

For a moment none of them spoke. Then Todd lifted the foil off the baking pan, filling the kitchen with the mouthwatering odors of meatloaf and roasted vegetables.

"Who's ready to eat?"

Chapter 10

Henry Coleman heard the sounds just as he lowered his aching body into his old recliner. The crushing humidity of the evening had set off his arthritis something fierce, making every movement a little slice of personal hell. Which was why the thought of getting up again annoyed him so. Sure the echo of breaking glass and shouting voices coming from the trailer next door hinted at something strange going on, but his seventy-three-year-old bones were offering a pretty strong argument for just turning up the volume of the TV and letting the Mackleys handle their own problems.

"Goddamned fools," he muttered, as he tried to concentrate on the classic John Wayne movie he'd just come across. He wanted to curse his own curiosity as well. After more than twenty years of living in Lowland Gardens, the mobile home park on the south end of the Lowlands, he should have been used to the sounds of family squabbles. Raised voices were as common as illegitimate children and welfare checks. Hell, before Alice had passed away, he and his wife had been known to contribute their fair share of arguments for the neighbors' listening pleasure. It was part of the scenery, just like the factories over the hill and the flock of pink flamingos in the Mackley's front grass.

Only difference between them and the rest of the trash around them was they'd never resorted to raising fists or using household objects as weapons of personal destruction.

Truth was, if you lived in Lowland Gardens, you learned quickly that it was better to stay out of other peoples' affairs. People who had no qualms about smacking their own kin around were as apt as not to bust a neighbor in the nose when that nose stuck itself where it didn't belong.

"Fuck 'em," was Henry's personal motto and he muttered it now as he turned up the volume. Then he said it again for the hell of it.

Problem was, even with the Duke's voice blasting his aged ears he still heard the next scream that came from the Mackley's trailer.

"Christ, it sounds like they're slaughtering each other." He knew the couple well enough. Typical trailer-park trash. Both of them approaching forty but looking ten years older. She worked down at the Shop-N-Save, he mostly sat home and drank beer. No surprise if they were the type to prefer knuckles to words when it came to making a point, but in the couple of years they'd been living there, he'd never heard anything like the ruckus they were causing now.

More glass shattered and a man shouted for help. That's when it hit Henry that maybe it wasn't a fight at all, maybe they were just drunk and had their own television turned up way too loud, watchin' some goddamned monster movie or karate flick.

"Inconsiderate bastards." With a groan he pushed himself from his chair and headed for his bedroom window, which he knew would give him a good view of the Mackley's living room. *God knows I've stared at their place enough times, hoping to catch a peek of Stacy Mackley in her birthday suit.* He grinned at his peeping tom tendency, one of the few joys left in his life. "Folks don't know enough to buy curtains, they're fair game," he liked to tell himself, while waiting for a glimpse of Stacy's titties. When you couldn't afford HBO you had to make your own entertainment.

A quick look now, just to make sure they were having a party and not a brawl, and then he'd head over there and give them a piece of what for.

Pulling the curtain aside a few inches, Henry peered across the tiny patch of so-called yard separating the two double-wides. Sure enough, the lights were off in the Mackley's living room but their big old TV - a twenty-year-old giant - was on, illuminating the room in grayish-blue light.

It only took a moment for Henry to determine that the TV wasn't the cause of the noises he'd been hearing.

Stacy's face was pressed up against the picture window so hard her features were deformed, like her face was melting against the glass. A man stood behind her, his arm wrapped around her neck in a chokehold. Her arms flailed back and forth, trying to dislodge his grip, and her tongue protruded from her mouth like a panting dog's, leaving snail trails of spit on the glass.

While Henry watched, the man used his free hand to grab Stacy by the hair and bang her head against the window. The second time he did it, a crack appeared in the heavy glass. The third time, she stopped struggling and went limp. He let go of her neck and she slowly slid down the clear surface, her face stretching even more as the glass pulled it out of shape, until her body came to rest draped over the television set.

Only then did Henry get a good look at her attacker, who up to that point he'd assumed was her good-for-nothing husband. Instead, the TV's flickering light revealed a large, powerfully-built man in a police uniform.

Jesus H. Christ. A cop just killed someone.

Henry backed away from favorite voyeur spot. What the fuck was he supposed to do now? Call the cops on one of their own? Who'd believe him? Plus, any time you called the police, they automatically got your name and number - he knew that much from watching television - and they sent out the nearest patrol car.

What if the lunatic across the way got the call to respond?

Something moved behind the cop and Henry focused his attention on the Mackley's living room again. At first he thought a child had entered the room, which was odd, since the Mackley's didn't have any kids. Then the figure moved closer to the TV and Henry had to clap a hand over his mouth to keep from screaming. He'd watched his fair share of movies over the years, especially after Alice passed and he had nothing else better to do, and he recognized the creature right away.

Aliens! It's a fucking invasion.

The egg-shaped head, glowing eyes and tiny arms - just like he'd seen in UFO movies and specials. As he watched, the alien reached out with its hands and grabbed hold of Stacy's face. The cop stared impassively while the deformity pushed itself into Stacy's throat. Her body twitched and convulsed as the dark form disappeared down her neck like a lizard squeezing into a hole.

Stacy stopped struggling and stood up, her face now wearing the same emotionless expression as the cop.

Shit on a stick. They've both been taken over. Now it made sense to Henry. The aliens were parasites and the cop already had one of the little gray bastards living inside him. He'd knocked Stacy out so his friend could have a home.

The alien-cop bent down out of sight and when he stood up he had Stacy's husband slung over his shoulder. Henry leaned closer to the glass, trying to see if Ed was alive. At that exact moment, his air conditioner kicked on, the whirring noise of the compressor sending his heart into overdrive. He instinctively turned to see what the noise was and in the process banged his elbow against the glass.

When he looked back at the Mackley's, Stacy and cop were both staring back at him.

Shit. Shitmutherfuckingshit!

Henry backed away from the window and ran across the small living room towards the door, then stopped. He couldn't go outside; his front door faced the Mackley's. That would be like jumping out of the pan and into the fire. He could go out the back, but he'd fenced his yard in years ago, when they'd still had their dog, meaning he'd have to either climb the fence - an impossibility with his arthritis - or use the gate.

Which faced the front.

"They're gonna be coming over here any second. Think, Henry, think." He looked around the trailer.

And saw the picture of the dog.

Sparky had been a big dumb-as-shit mutt Alice rescued from the pound. He'd died just a few months before Alice did and Henry often thought she'd given up the ghost just so she could be with Sparky again. God knew she loved that damn dog more than anyone, himself included.

Most importantly, they'd never gotten rid of his doghouse.

Henry ran for the back door and chugged across the yard as fast as his aching knees would carry him. Bending down to crawl into the musty sanctuary set his back to complaining something fierce but he ignored it, squeezing himself as deep into the dusty space as he could.

His knees and elbows howled in pain as he pulled his legs against his chest and wrapped his arms around his shins. Breathing in heavy pants, he sat among the spiderwebs, dead bugs and dried leaves, waiting. In the darkness, the glowing face of his watch showed ten to nine.

Across the yard, the gate squealed as someone opened it.

* * *

Cory and Marisol paused by Marisol's aging Toyota Corolla. She pulled her keys from her pocket but didn't move to unlock her door.

"What shift are you working tomorrow?" he asked, the soft, deep tones of his voice echoing the sultry, smooth atmosphere of the warm summer night.

"Day shift," Marisol said, wondering if she was having the same effect on him as he was on her. It had been an effort not to reach out and hold his hand or lean her head against his shoulder, as they sat next to each other on Todd Randolph's couch for the past several hours.

"So, um, maybe we could grab lunch? You still owe me."

God, yes. Yes! she wanted to say, but common sense overrode her feelings. "I'd love to but with everything that's going on I don't know what kind of day it's going to be. I might end up working overtime."

Cory gave her one of his lopsided, carefree grins. "All right. Well, I'll see you soon then." He stepped back so she could open her door.

Todd had made plans for everyone to get together again in two days to compare notes but Marisol had no intention of waiting that long. "Wait, how about this? I'll call you in the afternoon, let you know how my day's going, and then we can make plans for dinner? My treat."

"It's a date," he said. He stepped towards her and leaned down, his lips aimed towards a spot on her cheek.

Before she could stop herself, Marisol tilted her head and intercepted his friendly goodnight kiss by planting her lips firmly on his. Then, quick as she'd started it, she broke the stolen kiss and turned away, covering her sudden embarrassment by fumbling the key into the door lock.

When she looked up again, Cory was halfway to his pride and joy, a classic black Cadillac Seville he'd restored in his spare time. Marisol waited, her lips tingling, until he drove away. At that moment, the haunting wail of police sirens filled the night, making her jump. The ululating cries grew closer and for a brief moment she was convinced they were heading for Todd's house. Then the direction changed and she realized their goal was someplace even more familiar.

The Lowlands.

Where she'd spent the first eighteen years of her life.

That can't be good. Not that sirens in the Lowlands were anything new. She'd grown up with the cops visiting her house and those of her neighbors more times than she could count, usually for domestic disputes but on occasion to break up fights between drunken neighbors or to arrest someone wanted for a crime of some sort.

Yet there was something about these sirens that set her nerves on edge, something in their primitive howling that screamed *Beware! Danger is near!*

The feeling of impending doom washed away the giddy schoolgirl after-effects of her kiss, leaving behind nothing but a nameless anxiety that was all the more nerve-wracking for its lack of a source. With a sigh, Marisol started her car and headed home.

Todd Randolph happened to glance through the kitchen window just in time to catch Marisol and Cory as they kissed. A brief kiss, to be sure, but a kiss nevertheless.

Their first one? Wouldn't it be something if in the middle of all this, they finally got together after all this time?

He returned his gaze to the pot he was scrubbing, wondering if their burgeoning romance was a good omen or a bad one. He decided to take it as good, because the rest of the night had gone so well. Granted, John had stuck to his aliens-among-us theory. Todd still felt sure that the creatures had to be something from the depths of Hell. After all, he'd used Holy water and a Bible against them the last time. That had to count for something. Cory and Marisol were still on the fence, caught between Todd's previous success and the idea that there had to be a more logical explanation than demons.

But there'd been a lot less arguing than he'd expected and in the end they'd compromised - John would continue to research the alien angle while Todd would stick with the same line of investigation he'd been pursuing since he'd been committed. Over the next two days, each of them would put together a summary of what they'd learned and brief the rest of the group at the next meeting.

In the meantime, Cory's job was to go back and learn as much as he could about the murders from two decades ago and find any commonalities between them and the current killings. And Marisol would use her position with the ME's office to try and get copies of evidence and reports from all the cases.

Todd closed the door of the dishwasher and wiped his hands on a towel. Funny how things work out. Once the four of them had sat down, it was like no time had passed. They'd simply picked up where they left off twenty years ago, each of them assuming the roles they'd held as teenagers: John the quiet, reserved onlooker; Cory the shy, happy kid who was completely oblivious to how good he had things; Marisol, troubled and abused.

And me? I'm like the den mother. Back then I stole food and liquor because I was rebelling but also because I enjoyed playing host to the others. Now I'm doing the same thing.

"Hey, you okay?"

Turning, Todd found John staring at him, a concerned look on his face. "Yeah, I was just...I don't know. Reminiscing, I guess."

"I have a feeling we're going to be doing a lot of that the next few days. And not all of it good either."

"No, I'm afraid not. What are your plans for tonight?"

John shrugged. "I hadn't really thought that far ahead. Usually I just crash at one of the shelters."

"Well, you're welcome to stay here. The guest bedroom isn't much but it's got clean sheets and no roommates."

A ghost of a smile touched John's lips. "That'd be great." He held his arms out, indicating the clean clothes he'd just retrieved from the dryer. "I'd forgotten what fresh-washed clothes smell like."

"You want to watch a little TV? I've got more soda and food in the 'fridge."

"No, I think I'll turn in if you don't mind. It's been a pretty exhausting day and my belly's not used to being this full."

"Okay." Todd grabbed a soda for himself. "The spare room's right next to mine. I'm gonna stay up for a while; I always do. Nowadays I don't even think about closing my eyes before the end of Letterman. I've had trouble sleeping ever since...well, you know. "

"Yeah." John paused by the steps, as if he was going to say something else and then turned away and went upstairs.

Todd took his soda into the living room and sat down in the brown recliner that had belonged to his father. It was a déjà vu moment for Todd, one of many he'd had since moving in. Although he'd never lived in the house before, in some ways it felt as if he'd spend his whole life there. Everywhere he looked it was like seeing his old house, the one he'd grown up in, through a piece of flimsy lace. When his parents had moved they'd taken all their belongings with them and very little had changed in the intervening twenty years. The same brown rug on the floor; same brown and white patterned couch and love seat. When Todd's father had died the church had closed as well, taking with it the family's only source of income. Since then, Todd's mother had been living on Medicaid, Social Security and her husband's life insurance policy. After the mortgage and taxes, there wasn't much left.

Todd wondered if his father was looking down, watching him

from wherever it was people went when they died. Since the day Todd's great-grandfather had established Rocky Point's first official church more than one hundred and fifty years ago - he'd built the original Randolph house behind it at the same time - a Randolph had always served as Minister in the Episcopalian church, a role handed down from father to son without any break in service.

Until me, Todd thought, leaning back in the recliner. *Dad must be so proud.* On the floor directly in front of him sat the darker stain in the carpet where his uncle had spilled his coffee, a reminder of his father's death. *So much death because of me. So many changes. What would my life be like right now if I hadn't found that game?*

Thinking of the other Cemetery Club members, he added, *What would their lives be like?*

The guilt rose up again, the monster that lived deep inside him, a thing that refused to go away. Sometimes it burrowed down and hibernated for days or weeks but it always came back. And each time it appeared, it was stronger than ever.

Oh God, I wish I'd never met them!

A sad thing to think about his only three friends in the whole world but it was true. The Cemetery Club had led him down a dark road, even if the choices he'd made were his own. Being a part of it had turned him further away from the path his father and God had intended.

Outside, sirens howled pain-filled announcements of violence and death, startling Todd from his reverie. Judging by their vicinity to his neighborhood they were heading somewhere close by. Not his street; more likely the dangerous section of town. The factories, maybe. Or the Lowlands.

He flicked on the television and scrolled through the channels until he found one of his favorite movies from the eighties, some silly beach comedy starring Demi Moore and John Cusack. Turning up the volume so it drowned out the call of the emergency vehicles, he leaned back and tried to relax while Demi pretended to sing and play the guitar. He had a feeling it was going to be a long time before he got to sleep.

Chapter 11

Although the Monday morning sun had barely crested the horizon, Nick Travers was already on his fifth cup of coffee from the vile witch's kettle that had cleverly disguised itself as the station's coffee pot. He'd been called in just after three a.m., following several frantic reports of domestic violence from the Lowlands. Normally that wouldn't have been enough to warrant rousting him from his bed, but in the course of the investigations, Officer Manny Salvo had gone missing.

"Chief?"

Travers turned from the coffee pot and found Bud Marks, the morning shift desk sergeant, standing by the door to the break room with an unhappy look on his face.

"What is it now Marks?"

"Um, we've got a guy who says he's a witness to a kidnapping."

"He saw something? What? Where?" Travers downed his coffee and tossed the paper cup aside.

"Actually, he says...he says it was a cop." The rest of Marks' words came out in a rush. "Said a cop and some other folks were taken over by aliens and they're the ones that caused all the trouble in the Lowlands last night." Marks stepped back and cringed slightly, like a dog expecting a boot to the ass.

"Oh for the love of...Jesus Christ, Marks. Why are you bothering me with this shit?"

"The guy's old. Maybe a drunk. He could have seen something for real and just gotten it all mixed up in his head. I thought you might want to talk to him, just in case."

Travers closed his eyes and counted to ten, a trick for calming his anger that he'd been trying unsuccessfully to master ever since getting elected Sheriff. He reached six before he couldn't hold it in any longer.

"For chrissakes Marks. Give him to somebody else, anybody else. I don't care who. Give him to a rookie. Don't bother me unless you've actually got something better to report than this kind of nonsense."

"Yes sir," Marks said. He might have said something else but by then Travers had already pushed past him and gone into his office, slamming the door shut behind him.

Staring at the mountain of reports piled on his desk, Travers shook his head. "Just once I'd like to catch a fuckin' break. Just once."

He sat down and tried to focus his coffee-wired brain on how three cops could have disappeared in less than a week. Before he could open the first file, his intercom beeped.

"Sheriff? Deputy Mayor Smith is on line one for you."

Travers groaned and put his head in his hands.

Just fucking once.

"Have a seat right here," Bud Marks said to Henry Coleman, indicating the cheap plastic chair across from Manny Salvo's desk. Bud hadn't had any luck in finding someone available to question the old geezer, so he'd taken it upon himself to conduct the interview. He'd chosen Salvo's desk because from there he could answer the phones, talk to the witness and still have a view of the front door.

"Okay Mr. Coleman, why don't you tell me what you saw?"

The old man frowned. "You said you was gonna get the Chief."

"I'm sorry but he's very busy right now. If you don't want to talk to me, you'll have to come back another time."

Coleman pursed his lips as he considered what to do. "Fine," he finally said, just as Bud was about to ask him again. "But you ain't gonna believe me."

Marks stared at the grizzled countenance before him, took in the raccoon-mask dark circles around the man's eyes, his tousled hair and dirty clothes, and fought to keep from saying his real thoughts out loud. *You're probably right.*

"That's okay. Just tell it like it happened."

"Well, it all started when I heard this crashing and banging comin' from the Mackley's trailer. Shoutin' too. They're usually pretty quiet, so I decided to peek out my window and see what the ruckus was about. Had a good view, clear as day."

"You saw people's faces?"

"Yep. This big ol' cop had Stacy Mackley pinned against the window. He was stranglin' her, had his arm around her neck. Banged her head against the glass real good too. Thought he was gonna kill her right there but he dropped her to the floor soon's she passed out. That's when *it* came into the room."

"It?"

"The alien. Ain't you been listening? The goddammed thing that took over Stacy. Crawled right down her throat. Then her and this cop picked up her dead husband and went outside. They didn't catch me though. I hid my ass in the dog house. Waited there all night. Couple of times I heard people come into the yard and look through the trailer. I stayed put until the sun came up. Figured no aliens gonna be runnin' around in the daytime."

Bud Marks put down his pencil and sighed. Coleman was nothing but a drunken dead end after all. "This cop you saw. Can you describe him?"

"I don't have to," Coleman said. "That's him right there."

Marks followed the man's bony, shaking finger to a picture on the desk. In the print, Manny Salvo was holding up his citation for volunteer work.

"You're sure that's the man you saw?" Bud asked, grabbing his pencil again.

"Sure as shittin'. Saw him clear as day. Scared the piss out of me. Say, you got any coffee?"

Bud stood up and pointed to the break room. "In there. Help yourself. Just don't leave the station. I'll be right back." He headed for the Sheriff's office, fighting to keep a smug expression from his face.

Don't bother you unless I have something to go on? I think this is gonna count as one motherfucking big something.

* * *

Warner Dawes looked at the people taking their seats in the conference room and felt a tickle of fear run down his back, a creepy-crawly sensation that sent his body into an involuntary shiver. He fought the feeling down and took a sip from his coffee cup, happy to see that his hand didn't shake at all. As Mayor of Rocky Point, it behooved him to appear calm and in control, no matter what the situation.

And judging by the grim expressions on the faces of those around him, they had one shitfuck of a situation on their hands.

Deputy Mayor Jack Smith was the last person to enter the room and even he wore a serious look, a welcome change from the supercilious smile that was as much a part of him as his perfect hair and athletic body. Smith took his customary seat at the opposite end of the table. Dawes preferred to be as far away from his second in command as possible, mostly because he couldn't stand the sneaky bastard. But also because he knew he cut a more commanding figure by not sitting next to someone younger and better looking. There was also a business reason for the arrangement: it kept anyone they met with penned in between them, allowing no one else to think they had any kind of equality by sitting at the other head of the table. Pigs in a pen, as he liked to think of those who came looking for favors.

Today, they had four piggies boxed in: Sheriff Travers, Edwin Corish the M.E., Town Clerk Freddy Alou and Betty Smyrna, Dawes's secretary.

Dawes purposely took another slow, relaxed sip of coffee as everyone got their papers in order and then turned to the Sheriff. "All right Nick, how bad is it?"

Travers cleared his throat. "It's not good, that's for damn sure. Over the past two nights we've had eighteen reported disturbances in town, most of them in Lowland Park and the factory district. The same M.O. in every case. Neighbors hear noises, sometimes shouting. Figure it's just a domestic disturbance. But the next day, people are missing."

"How many?" Smith asked the question before Dawes had the chance.

Without glancing at his notes, Travers said, "At least twenty."

"At least?" Dawes frowned. "You don't have an exact number?"

"No, sir. There could be more that just haven't been reported. It is the Lowlands after all. On the other hand, we both know that in that part of town it's not uncommon for someone to go off on a bender for a few days or get some cash and hightail it out of town to Atlantic City, or maybe one of them Indian casinos. Hell, sometimes people just up and leave without telling anyone, never come back, and you don't hear from them again until years later. These aren't bankers and business owners after all. So it could be more or it could be less. However, there are the other cases, outside the Lowlands."

"Go on."

"Four missing for sure. I've got my men looking into them as top priorities. It kind of puts the Lowlands on the back burner but from a PR point of view we have to do it. Ten people disappear from a trailer park, most people either don't bat an eye or they say good riddance. One insurance agent disappears from a nice neighborhood and you've got all sorts of folks writing the newspaper, wanting to know what's being done to solve the crime."

"God fucking dammit." Dawes shook his head. "Any other good news?"

An angry expression took hold of Travers's face. "Yeah. I've got another cop missing. Manny Salvo. He responded to a call in the Lowlands two nights ago and we haven't heard from him since."

"How can a cop just disappear?" Smith asked.

"If I knew that, he wouldn't be missing!" Travers said, his voice rising to almost a shout. He took a deep breath and continued in a calmer tone. "We have a possible witness. Unfortunately, he's eighty-something years old and thinks aliens are abducting people."

Dawes didn't know what to say. Things were even worse than he'd thought. He glanced at Corish. "Is there anything you can add to all this?"

The M.E. shrugged. "All we can do is process the evidence that's given to us. So far, other than the patrol car that belonged to Foster and Harris, we haven't had anything to work on. Travers's men gathered forensic evidence from some of the alleged disappearance sites, but it's going to take a long time to separate prints and DNA traces from home owners and regular visitors and determine if there is anything substantiating intruders. What we need to find are commonalities between several of the potential crime scenes. Then I'll be able to give you some real information."

"So that's it then? We just sit around with our thumbs up our asses?"

"Goddammit, we're not just sitting around Warner," Travers said. "My people are doing everything they can. I've got everybody working double shifts but we're three men down and we can't ignore the regular calls we get in."

"Maybe it's time to call in some outside help, like the FBI or Staties?" asked Corish.

Travers and Dawes responded in unison. "No!"

"That would be a PR nightmare," Dawes continued. "For now we keep it to ourselves. Hell, as far as we know this might not be as bad as it seems. Like you said, a lot of the disappearances could just be drunks or people running away from bad marriages. Focus on the missing cops and the murders at Gus's place. Vandalism in the Lowlands isn't as much of a priority."

Smith cleared his throat. "Um, sir? There is one other thing we should discuss."

"What's that?" Dawes looked down the table. He hated when Smith sprang surprises on him, especially during meetings.

"I've been getting a lot of calls from the townspeople. Not just the usual loudmouths either. The Rotary Club, homeowners associations, even the Chamber of Commerce. Everyone's worried that nothing's been done about the murders at Gus's or the cemetery. I was thinking...maybe we should have a town meeting. Let everyone know we're not sitting on our asses. We can play up the missing officers angle - people hear that, they'll automatically believe we're putting all our resources into this."

"We are!" Travers slapped the table with his hand. Across from him,

Betty Smyrna jumped.

"I -*we* - know that Sheriff. But the constituents don't."

Dawes thought about it. If his deputy mayor was convinced a town meeting was necessary, it probably was. He was an asshole but he did have brains.

"All right." The Mayor glanced down at his schedule. "Set something up for...tomorrow night. Put a notice in the paper. A very small one. I don't want every yahoo in town showing up. Let's keep it short and simple. The fewer questions we have to answer the better."

"Yes sir." Smith typed something into his Blackberry.

Dawes looked around the table. "Anything else?" No one responded. "Then everyone get back to work. Sheriff, you've got the rest of today and tomorrow. See if you can come up with something that will make us look good at this meeting."

Everyone stood and headed for the door. As Betty Smyrna went past, Dawes placed a hand on her shoulder. "Um, Betty, could you come into my office for a moment? I have some memos for you to write up."

Betty glanced back, a knowing smile on her face. She'd only been working for him for six months but she'd learned very quickly what kind of memos he enjoyed dictating, and she'd proven very willing to put in the extra work required.

As he headed for his office, his eyes on Betty's shapely ass under her conservative skirt, Dawes rationalized his cheating the same way he always did: *It's a job-related necessity. Being Mayor is stressful. In order to perform my job well I need to eliminate the stress. Better a ten minute hummer in my office than being caught in a sleazy massage parlor. And it's not like my wife is going to drag her fat ass down here and crawl under my desk.*

The image of Abby's hefty bulk wedged under his desk caused him to snort laughter, which he covered up quickly with a cough, lest anyone think he wasn't focused on the serious situation at hand.

Only when his door was securely locked and Betty's mouth wrapped just as securely around his dick, did he allow himself to smile.

Chapter 12

Kush Pachuri was doing his usual Monday night inventory when he heard Ana, his daughter, shouting for him. Fearing another robbery, he dropped his clipboard and ran to the front of the combination gas station and convenience store.

Instead of a masked gunman or a group of drug-addled teenagers from the nearby Lowlands, he found his daughter pointing towards the gas pumps. "Help them papa! They're killing them!"

Kush looked out the window but it took a moment for him to register what he was seeing. A car was parked at pump three, its doors open. Four people stood by the car and at first it looked like two of them were embracing the other two. Kush had seen such vulgar displays of public affection many times since opening his business, men pinning their girlfriends or wives against the car and kissing them with a passion only appropriate in a bedroom, but never two couples at once. He was about to turn away when one of the men lifted a hand and drove his fist directly into the face of the woman he held.

A carjacking? Here? Kush looked back at the counter. No time to call the police. "Give me the gun, quickly!"

Ana, to her credit, didn't question him. She just handed him the pistol he'd kept loaded and ready under the counter ever since they'd been robbed last year.

Clutching the weapon he ran outside, shouting at the men. "Go away! Leave them alone. I have a gun!"

Instead of backing away or running, the two attackers dropped their victims and came towards him. As they passed under the gas island's lights, he saw fresh blood covering their faces, dripping from their mouths.

Allah save me. They are crazy. Kush immediately changed direction, now moving backwards as the two men kept approaching.

"Father?"

Ana's voice from behind him. Keeping his eyes – as well as the gun - on the two men, he called out to her. "Daughter! Run, now!"

He heard her footsteps behind him as she did as she was told. He thanked his ancestors that she wasn't a spoiled teenager like so many of her classmates, that she still knew to obey her parents. Then one of the men changed direction and started walking faster. Kush wondered if he'd made the right decision. He knew Ana would have run around the back of the building, to the employee parking lot. If the man reached her before she got to her car...

Deciding he had no choice, he turned and fired the gun at the man following his daughter. His first shot missed but his second hit home, sending the man staggering back against the propane tank cage that sat at the corner of the store.

Propane?

Kush's finger had already pulled the trigger two more times before the STOP signal from his brain reached his hand. He never heard the metallic ping of metal striking metal over the sound of the gun's firing. Just as he never saw the spark created by the last bullet hitting the metal screen of the cage.

He couldn't miss the effects that followed though.

Escaping propane from a punctured tank ignited, producing a plume of flame that sent the damaged tank bouncing around like an out of control rocket. The metal tank knocked the valve off another cylinder, creating a second flash of fire that caught the wounded man's shoulder and set his clothes ablaze.

Kush watched in shock as the stranger ignored his burning arm and the bullet in his chest and turned back towards the pumps.

Movement from the corner of his eye caught Kush's attention, reminding him of the second attacker. He tried to bring the gun around but the man was already on him, fingers curved like claws and mouth open wide, displaying blood-coated teeth. Kush managed to scream once before the man bit into his neck.

As he struggled to break loose, Kush felt the weight on top of him shift and he knew the crazed man had shifted position. Before he could break free, sudden pain, far worse than the bleeding hole in his throat, erupted in his groin as the lunatic bit down again.

Then everything went bright and the world disappeared in an

explosion of light and sound. A scorching wind whipped past, the sizzling gale sending Kush and his attacker tumbling across the asphalt, their bodies engulfed in flames. Metal shards filled the night air with razor-sharp death as more than forty propane tanks turned into red-hot shrapnel.

Kush had just enough time to call out to Allah before superheated air entered his lungs and incinerated him from the inside out.

Behind the building, Ana Puchari rose from her hiding place behind her six-year-old Nissan, stunned by the sound of the explosion. She saw that the propane cage and the side of the building facing it were on fire and reached back into the car to retrieve her cell phone and call for help.

Her hand was still moving down when a six-inch piece of steel shattered the windshield and lodged itself in her face.

In the time it took the fire department to put out the blaze and discover Anna Puchari's body, six more people disappeared within Rocky Point's town limits.

* * *

Tyler Lavine smoothed out the blanket and patted his hand on the soft cotton.

"C'mon, don't just stand there. Sit. I promise I won't bite."

I sure plan on nibbling though, he thought, staring up at Katie Reyes with what he hoped was an innocent expression.

Katie looked down at him. Although the quarter moon sitting low on the horizon didn't provide much light, it was still enough for Tyler to see there was no nervousness or animosity in her look, just distrust. And that was fine with him. Better they both knew what was going to happen over the next couple of hours than her be caught off guard and ruin the night by demanding he stop.

"If I sit down, you're going to be all over me like a shore leave sailor." She smiled as she said it, her teeth as white as the moon against her dark skin.

She's being a cock tease. That's okay, as long as teasing isn't all she does. "I swear I'll keep my hands off you until this is all gone." He held up the bottle of wine he'd swiped from his parents' cellar. It was the one promise he intended to keep, figuring it'd be a lot easier to get Katie's panties off if she was drunk.

"Really?" Katie knelt down next to him and took the bottle from his hands. She tipped it up to her mouth, pretending to drink from the still-corked container, her back arching and her large breasts sticking out as she did so. Tyler felt himself grow hard as he noticed she wore no bra.

Katie laughed, tossing it behind her. "Well, what do you know. All gone."

Before Tyler could say anything she let her body fall forward, landing across his chest and pushing him onto his back.

"No more games. We both know why we're here," she said, rubbing one hand across his crotch. Beneath his jeans, his cock twitched and jumped.

Tyler slid his hands inside her t-shirt, feeling her nipples harden against his palms. Katie moaned and gripped him harder, then pressed her mouth against his.

The next fifteen minutes were the best of Tyler's life, as he finally got to do all the things he'd only seen on internet web sites.

With the after-effects of his orgasm subsiding and his pulse no longer doing a demonic jungle drum beat in his ears, Tyler took a deep breath and leaned over Katie to grab the bottle of wine. "I don't know about you but I need a--"

"Quiet!" Katie grabbed his arm, her nails digging into his flesh in a way that was far less pleasant than the scratches she'd left on his back just a few minutes earlier.

"Ow! What--"

"Shhsh! I heard something. I think someone's watching us." She picked up her shirt and held it to her chest as she sat up, her eyes wide and round as an owl's.

"Where?" Tyler didn't want to say anything but he had a feeling he knew who it might be. He'd bragged a little – okay, maybe a lot_– to Jerry and Chris in gym class that he was taking Katie to the football field. They both had girlfriends and constantly teased him about his inability to get laid. Tired of sniffing last night's pussy stink when they shoved their fingers under his nose, he'd been more than happy to rub it in their faces that he was going to get something off one of the hottest girls in homeroom.

I should have figured they'd come sneaking around to see. Maybe even to ruin things for me.

"I think I saw something over that way." Katie pointed to their left, where the bleachers sat a good forty yards away.

"I'll check it out." Tyler stood up. Cold wetness against his leg reminded him he was naked and still wearing the first of the three condoms he'd hoped to use before the night was over. He pulled the sticky rubber off his cock and tossed the deflated balloon shape off to the side. Slipping into his pants, he headed across the field, leaving his shoes and shirt behind. If it turned out to be nothing he'd have that much less to take off when he returned to Katie. If it was Chris and Jerry getting ready to bust his balls, he'd make sure they went home bruised.

He'd almost reached the bleachers when two people emerged from the shadows, only they weren't Chris and Jerry.

Cops! Tyler almost said it out loud, then he saw that the second person wasn't a police officer, it was a fat lady in a nightgown. *What the hell, is one of Rocky Point's finest getting himself a little action under the bleachers?*

At first, nervous about getting caught trespassing by the police, he felt himself growing calm again. After all, no officer was gonna bust him if it meant having people find out he was getting a BJ while on duty. Tyler figured he would just tell him to pack up his shit and leave. And the whole episode might even make him look better to Katie – he'd be the guy who talked them out of trouble with the cops. She didn't have to know the whole truth.

Just as he was about to say hello, he noticed something strange. Both of them had dark stains on their clothes. And their faces. Stains that looked like...

Blood? Oh my God, is that--

They came at him before he could finish the thought, charging forward and smashing into him so hard it knocked the air out of his lungs. He tried to call for help but all that came out was a croaking gasp. Unable to shout or move, he could only lay there as a third figure appeared, a figure made of darkness except for its devilish eyes.

Even when the creature dug its way down his throat with icy fingers, Tyler's screams were only in his head.

Katie watched Tyler cross the field, his arrogantly self-confident attitude doing nothing to ease her fears of getting caught. What Tyler didn't know – and she had no intention of telling him – was that she'd been nabbed by Campus Security three weeks earlier, in the middle of an ankles-behind-the-ears fuck session with Andy Wilson. It hadn't meant anything, just an old fashioned booty call, but she didn't want Tyler to think she was some kind of slut. The guard, who'd probably gotten quite an eyeful before he made himself known, had let them go with a warning. But if he caught her again he might not be in such a forgiving mood. Worse, he might let it slip that he remembered her.

So as Tyler approached the bleachers on the far side of the field, she took a moment to put her clothes on and fold the wine bottle inside the blanket. When she looked up again, Tyler was coming back across the dew-damp grass, his pale naked chest and dark jeans turning him into a ghost sailing through the night.

"Tyler? Everything okay?" she asked.

He didn't answer, just kept walking. As he drew closer she saw that he had a serious expression on his face and she wondered if he'd encountered the security guard and gotten a lecture.

Hopefully that's all it was and not a phone call to Tyler's parents. If he gets in trouble--

Katie didn't have time to finish her thought as Tyler let out a loud growl and threw himself at her. For one brief moment she thought he was playing around, was maybe hoping for round two.

Then his teeth sank into her throat, crushing muscle and cartilage, and all she knew was pain, pain so great she never even tried to scream. She just laid there as he tore a huge chunk of flesh away, spit it out, and then stuck his face into the hole and started chewing.

Her last thought was of her parents and how disappointed they'd be to find out she'd been having sex with boys on the football field.

Chapter 13

Marisol held her coffee in both hands, trying to force the chill from her body. Outside the city offices the summer sun was already driving away the cool of the night, warming Rocky Point like a pie in an oven, an oven whose temperature would slowly rise throughout the long, hot day. Marisol's chill had nothing to do with the previous night's cool breeze that had blown through her windows while she tried to sleep. No, her shivers were the after effect of the secrets the night had nurtured, secrets the breeze had carried along on its whispering sighs.

Death. Violence. Unnamed horrors.

She'd heard the sirens all night long, knew what their high-pitched wails warned of.

They're back again. The *things* that lived underground, the things she'd tried so hard to drive from her memory and for the most part, she'd succeeded. Her nightmares of the creatures she and her friends had encountered beneath Gates of Heaven Cemetery had dwindled over the years to only occasional bad dreams, usually brought on by indulging in too many chili dogs or jalapeno pizzas.

Until now. John Boyd had seen them again, right by their old crypt. Add to that the violence and disappearances plaguing the town for the past week and even a stubborn fool - *like me!* - could see what was going on.

What the fuck was John doing by that crypt anyhow? They'd had an unspoken agreement to never go near it again, never venture into the cemetery at all unless absolutely necessary. Had his drinking really gotten that out of control? She'd known about his DWI; it had been in all the papers when it happened. She'd even sent him a letter - a short note really, - expressing her sorrow and asking him if there was anything she could do. Back then she'd still been married to Jack and had the power of the Mayor's office behind her.

But John had never responded and she'd figured he'd accepted his jail time as penance for what he'd done. During the months he'd been locked away she'd forgotten about him, the tragedies of an old friend pushed aside by the travails of daily life in a loveless house.

How many times did I pass him on the street, maybe even tossed him a handful of change at Christmas time, without recognizing him? Did he resent my good fortunes, the way I resented Cory for getting the hell out of this town?

She hoped he held no grudges; she hoped she hadn't been rude to him. Odds were if she'd been alone she'd dropped some coins in his cup or hat or whatever. Jack had always gone on at her about her caring too much for those less fortunate than them, forgetting completely that before she'd married him *she'd* been one of the less fortunate he looked down on.

Of course, in public, Jack always made a show of demonstrating his own concern for the underprivileged, especially around the holidays. He carried green pieces of paper in his coat pocket that resembled folded dollar bills and he'd drop them into hats or donation pots as he smiled broadly, wishing everyone within earshot a 'warm and safe holiday season.'

When unfolded, the paper was nothing more than a list of addresses for the town's soup kitchens and shelters, along with a vaguely biblical quote about God only helping those who helped themselves.

She hoped John had never been the recipient of one of those pieces of paper.

"Penny for your thoughts *chiquita*."

Marisol nearly spilled her coffee as the unexpected voice sent her heart into overdrive. She'd thought she was alone in the morgue, having come in two hours before first shift started. Turning, she found Freddy Alou standing by the door to the break room, his graying hair still damp from his morning shower, his eyes bright and alert.

The complete opposite of how I probably look. "Morning Freddy," she said, getting her heart under control. "What brings you in so early?"

"A sixty-year-old bladder that thinks it's my personal alarm clock," he said with a laugh. "Since I was up I decided to come in and get some paperwork done for the town meeting tonight."

"Town meeting? I haven't heard anything about that." Marisol topped off her coffee to warm it and then poured a second cup, handing it to Freddy, who took a few sips and sighed before responding.

"Last minute thing. Dawes and your ex decided yesterday it

would be a good idea to address the 'concerns of the populace' regarding the current disappearances and murders. But since those two *pendejos* don't actually want any of populace showing up and asking difficult questions, they're doing their best not to publicize the meeting, other than what's legally required."

"Figures. But how does this all concern you?"

Alou shrugged. "The powers that be prefer that all records and documents relating to our 'situation' touch no hands in the records department other than my own two *manos*. Your boss and me, we've kind of been sucked into this bucket of *mierda* against our will." He sighed, then narrowed his eyes. "But enough of my problems. What brings you here before the morning paper?"

Marisol smiled. "Nothing as bad as your reasons. I just couldn't sleep."

Freddy raised an eyebrow. "Out late with Mister Miles last night?"

"What? No I was not. How did you know Cory's in town?"

Letting out another of his infectious laughs, Freddy pointed first to the corner of his eye and then to his ear. "I see everything and hear everything that goes on in town *chica*. That's my job. Just like my father before me. I come from a long line of nosy men and women, going all the way back to the days when this place was nothing more than another stop on the Hudson River trading route."

"I don't doubt it. But this time you're wrong. There's nothing going on between Cory and I."

"Not yet." Freddy gave her an exaggerated wink and then exited the break room.

Marisol stared after him, her coffee churning slightly in her stomach. His words had hit a little too close to home. In fact, they'd echoed her own feelings pretty damn closely, like he'd read her mind. There was certainly an attraction between her and Cory and based on their kiss Sunday night, the feeling was mutual. She'd hoped to talk to him, maybe see him on Monday, but they'd ended up playing phone tag most of the day. And when she finally got home she'd begged off his dinner invite, preferring to eat a quick frozen dinner and go to bed early.

But they'd managed to make plans for an early dinner tonight, a quick bite before heading to Todd's house for their next meeting. Anticipation at seeing him again had kept sleep at bay until late the previous evening. Combined with the sirens and it was no wonder she was exhausted.

Tonight. The word reminded her of the town meeting Freddy had mentioned. *They don't want the public there? Nice try. We'll make damn sure the whole town shows up.*

She flipped open her cell phone and dialed Todd's number.

* * *

Todd Randolph hung up the phone and hurried across the hall to the guest bedroom, where the sound of snoring indicated John Boyd still slept on. Todd rapped on the door until he heard John's groggy voice call out, "I'm awake."

"Well, get your lazy butt out of bed my friend. We've got work to do."

Smiling at the thought of putting a wrench in the town leaders' plans, Todd went downstairs to start breakfast.

* * *

Todd and John were waiting in front of the City Building when Marisol and Cory walked up. They'd had to park two blocks away, a testament to the success of their hastily-planned effort to bring the meeting to the town's attention.

"Jesus. Half the damn county must be here. I've never seen the place so crowded," Cory said as they went inside and down into the basement of the old wing.

"I figure between the four of us we handed out over three hundred flyers," Todd told them. "I imagine there's gonna be a lot of people pissed off that the meeting wasn't publicized."

"I'm more curious to hear what kind of questions people will be asking." Marisol pointed to one of the flyers they'd made, which lay on the hallway floor. The large letters read:

Town Meeting Tonight
Mayor Dawes and Sheriff Travers to discuss the
more than two dozen disappearance plaguing Rocky Point.

Beneath that bold statement was the time and place of the

meeting, which Marisol had verified by calling the Mayor's office anonymously.

"The newspapers haven't been reporting the disappearances because the police haven't been giving out information on them," she continued, as they entered the room that doubled as a meeting hall and civil wedding chapel. Originally designed as a bomb shelter that could hold up to four hundred people, more than anything else the auditorium resembled a high school gymnasium, minus the bleachers and baskets.

"That's sure to ruffle some feathers," Todd said. "People might not care what happens in the Lowlands but they hate when politicians keep secrets, especially those having to do with town safety."

John opened the door to the auditorium, which was packed to capacity and beyond with people already taking standing positions along the side and back walls. The din of several hundred mouths talking at once filled the air with a sound reminiscent of the anticipatory murmur preceding a concert.

The four Cemetery Club members took spots at the back of the room, where they had a view of the entire auditorium. At the other end a young, busty woman, was busy setting out pitchers of water and glasses on the small table where the Mayor and his aides would be sitting.

At exactly seven p.m. Mayor Dawes and Deputy Mayor Jack Smith entered from a side door, with the members of the town board, as well as Freddy Alou and the Medical Examiner close behind them. Tagging along in the rear was Police Chief Travers, a violence-threatening scowl on his face. Marisol wondered if he'd been arguing with the Mayor's team backstage or if he just didn't want to be forced into providing information to the public.

Maybe it's both.

Smith was the first to speak, clearing his throat and tapping on the microphone to test it. "Um, good evening. Mayor Dawes and I want to thank you all for joining us tonight. We hadn't expected such a large turnout, so please bear with us."

Someone in the crowd called out in an angry voice. "That's because you tried to keep the meeting a secret!"

A chorus of shouts and boos followed.

Ignoring the interruption, Smith continued. "This meeting of the Rocky Point Town Board will now come to order. First on the agenda--"

"Forget the damn agenda. Tell us what's going on!"

"Yeah, how many people are missing? Are they dead?"

"It's a cover up!"

Smith raised his hands. Behind him Mayor Dawes and several of the board members looked unhappy. "People, please. The Board has an agenda to follow. After each item is announced, you will have the opportunity to voice your opinions before a vote is taken. Now--"

"Can the bullshit! Tell us what you're doing to keep the town safe!"

More shouting followed. Smith raised his hands again but that only succeeded in riling the crowd even further.

"This isn't going well for them," Cory whispered to Marisol. On stage, Smith returned to the table and leaned down to talk with the Mayor.

"No, it's not, is it?" Marisol wore a happy grin on her face.

Mayor Dawes stood up and approached the microphone. "Please, ladies and gentlemen, can we have some quiet?"

The crowd responded with even louder cries of 'We want answers now!' and 'Tell us the truth!'

"All right, everybody settle down!" Dawes shouted, his amplified voice setting off squeals of feedback that cut through the agitated din. This time the noise quickly diminished. When the room was almost silent, Dawes continued in a quieter tone. "In order to keep peace the Board has agreed to make a special announcement regarding recent events here in town. After that we'll allow twenty minutes for discussion."

There was a pause as Jack Smith handed the Mayor a sheet of paper. After clearing his throat, Dawes began reading from the document he held.

"Here are the facts pertaining to the so-called disappearances that have occurred over the past week or so. First, there is no verifiable proof that any of these disappearances are linked to foul play. While it's true that people have been reported missing, it's entirely possible these individuals or families have simply moved, or taken a trip and forgotten to inform people of their whereabouts."

Someone yelled "Bullshit!" and several people cheered.

"People! If we cannot continue in an orderly fashion, I'll be forced to close this meeting to the public."

"Let him try it," John said. "He'll have a riot on his hands."

Todd shushed him. "I want to hear this."

"Point number two," Dawes announced, holding up two fingers.

"The reported disappearances are in no way related to the unfortunate murders that took place at Gus's Bar or Gates of Heaven Cemetery. While those crimes were indeed heinous and we are doing everything in our power to find the perpetrators, I want to remind you that Rocky Point's rate of violent crime is far lower than the national average, a testament to the hard work of Sheriff Travers and his men. Now--"

An elderly man stood up in the middle of the room. "What about the aliens?"

A look of confusion crossed Dawes's face. "The...what?"

"The goddamn aliens I saw the other night. Ask Travers. I made a statement at the police station. Saw the little bastards kill someone with my own eyes."

Murmured voices, like the growl of distant traffic, filled the room as the people in the audience spoke to each other in hushed tones.

Travers rose from his seat and whispered something into the Mayor's ear. For a moment, Dawes looked as if he'd just smelled something rotten, his face contorting and his lips pulling to one side. Then he resumed his composure. "Mister, ah, Coleman, is it? Sheriff Travers tells me he does indeed have your statement and that his men are investigating the disturbance in your neighborhood. However, to speculate that--"

"Speculate this you sack of hot air," the old man said, grabbing at his crotch. "I saw a damn alien take over the body of a young woman. And what about the cop I saw that same night, the one that killed the man?"

Members of the audience started calling out questions and more than a few stood up, pointing at the Mayor, demanding answers to the 'alien sightings.'

A rotund woman in a red and yellow muumuu bellowed out a question in a deep voice that rose above the general clamor. "I live down to the Lowlands and I know for a fact Angie Negron is missing. She ain't on no vacation neither. She was supposed to help me bake cookies for the church social and she never showed up. When I went to her house, all the front windows was broken and the door wide open. How come I ain't seen no cops investigatin' that?"

"Aliens!" Henry Coleman called out. "That's how they do it. Came for me too, but I hid!"

The noise factor rose another level as more people stood, some shouting, some talking on phones and some arguing with their neighbors.

"Things are getting out of hand," Marisol said.

John nodded. "Maybe we--"

A Hispanic man with tribal tattoos running down both arms jumped to his feet. "It's racial discrimination! They doan want to do nuthin' about the shit that happens in our part of town."

Jack Smith went to the microphone and stepped in front of Mayor Dawes. "Racial discrimination? How can you say that when more than half the Lowlands is white?" he asked. "Now, if you'll all just sit down and listen, Sheriff Travers will tell you exactly what his department is doing to keep everyone in our town safe."

The angry voices died down. Jack glared at the audience and in twos and threes they slowly complied. Only when everyone was seated again did he motion for Travers to approach the podium.

"You've gotta admit, he's got stage presence," Todd whispered to Marisol.

She shot him a dirty look and then turned her attention back to the stage.

Travers gave his mustache a nervous stroke and then began speaking. "Contrary to what some of you believe, the Sheriff's department is out in full force and has been since the incident at Gates of Heaven. Not only have I got all my men pulling double shifts but I've called in several deputies from other substations to help us out. We have cars patrolling the entire town, including," - he stared at the man who'd accused the mayor of racism - "the Lowlands and the factory district."

"It's not enough!" someone called out.

Travers glanced around the room, his face solemn. "You're right, whoever said that. It's not enough. I could put a hundred men on the street and it wouldn't be enough. And do you know why?" He didn't wait for an answer. "Because I want to catch the bastards *yesterday!*"

"Bullshit!"

The Sheriff didn't flinch. "No, it's not bullshit. Someone has come into our town, *my* town, and murdered at least three people, maybe more. I want to stop it from happening again and I want to stop it right now!" He banged his hand on the podium and several people jumped as the sound of flesh striking wood echoed through the room.

In a quieter voice, he continued. "But I can't do it without your help. Even with the extra men there's a lot of ground to cover every night. There are too many places a person can hide, places where patrol cars can't go. Parks, backyards, empty buildings. So we need you, all of you, to do two things. One, keep your eyes and ears open. If you see anything suspicious, call the police. I promise you won't be ignored."

"What's the second thing?"

Marisol jerked as Todd yelled his question from right next to her.

"Stay inside at night. I don't want to impose a curfew on the town but I will if I have to. The fewer people out at night the better the chance that no one will get hurt."

"Sheriff?" A woman in the middle of the room raised her hand, a sharp contrast to the free-for-all attitude of previous questions.

"Yes?" Travers nodded in her direction.

"What about the convenience store fire last night?"

"As of right now that fire is still under investigation. However, so far there's no evidence it's related in any way to the tragic events at the cemetery or Gus's bar."

More people called out questions but Travers shook his head. "I'm sorry, that's the only statement I'm prepared to make at this time. Now, if you'll excuse me, I have to get back to work." He put on his trooper-style hat and headed for one of the side doors.

"He didn't say anything about the missing police officers." Marisol started to raise her hand but Todd held her back.

"No, and maybe we shouldn't bring it up either. First of all, it will probably get you fired, or at least suspended, and we need you at work. You're our only source of inside information. And second, putting all these people in more of a panic might not be the best idea right now."

Jack Smith returned to the mic. "You now have as much information as we do. If any of you would like to stay for the remainder of the Board's business tonight please feel free, but we won't be entertaining any more discussion about deaths or disappearances."

The murmuring chant of hundreds of voices all talking at once grew in volume again as people stood and headed for the exits.

"That's our cue," Cory said to his companions. "Let's go grab some coffee across the street before the diner gets too crowded. We can talk everything out over there."

Todd glanced at his watch. "I'd love to but I've got to get home and get my mother's evening medicine ready. It's Abigail's night off."

"I'll go with you," John said. "I want to get on the computer again."

Cory looked at Marisol. "Guess it's just you and me. You up for some coffee?"

She smiled. "Up for it? If I don't get some caffeine in me I'll fall asleep right where I'm standing."

"Have fun kids." Todd shot Marisol a wink when Cory wasn't looking. In return, she flipped her middle finger at him.

"Let's go." Taking Marisol's arm, Cory led her towards the stairwell.

John and Todd watched them exit the building into the warm, muggy evening.

"Sometimes it seems like nothing's changed since high school," John said. "Do you think he's ever gonna have a clue?"

Remembering the kiss outside his house, Todd smiled. "Oh, I think he's got a clue. The question is when is he finally going to make his move?"

Chapter 14

Nancy Harmon was putting the dinner dishes away when she caught a glimpse of movement outside her kitchen window. Normally she would've ignored it - after all, it was probably just neighborhood kids playing or maybe a dog searching for a garbage can to knock over. Or a deer. God knew there were plenty of deer wandering around; they liked to come down from the woods, drink from the stream at the town park, and then peruse the neighborhood for gardens or flower beds to eat.

But after attending the town meeting earlier the idea there might be someone - or more than one someone - roaming the town and attacking people, made her nervous. On the other hand she didn't want to appear hysterical, calling the police because of a hungry deer. Better to be sure than look stupid.

"Hank? I think someone's outside in the yard."

Her husband, who'd just finished his shift at the ME's office, didn't look up from his newspaper. "Probably just a deer," he mumbled.

"No really. I saw something. Can you go look? And while you're at it, take out the garbage?"

Hank rolled his eyes and put the paper down. "Fine. I'll check it out." He pulled the garbage bag from the canister and tied it off, then opened the back door. Before stepping outside, he turned to his wife. "Try not to see any--"

Two men emerged from the darkness and charged into the kitchen, knocking Hank to the floor in the process. They stopped just inside the threshold, glancing around the kitchen with wild eyes.

Nancy opened her mouth to scream but the words died in her throat. She dropped the dish she'd been holding and when it struck the floor, both men turned towards her.

Time seemed to freeze as she and the intruders stared at each other. Both of them wore clothes stained with dirt and something darker.

Their hair stood out in clumps and strange white marks marred their faces and necks. Pieces of bluish-gray flesh hung from their cheeks and foreheads, giving them the look of lizards shedding their skins. Their rank, heavy odor filled the kitchen, overwhelming the lingering scents of dinner.

Then time kicked into motion again as Hank rolled over and grabbed one of the men by the leg. The stranger fell to his knees but instead of trying to get up he turned and plunged his thumbs into Frank's eyes. There was a wet, splattering sound and Frank started screaming, a high, panicked cry unlike anything Nancy had ever heard.

That's when she found her own voice.

"Help! Help!" She took a step backwards, intending on running into the living room and out the front door, but the sight of Frank lying on the floor, bloody pieces of flesh hanging from the holes where his eyes used to be, stopped her. How could she leave him behind?

Her indecision gave the second attacker all the time he needed to grab her and slam her against the refrigerator. Her head hit the door and for a moment there were three men in front of her. By the time her vision returned to normal she was on her ass, her back against the cold metal of the icebox.

Then the third figure entered the kitchen.

At first she thought her eyes were still playing tricks on her. Then she remembered the old man at the meeting, shouting about aliens.

Oh my God. He was right! It's an invasion from space!

The short, charcoal-gray creature floated across the floor, its stubby feet never touching the ground. It reached out to her with tiny hands, ignoring her screams.

The last thing she saw was the two men bending over Hank and tearing his clothes away.

Then her whole world turned gray.

Nancy Harmon ceased to exist.

* * *

Cory and Marisol were on their second cup of coffee when the Medical Examiner entered the diner. As soon as he saw them, he hurried over to their table.

"Marisol! I'm glad I found you."

"Oh, hi Ed. This is my friend, Cory Miles," Marisol said. "Cory, this is my boss, Dr. Ed Corish."

"Pleased to meet you." Cory held out his hand.

"Likewise." The ME gave it a perfunctory shake and turned back to Marisol. "I hate to interrupt but the forensic team at the gas station just found some remnants of human bodies. They're down in the lab right now. I need you to run the DNA tests."

"Right now? Can't the night shift handle it?"

Corish shook his head. "Nope. They're all tied up running tox screens. I tried calling Hank Harmon but no one answered at his house."

Marisol sighed. "All right. Sorry Cory."

Smiling, Cory stood up and tossed five dollars on the table. "That's okay. I've got files to go through back at the hotel. I'll walk out with you."

Outside, the ME headed back across the street to the town offices. Marisol and Cory hung back.

"I had fun tonight, considering the circumstances," Cory said as he took her hands in his.

"Me too." She closed her eyes and leaned forward.

This time Cory was ready and the tender kiss lasted much longer than the one at Todd's house. When they finally separated, Marisol opened her eyes to find Cory staring down at her.

"I'll be up late tonight. If you finish at the lab early, come by my room."

She shook her head. "I've got a better idea. There's a spare key under the mat on my front porch. Why don't you just wait for me at my place?"

Cory's smile grew wider. "Sounds like a plan."

She kissed him again and then hurried across the street.

From the window of his second floor office, Jack Smith felt his anger rise as he watched his ex-wife kissing Cory Miles, right out on the street for all the world to see.

That bitch. The ink's barely dry on the divorce papers and she's already sucking face with her old high school sweetheart.

Jack knew all about Cory Miles and his relationship with Marisol. Over the years she'd mentioned him on occasion, how he'd been her first crush. He'd never really worried about Miles, especially since Cory's family had moved away before senior year, but Jack was a big believer in doing his homework and since he'd found out Miles was in town, he'd put his staff to work digging up everything they could on the hotshot lawyer.

He hadn't known Cory very well in high school; Cory hadn't played any sports or been a member of any school clubs. When he and Marisol had started dating, she'd still been bitter about Cory moving away and never staying in touch, been bitter as well about losing her only other friends, Todd Randolph and John Boyd. Jack had filed all the names away in his memory, a habit that served him well as time went on and he developed political aspirations.

And then, all these years later, he'd seen Cory's name in the paper as the lawyer representing Randolph. He'd known it was only a matter of time before Miles and Marisol met up, either accidentally or on purpose. So he'd made sure he was prepared.

Watching Marisol walk across the street while Miles headed for a mint-condition Cadillac parked nearby, Jack mentally reviewed what he'd learned about his unexpected rival.

Cory Andrew Miles. Born and raised in Rocky Point. His parents, both from fairly well-off families - although nowhere near as well off as the Smiths - had moved to Connecticut right before Cory's senior year. Supposedly that was because the senior Miles had gotten a promotion and transfer, but Jack was fairly certain the whole mess with Todd Randolph killing all those people had more than a little to do with it. Get the kid out of town and away from bad influences.

Miles's parents had died in a car accident while he was in college and he'd inherited a nice sum of money - more than enough to pay for college and law school and still have some left over.

No arrests, no record of drug or alcohol abuse. No divorces. No suspicions of homosexuality or perverted sexual habits despite his lack of any long-term relationships.

All in all, on paper, Cory Miles seemed to be a model citizen and businessman, the type of person Jack would have welcomed at his own country club.

So he's got nothing I can use against him. That's okay. I can still make his life difficult. And as for Marisol...well, she's got plenty of skeletons in her past. We'll see how long their romance lasts when the shit storm starts and they've got no umbrellas.

Jack went to his desk and jotted a note for himself to run Miles's plates in the morning.

Since he doesn't have any outstanding tickets, maybe it's time he got one. You messed with the wrong guy's wife asshole.

* * *

Marisol loaded the last DNA sample into the lab's state-of-the-art Beckman Coulter STR analyzer and hit the run button. It would take twenty-four hours for the machine to run the forty samples; two each from the fourteen pieces of human flesh recovered from the fire, plus controls and standards. The lab had already identified one of the victims - Ana Pachuri, age twenty-two - from her dental records. The police were assuming that at least some of the other remains would belong to her father. The family had provided hair samples for DNA comparison.

But there had also been a second car at the station when the fire started, parked at the pumps. No bodies had been found inside. So there was the distinct possibility that one or more of the samples could come up as unknowns, leading to a long identification process - especially if the car's occupants were from out of town and had just stopped for gas.

Marisol looked at the clock. Almost midnight. That meant another late night tomorrow. She sent a quick email to Ed letting him know the samples were running and she'd talk to him the following afternoon, when she came in for her shift. Then she grabbed her purse and went across the hall, where Jaime Snyder was running chemical analyses on various pieces of burned metal.

"Hey Jaime. I'm taking off. Do me a favor and just peek at the STR once in a while, will you? Call me if it jams or if there are any other problems."

"Will do," the anorexically-skinny blonde said, never looking up from her work.

Marisol thanked her and hurried out to her car, her stomach doing nervous flips. She'd managed to avoid thinking about Cory for the past few hours by concentrating on her work but in a few minutes she'd be alone in her house with him.

The first time we've been alone in private since...shit, since the day we decided to go into the tunnel.

The memory of that long-ago afternoon, when she'd kissed him on the cheek just before Todd and John had arrived at the crypt, was as fresh in her mind as if it'd been yesterday.

With a start, Marisol realized she'd initiated every moment of intimacy between them, from the first gentle hints back when they'd both been shy teenagers to the two times they'd kissed since he'd arrived in town.

Her nervousness increased as she thought about how to bring things to the next level. Would she have to seduce him? Could she? The image of her seducing Cory - *Let me slip into something more comfortable*, her mind drawled in Marilyn Monroe tones - was so...bizarre...that she had trouble wrapping her mind around it. They'd been the objects of each others' teenage crushes and shared two passionate kisses twenty years later. That hardly meant he'd be ready to bring their relationship to a whole different level. *Emotionally ready, not physically,* she amended to herself. *After all, he is a guy.*

What if he turns me down? What if I end up standing there, a naked fool in my own bedroom?

She turned onto her street, her house only moments away, and found her hands shaking so bad she had trouble working the turn signal.

Get a hold of yourself, girl! You're acting like a silly virgin.

She and Jack had stopped sharing a bed two years before the divorce, so in a sense...

Don't go there!

Cory's car sat in front of the house, leaving the small driveway clear for her. After leaving Jack she'd taken a portion of her ridiculously small settlement and purchased a nice two-bedroom cottage just off Main Street, technically in a good part of town, but in practical terms a million light years away from the mansion she'd lived in while serving her time as Mrs. Jack Smith.

Yet where most, if not all, of the people in Jack's circle would have been mortified to move into a residence smaller than their guest cottages, Marisol felt nothing but joy each time she pulled into her driveway. The house was hers and she was damn proud to say so. She'd earned it, both through her hard work in going back to college and getting a damn good job, and for all the shit she'd put up with as a trophy wife. She could have taken him to the cleaners; after all, he'd had affairs, verbally abused her and generally made her life miserable. Her lawyer had urged her to take half his money, half the belongings in the house and alimony larger than her current salary.

Instead, she'd asked for a cash settlement equal to what she estimated she would have earned had she been working the past twenty years, plus an alimony payment just large enough to cover her school loans and mortgage. In total, it came to less than what they'd paid in country club membership fees and vacation expenses while married. She figured Jack probably only had to cash one of his many bonds to pay everything.

And he'd still been frighteningly angry at having to do that.

Stop thinking about it, she told herself as she unlocked the front door. *It's over. Time to move on.*

Maybe with Cory? That thought was almost as terrifying as thinking about Jack.

The only light in the house came from the kitchen, where Cory had lit two candles and placed them on the L-shaped breakfast bar that divided the kitchen and dining room. Between the candles sat an open bottle of Chianti and one glass. As she got closer, she saw he'd placed a note by the bottle.

Pour yourself a glass and come into the bedroom.

Her stomach started tingling again and her hands trembled as she poured the wine. *This is it. This is it. Don't ruin it. Don't act like an idiot.* But how *should* she act? Should she take her clothes off before going in? What if he was simply watching TV? But if she went in fully dressed and he was naked, would he feel embarrassed?

Oh for Christ's sake, just go in!

Marisol downed her glass of wine and poured another before kicking off her shoes and undoing the top button of her blouse. The bedroom door stood three-quarters closed. Flickering shadows told her he'd lit more candles in there.

He'd certainly made himself busy. He'd have had to look pretty hard to find the candles and matches. Oddly, the thought of Cory rummaging through her closets didn't bother her in the least. She reached out to push open the door, paused just long enough to undo one more button, and then stepped inside.

Cory lay under the sheets, just enough of his chest exposed to show he wore no shirt. "Hello Ms. Flores," he said, one side of his mouth curving up in an enticing grin.

"Hello yourself Mr. Miles." Marisol set her wine down. "Pretty forward of you, getting naked in my bed."

"How do you know I'm naked? I could have my pants on." He took a sip of his own wine.

Marisol pointed to the pile of clothes on the floor. "Then you must have been wearing two pairs of pants."

He shrugged. "Maybe I'm in my underwear."

She glanced at the clothes but couldn't see any underwear in the pile. "Are you?"

Another shrug. "You'll have to get under the covers to find out."

She chugged her wine, enjoying the hot burn as it ran down her throat. It was already sending warm, comforting waves of pleasure from her stomach to her brain, each surge washing away more of her nervousness and leaving behind a welcome layer of alcohol-manufactured bravery. Feeling freer and less inhibited than she'd ever felt in her life, she removed her blouse and bra, trusting the candlelight to hide any awkwardness or imperfections. Then she dropped her skirt to the floor, revealing her naked body to him for the first time.

Approaching the bed, she whispered, "I don't wear underwear." Cory flipped back the sheets. "What a surprise. Neither do I."

Chapter 15

The heavenly scent of fresh coffee forced Cory to open his eyes, just in time to see Marisol tip-toeing towards the bedroom door. He took a moment to admire her body and then called out.

"Good morning beautiful."

Marisol came back to the bed, wearing a wide grin and a short, silky bathrobe that exposed almost as much as it hid. "Good morning yourself. Or should I say good afternoon?"

Cory ran his hands through his hair and took a sip from the steaming cup she had left on the nightstand. "Afternoon? What time is it?"

She laughed. "Almost twelve. Do you always sleep this late?"

He raised an eyebrow at her. "Only when a horny vixen keeps me up half the night, using and abusing my body." He stretched and sharp pains in his back and legs told him his statement wasn't far from the truth. He hadn't had marathon sex like that in a long, long time.

But it was worth every bite, bruise and scratch!

"Vixen? You were just as bad. *I* wasn't the one who wanted to do it standing up. Now, since you're awake, you can get your ass out of bed and I'll get breakfast started. We've got just enough time to eat before I go to work."

Cory reached out and undid the sash of her robe, revealing breasts that had managed to stay firm and proud, and a stomach that was still youthfully flat. He ran his fingers down her body, beginning at the base of her throat, moving between her breasts and over her stomach, and then trailing down to the smooth, soft area between her legs.

The area that quickly grew damp as he explored.

Marisol moaned. "That's not what I meant."

Moving his head forward, he breathed in her scent, a combination of wildflowers and soap that told him she'd already showered. "I guess my idea of breakfast is a little different," he said, his voice muffled as he pressed his face to her and substituted his tongue for fingers.

Marisol spread her legs and pushed forward with her hips.

"Mmmm. I think I like your idea better."

By the time Cory showered and dressed, and Marisol showered

again, it was close to two o'clock. "You're on your own for dinner," she told him, running a brush through her hair. "I'm working the late shift tonight, which means I won't be done until after midnight."

"I guess I'll have to suffer through the day alone," he said, an exaggerated expression of woe on his face.

She put the brush down and looked at him. He saw something in her eyes, something that looked like fear. "What's wrong?" he asked.

"I...I was thinking...if, um, you want, you could, bring your stuff from the hotel and..." she paused again, her cheeks growing red.

"Are you asking me to stay here, with you?" Knowing what he did of her traumatic breakup with Jack, he was surprised and flattered she'd even consider asking him.

"I just thought, staying in the hotel is expensive, and this way you'd be closer to the Town Hall, and...oh, crap, I sound like an idiot don't I?" She turned away from him.

Cory wrapped his arms around her and pulled her close, kissed the back of her neck. "Thank you," he whispered into her hair. "It means a lot to me. I'll bring my stuff over later this afternoon."

Marisol turned in his arms and looked up at him, tears threatening to overflow her wide eyes. "Really?"

He kissed her lips, her cheeks and finally her nose. "Really. I can't think of anywhere I'd rather be or anyone I'd rather be with."

She pressed her face against his bare chest and he felt the warm damp tears seep through the material of his shirt. She sniffled a few times, then took a deep breath and stepped back. "Just don't think you can start leaving the toilet lid up or drink from the milk carton."

Raising his hands in mock surrender, Cory said, "Yes ma'am! I'm just a humble sex slave."

Marisol laughed and gave him a playful slap. "Maybe tonight, if you're lucky. In the meantime I've got to get going."

He leaned over and gave her a kiss. "Have a good day. Stay out of trouble."

"I'll call you if I hear anything interesting," she said, and then she was out the door.

Cory poured himself another cup of coffee, leaned against the counter and whispered something he'd waited twenty years to say.

"I can't believe I slept with Marisol Flores."

And now he was going to be staying with her. In her house.

In her *bed*.

For the first time in as long as he could remember, Cory Miles felt truly happy.

* * *

"I can't believe I slept with Cory Miles." Marisol spoke the words then quickly glanced around the break room to make sure no one had heard her. She'd been half in a daze all afternoon, constantly replaying the events of the past night in her mind, events that started with her stripping for Cory and climbing into bed with him and ended with her asking him to move in.

Not move in, she corrected herself. *Stay over. It's only temporary.* She had to keep reminding herself of that, that Cory still lived in Connecticut, still had a job there. Once they put an end to whatever was wrong with Rocky Point, he'd have to go back. Sure, they could still date but it wasn't like he was dropping everything and moving back to town.

And as much as having him in her life thrilled her to the core, she had no intention of leaving her job for him.

Still, every time she thought of his hands touching her, his lips caressing her body--

Stop it! Get back to work. The last thing you need to do is screw up the samples. Then you will *have to find a new job.*

She'd checked the STR as soon as she'd gotten in. All the tests were processing correctly, so she'd turned her attention as best she could to the other work that had piled up during the night. Even with the town practically in a state of emergency and all attention focused on the murders, there were still autopsies to do and other crimes occurring around the county, which meant a full workload for everyone.

At six o'clock she and Pat McBride grabbed takeout from the diner. She'd thought about inviting Cory but decided not to bother. After all, it wasn't like she had time to sit and chat. Instead, she'd left a quick message on his voice mail, telling him she'd call when she got off work to let him know if he should open a bottle of wine or just have her pajamas waiting for her.

By the time the night was closing in on eleven o'clock the gas station samples were almost finished. Once they were done she could pass the results on to the police and head home. Tomorrow was an off day, followed by two weeks straight of day shifts - almost a vacation in itself, unless there was mandatory overtime. Which seemed likely given the current circumstances.

Marisol downed the rest of her coffee and tossed the cup into the trash. As she opened the door to the DNA lab, the STR began beeping, announcing the first batches were ready.

One by one the reports emerged from the printer, each detailing a DNA profile. Marisol reviewed them as they came out, to ensure there'd been no contamination. Once they'd all printed, she laid them out on the table and analyzed them in more detail.

As she'd expected, some of the samples matched the gas station's owner and his daughter, based on hair the family had provided for comparison. Marisol shook her head as she set the papers aside, thinking about the bad news that poor family was going to receive.

The remaining samples represented three different individuals, which she assumed were the passengers of the car at the pumps. Although she expected no hits, Marisol followed standard procedure and ran the results through the FBI's Combined DNA Index System, commonly referred to as CODIS, and the New York State DNA Databank. The system contained not only the DNA profiles of known criminals but also missing persons, law enforcement officials and previous victims of crimes.

Marisol considered getting another coffee. With more than five million profiles to review, it could take several hours for the search to finish. She was halfway across the lab when the computer beeped.

Sudden dread blossomed in Marisol's guts and she had no idea why. The odds were that one of passengers had a criminal record.

So why did she have the feeling she was about to receive bad news?

With a pounding heart and a dry mouth, Marisol approached the computer. When she saw the name and picture displayed on the screen, her premonitory fear quickly became a reality.

Manuel Salvo, age 32.

Last known residence: Rocky Point, New York.

Occupation: Police Officer, Rockland County Sheriff's Department.

"Holy shit." In the empty room, her voice seemed unnaturally loud; the sound of it actually made her jump and set her heart beating even faster.

The name was instantly familiar. You couldn't work in the county offices and not know the name of a missing police officer.

How could Manny's DNA be at the scene? Scenarios flashed through Marisol's head. Had he been the victim of a crime, possibly locked in the trunk of the car when it caught fire? If not, why had he been there after being missing for days?

Realizing the sensitive nature of the information, she decided to call Dr. Corish. *Let ME bring this one to Chief Travers.* He answered on the third ring, his voice groggy with sleep.

"Ed? It's Marisol Flores. Sorry to wake you but I just got the results of the DNA tests, and...well, you're going to want to talk to the Chief personally. I'm going to fax them over to you right now."

After sending the fax, Marisol waited next to the phone, knowing Corish would be calling back momentarily. Even so, she jumped a little when it rang.

"Marisol?" The ME was wide awake now but sounded as confused as she felt. "You were right to call me. Chief Travers and I will be there in fifteen minutes."

"All right." She hung up the phone and gathered the printouts and CODIS report. The system was still searching for matches against the remaining two samples, so she decided to wait until the last minute before heading upstairs, in case more information came up.

Movement outside the lab caught her eye and she turned to see Jake Spencer, one of the night shift techs, waving at her through the window of the door. She signaled for him to come in.

"What's up Jake?"

The skinny tech, only a few years out of college, shrugged. "Not much. I was heading to the break room. Saw you sitting there and figured I'd ask if you want a cup of coffee."

"Thanks, but I--" Marisol stopped at the sound of breaking glass down the hall. A moment later, someone screamed.

"What the hell was that?" Jake asked. Eyes wide, he turned and looked down the hall.

"I don't know." Marisol moved towards the door as Jake stepped into the hallway.

"I don't see - holy shit!"

He jerked backwards, one foot crunching down on her toes as he tried to push back into the lab. Marisol caught a quick glimpse of movement, but those few seconds were more than enough for her to understand Jake's sudden fear.

Two men, maybe more, their flesh bluish-gray under the harsh hallway lighting. Torn clothes covered in blood. And their faces...horrible masks, like something from the monster movies she loved to watch on Saturday mornings as a kid.

The worst part was that she recognized them. Not the men themselves but what they'd become. She'd seen their kind before, back in high school.

Under the cemetery.

"Hide!" she shouted to Jake, who was staring glassy-eyed at the doors. She ran past him and looked around, wanting to heed her own advice to find safety, but the small room offered no escape. There was only the one set of doors and the closest thing to a hiding place was in the foot space under her lab station.

Before she could slide the lab stool out and cram herself into the cubbyhole the doors burst open and three figures stormed into room. They paused just inside the doors, looking back and forth. In that instant Marisol was reminded of the scene in Jurassic Park, when the two raptors had the children trapped in the kitchen. Then she got a good look at their faces and a new word jumped into her brain.

Zombies.

There was no mistaking the three men for anything else. She'd seen too many corpses not to recognize the pallor of dead flesh. And if that wasn't enough, two of them showed signs of advanced decay, with skin hanging in flaps from their foreheads and cheeks, exposing bloodless muscle and connective tissue. Their eyes were evil orbs, the normally white sclera a puss-yellow color with patches of red where capillaries had burst.

Todd and John were both wrong, she thought. *They're not aliens and they're not demons. They're monsters, just like in the movies.*

Jake's temporary paralysis broke; he jumped to one side and tried to dodge around the three creatures. Two of them tackled him before he got anywhere close to the door, their lifeless bodies moving faster than Marisol thought possible. Jake screamed and flailed his arms but the two zombies pinned him to the ground and held him there, their mouths open in unnatural grins that dripped fresh blood.

The third creature moved towards Marisol, its face totally devoid of any human expression.

"No," she whispered as she retreated. She managed to take four or five steps before her back hit the lab wall. As the zombie came down the narrow aisle, her only choices were to dodge left or right. She forced herself to wait until the last second, knowing that if she moved too soon the monster wouldn't be fooled.

When the zombie was four feet away, its fetid stench filling the air around her and its face so close she could see bits of flesh stuck between its teeth, she made her decision. A quick fake to the right and then she dodged left, the way she'd seen football players do on TV.

The monster fell for it, committing itself in the wrong direction. She grabbed the corner of the lab bench to keep her balance as she turned and sped down the next aisle, sprinting for the door. Something crashed and broke behind her but she kept her eyes straight ahead, focused on her one chance for escape.

I'm going to make it! Thank God, I'm going to--

A cold hand grabbed her by the neck and slammed her sideways into a bench. Pain exploded in her ribs, her feet tangled and she fell to the floor. Her elbow struck the hard tile, sending another wave of agony up her arm.

She tried to push herself up with her one good hand but she'd only gotten to her knees when the zombie twisted her around and forced her down onto her back. It knelt on her, its knees digging painfully into her thighs and its hands pinning her wrists to the cold floor.

Fiery malevolence glittered in its eyes as it leered over her, its smell so vile she felt her dinner threatening to erupt from her stomach. Bloodstained drool hung from the creature's mouth in long, slimy strands, adding to her panic as she wondered if whatever had infected the thing might transfer to her through its saliva.

Or its bite, she thought, as a piece of its last victim fell from its teeth and landed on her chest. Her bladder released at the idea of being eaten alive or turned into some kind of undead thing for all eternity.

Then something moved behind the zombie, came into her field of vision and being eaten alive by a monster suddenly didn't seem so bad.

Oh, lord. John was right after all.

The alien stood about three feet tall. Its slanted, almond-shaped eyes burned hellish red and its mouth was a black slit against a dark gray background. A wave of numbing cold preceded it as it approached her. The chill sank into Marisol's bones, filling her with a dread worse than anything she'd ever known.

It motioned with one stubby hand and the zombie slid to one side, still holding her. The alien moved closer and the pain in Marisol's bones increased until she thought they might break, the way a flower would shatter after being dipped in liquid nitrogen. She tried to open her mouth to scream but couldn't move her jaw.

She remembered the old man at the town meeting screaming about aliens taking over people. *That's how they turn people into zombies, by possessing them somehow.*

The abrupt image of being taken over by the alien was too much for Marisol. Her mind retreated from the events around her. She could still hear Jake's screams, still feel the freezing ache in her bones, still smell the monster on top of her, but all of it seemed distant. Instead, she found herself returning to the time she'd spent so recently with Cory in her bedroom. She saw his face, smiling as he motioned for her to join him in bed. The way he'd touched her, held her, rode her and stroked her body until it exploded with pleasure again and again.

In that moment, she knew she loved him, really loved him, and a bittersweet feeling surged through her bones, a combination of joy and regret - joy for the time they'd shared, regret that it would never happen again. She closed her eyes, resigned to becoming another victim of the plague they'd let loose so many years ago. In a weird way, it seemed almost meant to be; she was partly responsible for so many deaths and now she was paying the ultimate price for them.

Time slowed down until it stopped altogether as she waited for the alien being to touch her, or enter her, or whatever it did to its prey.

Then something changed. It took Marisol a moment to understand the cold was receding, the throbbing torture in her bones lessening. She opened her eyes and saw that the alien had moved away from her, was instead heading towards Jake, who still shouted and thrashed under the weight of the other two zombies. The alien rose up in the air and floated over Jake until it hovered above his chest. It paused and then dove down faster than a cobra's strike, its body twisting and shrinking as it poured into Jake's open mouth and into his throat.

The technician choked and gagged, his body seizing wildly, but his spasms had no effect on the thing, which now looked like one of the used condoms she'd occasionally found in Jack's office, her first clues to his affairs. In seconds the gray being disappeared into Jake, who convulsed once more and then went perfectly still. The two zombies let go of him and stood up.

Marisol had time to take three rapid breaths before Jake moved again. He sat up, his eyes wide and sniffed at the air like a dog.

"Jake?" she heard herself ask in a trembling voice. The zombie holding her tightened its grip on her shoulders. Jake turned and looked at her and her relief at not being possessed by the alien shattered under his cold gaze.

The man who'd been so quick with a joke, who always had a smile on his face, who sometimes brought homemade brownies to work on Saturdays, was now a stranger. His normally pleasant expression had mutated into something filled with a dark, hungry malevolence. He stared at her for a moment and then his lips slowly curled up in a wicked smile.

He stood up and walked towards her, the other two zombies following. Cold, dead fingers dug into her arms as the monster behind her leaned forward. She could hear its teeth gnashing together as it prepared to take a bite of her flesh.

Marisol kicked her legs and arched her back, knowing even as she did so that she wasn't strong enough to break free.

Jake knelt down and tore her lab coat and shirt away, exposing her chest and belly. He licked his lips and lowered his head towards her stomach.

His mouth opened.

The lab doors banged open. Someone shouted.

Marisol screamed as the zombie bit into her.

Section III

Actions

Chapter 1

Edwin Corish and Nick Travers stepped out of the elevator and stopped short. Crimson splashes covered the walls of the morgue hallway, the fresh blood still dripping down and forming puddles on the floor. Broken glass and pieces of lab equipment lay scattered down the hall. Red handprints and footprints covered the floor and walls.

"What the fuck happened here?" Travers asked.

Before the Medical Examiner could answer, a woman screamed from inside one of the lab rooms.

"Stay behind me," Travers said to the ME. He drew his gun and moved down the hall, keeping as close to one side as he could without actually touching the blood-spattered wall. He paused briefly by each door to peer through the windows before moving on to the next room. With each step, the pounding of his heart grew louder and the twisted feeling in his stomach grew stronger. The palms of his hands started sweating and he had to tighten his grip on his gun.

When he reached the door marked DNA LAB, he motioned for Corish to stop. "There's people inside," he whispered. With one foot, he pushed the door open. He entered the room as fast as he could, stepping to one side they way he'd been taught at the academy.

He'd expected the people to turn towards him, perhaps even aim a weapon at him. He'd expected to confront teenagers, high on drugs maybe and looking to steal more, or an employee who'd gone postal.

He hadn't expected four men covered in blood, so focused on their victim that they ignored him.

"Stop! Get away from the girl!" Travers shouted, pointing his gun in the general direction of the men surrounding the pretty lab tech. *Marisol Flores*, he remembered. He took aim at one who looked ready to take a bite out of her stomach.

The man - who wore a white lab coat just like the Flores woman - ignored the warning and bit down, his teeth puncturing the flesh of the girl's stomach. She screamed again. Blood flowed from the wound, dark red against her tan skin.

Travers pulled the trigger. The .9mm roared, the sound louder in the confined space than at the practice range, which was the only place he'd ever had to fire it before. The girl's attacker fell sideways, blood and tissue exploding from his side as the heavy slug tore through his body.

The other three men finally turned, giving Travers his first real look at them. Their Halloween masks caught him by surprise. Then he felt a chill as he realized they weren't wearing masks.

He was looking at their real faces.

"What the hell...?" he said, unaware he'd spoken out loud.

Behind him, Edwin Corish shouted, "Shoot! For Chrissake, shoot them!"

Travers's finger twitched and the sounds of Marisol's next screams disappeared in the multiple blasts. One man - *monster!* Travers' mind cried - crumpled to the ground, the back of his head disappearing in a wet red spray. The next round went wide and shattered the glass door of a cabinet but the following two found their targets, catching one man in the stomach and the other in the chest. Both men fell to their knees and then tumbled over.

Travers hurried to the lab tech, who was crying and clutching at her mid-section. "Are you all right?"

Before she could answer, Corish shouted again. "Look out!"

Travers glanced up and saw the two men he'd just shot running towards him. He dove to the side, his shoulder striking painfully against one of the lab benches. His arm went numb and he dropped his gun.

No!

He scrabbled his fingers against the tiled floor, trying to locate his weapon before the *things* got to him. But instead of attacking him they ran past, heading towards the door. His hand closed on the hot barrel of the gun just as the man who'd bitten the lab tech stood up, a gaping hole in his side revealing broken ribs and bloody organs. Travers reversed his grip on the gun and fired upwards but the bullet missed the mortally-wounded man, who leaped over the girl's body and followed his grotesque companions out the door.

Travers leaned back against a bench and did something he hadn't done since the time he'd almost drowned in the Hudson River when he was eleven.

He thanked God for sparing his life.

None of them saw the black, smoky figure rise up from the dead man's body and disappear through the ceiling.

* * *

The next few minutes were the strangest of Marisol's life. Faces loomed over hers, shouting her name. She thought one of them was Edwin Corish. Then the lab room faded away, replaced by a scene just as familiar but much more frightening.

Gates of Heaven Cemetery.

It was two weeks after the first murder in town and there'd been three more since, along with several disappearances. Herman Davis, the Chief of Police before Nick Travers, had already implemented a mandatory curfew for anyone under the age of eighteen.

But of course the Cemetery Club hadn't obeyed curfew any more than they did their own parents' rules.

It'd been Cory's idea to take their usual Friday night party out of the crypt.

"It's a beautiful night," he'd said, and he'd been right. Not too hot, not chilly. Very little humidity, which was always a relief in the middle of a New York State summer because it meant there wouldn't be too many mosquitoes.

Cory's idea, yes, but none of them had put up any argument.

They'd spread a blanket out on a small area of flat, grave-less grass not far down the hill from the crypt. Passing a joint around and sharing the two bottles of beer John had stolen from his refrigerator, they talked about the same things teenagers around the world were probably talking about at the same time: music, the teachers they hated, how much their parents bothered them. At some point Todd finished one of the beers and tossed the bottle into the center of their circle. It spun twice and came to rest pointing at John.

"Good thing we're not playing spin the bottle," Marisol had said. "You'd have to kiss each other."

"Maybe we *should* play," Cory said, giving the bottle a tap with his finger. It moved ninety degrees and stopped, the open end pointing right at Marisol.

"You did that on purpose," she said. Todd and John laughed and made kissing noises at her.

"Pay up." Cory leaned forward and Marisol found herself leaning towards him as well. It was the opportunity she'd been waiting for and she wasn't about to let the presence of John and Todd keep her from her goal of making out with Cory. They could watch or leave; at that point, she didn't care.

Her lips were so close to his she could smell the beer and pot on his breath, when something stumbled out of the bushes not ten feet away.

"Hey!" John stood up and all three of them joined him. Marisol was prepared to run, in case it was a night watchman or a cop.

Instead, it was something that looked like it had just dug itself free from one of the fresher graves. Moonlight illuminated dead flesh, turning it bone-white. The thing's clothes were torn and filthy, a rank foulness rolled off it in nauseating waves.

"Oh shit. Run!" Cory grabbed Marisol's arm and jerked her around, putting action to words. John, the fastest of them all, quickly disappeared ahead, while Todd brought up the rear.

They ran down the hill to the main drive, climbed the rusty iron gate and dropped down onto the sidewalk.

Right next to a police car parked by the curb.

"Hey you! Stop!" A spotlight came on, pinning them to the wrought iron. Marisol and the others froze as the two police officers got out of the car, hands hovering over their guns.

"Help! There's a monster chasing us!" There was no hesitation on Marisol's part, no moment where she considered what she was saying. The words just came out. Next to her, Cory muttered, 'Oh shit.'

"What are you kids doing in the cemetery?" one of the cops asked. With the car's spotlight behind him it was impossible to make out his face.

"She told you, someone's chasing us," Cory said, giving Marisol's arm a squeeze. She understood his silent command to keep quiet but all she wanted to do was dive into the safety of the policeman's arms and get driven away. Even if away meant a trip to the station and a call to her parents.

Anything that got them the hell away from the thing in the cemetery.

"She said a monster. I think you kids are high." The cop shined his flashlight casually across the gate. At the same time, the second cop leaned back into the car and started talking on the radio. John glanced over his shoulder at the cemetery and his whole body went tense.

She didn't know if he saw something or was just scared, but Marisol was getting ready to say the hell with the cops and start running. Let them chase her. Better them than it.

Then the second cop, a stocky man with a mustache, came back. "Chief says to bring all four of them to the station."

As Marisol climbed into the back seat she took a last look at the cemetery.

I'm never going back in there again.

But of course, she did. They all did.

* * *

Marisol was trying not to watch Doctor Corish put in the last of her stitches when Cory burst into the M.E.'s office. She'd called him as soon as the M.E. and Chief Travers had helped her to Corish's office and started cleaning her wounds.

"Are you all right?" he asked, pushing past Chief Travers and kneeling next to her.

"Oh God, I'm so glad to see you!" She gave him a hug with one arm. "And yes, I'm fine."

"You won't be if you keep moving," Corish said, a mock angry look on his face. "Just stay still until I'm done, will you?"

"What the hell happened?" Cory asked.

Marisol opened her mouth to answer but it was Travers who spoke first. "Addicts."

"What?" Cory looked confused.

"A bunch of them, probably hopped up on meth or coke or some shit. We think maybe one of the techs here was supplying them. They got wasted and attacked your girlfriend."

"You were attacked?"

"I--"

"She got bit by one of them," Ed Corish said as he used a cotton ball to apply Betadine to Marisol's stitches.

"Bit?" Cory looked from Marisol to the M.E. and back again. "By who?"

"One of the druggies," Travers said.

Marisol shook her head. "Jake Spencer didn't do drugs." She was getting tired of repeating it. No matter how many times she told her story, the police chief seemed convinced he had the whole thing figured out.

Travers glared at her. He'd been doing that since the first time she uttered the word zombie. "They sure looked like addicts to me. Eyes all weird and shit. They didn't even care when I started shooting."

"Will somebody please tell me what the fuck is going on?" Cory stood up, one hand resting protectively on Marisol's shoulder. She could feel the heat from his palm through the cotton scrub shirt she'd put on to replace her ruined top.

Corish stripped off his latex gloves and threw them on the desk. "For God's sake Nick, it wasn't drugs. You shot Jake Spencer in the chest and he got up and ran away."

"Meth or crack'll do that to you. Body runs on pure adrenaline." Travers crossed his arms, daring anyone in the room to contradict him.

Marisol looked up at Cory and found him staring at her. She knew what he was thinking. She gave him a quick nod and he returned it.

"We'll know if it was drugs soon enough," Marisol said to the Chief. "I'm going to run samples from the dead man and Jake. If there were any drugs in their systems, they'll show up."

"No, you're going home and going to bed," Corish said. "You've been through enough tonight, on top of all the extra hours you've been putting in lately. You need rest."

"As soon as I run the samples." Now it was her turn to be stubborn. Her boss stared at her but in the end he backed down, as she'd known he would.

Corish turned to Cory. "You've got yourself quite a little bulldog."

Cory smiled. "I wouldn't have her any other way." He turned his gaze down toward her. "How's this sound? Marisol runs the tests and then I'll make sure she goes home and stays in bed for the rest of the day."

"Two days. With pay," Corish added, holding up two fingers.

"Fine. Two days." Marisol fought to keep from smiling. Two days off, with Cory and with pay? It was almost like a vacation.

Of course, we'll probably spend the whole time chasing zombies or aliens or whatever the fuck kind of monsters are living under the cemetery again.

Marisol stood up and started for the door, Cory still right next to her.

"Wait a minute." Travers moved to block their exit.

"What now?" Marisol asked.

"I'm gonna need you to come down to my office at some point, so you can fill out an official report of what happened here."

"It wasn't drug addicts."

Travers rolled his eyes. "Whatever you say. But let's wait for the results of your tests. Then you can give whatever whacked out statement you want."

"I'll be there tomorrow." She took Cory's hand. "Let's go."

Travers followed them out into the hallway where four uniform officers stood next to yellow crime scene tape. Bright flashes from the DNA lab indicated other investigators were still busy taking their pictures and measurements.

"You'll have to wait outside until they're done," Travers told them. "Be at least an hour or two."

"We'll grab a coffee across the street," Cory said. "You want us to bring you back one?"

Travers stared at the bloody walls, where an officer was taking samples. "Make it two. Black." He sighed. "It's gonna be a long day."

* * *

Jack Smith was parking his car in front of the city building when he saw Marisol and Cory coming down the front steps of the new wing, hand in hand. *Four o'clock in the morning? What the hell are they doing here?*

He ducked low, hoping they wouldn't notice him amid the red and blue lights spraying the walls of the buildings on Main Street. He'd received the emergency call less than half an hour ago. A break-in at the morgue, with several deaths. He'd immediately hopped out of bed and had gotten dressed, his brain already in damage-control mode. The idea that Marisol might have been a victim had never even crossed his mind.

Guess I really am over the bitch. Then the picture of his ex-wife parading around town with her high school sweetheart appeared in his head again, and his anger blossomed anew. *Maybe she was thinking about him while we were married. How else could she put being his wife behind her so quickly?*

That galled him the most, that it was apparently so easy for her to forget him and move on with her life. It was different for him; he hadn't really lost anything. He still had his money, his job, his connections. By contrast, Marisol had lost everything. He'd taken her from rags to riches, taught her etiquette and how to enjoy the good things in life. When you thought about it, he'd literally handed her the keys to not only the city but to a whole different world.

And it still hadn't been enough.

No, she'd wanted love and respect on top of everything else. She hadn't gotten it - just because he'd married her didn't mean she was his equal after all. So many girls would have been happy to settle for what she had. Why couldn't she?

In retrospect, his parents had been right. She hadn't been worth the effort, hadn't been smart enough to realize how lucky she'd been.

And now she flaunts her new man, as if she'd never been happier.

It just wasn't right. It made him - Jack Smith the Deputy Mayor - look bad, because if people saw that Marisol was happier without him, they'd start to think that maybe some of the things she'd said were true, that Jack Smith might not be the nice guy everyone thought he was. He'd gone to great lengths to cultivate his public image and he'd be damned if some two-bit spic from the Lowlands was going to tarnish it.

No, in order to keep things right, it was necessary that Marisol's public face be a sad one. Or at least untrustworthy.

Which meant it was time to put the heat on Mister Cory Miles and his friends.

His lips pursed in grim concentration, Jack pulled out his Blackberry and dialed his assistant.

Chapter 2

Cory closed his cell phone and turned to Todd Randolph. "Marisol's still in the lab. She said that when she finishes her work, she'll call me so I can drive her home." He looked at his watch. "It's only nine; the library doesn't open for another hour. What do you want to do until then?"

Todd wiped his mouth. They'd just finished a quick breakfast of coffee and donuts Cory had picked up from the bakery and taken back to Todd's house. John was already in Todd's study Googling reported cases of alien abduction and possession in the New York Tri-State Area.

"I'd like to go to the police station and talk with Chief Travers. I think it's time we came clean about what happened in high school. Maybe something we know will help him with his investigation."

"You think Travers will talk to us?" Cory rolled his eyes. "The man's as stubborn as a two-year-old. He wouldn't believe something supernatural was going on if a zombie came up and bit him on the ass. Which almost happened last night, from what Marisol told me."

Todd shrugged and downed the rest of his coffee before answering. "We owe him the opportunity to listen. If there's the slightest chance something we know prevents someone else from being killed..." His words tailed off and he stared at Cory, an earnest expression on his face.

"What the hell. We'll go see him. Marisol's lab is right next door anyhow."

"I'll tell John," Todd said. Before he could leave the kitchen Abigail Clinton came downstairs.

"Mister Todd? You get those medicines for your mother?"

Todd patted his shirt pocket. "I've got the prescriptions right here. I'll drop them off today. She's still got enough for a few days."

"You sure? I can do." The home health aide held out her hand.

"No, that's okay. Cory and I are going out for a few hours

anyhow."

"Okay Mister Todd." She turned and went back upstairs.

"How's your mom doing?" Cory asked.

Todd sighed. "Not good. The drugs keep her pretty much out of it most of the time. She doesn't even get out of bed anymore. And my arrest didn't help."

"I'm sorry man. That sucks." Cory stood by the table for a minute, coffee in hand, not knowing what else to say. Losing his own parents had been a tragedy that left a big hole in his life, but he'd always been comforted by the fact that death had been quick and painless for them. The idea of watching a loved one slowly fade away like Todd's mother was doing, it seemed wrong somehow. He didn't know how Todd could stand it, especially considering he'd never had the chance to spend much time with her when she was healthy.

Thanks to us.

"Yeah. It does." Todd turned away and started cleaning the table.

Cory waited another moment, in case his friend had something else to say, then left the room when the silence began gaining the heavy weight of awkwardness.

As he walked down the hall to the study, it struck him that all four members of the Cemetery Club had lost their parents. The only ones left were Todd's mother, clinging to life by her aged fingernails and Marisol's father, who'd left town - and possibly the country - not long after she'd graduated high school. She assumed he was still alive, since she'd never heard anything from Social Security about his passing away.

"Probably rotting in a jail cell somewhere," she'd said when he'd asked her about it. The deep bitterness in her voice stopped him from pursuing the matter.

I wonder if there's any significance to that, he thought, as he walked up the stairs. *None of us are even forty yet.* It sure was an odd coincidence that six out of eight of their parents were not only dead but had died young. And when it came to the Cemetery Club and Rocky Point, he had a feeling there were no coincidences.

* * *

The first surprise Cory got when they arrived at the police station was finding Chief Travers alone in his office. The second was when the

Chief looked up at Cory's knock, saw them, and still motioned for them to enter.

"Take a seat," Travers said, gesturing towards the two uncomfortable wooden chairs by his desk. "What can I do for you?"

Cory eyed the police chief carefully, alert for some kind of trick. But try as he might, he couldn't see any malice in the man's square face, only a weariness expressed in gray pallor, dark bags under the eyes and hair that looked as if it hadn't been combed that morning. Even his mustache seemed unkempt.

"You look like you could use some sleep," Cory said, then wished he could've taken the words back. The last thing he wanted to do was antagonize the man.

Travers gave him a half-hearted glare, his breath escaping in a long, drawn-out sigh. "Tell me something I don't know." He rubbed his eyes with his fists. When he stopped, they were more bloodshot than when he'd started, but they had also regained a little of their customary fire. "I'm busy Mister Miles, as you might have guessed. I hope you didn't just drop by to shoot the shit."

"Actually, we wanted to talk about the murders," Todd said.

"What about them?" Travers looked at Todd the way most people look at Jehovah's Witnesses when they came to the front door.

"Not the current murders, the ones twenty years ago. We think there are some, uh, facts about them you might not know, facts that might be helpful with what's been happening lately."

Travers scowled. "Well, if anyone knows about how those poor people died it would be you, wouldn't it?"

Todd gave a slow nod of his head. "Yes, you're right Chief, but not in the way you think you are. I didn't kill any of those people, just like I haven't killed anyone the past few days. But I hold myself responsible just the same."

"Not just him," Cory added. "All four of us played a part."

Travers stared at them, his gaze suddenly alert. "What do you mean?"

Cory looked at Todd, who nodded. "We agreed to tell him everything."

"It's like this," Cory said. "We - Todd, myself, Marisol and John Boyd - did something twenty years ago, something we shouldn't have done. But we were just kids, we didn't know better."

"We didn't believe," Todd interrupted.

"Believe in what?" Travers asked, his gaze darting from Todd to Cory and back again.

"The supernatural." Todd's face remained impassive as the Chief's eyes went wide and then narrowed in anger.

"What the fuck are you doing, wasting my time with this bullshit? Get the fuck out of here!"

"Chief, listen to him." Cory leaned forward. "It's true. We were messing around in the cemetery, using a Ouija Board. We...made contact with something. It scared the shit out of us and we ran away. But the next day..."

"The next day the first murder happened," Todd finished. "And they went on all summer long, until we stopped them."

"*You* stopped them?" Travers looked from Todd to Cory and back again. "You? Not the police who worked their asses off day and night. You did it. Four teenagers who spent more time stoned than awake, from what I remember."

Cory ignored the sarcasm. "That's right. In fact, it was Todd who put an end to things."

"And I suppose being found with the half-eaten bodies of the victims was part of solving the case?"

"We went into the tunnels and confronted the demons," Todd said. "I used Holy water and the Bible. The tunnel collapsed. When they found me--"

"You mean, when they caught you," a new voice said. "The police - the real heroes - captured a sick little bastard and put him where he belonged. In the nuthouse."

Cory jerked around and saw Jack Smith standing in the doorway. Cory started to rebut the accusation but Smith kept talking, raising his voice over Cory's.

"Say Chief. Did you know that while Mister Randolph was in Wood Hill, they fried his brain? Gave him the ol' zapper-oo? Or that he allowed himself to be used as a guinea pig for experimental drugs? I've got copies of his medical records in my office, if you want to see them."

"Those were confidential," Todd said.

"Confidentiality doesn't apply to murder suspects."

"That's enough!" Cory shouted. "Everyone has rights and if you violated his--" He started to get up from his chair but Todd placed a hand on his arm.

"It's okay Cory. He's right."

"What?"

"When I was in the sanitarium, they did do shock treatments on me. Three times I think. And I willingly took part in several pharmaceutical protocols during my time there. The drugs were simply new types of sedatives, not narcotics or hallucinogens. And by agreeing to participate in the trials I earned special privileges, such as extra library time and a chance to work in the kitchen."

"How 'bout that Chief? Right from the horse's mouth. Any wonder he's talking about demons living under the city? He's as nutty now as the day they took him away." The Deputy Mayor leaned against the door frame, a shit-eating grin plastered across his face.

Travers, who'd been looking back and forth between Smith and Todd as they spoke, finally opened his mouth. "Mister Randolph, I appreciate you and Mister Miles coming down here today. But I'm afraid I'm going to have to ask you to leave now."

Cory leaned forward, his hands on the Chief's desk. "We're telling the truth. There was something under the ground that day, something - I don't know if it was supernatural or not - that killed all those people. And --"

"That's enough Miles." Travers held up one hand. "It doesn't matter what you saw. It doesn't matter if you're telling the truth, full of shit or just plain crazy like your friend. Fact is, I can't trust anything either of you tell me. He's spent the past twenty years in the loony bin and you're too personally involved in the case, as his lawyer and the Flores woman's lover. Neither of you are credible as witnesses in any shape or form. Now, unless you have some real hard evidence you can show me, instead of all this hearsay and crazy talk, you're gonna have to leave me to my work."

"Please, you've got to listen to us."

"Yes, listen to him Chief. He's got a real good team. A mental patient, a homeless drunk and a lab tech who can't keep her pants on. Quite a crew. Maybe you should hire them."

Travers didn't even have the decency to cover his mouth when he laughed. "You heard me. Get out of here."

Cory shook his head. "You're making a big mistake. C'mon, Todd, let's go."

"Yes, go hunt some demons or something and leave the real work to the police," Smith said with a snicker, as he moved aside to let Todd and Cory exit the office.

"I know why you're doing this," Cory said. "But just because you have a problem with me, don't let innocent people suffer the consequences."

Smith stepped into the hall and shut the door before replying. "Listen, Mr. Fancy-Pants lawyer. You messed with the wrong guy. I'm making it my personal mission to make life a living hell for you and your wacko friends. This is just the beginning." He turned and walked down the hall, flashing his best campaign smile as he said hello to the police officers he passed.

Cory started after him but Todd grabbed his arm. "Don't Cory. All you'll do is get in more trouble. Smith runs this town, probably more so than the actual Mayor. Best thing to do is lay low and hope he gets too busy to worry about us."

"Too busy?" Cory stared at Todd. "If he's too busy, it'll be because those things are killing more people."

Todd slowly nodded. "I know. Believe me, I know."

Chapter 3

"So what do we do now?"

They were gathered around Todd's kitchen table. John, who'd posed the question to the group, was nursing his third soda of the day, on top of several cups of coffee. Todd didn't say anything, figuring if the caffeine fix helped him keep the DTs away it was an acceptable solution, even if John's hands constantly shook so much he was in danger of spilling soda all over the table.

"Maybe we should do what the Chief said and stay out of it. Serve 'em all right," Marisol said. She'd already informed them of the test results she'd obtained in the lab. As she'd predicted, no traces of drugs or alcohol had been found in the dead body, nor in the blood left behind by the two men who'd gotten away. Of course, Marisol knew that wouldn't mean anything to Travers. He'd just say that maybe the tech had been straight but stealing drugs for his friends who were high on some new, undetectable kind of drug.

She'd filed her report with the M.E. and then gone straight to Todd's house with him and Cory, where Todd had filled everyone in on the events in the Chief's office.

"How can you say that?" Todd asked. "This is our town too. Just because Travers and Smith are being assholes doesn't mean the whole town should suffer."

"There are still some good people here," John added.

"Good enough to sacrifice ourselves for?" Marisol looked around the table. "Good enough to risk our lives for?"

"We have to do what we can," Cory said.

Marisol glared at him. "Why?"

"Because it's our fault," Todd said in a low voice.

"Exactly." Cory pointed to each of them in turn as he spoke. "We all share the guilt for what's happening. We started it. It's up to us to finish it, for good this time."

"More importantly," Todd said, "I believe we might be the only ones who *can* stop it, because we started it."

"Which brings us back to my question." John took another sip of soda. "What do we do now?"

"We need more information," Todd said. "We're doing all this research, learning about aliens and demons and possession but we don't know if we're on the right track."

"I do," John interrupted. "Don't forget, I've seen them."

"We've seen things too John," Marisol said. "Like the undead walking. One of them bit me, remember? I've heard of aliens abducting people, experimenting on them, but never possessing someone. Or trying to eat them alive."

Cory patted her leg, a not-so-subtle hint for her to ease up. She did, mainly because deep inside she knew her anger was just camouflaging her real emotion: fear.

"Maybe the aliens turn people into zombies."

"That's the problem," Todd tried to placate them. "Conflicting experiences. We need definitive proof one way or the other. So I think we should take a visit to Gates of Heaven."

"No!" John jerked back in his chair. His soda can fell from his hand, splashing cola across the small table.

Todd shrugged. "It's the only way to be sure of what we're dealing with."

"The cemetery's a big place. Where would we start?" Cory asked, mopping up soda with some paper towels.

John shook his head. "Don't even say it."

"Where it all started. The crypt."

"I knew it. This is just plain foolish. We're all gonna end up dead, or worse."

"John, be quiet." Marisol touched his hand to take the sting out of her words. "Much as I hate to admit it, 'cause it's the last place I ever want to see again, I think I agree with Todd. If we have to get involved we need as much information as possible. I think this is something we have to do."

"Not you," Cory said. "At least, not until you go home and get some sleep. Doctor's orders, remember?"

Todd stood up. "All right. We'll all meet here at eight o'clock tonight. That will give Marisol time to rest, while John and I gather the supplies we'll need."

Looking more despondent than usual, John said, "I hope you know what you're doing."

Cory tossed away the wet paper towels and took Marisol's hand. "And on that sunny note, we're out of here. See you all tonight."

* * *

Gina Torelli was pouring herself a second glass of wine when her front door crashed open. She screamed, dropped her Merlot and backpedaled across the kitchen as three intruders stormed through her small living room. Only when her back hit the kitchen counter did she remember the phone she'd left next to the sink when she finished talking to her son Michael, who was spending the week with his father.

She grabbed the phone and ran for the dining room, fumbling for the redial button. Behind her, the three men - Oh God, was that blood all over their clothes? - knocked aside the kitchen table, their faces contorted and their wild hair matted to their scalp.

"Hello?" Her ex-husband's voice, tinny and distant from the phone's speaker. It was the first time in five years she'd actually been glad to hear it.

"Help! Jim! Someone's here! They--"

A heavy blow struck her back and she fell, losing the phone in the process. It sailed through the air, Jim's voice shouting - "Gina! Gina, what's wrong? Gina--" - and then her head hit the floor and the world exploded into colored lights. She tried to cry out again but a heavy weight landed hard on top of her, driving the air from her lungs.

Daggers of pain lanced through her neck and she clawed at the ground, trying to pull herself away. The phone lay just out of reach, Jim's impotent voice still shouting her name. Strong hands gripped the sides of her head, digging and clawing and pulling. Fresh agony detonated in her skull just as she found her breath. Before she could call out for help, something landed on the floor, directly between her and the phone.

It took her a moment to comprehend that the object was one of her own ears.

A mud-splattered foot came down on the ear and more hands dug at her body, tearing away clothes and flesh with equal ease. She had time for one more scream before teeth clamped down on the back of her neck and all the pain disappeared.

Gina closed her eyes and tried to ignore the gravelly sound of teeth on bone.

Then there was only quiet darkness.

Jim Torelli arrived at his ex-wife's house less than a minute after the first police car got there. He was running up the front walk when one of the officers emerged from the house, hands over his mouth and vomit spraying out from between his fingers.

"Gina!" Jim rushed past the officer, who ignored him and continued puking.

The living room and kitchen were in shambles, furniture overturned and broken, shattered glass everywhere. In the kitchen, spaghetti sauce covered the walls and floors in red splatters.

Something important tapped on his brain for attention. *Gina doesn't eat spaghetti sauce.*

"What...?" The truth of it hit him just as he turned and saw the scraps of flesh, bone and clothing scattered across the room, standing out like islands in the sea of red that covered the tiles.

"Nooo!" The cry tore from Jim's throat as if he could put things right by shouting loud enough. He fell to his knees in the tacky blood, put his head down and cried out again. And again and again, until the paramedics arrived and sedated him.

Even then, his screams didn't stop. The difference was, only Jim could now hear them.

* * *

At two o'clock in the morning, the B-Line Diner was doing a typical business. Nightshift workers from the nearby machine shop, their hands tattooed with years of accumulated grease and grime, occupied four of the twelve counter seats, gulping down burgers and coffee before their lunch break ended. A group of mildly drunk college students took up two booths in the back, working their way through stacks of pancakes they hoped would soak up enough alcohol to prevent morning hangovers. A smaller booth, closer to the cash register, held two elderly men dressed in ragged, dirty clothes who cradled cups of coffee in grimy hands, as if it was winter outside instead of a warm summer night. They took only occasional sips between short bouts of conversation, doing their best to extend their stay in the relative comfort of the diner. While summer normally posed no hardships for the homeless, there'd been rumors going round lately that it wasn't safe on the streets. The diner represented temporary safety and they were loath to leave.

Darcy Ellison, the only waitress on duty from midnight to four a.m., stood by the coffee machine, counting her tips. Where most people might have hated working the night shift at a cheap diner in the heart of the factory district, for Darcy it was the perfect job. She lived two blocks away, in a neat trailer in Lowlands Park. A chronic insomniac, she was up most nights anyhow. Working at the B-Line allowed her to make some money without having to bust her ass like the dinner or breakfast crews. The tips weren't great but between them and her dead husband's pension, she managed. Plus, Curt, the night cook, usually sent her home with a couple of to-go containers.

After more than five years at the B-Line, Darcy figured she'd seen it all. Drunken frat boys with sassy mouths, fights and more than a few couples in the back booths who thought they could get away with a little sex under the table when no one was looking. She'd even had a gun pointed at her during a robbery. So when the front glass came crashing down Darcy's first thought was that a car had plowed into the building, like had happened three years earlier when a drunken factory worker never hit his brake while parking.

Then she got a look at the people climbing through the broken window and she realized there were still surprises left in the world. Staring at them, all she could think of was the scary movie she'd watched the night before, the one about the dead people in the shopping mall.

The sound of screaming filled the air. It took Darcy several seconds to realize the screams were hers.

The four men at the counter stood up and formed a clumsy line facing the things that had broken in. They were outnumbered three to one but they had years of metal-working muscles in their arms and tempers as hot as the flames of their welding torches. None of them showed any fear as the dead-looking people surged forward.

The first couple of attackers went down quickly as the factory workers dealt out swift, hard punches. The crunch of noses and jaws breaking was like music to the men, who shouted encouragement to each other and swung their calloused fists with something approaching manic glee, as if the act of hitting someone's face was some sort of cathartic release.

The college boys cheered and hollered from the back; the two elderly men had disappeared the minute the window shattered, running for the back door. Darcy told herself she should do the same but her feet seemed frozen to the ground.

Chet burst out of the kitchen, a cleaver in one hand and an iron skillet in the other. "Call the police!" he shouted to Darcy as he joined the fight.

Darcy tried to force her feet to move but they still refused to listen. *I can't!* She wanted to cry but her mouth - still hanging open from her previous screaming - stayed as immobile as the rest of her. Held captive by her own body, she could only watch as the tide of the fight quickly turned in the monsters' favor.

Three more walking corpses climbed through the window, as if drawn by the sounds of the fighting. At the same time, the ones who'd been knocked to the ground started to rise, showing no effects from their beatings.

"Son of a bitch!" one of the workers said, his breath coming in heavy gasps. "Fuckers won't stay down."

Chet struck a blow with the skillet, the impact of metal-on-skull sounding like a muffled musical note. Instead of collapsing, the corpse grabbed Chet's arm and bit into it. The lanky cook cried out and swung his cleaver, burying it in the other man's back. The dead man straightened up, blood running from his mouth, smiled, and then bit Chet's arm again. Two of the factory workers tried to pull the creature off him but almost immediately had to let go when other dead people jumped on their backs, digging and tearing with nails and teeth.

An old man, his pale face covered in savagely-deep cuts and a black hole where one eye should have been, darted past the melee and approached the counter. He opened his mouth, exposing crooked, yellowed teeth that had bits of flesh hanging from them. Darcy leaned back as the man placed bloody hands on the counter and prepared to leap across.

A surge of adrenaline ran through her and her muscles came to life. She dropped the tip jar and reached behind her, feeling around until she found the handle of a coffee pot.

"Get away!" she shouted, and swung the pot as hard as she could into the creature's face. Glass broke and steaming hot coffee sprayed across her attacker. Hot droplets burned her hand but she paid no attention. Relief and a feeling of victory filled her as she turned to run into the kitchen. From there, a short sprint would bring her to the back door and the back parking lot where her car - and safety - waited.

She'd managed two steps when a hand clutched her shoulder and pulled her backwards. Her feet flew out from under her and she landed hard on her back, knocking her breath away.

The old man's face, droplets of coffee still dripping from it, loomed over her. She screamed, thinking it was about to sink its vile teeth into her.

What came next was far worse.

From over the man's shoulder a new face appeared, this one in no way human. Eyes that burned with the fires of Hell looked down at her, seeming to stare into her very soul. Darcy's next scream turned into a choking sound, the last sound she ever made, as the creature forced itself into her mouth. Her lungs fought for air and her hands pounded impotently on the dirty floor tiles.

Then the evil was inside her and Darcy ceased to exist.

Instead, there was only the Horde.

Chapter 4

"Morning John," Todd said, noticing his friend enter the kitchen. It was just after ten. Todd had risen twenty minutes earlier and started the coffee pot. Abigail was due at eleven and he liked to be done with breakfast and out of the way before she got there.

"Uh." John sat down at the table, accepting his cup of coffee without any other comment.

Todd knew how he felt. They'd spent nearly the entire night in Gates of Heaven Cemetery, camped out twenty yards from the old crypt, without seeing a single zombie or alien. Still, they'd stuck it out until four a.m. before admitting defeat and going home.

"Why weren't they there?"

Todd turned away from the sink as he pondered John's question. "I don't know. Maybe they don't come out every night. Maybe they have more than one route. Hell, maybe they saw us and didn't want a confrontation."

"Confrontation?" John gave a sarcastic laugh. "The motherfuckers *eat* people. You think they're scared of us?"

"It's possible. Not us per say but the public in general. Think about it. Whoever, *whatever* these things are, they only attack at night and never in a crowded or public place. They obviously don't want to be seen."

"What about that bar? That's a public place."

"Yes but it was late and only a few people were inside."

John frowned. "All right, but what about the attack on Marisol?"

Todd shook his head. "Again, late at night. Only Marisol and a couple of other people were working. I doubt the monsters expected the police to show up so fast."

"I still don't--" John broke off as someone knocked at the back door.

"It's Cory and Marisol," Todd said, glancing out the window. "I wonder what they're doing here so early."

Cory wasted no time in telling them. "Did you see the news?" He hurried into the living room and turned on the television, not waiting for an answer.

"No, we just got up." Todd said, as he and the others followed him.

The TV came to life in the middle of a reporter's dialog. "...continue with our breaking story. We're here live at the B-Line Diner in Rocky Point, where four people are confirmed dead and at least five others are missing. Among the missing are Darcy Ellison, a waitress, and Kip Weals, a nineteen-year-old student at Rockland Community College. Police say the attack occurred sometime between two and three in the morning and that several people, perhaps as many as ten, may have been involved. Sheriff Nick Travers--"

Cory hit the mute button and turned to the others. "While we were playing fucking detective in the cemetery, those things were out killing more people."

"Jesus Christ," Todd whispered.

"How?" John asked. "We know the mausoleum is where they come from."

"They must have another den, or lair, or whatever you call it," Marisol said.

Todd shook his head in frustration. "Now we have no idea where to find them. We're back to square one."

"We'll have to split up," Cory said. "Two of us can watch the cemetery, while the others drive around town and hopefully catch sight of the creatures on the streets. Then we can follow them back to their hiding place."

Marisol frowned. "That could take weeks."

"I know." Cory shrugged. "But what else can we do?"

"We'll still have the daytime," Todd said. "We can do more research."

John gave a sarcastic laugh. "How much more reading about monsters can we do? Cory hasn't found anything in the town records. None of what we've learned has helped us find them."

"That's 'cause we've been going about it all wrong." Todd glanced at each of them in turn. "Instead of trying to figure out what they are, we should be trying to learn *why* they're here."

"We already know that," Marisol said. "It's because of us. What we did that day."

"Is it?" Todd sat down in his recliner. "I'm not so sure about that anymore. People - especially teenagers, like we were back then - have been fooling around with Ouija boards and all sorts of other mystical toys for decades. Séances. Spells. But you never hear of anything bad or evil happening. How is it we had the power to call something so evil into our world?"

Cory frowned. "What are you getting at?"

"I think perhaps instead of creating these creatures, what we did was wake something up, something already there, something just waiting to emerge again."

"Again? You mean, this has happened before?"

Todd shrugged. "I don't know. But I think it might be a good idea for us to start reading about the history of Rocky Point before twenty years ago, beginning with that mausoleum."

Marisol rubbed her eyes. Dark circles hung underneath them, evidence of her lack of sleep. But her voice was still filled with energy. "Can't hurt. Where do we start?"

"I'll stick with the county records," Cory said. "I'm already familiar with how the files are set up."

"John and I will check the old newspapers." Todd smiled. "We might be pariahs in our own community but we haven't been banned from the library yet."

"What about me?" Marisol asked.

"Police files," Todd said. "You're the only one with access to official reports that might not be in the public records. See if you can find anything there."

"I'll try but I'm not exactly in good with the cops right now."

"Just give it your best shot. If that doesn't work you can help Todd and John. It's probably best if no one sees you with me in the records room."

Cory stood up. "I don't know about the rest of you but I'm dog-tired. What say we stock up on coffee and some nice, sugary donuts before we get to work? My treat."

Marisol gave a wan smile. "Sure, why not? What better way to spend my last day of enforced vacation?"

John cast frequent glances around them as he and Todd approached the mausoleum. At that moment, there was no place on Earth he wanted to be less than Gates of Heaven Cemetery. Even with the sun shining and the birds singing their summer songs, he more than half-expected reanimated corpses to come leaping out from hiding places behind crypts and monuments, fangs bared and ready to chow down on human flesh.

The fact that they were also planning on tampering with a crime scene didn't help his anxiety level.

"All those days and nights we spent hanging around here and we never wondered who was buried inside," Todd said. "Why is that?"

Although he knew his friend was being rhetorical, John answered anyway. "'Cause we were wise-ass teenagers who didn't give a shit. The real question is how do you know there's a name on that?" He pointed to the small brass plaque next to the mausoleum's door. Decades of rain and snow had created layers of corrosion on the metal until not a single letter showed through.

"That's why we brought this." Todd opened the plastic bag he carried and removed a bottle of brass cleaner and a scouring pad. "Don't forget, I went to a lot of funerals here, more than I can remember thanks to my dad being the minister. He always insisted that me and my mom be there for every one of them, because it showed the congregation we were one big family. Along the way I learned that crypts always have a marker, with a number. That's so the cemetery or the church can keep track of who's buried where. A lot of people put their names on them too."

"Well, let's hope this family remembered to do that," John said, while Todd poured cleaning solution on the rough pad and began scrubbing at the metal.

"Even if they didn't we'll still have the plot number. We can look it up in the old records and find out who was buried here."

"If they let us. I have a feeling our little group will be wearing out its welcome at Town Hall real soon and those records probably won't be available at the library."

Todd grunted as he scrubbed the pad across the metal. "We'll figure something out. We...hey, I see letters. Maybe we're going to get lucky after all." He poured more solvent on the pad and resumed scrubbing.

John tried to contain himself but after another minute he gave up. "Well? What does it say?"

"Hmf. Gimme another...there, that should do it." Todd pulled a dry cloth from the bag and wiped away the wet sludge from the plate. "Let's see... 407 dash Z5A. That's the plot number."

"That's it?" John asked, writing the information on a scrap of paper.

"Yes, no name."

"Figures. Well, call Cory and see if he can look that number up."

Todd pulled put the cleaning supplies in the bag and they started down the path to where they'd left his car. "I'll call him on the way to the library. Reception's never good on this side of the hill. I...hey, who's that?"

John looked where Todd was pointing. A police officer was standing behind Todd's Toyota, staring at them as they came down the small hill. "Uh-oh. Do you think he saw what we were doing up there?"

"I don't think so. The crypt is out of sight from the car." Todd raised his voice. "Excuse me officer, is something wrong?"

The man continued to stare at them, his expression hidden behind aviator-style mirrored sunglasses. A little shiver ran through John's belly and up his back.

"He's creeping me out," John whispered.

"Yeah." Todd stopped walking. "Something's not right here."

The officer chose that moment to step out from behind Todd's car. John felt a chuckle rise up as he saw the mess on the man's uniform - it looked like the poor guy had spilled his lunch on his lap. It was only when Todd muttered a startled curse that John thought to take another look.

"Jesus fucking Christ," he heard himself say, as he realized what he'd thought was food stains was actually clotted blood.

"Run," John said. When Todd didn't move, he reached out and hit his friend on the shoulder. "Run!"

Not waiting to see if Todd took his advice, John turned and sprinted back into the cemetery. A moment later Todd caught up to him and passed him by, something he'd never been able to do when John was in high school.

Damn that booze!

"Follow me," Todd said, his breath already coming in heavy gasps. "We'll cut through the woods to the church."

John risked a look back, saw that the thing was coming down the path after them, moving as fast - if not faster - than they were. He tried to remember how far it was to the old church. His heart was already pounding in his chest and he pictured it getting ready to explode, its walls too deteriorated from years of alcoholism and malnutrition to stand the sudden strain he was putting on it.

I will not die today. I will not become food for an alien cannibal thing.

He willed his legs to pump faster, ignoring the pain growing in his lungs.

Then something caught his leg and he was flying through the air.

Chapter 5

Cory's phone rang just as he was opening the next file in the stack he'd put together. He glanced at the caller ID, saw that it was Marisol.

"Hey, what's up gorgeous?"

"You wouldn't say that if you could see me right now," she said. "I've spent the last two hours driving myself crazy looking through filing cabinets. First in the lab and now I'm hiding in the records room at police headquarters."

"What? How'd you manage that?"

"I got someone to let me in without Travers knowing but now that I'm here, I've got no idea what the hell I should be looking for."

"I guess you could start with murders. A town this small, there can't have been too many of them."

She snorted. "You'd be surprised. The little bit of skimming that I've done you could fill a notebook with the people who've been killed just down in the Lowlands. On top of that, all the records for the whole damn county are here, not just Rocky Point."

Cory frowned. "Shit. I forgot the Sheriff's Department covers the whole county. All right, tell you what. Forget the police files. Head down to the morgue and see if they've got any results yet from last night's crime scene."

"Okay," Marisol said, her relief evident even through his cell phone's tiny speaker. "Have you heard from Todd and John yet?"

"No. They're probably at the library by now. I'm sure they'll call soon."

"All right. Are we still meeting back at Todd's for dinner?"

"Unless we hear different. It's my treat tonight. How's Chinese sound?"

"Make mine sweet and sour chicken with brown rice. I'll see you there."

"'Bye," Cory said. He thumbed the disconnect button, surprised to find the words "Love you," sitting at the edge of his tongue. He'd almost said them out loud; the only thing that had stopped him was a feeling that the time wasn't right. He was certain Marisol liked him, perhaps even loved him. He knew he loved her. He also knew that telling her too soon might send her running for the hills, especially after how badly her marriage had ended.

There's no rush, he thought. *When this is all over and we can spend time together without worrying about the town falling apart around us.*

Of course, who knows when that will be?

With a sigh, he opened the next file and started reading.

* * *

Beneath Rocky Point, in tunnels and caverns both man-made and natural, the Horde opened its many eyes in response to a disturbance on the surface.

The cemetery. One of the appendages had come upon humans near a point of egress.

"**Return home,**" the Horde told itself.

Dozens of faces frowned as one. The Horde remembered the last time humans had descended below the surface. Many decades ago but still the memory burned, as painful as the damage the interlopers had wrought.

The Horde considered the possibilities. Their numbers were strong again but not strong enough. Not yet. It sent a message throughout itself, imprinting the orders in the minds of all the appendages.

"**Do not use the cemetery to exit or enter the home.**"

The Horde considered the town above and the humans that infested it.

Soon, it thought. *Soon we will be free. Free to grow.*

And feed.

* * *

John threw his hands up, cushioning his fall just enough that he didn't hit his face. He felt like he'd taken a bowling ball to the chest but was still able to move. He rolled to the side, kicking out with both feet, expecting to find the reanimated cop clutching him with dead fingers.

Instead, all he saw were the gnarled, bulging roots of an old tree rising from the dirt path Todd had chosen.

"John!" Todd's frantic voice seemed like it was a mile away. It took a moment for John to realize that was because the pounding of his pulse in his ears was overpowering all other sounds.

"I'm...I'm okay," he said, fighting to get the words out while his lungs struggled to take in enough oxygen.

"C'mon." Hands grabbed him under the arms. "I don't know why but that thing stopped chasing us and turned around. I don't trust it though. I still think we should take the long way back into town. We can come back for my car later."

"Whatever you say." John coughed and wheezed as Todd led him up the hill. When they reached the top, he saw the old church standing there, its whitewashed walls stained a dismal gray from decades of exposure to the elements. Those same elements had stolen several shingles from the roof. Plywood covered the windows and front door, and the cement steps were cracked and broken.

Todd paused. "John, if you're feeling up to it, maybe we should go into the church and check the old records. We might find something about that crypt."

John held back a groan. The last thing he felt like doing was going inside a run-down, spooky old church, especially after they'd already been chased by one monster. Who knew what was waiting inside for them? But the look on Todd's face told him his friend was going in with or without him.

And friends didn't desert friends.

"I'm fine. Let's go."

As they walked up the crumbling stairs, he hoped they weren't making a mistake.

Two hours later, John's worries had changed from sudden death by monster attack to slow, lingering death from toxic mold poisoning. Digging through the file cabinets and boxes in the church storage room - not in the basement thank God, he didn't think he could have dealt with that - had churned up clouds of dust and fungal spores worse than anything he'd endured living on the streets. Thanks to years of abandonment, a leaky roof and too many humid seasons, half the papers they needed to look through were stained black and gray with mildew and worse.

"Jesus, this place reeks." He opened another drawer, exposing more yellowed, mildewed files. The upwelling of fresh dust tickled his nose and throat, sending him into yet another coughing fit.

"I know, I'm sorry. But we have to find out who that crypt belonged to. There must be a reason those creatures chose it for their lair."

"A reason?" John let out a short laugh that turned into another cough. "What makes you think there's a reason? Maybe it was just the first place they came across."

"No, that's too random for me to believe. I'm thinking perhaps it lies over a mystical place or the owner was someone who...Hello, what's this?"

"What do you have?" John dropped his files to the floor and joined Todd by another file cabinet. Todd's dirt-encrusted hands were busy flipping pages in what looked like an old-fashioned ledger.

"It's the old caretaker's book. It lists all the graves in the cemetery." A note of excitement crept into Todd's voice. "The information about that crypt must be in here!"

"But how are you going to find it?" John pointed at a column, which held nothing but dates listed in day, month and year order. "It's in date order. And we don't know what year the mausoleum was built."

"Well, we know it has to be before our junior year in high school." Todd flipped back through the pages until he reached a point twenty years in the past. Then he went to a page halfway between the open page and front cover. "Now we split the work." Gripping the book with both hands, he pulled it apart, tearing the binding. A huge cloud of dust flew into the air and more than a few silverfish fell to the floor.

"Here." Todd handed half the book to John. "You get from nineteen-forty on. I'll take the earlier half."

"Damn Todd. That was church property you just destroyed. What would your father say?"

Todd gave him a weak smile.

"Since when did I ever care what he thought?"

Chapter 6

Cory was almost ready to give up and head back to Marisol's for a shower and a beer when his cell phone rang. His first reaction after hearing about Todd and John's near-attack at the cemetery was to call Marisol and tell her to join them, in case there were further threats. But Todd dissuaded him from doing anything hasty.

"I don't think it was after us specifically," he said. "We know they've been using the crypt. It was probably just returning to its nest or lair or whatever and we happened to be there. But none of that matters. We found out who the crypt belongs to."

"What? How?" Cell phone tucked between his shoulder and ear, Cory hurried back to the computer he'd been using to access the town's files.

"We got an ID number on the crypt and then found the old cemetery records in the church storage room. Thank heavens my father never threw anything out. Anyhow, it took a while, but we were able to match the number to a name. Grover Lillian. He was buried in 1922."

"I'll get right on it."

"Good. We're heading to my house to wash up. Are you still bringing dinner?"

"Yeah. I'll call you when I'm on the way." Cory hung up and scrolled through the options in the records system until he found Obituaries. Keying in the name and date Todd had given him, he hit enter and waited for the death notice to pop up. He'd expected a standard notice, possibly a two-column layout, given that the man must have been at least fairly well-to-do, based on his expensive burial site.

Instead, he found himself looking at a list of more than fifteen newspaper articles. He opened the first one.

Doctor of Death commits suicide in secret burial ground.

For the next twenty minutes, he kept the records room printer running non-stop.

"This is unbelievable." Marisol put down one of the articles Cory had found on Dr. Grover Lillian.

"Not really." Todd washed down a mouthful of sesame chicken before continuing. "In the twenties and thirties, many mental institutions doubled as experimental laboratories for physicians. And not just for mental illnesses either. Small pox, tuberculosis, syphilis, cerebral palsy - you name it and likely someone was working on a cure at an asylum. And in the absence of good government controls, many of those experiments bordered on sheer barbarism."

"So, is that what we're dealing with? The ghosts of all those people he killed?"

"Ghosts don't turn people into zombies," John said. He picked up a carton of moo goo gai pan and scooped some onto his plate, topping it off with a dollop of hot mustard.

"Well, that's just it. We don't really know what ghosts do or don't do. Or," Todd held up a hand to stop John's argument, "even if we're dealing with ghosts at all. I think we need to find out more about this Dr. Lillian. For instance, where under the hospital was this burial ground? The articles don't say."

"Good question." Cory finished his beer. "First thing tomorrow morning, we meet at the library and do some serious research."

"Not me." Marisol stood up. "It's back to work for me tomorrow, which means early to bed tonight."

"Are you sure you're okay to go back?" Cory stood also. "You're stitches aren't even out yet."

"Gotta pay the rent," she said. "Besides, I'll be able to keep up with any new information the police gather. Gossip spreads faster than light in a government building."

"Goodnight Marisol," Todd said.

Still eating, John merely waved.

"Coming?" She looked at Cory, who glanced at the others.

"Go ahead." Todd smiled at him. "We all know."

"See you in the morning then," Cory said, a relieved smile on his face.

After they left, John looked at Todd.

"You're not really planning on waiting until tomorrow, are you?"

Picking up his soda, Todd shook his head.

"That's why God gave us the internet."

* * *

Doctor Eli Sloan put his car in park and stared out the windshield. In the white glare of the car's headlights, Wood Hill Sanitarium took on a sinister appearance and he imagined it wouldn't take long for it to gain a reputation for being haunted. Although the walls were still free of wild ivy and moss, and none of the windows or doors had been broken by drunken teenagers, it was easy to picture how the reflections of trees and clouds on the institutional glass would be interpreted as ghostly shapes. How the whispering night breeze would be construed as the voices of the dead calling for release.

Even knowing there was nothing inside except the usual detritus of *Homo bureaucratis* - tons of files and abandoned office furniture - Sloan still felt an almost instinctive dread at the idea of going back inside the hospital. *If ghosts do exist, then Wood Hill ought to be filled with them. And more than a few would be there because of me.*

Not the best thoughts to have before going inside. Except that not going in might lead to something far worse than encountering an angry spirit or two. As in, losing his medical license. Or maybe even going to jail.

Given those choices, there really was no decision.

He'd gotten the phone call a few hours earlier, just as he was about to pour himself a nice after-dinner glass of sherry. The speaker hadn't identified himself. Hadn't needed to. Sloan had recognized the voice right away: Dan Remoso, Manager of Building Facilities. Not a person he'd have normally associated with, let alone known on a personal basis. But several years earlier they'd discovered a mutual fondness for a certain white powder after Sloan had walked in on Remoso cutting a line in the men's room. Since then they'd shared many a bag, sitting in the parking lot at the end of a long work day.

"Sloan, you should stop by the hospital. Tonight. Check the files in the administration's storage room. Sublevel One. They're coming tomorrow morning."

The connection had clicked off before he'd been able to ask any questions. Who was coming? The FDA, looking for evidence of misconduct? The senior administrators, intent on placing falsified evidence in the files? And what files had he missed? He'd submitted no written reports that contained anything relating to his human trials, only verbal updates. And he'd kept his data in his briefcase, not his office.

Did I miss something? Or worse, did they record me? Or maybe have meetings without me, meetings where they discussed all *the aspects of my work?*

And how did Remoso know about any of this?

There'd been no question of whether or not to go back to the hospital. Thanking his lucky stars his drug habit had created an unexpected confidant, he'd grabbed a flashlight and headed back to Rocky Point without even telling his wife he was going out.

Now, an hour later, he was sitting in the parking lot, suddenly afraid to enter an empty building.

Get a grip and move your ass. You've got six hours until sunrise and maybe an hour or two at the most after that before they - whoever they are - show up. And by then you need to be long gone.

Flashlight in hand, Sloan turned off the car and got out. After removing his tire iron from the trunk, he walked around to the building's maintenance entrance. Unlike the big front doors, it only had one simple lock above the knob. He jammed the pry bar between the door and frame, using a rock to hammer it in. Two heaves later the door opened with a loud metallic squeal. Sloan paid no attention to the noise; the hospital was well away from any neighborhoods or streets so there was no chance anyone would hear him.

Once inside, he made his way to the nearest stairwell and headed down to Sublevel One, the lower of the two basement levels. Sublevel Two held the morgue, the Chemistry Lab and the Dental Department. Sublevel One was strictly storage and maintenance, the guts of the building. Generators, HVAC, waste disposal and plumbing took up the wide center area, with small offices along the sides.

He groaned as he saw there had to be a dozen or more storage rooms, all filled with filing cabinets and cardboard boxes. Which ones belonged to Administration? Was there an order to the way things had been stored or had files simply been carted down and placed from oldest to newest?

Sloan realized he was in for a long night.

"Well, let's hope the room closest to the elevator has the newest files." In the cavernous space, his words came back to him from multiple directions, bouncing off concrete and metal until it sounded like several people were mocking him from the darkness. Already creeped out by the empty building, he made a silent note not to speak out loud again.

He was halfway through the first box of files he'd opened when a sudden thought came to him.

This is the floor that connects to the old power plant.

The power plant where the bodies had been buried.

In his mind's eye, he saw how they must have done it. Waiting until the dead of night to take the lifeless forms from the morgue down to Sublevel One and then wheeling them through the tunnel that connected the current hospital to the old building, the one not in use any more.

Dumping them in the Pit.

The bodies are all gone asshole! he chided himself. They'd been carted away by the police long ago. Still, he couldn't shake the image of corpses piled on each other, eyes opening in the dark, hands digging their way free.

Bodies rising from the ground.

Stop it! You're acting like a child who's afraid of the dark.

Opening the next box, he saw the Chief Administrator's name on a folder. *Bingo! This has to be the right room.*

That's when he heard the noise.

A soft whispering, like the voices of children playing hide-and-seek.

He paused, hand halfway to a file. Listened.

Nothing. Just endless quiet.

Deathly, tomb-like quiet, his mind supplied, and he quickly told it to shut up.

You're imagining things. Or maybe it was his blood pulsing in his ears, an internal white noise only audible because the building was so silent.

He resumed flipping through the files, checking the papers inside each one for his name since it was unlikely anything relating to him would be conveniently labeled as Human Trials or Illegal Activities.

As he prepared to open the third box, he heard it again.

Whisper-sshhh-shush

Not words. More like distant waves lapping at a sandy shore. A sliding, shuffling sound.

Like someone scuffing their feet while they walk?

Just like that, a new picture appeared in his brain: zombified corpses dragging themselves through the pitch black hallways, seeking...

Me.

Unable to control his imagination any longer, Sloan went back into the hallway. His intention was to prove to himself nothing was there. A quick look in both directions with the flashlight and then he could return to the real job at hand: saving his career.

He aimed the flashlight towards the elevators, casting the beam back and forth across the hall, alert for any movement.

Nothing.

See? You're being what your son would call a real wuss.

Turning the other way, he brought the light around.

For a moment, the scene before him didn't even register; his rational mind was already telling him nothing was there. Then it actually processed what his eyes were seeing and he gasped. The instinctive areas of his brain tried to take over, tried to kick his fight-or-flight response into high gear but all that happened was his bladder emptied a stream of hot piss down his legs.

As the approaching monsters drew closer, Sloan's mind regressed into total chaos. Thoughts and commands mixed together, creating a jumble of conflicting messages that left him standing like a statue, helpless as the dead hands reached out for him. His mouth opened but instead of a scream, all that came out was a long, thin rope of saliva. His legs quivered but instead of propelling him away from the danger, his sphincter relaxed and his bowels released.

In the end, as the living nightmares bit into his flesh, he died like so many of his patients had - deathly afraid, unable to speak and covered in his own shit.

Chapter 7

"Attention all units. Ten-thirty-three at four-fifty East Main. Possible two-eleven in progress. Repeat, possible two-eleven in progress."

Bud Marks froze with his coffee cup halfway to his mouth. A ten-thirty-three was a security alarm going off; two-eleven was the code for a robbery. Although he was only filling in for one of the officers who was out (he refused to say missing, even to himself), he knew the codes. He'd dispatched people for plenty of them.

Four-fifty East Main. That's only two blocks from here. His hand shook as he reached for the radio. He was about to respond to a potential violent crime for the first time in his career. He had to clear his voice twice before he thumbed the mike.

"Car zero-seven. I'm on it."

Although he'd never seen an actual robbery in progress, it only took Officer Marks two heartbeats to know this wasn't one. Four-fifty East Main had turned out to be the Pastry House, one of Rocky Point's two bakeries. Marks arrived to find the front window was smashed in, a human arm draped over the ragged edges of the glass. As he was about to call for backup, terrified cries came from inside the building - shrieks, really, sounds human throats should never make. Pulling his gun, Marks stepped over the bloody limb and moved through the bakery, the slippery floors tempering his desire to rush forward at full speed. Whoever had broken in had left a trail of destruction behind, with smashed cakes and pastries littering the floor. Marks did his best to avoid stepping on any of the perps' footprints but it was an almost impossible task. He quickly found himself trying to hop from one clear spot on the floor to the next.

Behind the glass counter a doorway led into the kitchen. The horrible cries ended while he was still only halfway across the room and he feared he was too late to save whoever had been in the source.

Was it Mrs. DeAngelo, the hefty woman who'd owned the bakery for so many years? Or her equally-stout daughter, Maria? He hoped neither. Of course, he didn't want it to be one of the kitchen or counter help either but he knew the DeAngelos personally, would hate to see anything happen to them.

Marks stopped at the doorway. Technically, he should wait for backup to arrive. Or at least call in and report on the situation. But using his radio would alert whoever was back there. And if he waited, someone might die.

Screw it.

Crouching down, he edged around the door frame, gun out and aimed forward. "Police! Stand still and put your hands..."

The rest of his words trailed away as Marks took in the scene before him. Three men, one of them wearing what looked like a police uniform, had Carmen DeAngelo pinned to a long metal table. At first glance it looked like they were licking strawberry sauce off her ample stomach.

Then he realized it wasn't sauce and they weren't licking.

Jesus! They're...eating her!

Even as he thought it, his brain took in other details, things that made no sense but he couldn't ignore.

One of the men was missing an arm.

Maria DeAngelo's head was on top of the stove but her body was on the floor, a gaping hole where her stomach should be.

The man with the police uniform was Manny Salvo.

Marks was about to call out to Manny, ask him what the hell was going on, when something hit him hard from behind. His gun flew from his hand and he found himself face down on the cold ground, his nose and lips split and bleeding, before he had a chance to understand what had happened.

Rough hands grabbed his arms and legs, turned him over. Through tears of pain, he saw a face above him. An impossible face, with horrible red eyes that seemed to burn into his very soul.

The creature bent closer and an icy blanket of winter cold descended on Marks. Like a balloon deflating, the thing collapsed into a long, coiled shape and pushed itself into his throat. Bud Marks had time to wish he'd never offered to ride patrol.

Then everything that made Bud Marks human was consumed.

* * *

Cory arrived at Todd's house the next morning with a box of donuts and three extra-large coffees.

"Nothing like sugar and caffeine to prime the engines for a long session of research," he said, placing the food on the table.

"Or to keep you awake after a long night of it," John replied, grabbing a chocolate glazed and a coffee.

"What?" Cory glanced at Todd. "You guys found something last night? Why didn't you call?"

Todd gave him a tired grin as he spooned sugar into his coffee. "Well, considering we didn't really hit pay-dirt until well after midnight, we figured you'd either be asleep or, um, otherwise occupied."

"Asleep, thank you very much," Cory said around a mouthful of jelly donut. "So, what'd you find?"

"I printed everything out." Todd pointed at a pile of papers on the kitchen table. "But I can give you the highlights."

Intrigued, Cory took a seat next to John, who was already well into his second donut. After grabbing milk from the refrigerator, Todd joined them.

"It seems that Rocky Point and the area in and around the Lowlands in particular, has a very nasty past. How old do you think Wood Hill Sanitarium is?"

"I know there are buildings on the property that are pretty old, the ones that aren't used anymore. They go back to what, the forties?"

"Keep going." A blob of jelly fell out of John's donut and he scooped it up with his finger. "The original Wood Hill was built in nineteen nineteen."

"Wow. I never knew."

"Me either," Todd said. "They called it a sanitarium but back then it was more like a concentration camp. A place where the feeble, the retarded and the insane were locked away in squalid conditions forever, by relatives who wanted nothing to do with them. Those poor people often ended up being used for medical experiments."

"That's terrible," Cory said, well aware that at least part of Todd's empathy was a result of his own experiences. "But what does it have to do with this Dr. Lillian fellow?"

"They say there are no coincidences in the world, only related incidents that don't, at first, seem related."

"Todd, get to the point." John reached for a third donut, paused, and then muttered "what the hell" and took it.

"Okay. I'm just still a bit amazed by what we learned. Anyway, Dr. Grover Lillian was supposedly a brilliant scientist. A medical doctor and also a researcher who was trying to find a cure for polio.'"

"Don't tell me he experimented on his patients."

Todd shrugged. "Lillian was as immoral as he was brilliant. He injected patients, including children, with his own untested serums to see if they were lethal or not."

"Oh, shit." Cory didn't like where the story was going. "What happened?"

"Many of them died. Too many to be covered up apparently. The police caught on to him and the FBI was brought in. Except instead of surrendering, Lillian killed his assistant and then himself."

"And that's not the half of it," John said, taking up the story. "Turns out Lillian wasn't just covering up the deaths. He was also secretly disposing of the bodies. Want to guess where?"

Cory was about to say he had no idea and then the articles he'd read about Wood Hill's recent troubles came back to him. "Don't tell me he buried them under the hospital?"

"Winner, winner, chicken dinner," John said in his usual somber tone.

"Under one of the old buildings," added Todd. "Listen to this." He picked up one of the print outs and read from it.

Officer Shaun O'Haney, one of the first men on the scene, described it as something no sane person should have to experience. "Them bodies was piled on each other like fire wood. Even before we got to them, we could smell them in the tunnels. Like rotten meat in the summer. But as bad as they stunk, seeing them was worse. I'll never forget what that maniac did, not for as long as I live."

"Jesus." Cory shook his head. "How many?"

"According to the newspaper accounts, forty-seven. But there may have been more. None of them had families - at least, none that came forward to claim them. They ended up buried in a Potter's Field at the ass end of Gates of Heaven."

"That section with the tiny iron markers that only have numbers, not names? We always wondered what those were."

"And our parents always said they didn't know. Except they had to have. A scandal that big in a small town like this?" John shook his head.

"That's amazing. I'll call Marisol right now. Maybe she can find something in the police files."

"We're not done yet."

"What?" Cory looked from Todd to John and back again.

"Remember I said the town has a nasty past? It begins way before Grover Lillian."

Cory leaned back and sipped his coffee. "I'm all ears."

"Well, it seems the plot of land where Wood Hill sits used to be a leper colony back in the mid-eighteen hundreds. A leper colony that was burned to the ground by the townspeople."

When Todd didn't continue, John spoke up. "What Todd doesn't want to tell you is that dozens of people died in that fire. And the man who initiated the burning was none other than Todd's great-grandfather."

"What?" Cory knew he was repeating himself but his two friends kept springing surprise after surprise on him.

"It's true." Todd's face sagged, giving him the appearance of a man ten years older. "Apparently my family has a history as sordid as the rest of the town. My great-grandfather, Hollister Randolph, the first official reverend in town, together with Percival Boyd--"

"My great-grandfather," John interjected. "Todd's not the only family with issues."

"--the mayor at the time," Todd continued, "led the destruction of the leper colony because the physician in attendance refused to move the it outside town limits. They believed the disease would spread throughout Rocky Point."

"Jesus Christ. Neither of you knew?"

"No." Todd shook his head. "Just like I didn't know that Hollister Randolph's father, Nathaniel, was also crazy. A self-anointed preacher, he burned down a whorehouse in seventeen-seventy-nine. Killed himself in the process."

"Want to guess where the brothel was?" John asked.

"Wood Hill?"

"Close enough. Near as we can tell, it was dead smack in the middle of where the cemetery is now."

"Wow." Cory rubbed his eyes. He'd had a good night's sleep;

Marisol had wanted to be fully rested for her first day back to work. But now he felt like he'd been up all night, as if his brain had exhausted its store of energy trying to take in too much new information in such a short period.

He could only imagine how tired John and Todd must be.

"So, we have a ton more information than we had before. But how does it tie in with what's going on now and what happened when we were kids? Are there other episodes of killings or monster sightings? I didn't find anything in the town records but I wasn't looking back as far as you guys."

Todd shook his head. "That's the weird thing. We couldn't find anything about mass murders or strange occurrences. But I can't shake the feeling it's all connected somehow, with the land between the cemetery and Wood Hill doing the connecting."

"I think you're right." Cory tapped the papers. "Why don't I read through these and you guys see if you can dig up anything else?"

John groaned and rolled his eyes. "More computer work. Great."

Todd laughed. "Think of it as a work training program. When this is all over, you'll have new job skills."

"Ugh. When this is all over, I think I might go back to living on the streets. It's less stressful."

Chapter 8

When Cory picked Marisol up after her shift it was hard to tell which of them was more exhausted. Nine hours of reading printouts and performing fruitless internet searches had left Cory with a massive headache and dark circles under his eyes. Marisol wasn't looking much better. As soon as she got into his car, her strained expression told him she was in pain.

"C'mon, let's get you home," he said, after a quick kiss hello. "Shower, food and bed."

"Sounds good but there's nothing in the house to make. We need to go shopping."

"Shopping can wait. While you're in the shower, I'll grab a pizza. After that it's straight to dreamland, do not pass go, do not collect two hundred dollars and do not think about jumping my bones."

That drew a small smile from her. "Long day for you too?"

"Long and boring." He'd called her at lunch and told her what Todd and John had found out the previous night. "We didn't learn anything else today, which is pretty frustrating."

"I've been thinking about that." Marisol chewed her bottom lip, something she always did when concentrating. "Maybe you're looking in the wrong direction. Maybe it's not their connection to the town that's important but their connection to us."

Cory knew by 'their' she meant Grover Lillian and Effram Charles. "What do you mean?"

"Well, Todd's ancestors were involved in two events: the burning of the brothel and the burning of the leper colony. What about the rest of us? We all have family that's been in this area as long as Todd's."

"Hmm. That's an interesting thought. I'll hit town hall again tomorrow and look up our families in the records."

"Why not call Todd tonight?"

Cory shook his head. "No way. Those two looked worse than us when I left. I doubt they've had more than a couple hours sleep the last two days. I think tonight needs to be a recuperation night for all of us."

"Sounds good to me."

Glancing over at her, Cory found himself smiling.

Snuggle and sleep sounding better than sex? Either I'm more tired than I thought or there really is something more between us than just a physical attraction.

* * *

If Chief Travers had been asked to predict where the next violent attack would occur, Restaurant Row would have been last on his list, despite its general proximity to the factory district and Lowlands. The two-block area on the west side of Main Street was one of the poshest parts of town, comprised mostly of high-end eateries and gourmet food shops. Not the kind of place where you'd expect a gruesome murder.

Yet here he was, standing in front of Martel's Steak and Seafood, thinking the place resembled the aftermath of a mob hit.

"Good thing it happened after closing, huh?"

Travers turned and saw Kyle Overton, one of the junior patrol officers, approaching. Waving his hand at the overturned tables, broken bottles and glasses, and scattered body parts, Travers asked, "A good thing? What in hell is good about this, Overton?"

Overton's face turned red and his eyes went wide. "I, um, I just meant that it could have been a lot worse if the restaurant was open and crowded. Sir."

He's right. Three dead is a helluva lot better than twenty or thirty. But he also needs to learn when to keep his mouth shut.

"Tell you what rookie. Go help the crime scene boys bag the pieces. Then talk to me about how lucky we were."

Overton had enough sense to look embarrassed - and afraid - as he walked away. Watching him, Travers gave a silent curse. He'd probably been too hard on the kid but it would make him a better officer in the long run.

Then his thoughts turned to the mess inside. They *had* gotten lucky. Not only had there been just a skeleton crew cleaning in the kitchen but one of them had escaped and called 911. The officers who'd responded managed to kill two of the perps. No one was saying anything out loud about the condition of the two assailants but from the brief look Travers had of the bodies, he'd seen they were just like the ones in the morgue.

Monsters, his mind supplied. *Zombies.*

Bullshit. There's no such thing. They're just wacked out on some new drug, something we haven't been trained to look for. But that's gonna change tonight.

Pulling out his cell phone, he scrolled through his contacts for the Medical Examiner.

"Corish? It's Travers. Get your troops together ASAP. We've got bodies coming in and I want tests run for every known and unknown drug possible. Legal and illegal. Something's turning people into walking death machines and I want to know what it is."

* * *

Marisol was enjoying a wonderful dream. It was the last day of school. As soon as classes were over, she and Cory were going to the beach for a month with Cory's family, a whole month with her boyfriend - and just as important, a month away from her own family.

The strident ring of the school bell signaled the start of summer vacation. Grabbing her book bag, she ran outside. Except the bell wouldn't stop ringing. If anything, it grew louder.

What's wrong with it? And where's Cory?

"Marisol?"

Someone grabbed her shoulder. She turned her head, expecting to see Cory standing there.

Instead, it was a skeleton dressed in a gray robe.

"No! I don't want to die!" She tried to pull away but the bony hand shook her harder.

"Marisol!"

She sat up and the Reaper disappeared, replaced by the dark outlines of her bedroom.

A dream. Oh, sweet Jesus, it was only a dream.

The ringing continued.

"Marisol. The phone."

Cory gave her arm one more shake. Her heart still beating in double-time, she reached out and picked up the phone.

"Hello?"

Five minutes later she was heading for the door.

Marisol stared at the corpses and wondered if she was still dreaming, a nightmare about the end of the world, like in one of those movies where the dead rise up and take over everything.

Not for the first time since reuniting with her old friends, she wished she could just pack her things and leave Rocky Point far, far behind. Common sense told her to say the hell with her town but her conscience wouldn't hear of it. Forget her burgeoning relationship with Cory; there was no way she could abandon Todd. Not again.

We did that once already and ruined his life.

No, the four of them were stuck with the mess they'd made, doomed to see it out to the end, whatever that might be.

*Please God, just don't let it be at the hands of one of these...*things, *with its teeth tearing my stomach open.*

She hadn't had any nightmares about her attack - yet. Maybe because three days had passed and she hadn't turned into a walking corpse. But she knew it was just a matter of time before the zombie-things appeared in her dreams. She'd always been that way. The problems of her waking hours became the stuff of her nightmares.

"Marisol, which one do you want?"

"What?" Startled from her musings, Marisol glanced to the side, where Ned Felson, who usually worked opposite shifts from her, was standing between the two bodies, a tray of tubes and syringes in each hand.

"Left or right?" he asked, unfazed by the gruesome condition of the corpses. Their skin was gray and mottled, their eyes a vile yellow, worse than jaundice could explain. Although they looked like week-old corpses, the fresh blood around the bullet holes in their bodies was clear evidence they'd been alive when shot.

"I'll take left," she said, accepting one of the collection kits. She'd only worked with Felson on a couple of occasions but he seemed like one of those people who are always cheerful, even when handling a stinking, rotting body. She wasn't sure if that was a good or bad thing, given that her current mood was one of barely-controlled terror. She decided that maybe focusing on work would be a good way to blot out both her anxiety and Felson's already irritating whistling.

Although their job was simply to collect samples, Marisol couldn't help doing her own unofficial examination she gathered specimens of blood, body cavity fluids, cerebral-spinal fluid and saliva. Corish himself would be in later to perform the autopsies and collect further tissue from the brain and other organs.

The brain might be a tough one, she thought. Both men had been shot in the head, resulting in tremendous damage to the skull and its contents.

You have to shoot a zombie in the head to kill it.

Forcing the thought away, she scraped under the fingernails, gathering potential evidence into small brown envelopes. At the same time she took a closer look at the man's skin. While his paleness could be explained by loss of blood, there was no hiding the dark mottling covering his body, the same mottling that usually occurred when decomposition began to set in. Also, the skin had no yellowish tone to it at all, in direct contrast to the eyes.

Definitely not a liver issue.

The smell was all wrong too. There was the usual stink of fresh death - shit and blood and piss from the damage to the stomach and intestines, and the associated relaxing of the bladder and sphincter muscles. But based on the visual clues, the body should have reeked of decomposition. Yet the only other odors Marisol picked up were a mélange of body odor and dirt, as if the man had been living in the woods for weeks.

Or underground. Like in a cave or tunnel.

"You ready Freddy?" Ned asked, his overly-cheerful voice actually a welcome break from the pop tunes he'd been whistling.

"One second." She ran a final swab under the eyelids. She thought about sticking the eye as well, to collect some of the aqueous and vitreous humors, but that was traditionally the ME's job, performed when he did the cranial autopsy. She made a note on her sheet of the samples that still needed collecting and then handed the kit box to Felson.

"There you go. While you process them, I'll get the equipment up and running."

He frowned. "I thought we'd process together and then run them together."

The thought of spending more time than absolutely necessary with Mr. Sunshine made Marisol want to cringe. "Ed said he wanted everything ASAP. It'll be faster if I warm up the machines and then load small batches as you set them up, rather than waiting to do a big batch all at once."

"Oh. Yeah, that makes sense. Catch you in a little while then." Completely unaffected by her gruff tones or the late hour, Felson started gathering the chemicals he'd need to prep the samples for Marisol's chemistry and DNA analyzers.

Lord, save me from the perpetually cheerful.

Glad to be out of the autopsy room, Marisol headed for the analysis lab.

It was only when she realized she'd be alone in the room for the first time since her attack that she regretted - just a little - her decision not to stay with Felson.

By four a.m. the initial blood and tox screens were done and the results emailed to the ME. With the DNA tests not due for hours, Marisol dragged her aching body to the break room for another in a seemingly endless line of cups of coffee. While sipping the bitter brew, she sent a quick text message to Cory's phone, highlighting the results of her tests. As she'd expected, neither body showed any signs of drugs or poisons. In fact, there'd been no foreign substances of any kind in any of the fluid or tissue samples. The only anomalies had been drastically elevated BUN and creatinine levels, along with low blood glucose, evidence of an extremely high protein diet.

And I have a feeling I know what they've been eating, she thought, rubbing her hand across her stitches. She wondered what Chief Travers would say when the stomach contents came back positive for human flesh. Then maybe he'd listen to them.

Probably not. He'll find a way to rationalize it. A new drug we can't detect. Satanists. Anything but the truth.

Even with the caffeine in her system, she found her eyes starting to close. *Maybe a quick nap will be good. Refresh my brain.*

As she drifted off, Marisol's last thought was an image of Cory standing in front of a court room, his finger pointed at Chief Travers while quoting that famous line from *A Few Good Men*:

"You can't handle the truth!"

* * *

Marisol arrived at Todd's house just after 5 p.m. The others were already there. Cory gave her a quick hug and kiss before they all sat down at Todd's kitchen table. Her stomach growled as she got a whiff of the turkey breast Todd had roasting in the oven.

"Like I told Cory earlier, the tox screens showed nothing unusual. No foreign substances of any kinds. Edwin is still working on the brain and eye samples but I doubt they'll show anything."

Cory summed things up. "So, what we're dealing with, at least for now, are cannibals who seem to be alive and dead at the same time."

Marisol nodded. "They bleed. Their organs function. They can see and think and breathe. They digest food. But their skin and muscles show signs of decay, as do some of their internal organs. It's like they're going through decomposition before they die."

"Is that why you can shoot them but not kill them?" Todd asked.

"I don't think so. Remember, some of them have been killed."

"Head shots," John said. "Like in the zombie movies."

"Yes. I haven't seen all the autopsy results or police reports but I have a theory. I think they just don't feel pain. Shooting them in the stomach or lungs probably does kill them. But not right away. Unlike a normal human, they can ignore a horrible wound and keep going until they bleed out. My guess is a bullet through the heart would kill them just as well as a head shot."

Just then the timer on the stove dinged, indicating ten minutes before the turkey was done.

"That's because they've been taken over," John said, placing a bag of frozen vegetables in the microwave. After starting the timer, he set a basket of rolls on the table, along with a tub of imitation butter.

"That much we can agree on," Todd said. "Now we just have to figure out by what." He looked at Marisol. "Is there any way you can get copies of the evidence files, including the police reports?"

"Christ, I don't know." She rubbed her hand along her neck. Just being caught looking through the files would be enough to get her fired. But printing them out for private use?

Then she remembered what Todd had sacrificed for them. Without him, she wouldn't even have a job. Or a life.

"Maybe there's a way. We'd have to go back tonight, real late. Find an empty lab. I know some of the ME's pass codes. We all do, in case we have to get information for him when he's out in the field."

"I'll go with you," Cory said.

"No." Todd shook his head. "I'll go."

Cory tried to object but Todd kept talking.

"If we get caught we could get arrested. I've got nothing to lose by spending a night or two in jail. But we'll need you to stay free so you can get us out."

Marisol looked at Cory. "I hate to say it but it does make more sense."

Cory looked like he might continue his argument but then he sighed and sat back in his chair. "Fine. You guys go ahead."

A series of beeps sounded. signaling the vegetables were ready.

"And with that," John said, "we eat."

Chapter 9

At three in the morning, the morgue and adjoining lab were as quiet as ever. With the rush work completed, both buildings were back to skeleton crews. Marisol's knowledge of the layout allowed her and Todd to make their way unnoticed to an unoccupied lab room. In order to keep their presence a secret, they left the lights off, with Marisol using the light from the computer screen to see the keyboard.

"Keep an eye out," she told Todd. "If you see anyone coming let me know and I'll turn the monitor off."

"Got it," he said, stationing himself in the doorway.

Marisol brought up the reports folders and entered the ME's personal password. She knew he had other passwords, allowing him access to even more sensitive information, but she was hoping that she'd be able to find what they needed in the folders the morgue and police department frequently shared.

It only took a few moments for her to locate the ones relating to the recent murders. "Bingo," she said, plugging a memory stick into one of the USB ports. "This is it. Autopsies, names, times. I think we have...oh, holy shit."

"What?" Todd made his way across the dark room to her side.

"Look at this. There've been more than three dozen reports of missing persons or break-ins in the last week. And that's on top of the ones released to the press."

"Jesus. We're living in a war zone and no one even knows it."

"I'm going to copy all these too." Marisol tapped some keys. "Maybe we can find a pattern and use it to locate the main hive or nest or whatever."

"All right. But hurry. This whole breaking and entering thing is making me nervous." Todd turned to go back to the door and then froze as the lights came on.

"You should be more than nervous."

Marisol gasped at the sound of her ex-husband's voice. Looking up, she saw Smith standing in the doorway, Chief Travers and Edwin Corish behind him.

"I had a feeling I'd catch you sooner or later," Smith said, walking to where Marisol sat. "You and your friends have gone too far this time."

"We're not doing anything wrong Ed," she said, ignoring Smith and looking at the Medical Examiner. "We just wanted to examine the files and see if we could find a pattern or a clue the police missed."

Travers scowled. "You're using someone else's pass codes to access restricted information. That doesn't seem on the up and up to me."

"Why else would we need it?" asked Todd. "We have no intention of going to the press. This was just for our own investigation. The more information we have, the more we can help. We're on your side."

"On our side?" Jack Smith let out a sarcastic chuckle. "I don't think our fine police force needs criminals on their side."

"It isn't like that," Marisol insisted, still speaking to her boss and the Police Chief.

Before either of them could speak, the Deputy Mayor continued. "Let me tell you how I see it. Mister Randolph here managed to rope you and your so-called friends into his delusions, delusions either brought on or compounded by the psychotropic drugs and brain zapping he received in the mental hospital. Now he's got you all believing his crazy tales, to the point where you're attempting to falsify evidence just to support his theories."

"No!" Marisol stood up. "All we were doing was--"

"Chief, were these two caught trespassing and stealing?"

"Absolutely." Travers nodded his head, a stern expression on his face. "Should I take them in now?"

Looking right at Marisol and smiling, Smith said, "No. We got here before they could do any harm. I'm willing to be lenient. If Doctor Corish suspends her without pay until this whole case is settled, no arrests will be necessary. And, of course, this building and all other public and government buildings are off-limits for these two, along with Cory Miles and John Boyd."

"You can't do that!" Marisol stomped her foot, hating herself for resorting to a childish gesture but unable to stop it.

"Actually, I can. Or would you prefer jail time?"

Marisol looked at Corish, who shook his head. "I'm sorry, Marisol. My hands are tied."

She could see in his eyes that he meant it, that he knew she was innocent but couldn't help her.

"All right." She motioned to Todd. "Let's go."

Travers and Corish stepped aside so they could pass. They were halfway down the hall to the exit when Smith called out to them.

"Marisol, give your friends a message. Next time any of you screw up, you're all going to jail."

* * *

Jack Smith watched the bitch and the nutcase trudging down the hall and had to bite his lip to keep from laughing. In his wildest dreams he couldn't have imagined things working out so perfectly. After the attack in the morgue, he'd authorized putting alarms on all the civil servants' swipe cards, ostensibly for protection and - God forbid - body identification purposes, if need be. Of course, his real reason had been to keep tabs on Marisol's comings and goings. He'd assumed he'd catch her and her new boyfriend up to shenanigans in the lab. Something mildly embarrassing, like getting caught with her pants down, but still enough to ruin her reputation.

But this? It was as if God had decided to hand him an early Christmas gift. Caught red-handed breaking into police files? Once it became public, she'd be lucky to get a job flipping burgers. And Mister High-and-Mighty Lawyer might find himself chasing ambulances, if he didn't end up disbarred.

As for the other two, the drunk and nutcase, well, neither one of them mattered in the least. They could go back to their ridiculous fantasies. Who was going to listen to them?

And maybe when I'm mayor I'll pass a referendum to send all the homeless scum packing. Clean up this town, finally.

This time his smile managed to creep through and he quickly covered his mouth and pretended to cough.

All in all, a damn fine night.

* * *

Marisol could feel Jack's gaze on her neck as she walked down the hall, purposely keeping her pace fast to get them out of the building quickly but not so fast as to seem suspicious.

"I can't believe you just gave in like that." It was the second time Todd had said it and for the second time Marisol answered, "Just keep walking. Don't stop. Don't look back."

She could imagine what was going through Jack's mind. How he'd gotten the best of his ex-wife, disgraced her, showed the town her true colors. That was good. Let him keep thinking that way, at least until they were out of the building and on the way back to Todd's.

Fingering the memory stick she'd slipped into her pocket, she added *Then we'll see who's gotten the best of who.*

"Marisol?"

She stopped as Freddy Alou rounded the corner.

"Freddy? What the hell are you doing here?"

"I actually came to see you. I thought you were still working nights." He frowned. "Chica, what's the matter?"

"Nothing. Well, something, but it's too late to worry about it now. I won't be around for a few days though. Maybe longer, if our Deputy Mayor has his way."

"Oh no. What's that *idiota* done now?"

She shook her head. "Nothing you should get involved in."

Todd cleared his throat. "You said you were coming here to see Marisol?"

"Huh? Oh, yes. We need to talk *chica. Muy importante.*"

"Now is not the best time," she said, risking a glance back down the hall. Jack and others were still looking their way. "I - we - need to go. But I'll call you tomorrow. I promise."

Without waiting for an answer, she grabbed Todd's arm and pulled him towards the door. Only when they were back in her car and heading down the road did she relax.

"Can you please tell me what's going on?"

"This." She handed him the memory stick. "I managed to palm it while Jack was pontificating. I don't know how much got copied onto it but it's more than we had before."

Todd smiled and shook his head.

"I hope it was worth losing your job over."

Chapter 10

Before going to bed, Abigail Clinton had laid out her clothes for the next day. In the entryway, her purse and keys sat in their regular places, the only deviation from the norm being the bag of prescriptions for Mrs. Randolph that stood next to her purse. She'd noticed when leaving the Randolph's that Todd had forgotten to refill them, even though he'd promised to do it. Of course, she'd half-expected him to forget. After what they'd done to his brain in the asylum, it was a wonder he could walk and talk, let along think. So she always made sure to check the medicines and food each day.

Abigail believed in being neat and orderly. Before she left her house each morning, Abigail took ten minutes to go through each room of her small, two-bedroom home on the outskirts of the Lowlands, checking that everything was in its place and all dirty dishes, clothes and food containers were cleaned and put away. Unlike most of her neighbors, Abigail was proud of her modest home. She still remembered the house she'd grown up in back in Trinidad, a three-room shack filled with screaming children, dirty clothes and the crumbs from a thousand meals taken in a kitchen so small the children ate in shifts while Mother cooked a seemingly endless supply of fried chicken or goat, supplemented by rice or potatoes or plantains.

So when Abigail arrived in New York with one suitcase and forty dollars to her name, she'd vowed that no matter where she lived, she would create the type of home she'd only seen in magazines.

Which was why she knew something was amiss the moment the sound of glass breaking in the kitchen woke her from a sound sleep. With nothing on her counters for her cats to break, there could only be one explanation for the noise.

Someone was in the house!

Twenty-three years in the United States hadn't eroded instincts for self-preservation honed by growing up in a city - and country - filled with social unrest. Abigail had learned at an early age how to defend herself; living in the Lowlands the past seven years had only reinforced those lessons. Rising quietly from her bed, she reached out and felt for the short aluminum bat she kept behind the nightstand. There was no need to turn on a light, another benefit of always having everything in its place.

A nervous tingle ran through Abigail's body as she moved towards the bedroom door, her feet sliding silently across the carpet. The last time she'd had to resort to physical violence was when she was eighteen and two boys had grabbed her behind the school. When the police arrived, they'd found Abigail sitting on the steps, two fingers broken and a tooth missing. Her attackers had been lying on the ground, one screaming and holding his hands over his damaged eyes, the other clutching the bloody mess between his legs.

Something else shattered in the kitchen and Abigail felt her anger rise. How dare someone break into her home and destroy her things? Stepping into the short hallway, she hit the light switch and hefted the bat, calling out a warning at the same time.

"Whoever you are, you get yourselves out of my house!"

Two figures, a man and a woman, emerged from the kitchen. The moment she saw them, Abigail's rage metamorphosed into heart-pounding dread. Pale faces covered in gray, dead-looking spots. Wet blood covering their shirts. The vacant look of their eyes. It all shouted one thing to Abigail: Zombies!

Abigail didn't hesitate. She dropped the bat and ran for the basement door at the other end of the hall. She took the steps two at a time, dashed across the small space, and then hurried up the three stairs to the steel hurricane door that exited into her backyard. The bang of metal on metal sounded like an explosion as Abigail slammed the door open and emerged into the darkness of the summer night.

Right into the arms of four more strangers.

They attacked before she knew what was happening, forcing her to the ground and easily tearing away her cheap nightdress. Abigail screamed as she thrashed on the dew-wet grass of her neatly-trimmed lawn. In the midst of her struggles, ice-cold fingers grabbed her face and she opened her eyes to see a demon from Hell hovering over her body. Abigail cried out again, providing a perfect entry for the twisting, roiling gray mass that poured into her mouth. Abigail found herself choking and gagging as the spectral intruder violated her from the inside, forcing its frigid way down her throat and into her very essence.

They're turning me into one of them! she had time to think and then everything disappeared as her mind and soul exploded into icy fragments. When Abigail sat up a moment later, many more thoughts filled her head.

But none were her own.

* * *

After a few hours of sleep, the four members of the Cemetery Club had gathered again at Todd's house.

"You two look as exhausted as I feel," Cory said, taking in his friends' sallow complexions, shadowed eyes and slow movements.

"Between the hours of research and the constant fire and police sirens, who the hell can sleep in this town?" John groused, pouring himself a cup of coffee.

"Things are getting bad. We need to do something," Todd said, putting a plate of bagels on the table. Cream cheese and butter followed.

"But what?" Cory sat down with a sigh. "We know more about the history of the town. We know more about the zombie-things, how to kill them at least. But we don't know where the Grays come from or how to stop them."

"Todd does," John said. He pointed his bagel at Todd. "He did it once and they didn't come back for twenty years. I say all four of us go down there. If we can't kill 'em, maybe we can put enough of a hurting on them to knock 'em out for eighty years this time. Who the hell cares what happens after that? We'll all be long dead."

"Going into the tunnels and facing those things again?" Marisol shuddered. "I don't know if I can."

"You think I want to?" John asked. "I'm scared shitless. But better to do it our own terms, armed to the teeth, than get a surprise visit in the middle of the night. Besides, before long the whole town will be either dead or possessed. Then we won't stand a chance. We have to do it now."

Todd nodded. "I'm with John."

Cory took a deep breath. "Okay, so we do this. How and when?"

"Tonight," Marisol said. "We can't wait any longer."

"We'll need Holy water, Bibles and Eucharistic wafers," Todd said. "That's what I used the last time."

"And flashlights," John added. "I'm not going down there without a lot of light."

Todd glanced at Cory. "If you can get the flashlights and anything else that might help us in the tunnels, we'll take care of the religious supplies."

"We're on it," Cory said. "Flashlights, batteries and squirt guns."

"Squirt guns?" John asked.

"Yeah. We can put the Holy water in them. Better than just tossing it around."

"Speaking of guns, does anyone have a real one?" Marisol asked. "We know bullets stop the zombies."

They all shook their heads.

"Bring whatever other weapons you can scrounge up," Cory told them. "We'll meet at Marisol's in four hours, go over our strategy, eat something and then drive to the cemetery at midnight."

"Sounds like a plan," Todd said.

John poured more coffee. "No, it sounds like suicide. But it's all we've got."

* * *

After Cory and Marisol left, Todd checked on his mother and then left a note for Abigail, who wasn't due for another hour.

Their first stop was St. Anthony's church. While John filled several jars with Holy water, Todd went to the rectory and located Father Ramirez, who'd been a good friend of his parents. He'd expected Ramirez to put up an argument about handing over some of the blessed wafers but Ramirez surprised him.

"Your mother and I had many conversations after your father passed," Ramirez said, handing the package over. "She told me why you'd gone into those tunnels. What you thought was going on. I'm not going to ask you to explain yourself but if you think this is something that can help our town - or at least absolve you from any guilt that these deaths might be your fault - then I stand by your actions. God be with you."

"Thank you, Father."

On the way out, it struck Todd that for someone who'd turned his back on religion more than twenty years earlier, he certainly had no compunctions about utilizing its trappings when the situation called for it. Did that make him a sinner? A closet believer? Or just a pragmatist?

If we live through this, maybe I'll have to consider making some changes in my life.

Then he thought that maybe change was better done sooner than later and he paused at the last pew.

While John waited, Todd whispered a short prayer for their safety.

* * *

The first thing Cory and Marisol noticed as they approached the super-sized CVS on Main Street were the signs announcing a mandatory ten p.m. curfew for anyone who wasn't going to or from work. If that wasn't enough warning, the front page of the newspaper carried a headline about the drastic step.

"Good thing we know how to sneak into the cemetery," Cory said. "If the cops caught us breaking curfew tonight, your ex-hubby would probably throw the book at us."

"He'd throw the whole damn library."

"Do you think he's dangerous?" Cory asked.

"Dangerous? No, I can't see him getting into a fight or coming after us with a gun, if that's what you mean. Something like that would dirty his oh-so-spotless reputation."

Cory tossed a few flashlights and some battery packages in his basket. "Actually, I was thinking more along the lines of him really having us arrested or having me kicked out of town. Maybe even framing us for some of the murders."

Marisol frowned. "A few months ago I wouldn't have thought so. But now? I wouldn't put anything past him. He's a sneaky bastard."

"That's my impression too. One more reason to get this whole mess settled."

* * *

From his table outside Rosie's Café, Jack Smith watched Marisol and Cory enter the CVS. Finishing his coffee, he dropped a five-dollar bill on the table and crossed Main Street, keeping an eye on the pharmacy in case they came out before he got there. He wanted an opportunity to see what they were up to before they noticed him. Odds were they'd just stopped in for something innocuous but there was always the chance he'd see or hear something he could use against them.

Of course, they might be buying condoms or body oils. He hated his brain for providing the image of them fucking in the bed his hard-earned money had bought, their sweaty, naked bodies rolling back and forth. That they were sleeping together he had no doubt. Once a slut always a slut.

After peeking through the doors to make sure they weren't by the registers, Jack went inside and scouted the aisles until he saw them in the row containing children's toys. He hurried down the adjacent aisle until he was parallel to them. Peering carefully through the gaps in the shelves, he saw they had baskets filled with flashlights and batteries and were now looking at squirt guns, of all things.

A gleeful shiver ran through him.

They're up to something. I don't know what it is but I'm sure of it. I think I'll drop in on Chief Travers and mention what I saw.

Jack Smith smiled at the thought of Marisol and Cory sitting in jail.

What a great way to end the day.

* * *

When the alarm on Cory's cell phone signaled five p.m., he was already wide awake. Still, he made no move to get up. Everything he wanted out of life, everything he'd ever dreamed of, was in his hands at that moment, and he was loath to let go.

Marisol shifted slightly beneath his arm, a miniscule movement that nevertheless brought him semi-erect again as the smooth flesh of her ass rubbed against him. Without conscious thought, his hand slid from her hip to her breast, carefully avoiding her stitches, and gently caressed the nipple until it grew hard beneath his fingers.

"Mmmm, now that's how I like to wake up," she whispered, pushing herself back against him.

He gripped her breast more firmly, surprised to find himself ready again after the love-making session they'd finished earlier. What had started as something tender had morphed into animal lust, both of them taking turns on top until Marisol had screamed with the force of her orgasm and Cory duplicated her moments after.

Is it because we'll soon be risking our lives against monsters from some unknown Hell? Is there really truth to the old saying that danger makes you extra horny?

He had no idea, but if this was his last time with Marisol, he intended to make every moment count.

Thirty minutes later, satiated and showered, Cory joined Marisol in the kitchen. She'd already placed out flashlights, Swiss Army knives and rifle-sized squirt guns on the counter, along with the knapsacks they'd bought. Despite the lingering heat outside, they both wore jeans, hiking books and long-sleeved t-shirts.

"I guess this is it," he said, placing his hand over hers. "John and Todd will be here soon."

She looked up at him. "Cory, there's something I want to say--"

"Me first," he interrupted. "You probably know it already but I love you. I always have. When this is all over, I want us to go away somewhere. Someplace where we can drink cold beer and walk around naked on the beach all day and night."

Marisol wrapped her arms around him. "I'd like that too. I...I feel..."

"You don't need to say it." He'd heard something in her voice, a mix of relief and joy and sadness and fear all rolled into a muffled sob. "I know what you've been through. Me saying I love you is probably the last thing you want to hear."

He gave her a long, strong hug and then stepped away. "I wanted you to know how I felt, so that we both had a little...extra incentive to come back alive."

"What if we don't? I don't want to die without telling you I love you, but I don't want to say it right now just because...you know."

"We will not die tonight." He wiped a tear from her cheek. "I promise."

"Don't. You might jinx us."

"Too late. I already said it. And I always keep my promises."

With that, he opened the refrigerator and took out the chicken breasts he'd had marinating. "Now, time to cook. Lots of protein tonight. We have monsters to kill." He gave her a smile that he hoped didn't look too fake.

As he placed the chicken in a baking pan, he prayed she was wrong about jinxes.

*   *   *

They arrived at the crypt just before twelve-thirty. The short walk from the old church to Gates of Heaven Cemetery was uneventful, but John still breathed a sigh of relief when they reached their destination without encountering any zombies or Grays. He'd been certain there'd be some waiting for them but the cemetery was silent and empty. Only the scattered howls of police sirens in town let them know the creatures hadn't taken the night off.

"Well, one good thing," Cory said, as they stood in front of the heavy door. "At least some of the monsters will be occupied elsewhere. That helps our odds for survival a bit."

"Unless they come back and block our escape," John said, his face paler than ever in the reflected glow of their flashlights.

"Always the voice of optimism." Marisol gave him a light punch on the arm to let him know she was kidding.

"If we're going to do this, let's get a move on." The beam from Todd's flashlight jiggled back and forth, evidence of his shaking hands. He leaned forward and pushed the door open.

Metal scraped on metal with a squeal that vibrated the fillings in John's teeth. In the center of the floor the pit looked just as menacing as it had twenty years ago, the cement around it cracked and crumbling. A fetid stench rolled past them, a stink John remembered all too well even though he hadn't smelled it in two decades.

Maybe my nose hasn't smelled it, he thought as he covered his face with his hand, *but I've relived it too many times in my nightmares to ever forget it.*

Next to him, Todd gasped and backed away. Marisol coughed and muttered "Oh, Jesus, that is fucking awful."

The foul odor seemed to grow worse, a horrible invisible monster climbing out of the pit to smother them in coils of evil. John placed his hand against the cold metal of the door frame to steady himself, the combination of smell and touch suddenly too much for him. Something opened in his brain, unleashing a flood of memories from that fateful night twenty years before.

And transported him back to the place where all his nightmares lived.

Section IV

The Circle Closes

Chapter 1

In the tunnels, twenty years ago

In the aftermath of the tunnel's collapse, John heard nothing except his own cries for help, cries that turned into choking gasps as dirt fell into his mouth, bringing with it the rotten meat taste of the tunnel. He flailed around with his arms, desperate to free himself, praying he was digging up and out rather than down.

Then his head and shoulders broke free and he realized they'd had no more than a few wheelbarrows worth of dirt dumped on them. When he stopped his shouting to spit out grave-flavored dirt, he finally heard Cory and Marisol yelling for help.

"It's okay," he called to them. In the total blackness, distance and direction seemed all mixed up. Dropping to his knees, he started digging, doing his best to find where the sounds were coming from. A few seconds later, his hands touched moving flesh and he jumped back.

It's a monster! the primitive part of his brain shouted at him even as he realized it was just one of his friends, not some bloated, maggot-filled undead thing waiting to devour him. Still, the image wouldn't leave his thoughts and it took all his willpower to lean forward again and resume digging.

It only took a few more scoops to uncover a gasping, crying Marisol. Together they freed Cory from the shallow pile of grave dirt covering him.

"I can't do this. I can't go any further," Marisol said.

John heard the tears in her voice, knew he was one more scare from breaking down himself. The only thing that kept him from suggesting they turn around and go back was the knowledge that they'd all think of him as a coward. The pussy who wouldn't save his friend.

But if Cory suggests it... That hope died before he even finished the thought.

"We can't go back," Cory said, his voice raspy from the foul air and dirt he'd swallowed. "Todd needs us."

In the darkness, John heard Marisol take a whimpering breath. When she spoke, some of her old spunk had returned.

"Okay. For Todd. But let's hurry, before I crap my pants."

Cory let out a weak laugh. "Down here, who'd smell it anyway? Take my hand. John, take her other hand."

Warm flesh touched his arm, slid down to his palm. He clutched at it.

Unbelievable. He says jump and she asks how high. And yet neither one of them will admit their feelings for each other.

Marisol's grip tugged his and he realized they were moving forward. As they walked, he kept his free hand against the tunnel wall and hunched himself over as much as he could. Even then, dangling roots still grabbed at his hair and tapped against his forehead, each encounter frightening him anew with visions of groping corpse-fingers.

After thirty or so feet, the tunnel opened up enough for them to stand upright. It widened as well, so much so that he was able to stretch his arms out and barely touch the walls.

"I think I see light," Cory said, and at the same time John noticed he could see Marisol's shape in front of him. A few steps later and they could all make out a strong, flickering glow coming from ahead of them.

"It looks like the tunnel turns up there," Marisol said.

"Do you think that's Todd's flashlight?" John asked.

"No." Cory's voice held a note of uncertainty. "It looks more like a candle or maybe a whole bunch of them. C'mon."

Still holding hands, they made their way around the bend and then stopped, stunned by the scene before them.

Like some apocalyptic preacher, Todd stood in the center of a small cavern, holding a large jar of Holy water in one hand while with his other he flicked the blessed liquid at the creatures surrounding him. Each time droplets hit one of the floating monsters, tiny explosions of bright white light resulted, and the creature would back away.

Jesus Christ, they really are aliens! John's mind screamed as he took in their evil, over-sized eyes and tiny limbs. It was the closest they'd been to the creatures since catching sight of one in the cemetery.

Marisol screamed and pointed at something on the other side of the cave. From another tunnel, more shapes were moving towards them, only they weren't Grays.

With a shaking hand, John pulled his father's pistol from his pocket.

The zombies had arrived.

* * *

Present Day

"John? John!"

Cory looked at the others, unsure of what to do. John had taken one step into the crypt and collapsed.

"Do we keep going without him?"

Marisol's question was the same one he'd been asking himself. He hated the thought of leaving John at the mercy of anything that came along. But if one of them remained behind to guard him, the other two would be severely outnumbered in the tunnels.

"I don't think--" Todd began, but just then John let out a low moan and opened his eyes.

"What...what happened?"

"You passed out on us. How do you feel?" Todd asked.

"I'm okay." John held out his hand and Cory took it, helped him up. To his credit, John didn't seem unsteady on his feet.

Marisol stepped forward. "Are you sure you're all right?"

"Yeah. That was weird. I remember stepping inside and then, boom! It was like I went back in time, to when...the first time we went down there."

Cory put his hand on John's shoulder. "Can you handle going down there again?"

John slapped Cory's hand away. "I can handle it. I'm not a pussy."

Taken aback by the vehemence of John's reaction, Cory stepped away. "Relax. I didn't say you were. But we can't have you passing out once we're in the tunnel."

"I'll be fine. You just watch out for yourself and don't worry about me." Before anyone could stop him, John pushed past them and descended into the hole.

Cory looked at Todd and Marisol. "Was it something I said?"

Todd shook his head. "We're all scared but John is terrified. He's putting up a brave front but he's been having nightmares. I've heard him moaning at night, even shouting in his sleep. I think he's been suffering from them long before this all started up again."

"Shit." Cory hitched his pack up on his shoulder. "Well, then I guess we'd better not leave him alone down there. Ready?"

"Ready as I'll ever be." Todd walked past and climbed into the hole.

Marisol started after him, and Cory stopped her.

"What--?"

He cut off her question with a long, hard kiss that ended up more desperate than he'd intended.

"Just in case," he said, as they separated.

"There's no just in case." She looked him in the eye. "You promised."

Then she was gone, following Todd into the darkness.

Chapter 2

On the corner of Elm and Maple, three figures paused in the act of devouring an elderly man they'd attacked as he too out his garbage.

At the Bayside Marina, a massacre was avoided when the group of dead-looking people who had just crashed through the front window of the banquet hall suddenly froze in place, enabling all the guests gathered for Tim Henderson's fiftieth birthday party to escape.

In Griffith Park, a young couple narrowly escaped death when the four men chasing them stopped dead still on the path.

All across and beneath the town of Rocky Point, the Horde halted what it was doing as something registered on its consciousness.

In the tunnels.

Coming.

Too soon. Stop them.

Protect.

Summoned by its own command, the Horde began moving towards the cemetery.

And Wood Hill Sanitarium.

* * *

Cory had expected the tunnel to be smaller than he remembered it - the same way the hallways of your old elementary school always seemed smaller when you went back to visit. After all, it had seemed narrow and claustrophobic at the time and they'd only been teenagers.

Instead, the tunnel was both wider and taller, making him think that the zombie-things had been pretty busy clearing it out.

Either that, or there are a lot more of them than we thought.

They caught up with John right around the same place where the tunnel had widened the last time. He'd stopped and was casting his flashlight around, illuminating the dark earth. Although further away, roots still protruded from the ceiling and walls, grayish fingers and tendrils that Cory half-expected to wriggle free and grab them.

By unspoken agreement, they started forward in the same order as last time, with Todd going first followed by Cory, Marisol and John. When they reached the point where the tunnel turned, Cory whispered for them to turn off their lights so they wouldn't give their presence away. The resulting blackness caused him to shiver and his body jerked slightly when a groping hand found his in the dark. Marisol's. He reached out with his other one and found Todd's waiting for him.

Creeping forward in the lightless void was more of an ordeal than Cory expected. Every sound seemed simultaneously muffled and magnified, with no way of telling the point of origination. Someone whimpered, either Marisol or John, he couldn't be sure. At least, he hoped it was one of them. Did zombies whimper? Was it anxious hunger for human flesh he'd heard rather than human fear?

Just keep walking. Nothing is behind us.

The muted crunch of dirt beneath their feet filled Cory's ears, along with the bellows sound of everyone breathing in the small space. He heard his own lungs wheezing slightly as they struggled with the dual assaults of dust-and-dirt filled air and the foul stench of rotted flesh that seemed to grow worse with each step. He wished he'd brought a handkerchief or bandana to cover his face.

How could anything smell this bad?

Something tickled down his neck and beneath his shirt, and he fought the urge to slap at it, afraid of losing Todd or Marisol if he let go. He told himself it was only a piece of dirt falling from the ceiling but his already over-active imagination created images of ants and beetles skittering above and around them, dropping down onto heads and shoulders.

Nipping with their little pincers and claws.

He felt a scream forming in his throat and forced it down.

Without warning, he bumped into Todd's back and this time he had to clamp his teeth shut to keep from crying out. Then Marisol walked into him in the dark. She emitted a short squeak of terror and John gasped.

"What--?"

"Shh," Todd whispered. "The cavern."

He didn't have to say more. An involuntary shiver ran through Cory. They'd reached the cavern, the place where twenty years earlier they'd had their showdown with the monsters. Cory tried to remember what had happened but his mind refused to go back, leaving him with only half-seen images of Todd throwing Holy water and John shooting...something.

"Cory. *Cory.* Are you ready?"

Todd's voice. Cory nodded, remembered no one could see him. "Yes."

"Okay. Just like we planned. Cory and I go left, Marisol and John right. On three. One...two...three!"

Cory moved to his left and turned on his flashlight. Around him, the others turned theirs on as well as they took their positions. The sudden light blinded him momentarily and he cursed his own stupidity for not shielding his eyes. He peered through the haze of colored spots, searching for any immediate threats. When nothing presented itself, he stepped forward.

His foot encountered something soft and wet and he recoiled. Immediately a horrible odor, so rancid it made his stomach churn, filled his nose.

Marisol screamed.

Cory shined his light at her and then almost dropped it when he saw the corpse on the ground in front of her, as bloated and rotten as the one he'd stepped on. As the others played their lights around, he grasped the enormity of what they'd stumbled into.

Dozens of bodies littered the cavern, some in various states of decomposition, more of them nothing but bones and gristle inside tatters of cloth.

All of them looked like they'd been meals.

Forgetting their plan to spread out, Cory ran to Marisol and wrapped his arms around her. "It's okay," he whispered. "It's okay." She clutched at him, making her flashlight beam dance across the walls and floor.

Todd joined them and John came over a second later.

"Look. Over there."

Cory followed Todd's flashlight beam. Across the cavern was a darker shape against the earthen wall.

"Another tunnel."

Todd nodded. "I'll bet it leads to the old asylum."

Cory started to move his flashlight away then paused.

Was that movement in the tunnel? Just the quickest of flickers, something gray back in the depths. He brought the light back up. Definite movement, too far back to see what it was.

"Guys, there's something in that tunnel." Even as he spoke, the shape moved again, closer now. Close enough to see what it was.

A zombie.

With more behind it.

"Shit!" They'd come prepared more for Grays than zombies. Had Holy water worked against them the last time? He couldn't remember. His memories of that fight were still shrouded in fog.

"We've got a problem here, too," John said.

Cory turned around. Back in the tunnel they'd just left, just coming around the last bend, were more zombies.

"Into the center!" Todd shouted. They followed him, no longer caring about the dead, putrefying bodies underfoot, terrified of becoming another meal for the undead.

"Backs together," Cory said. They grouped shoulder to shoulder, two facing each tunnel. Cory caught a whiff of something summer-sweet in the midst of the death-smell. He looked to the side for a second, saw Marisol next to him, her squirt gun already in hand.

Instead of Holy water, Cory opted for one of the three-foot pieces of PVC pipe he'd snagged from Todd's garage. Each of them carried one. If the Holy water didn't work, at least they'd have weapons to defend themselves with.

Weapons. The last time we were here John had a gun. His father's gun. He remembered that much; remembered the sound of the gun as John fired it.

Dammit! Why can't I remember it all?

Although he had no idea what, he was sure there was something about that night that was important, something that could help them.

"I've got about fifteen on this side," Todd said from behind him. Cory peered at the tunnel, trying to count the dim shapes emerging from the darkness. Ten? Twenty? It didn't matter. They were badly outnumbered no matter what.

"At least that many here," he said.

The zombies moved forward slowly but easily, their lack of speed seemingly more due to caution than dexterity problems. Cory raised his pipe and braced himself for a fight. If these monsters were anything like the ones who'd attacked Marisol or Todd and John, they'd be as fast and strong as living people. Maybe stronger, since they didn't feel pain.

"Get ready," he told the others. "Shoot them as soon as they're in range."

The first zombies stepped out of the tunnel and began closing the distance to their prey. They paid no attention to the dead bodies they stepped on, marching forward with a singular purpose.

To kill us.

At a distance of ten feet away, they stopped. Illuminated by the flashlight beams, their slack faces were portraits of death, ashen, mottled flesh that looked like boiled pork. Several of them had pieces of skin hanging from where it had been cut or simply started to rot.

Cory was shocked to see women and children among the undead. *Which only makes it harder to kill them,* he thought. *How do you slam a piece of pipe into a grade-schooler's skull? A child who just a day or two ago was someone's son or daughter?*

As if reading his mind, a young boy took a single step forward.

"What should I do?" whispered Marisol.

The boy bared his teeth and growled.

"Shoot it," Cory said.

Holding the squirt rifle in two hands, flashlight braced under the nozzle, she aimed and fired at the child. Cory couldn't see the line of water, but he saw it splash across the boy's face and chest.

Nothing happened.

"It doesn't work," Marisol said.

The boy growled again and charged forward, his hands held out, fingers curved into claws.

Cory swung his pipe, a direct shot to the forehead that split the child's skull open with a horrendous, wet *crack._*The boy collapsed to the floor. A second later a dark-gray shape, ghostly and twisted, poured out of the boy's mouth.

"Shit! Shoot it, shoot it!" he cried, remembering how Todd had been able to kill the gray things with his Holy water. Marisol pulled the trigger and white light, brighter than all their flashlights together, exploded as the water hit the beast.

"What the hell was that?" John asked.

"The Holy water. It only works on the Grays, not the zombies. But killing the zombie releases the thing inside."

"We have to kill both or the demon will just find another host," Todd said.

"Yeah, like us." John's voice cracked but he kept his position.

"We are fucked," Marisol said as the remaining zombies all took a step forward in unison.

Cory raised his pipe. "I'll take care of the bodies, you take care of the Grays." In his mind, he knew she was right. They didn't stand a chance. He glanced at her, found her staring back at him. Saw the truth in her eyes.

They were going to die.

At that moment, the zombies charged.

Cory managed two swings with the pipe before they overpowered him. Hands grabbed at him, nails clawed at his clothes. He heard the others shouting. Something hit him from behind, knocking him to his knees. His flashlight fell. A reeking body tackled him and he ended up on his back. He brought the pipe up just in time to stop the dead woman's teeth from biting his face. Holding the pipe sideways against her throat, he pushed upward with all his strength, barely managing to keep her away. Waves of filthy, rank, dead breath poured out of her mouth and he struggled to inhale. Something bit into his thigh and coarse fingernails scraped the back of his neck.

Marisol screamed for help. He couldn't see her, couldn't even turn his head. More weight piled on him and the zombie's gnashing jaws drew closer. He knew he wouldn't be able to hold the thing off much longer. He cursed John for suggesting they enter the pit, cursed himself for listening. Cursed Todd for bringing that damned Ouija board in the first place.

His arms quivered, the muscles starting to cramp. He had no more strength left. He closed his eyes.

"Marisol! I love you!" he shouted, hoping she would hear him.

Something exploded nearby and he wondered if the cave was collapsing around them. Another explosion followed, then another and suddenly the weight on him was gone. He opened his eyes and instead of a dead face saw darkness broken by strobe lights. Another explosion, this one louder, almost deafening. He recognized the sounds as gunshots.

None of us brought guns.

Cory rose to his knees, looked around the cave. The light came from Marisol and John's flashlights. They were standing by the tunnel they'd entered, flanking someone - Chief Travers? - who was methodically aiming at and shooting zombies.

"Get up!" Hands grabbed Cory's arm and he cried out, afraid another zombie had found him. But it was only Todd.

"We have to get out of here. C'mon!"

He struggled to his feet and let Todd lead him to the others. John pointed behind them.

"Todd! The Holy water!"

Cory turned around. Several zombies lay on the floor, fresh additions to the corpses already decomposing there. From each one a twisting python of gray smoke was emerging and turning into a nightmare - stubby limbs, hellish red eyes, gaping mouths.

"What the fuck is going on?" Travers cried.

"Just keep shooting," Marisol told him, pumping her water gun. She and Todd started spraying Holy water at the advancing creatures, each hit resulting in an explosion of white light and one less apparition.

"I'm almost out of ammo," Travers said. "We need to get the hell out of here."

"Back through the tunnel." Cory took Marisol by the arm and guided her backwards so she could keep a watch for more Grays. The others followed, keeping their weapons ready, but the zombies, perhaps sensing they'd lost their advantage, remained in the chamber, their faces twisted with hate.

"Watch for an ambush," Todd said.

Cory kept his eyes open, especially when they rounded the corner in the tunnel, but nothing lay in wait for them. When they reached the spot where the cave-in had once occurred, he took Marisol's hand and practically pulled her through the tunnel, suddenly desperate to get out. At that moment, he didn't care if an army of zombies waited for them. He needed to get outside *now!*

In his haste to escape he almost ran into the wall at the end of the tunnel.

"Grab my shoulders," he told Marisol. Bending, he gripped her hips and then boosted her upwards. As soon as she was through the opening, he jumped up, grabbed the edge of the hole, and pulled himself through. By the time he'd turned around and reached down again, Todd stood underneath, ready to be pulled up.

Two minutes later, they all stood outside the crypt, sucking in untainted air in an attempt to rid their lungs of the horrendous stench they'd been breathing.

Once he could speak, Cory turned to the others.

"Is everyone okay?"

Todd and Travers managed to gasp affirmative answers. Marisol merely nodded. Cory glanced at John.

Just in time to see him collapse to the ground, a bloody stain covering his shirt.

Chapter 3

"He lost some blood and took eighteen stitches in his chest but he'll be fine."

Todd felt something in his chest relax at the doctor's words. They'd rushed John to the hospital in the Chief's car and Travers had shocked them by using his badge to get John bumped to the top of the list in the ER. He'd shocked them a second time by leaving the hospital without demanding any explanations about what had happened beneath the cemetery.

"Can we see him?" Todd asked.

The ER doctor shook his head. "We gave him a sedative. He'll probably sleep the entire night. Want to tell me what happened?"

Todd opened his mouth but stopped, unsure of what to say.

Cory came to his rescue. "Nothing criminal on our part, if that's what you're worried about. C'mon guys, we'll come back in the morning."

Todd followed Cory and Marisol out of the ER, conscious of the doctor's gaze on them. He knew what the man must be thinking. Three filthy, bruised people and an equally dirty cop bringing in a bleeding, unconscious man at three in the morning. It practically screamed trouble. He assumed the doctor would be on the phone to Travers as soon as they were out the door.

And what will Travers say? Will he vouch for us? Arrest us?

"What now?" Marisol asked as they stopped outside the main doors. She and Cory looked a lot like zombies themselves, with dark rings under their eyes, mussed hair and slumped shoulders. Todd imagined he looked just as bad.

"Back to my house. We can--" he cut himself off in mid-sentence as he realized they had no car.

Cory caught on at the same time and pulled out his cell. "We'll call a cab. My treat. It's at least four miles to your house and I'm not walking another step."

"I second that," Marisol said, taking a seat on a nearby bench. Her movements were slow and careful, like an arthritic old woman's. "I plan on soaking in the tub and then sleeping for a day. Maybe two."

When the cab arrived, Todd thought for a moment the man might not let them in. But aside from a startled expression, he ushered them into the back seat as if nothing was wrong.

Maybe it's because we're at the hospital. Bruised and beaten is an acceptable look here, even at this hour of the morning.

None of them spoke for the ten minutes it took to get to Todd's house. When the cab stopped, they just stared at each other. Todd figured Marisol and Cory felt the same mix of despair and exhaustion as he. Even saying goodnight took more energy than he felt he could spare.

"Do you want to come in for a night cap?" Todd asked, while silently praying they said no. All he wanted was a shower and his pillow.

"No thanks," Cory said, so quickly that Todd knew they were desperate for sleep as well.

"Goodnight Todd. We'll call you when we get up in the morning." Marisol lifted her hand in a weak wave.

"Or the afternoon." Cory's joke drew weak smiles all around.

"Goodnight then." Todd went up the walk and fumbled his keys from his front pocket. Even the muscles in his fingers ached and it took him two tries to get the key into the lock. He heard the cab leave but he didn't look back.

Inside the kitchen, he dropped his keys on the table and opened the 'fridge, desperate for a cola or juice, something to wash the lingering taste of dirt and death out of his mouth. The soda can was almost to his lips when he paused.

Something wasn't right.

Something about the table.

Even as he turned his head, a sick feeling erupted in his gut, a sense of terrible foreboding.

Next to his keys sat the note he'd left for Abigail.

Todd stared at the piece of paper, his mind like a car stuck in the mud. Wheels spinning but going nowhere.

It's no big deal. She read it and left it there.

Abigail never leaves a mess.

She didn't come here today.

She had to have. It wasn't her day off.

Maybe it was.

He had to think hard to remember what day it was.

Then his mental wheels got traction and he ran up the stairs, taking the steps two at a time, his exhaustion wiped away by terror-born adrenaline.

"Mother!"

She was on her bed, head resting on her pillows, eyes closed. For one brief second, everything was all right, she was simply sleeping, he'd been a fool.

Then he saw her uneaten breakfast still on the nightstand.

And noticed her arm hanging over the edge of the bed.

This time, his scream was much louder.

* * *

The feeling of déjà vu was so strong that Cory actually stumbled as he entered the hospital. It only grew worse when he approached the nurses' station and the woman at the desk pointed down the hall. "Curtain five," she said, before Cory even had a chance give Todd's name.

With a start, he realized it was the same nurse who'd been on duty when they'd left less than two hours ago.

"Cory c'mon." Marisol tugged at his arm. Like him, she was dressed in sweatpants and a t-shirt, her hair still damp from the shower they'd just finished when Todd's call came. He nodded and followed her to the circular examination area, which was sectioned off into curtained cubicles, each with a number above it. As they approached number five, the curtain parted and Todd stepped out. Cory caught a glimpse of three people in green scrubs standing around a bed and then a gloved hand closed the curtain.

"How is she?" Marisol asked, reaching out to Todd.

"In a coma thanks to me." Todd practically slapped her hand away and pushed past them, heading towards the waiting area.

Marisol's eyes went wide and she made to follow but Cory stopped her.

"Give him a minute."

"But--"

"I know you meant well," he interrupted. "but he's not thinking clearly right now. He needs to cool off. Let's see if the doctor will talk to us."

He approached the curtained area and tapped on one of the metal poles. "Excuse me? I'm a close friend of the family. Can I speak to someone for a moment?"

The curtain slid open and a nurse stepped out. Behind her, the doctor and the other nurse continued their examination of Mrs. Randolph, who was completely obscured by an oxygen mask and an assortment of tubes and wires that connected her to various machines.

"I'm only supposed to speak with family but I saw Mr. Randolph with you earlier, when you brought your other friend in."

"How is she?" Maria asked.

"Unresponsive. The EMTs had to use the defibrillator on the way here to restart her heart."

"What happened to her?"

The nurse shook her head. "Apparently, there was a mix-up with her medications and she didn't receive them. We see things like this happen all too often."

Cory felt his stomach clench. If Todd's mother missing her meds had anything to do with their being out all day and night, it was no wonder he was blaming himself.

"Will she recover?"

"It's too soon to say. She was already seriously ill."

Damn it. That's not what I wanted to hear. "Okay, thank you." Cory turned to leave but the nurse stopped him.

"Wait. Please tell Mr. Randolph this isn't his fault. In her condition, it was only a matter of time before her body shut down anyhow."

Cory nodded his acceptance of her statement without agreeing. "I'll tell him but it's not going to matter."

Marisol took his hand as they exited the ER. "What do we do now?"

"We help Todd through this." Cory shrugged. "I don't know what else we can do. John's out of commission until at least tomorrow. Todd isn't going to be much use. That means it's just us and I don't have a damned clue as to what to do next."

"Maybe that means we should do nothing," Marisol said. "Step back. Take a breath. Regroup, instead of just jumping into the water without looking."

Cory was about to respond when the doors to the ambulance bay swung open and two sets of EMTs came barreling in, each duo wheeling a gurney.

"Multiple lacerations and broken bones!" one of the EMTs shouted. "BP dropping fast. He's bleeding out!"

"So's mine," one of the other EMTs said. "We need lots of blood and a couple of surgeons."

Several nurses magically appeared, as if summoned from thin air. The gurneys were wheeled into the ER, each one surrounded by four or five people all working and shouting at once.

Cory almost gagged as one of the bodies went past. A loop of greenish-tan intestine hung over the edge of the gurney, splattered in red. More blood covered the person's clothes and limbs.

"I need hands in here," a doctor yelled from inside the ER.

"Can't spare any," one of the nurses replied, heading back to the ambulance bay with two of her co-workers. "We've got more coming in!"

"This is all our fault," a voice said behind Cory, making him jump. He turned and saw Todd standing a couple of feet away.

"Todd--" Marisol began, but he cut her off.

"Don't deny it. This shit all started because of us. The goddamned Cemetery Club. I wish I'd never found that Ouija board, never showed it to you all. Then I wouldn't have had to sacrifice my whole damn life for you people. Hell, as long as I'm at it, I wish I'd never met any of you. Then maybe none of this," he spread his arms, indicating the craziness in the ER, "would have ever happened."

Before anyone could respond, Todd did an about face and walked back into the ER.

Cory turned and looked at Marisol.

"Still think we should take things slow?"

* * *

The cab ride back to Marisol's was silent, although not uncomfortably so. Marisol stared out the passenger window, her eyes half-closed. That suited Cory just fine. He was preoccupied with his own thoughts, so much so that they'd already pulled into the driveway before it registered on his exhausted brain there was a car parked in front of the house.

"Who's that," he asked, tapping Marisol on the leg and pointing at the late-model SUV.

She leaned across him and looked out the window. Her frown quickly changed to a confused smile.

"It's Freddy. Freddy Alou, the Town Clerk? You met him once. I wonder what he's doing here?"

"One way to find out." Cory paid the driver and they got out, alert for any sudden movements. He'd kept his tone light but in truth the car made him nervous. There was too much going on - most of it dangerous - for him to think this was a harmless social call.

The SUV's driver door opened a second later and a stocky, gray-haired Hispanic man got out, dressed for work in gray slacks and a brown sweater vest over a white shirt.

Marisol took Cory's hand. "Freddy. Kind of early isn't it? Is everything all right?"

Their unexpected visitor gave them a smile but shook his head in the negative. "No, _chica_, it's not. I been trying to talk to you for like a week now, and I can't wait any longer. Things have gotten too out of hand. The whole town is *loco.*"

As if to emphasize his words, the *crack-crack-crack* of distant gunfire echoed through the relative quiet of the early morning air. After a pause, the all-too-familiar howl of a police siren started up.

"Maybe you'd better come inside. We'll put some coffee on." Coffee was the last thing Cory wanted, considering they'd been up almost twenty-four hours straight. And he didn't want to hear what was sure to be more bad news. Except he had a feeling it was information they needed to know.

As it turned out, he was right on both counts.

By mutual unspoken agreement, they kept the conversation to anything except the town - mostly Freddy apologizing to Marisol for showing up so early and saying how stupid Jack Smith was for suspending her - until the coffee was made and they'd sat down in Marisol's small but comfortable living room.

"So, where do we begin?" Cory asked.

Freddy wasted no time. "I know you and your friends have been investigating the strange things happening around here. But I don't think the four of you know how closely you're linked to what is going on."

"Oh, do tell," Marisol said, her tone more sarcastic than Cory had ever heard from her. "We've been getting that shit from John and Todd already. Now you're jumping in?"

Freddy frowned in confusion. "You mean, you know?"

"That it's our fault? Yeah, we're well aware of that fact. Who else knows?"

"I...I don't think anyone but me. I am the last. But how did you find out?"

"Wait a minute," Cory interrupted. "Are we talking about the same thing? The attacks that happened when we were in high school?"

Comprehension replaced confusion on Freddy's face. "It was the four of you! *¡Dios santo!* I thought so. To answer your question, yes and no. No doubt you had much involvement then. And to your credit, you were strong enough to stop them for a while. But your involvement goes back further. Much further. Before you were born, actually."

"Wait a minute." Marisol put her coffee down. "Before we were born? That doesn't make sense."

Cory patted her hand. "Let him explain."

"*Gracias.* The four of you, your families, you go back a long ways in this town. Back to the beginning, when Rocky Point wasn't much of a town at all. My family was there too. In fact, *el padre de mi abuelo,* my grandfather's father, came here with your grandfather's grandfather *chica*. They owned the town's first tattery."

"What the hell's a tattery?" Marisol asked. Cory had a feeling she had other questions, larger ones, but wasn't ready to ask them yet.

"A leather maker," Freddy said. "I have letters I can show you someday. Mr. Miles, your family was represented as well. Also business people. Of course, by now you've surely found out that a Boyd was one of the first mayors of Rocky Point."

Cory nodded. "In 1847, when..." His voice trailed off.

"What?" asked Marisol.

"When he and Reverend Randolph gave the order to burn down the leper colony," Freddy finished. "The colony that was built, mind you, on land that one Archibald Miles sold to Effram Charles for the sum of seventeen dollars and rights to the lumber."

"That's very weird," Marisol said.

Weird isn't the word for it, Cory thought, as Freddy kept talking. He listened with growing incredulity as the Town Clerk told the story of the founding families of Rocky Point. Along with their four and the Alous there had been five others, but those lines had died out along the way, lost in the usual tragedies that strike towns and families over the centuries. During the research done by the Cemetery Club members, Cory had noticed an odd rate of major incidents - fires, scandals, murders - in the historical records, but he'd attributed it to a combination of coincidence and the violent tendencies of the times.

Now he was suddenly sure there were no coincidences, not when it came to Rocky Point.

As Freddy's tale unfolded, Cory tried to mentally highlight the key points, the way he'd highlight a court document or witness testimony when preparing for a trials. The town had always had a Randolph as a preacher, with Todd's father being the last. The Boyds had always been involved in politics and business. John's father had managed the bank and been on the town board. And Cory's own family had remained true to their roots, apparently, with almost everyone - right up until Cory had gone into law - being involved in real estate or finance.

"What about my family?" Marisol interrupted. "My parents came over here from Puerto Rico. But you said my great-great grandfather was one of the town founders."

"He was," Freddy said. "His name was Jesús Rafael Carrasquillo. A moderately wealthy man in Spain, it was his dream to expand the family's fortune in the new lands. And he did. So much so that in 1925, his only son sold the business and moved to Cuba to live out the rest of his days in luxury."

"I never heard of him. What happened to him? Where did this so-called fortune go?"

Freddy shrugged. "Like so many, he lost everything in *La Revolución*, when Castro took over. He escaped with his wife and children to Puerto Rico. Changed his name to Ortiz."

"Ortiz? That's my mother's maiden name!"

"Yes. And many years later, she met your father and they returned to Rocky Point, probably never knowing your family's true history."

"So our families are tied together with the town's history. What does it have to do with..." Cory stopped, not sure of what word to use. Zombies? Monsters? Ghosts? They still had no idea what Alou knew and didn't know.

"The walking dead?" Freddy answered Cory's question, and the unspoken ones as well. "The things that possess them?"

"You've seen them?" asked Marisol.

He shook his head. "No, I have not. But my great-grandfather did, in 1922. He wrote it down."

"That was when Grover Lillian killed himself," Cory said.

"*Sí*. Until then, the Shadows were rare. After Lillian's experiments, though, they began to appear more often. Scaring people. But back then people believed in spirits. Took precautions. Our grandparents' parents, they did what they had to. Ended the problem before it grew too large. And in 1947, our *abuelos* did it again. The town was safe until..."

"Until we woke them up in the cemetery," Cory finished.

"I believe so, yes. But it would have happened again, sooner or later. Whenever there are violent deaths, the Shadows appear."

"Violent deaths happen all the time, all over the world. Why do the...Shadows...appear in Rocky Point?"

Freddy tapped a chubby finger against his temple. "It is not just the deaths, but the concentration of so many in one area. The experiments. The fires. All in the same place. All that negative energy, it is like fertilizer to seeds."

"Wait a minute!" Cory jumped up, ran for his notebooks. Something had been tickling the back of his brain for several minutes, something Freddy had mentioned.

Shadows. Spirits. He scrolled through the pages. Something Todd had told them...Yes!

"Here it is!" He held up a piece of paper with notes scribbled across it.

"What is it?" Marisol took it from him, frowned, and handed it back. "I can't read that chicken scratch."

"Todd gave me a lot of his old research to read through, so I could kind of catch up on everything he and John had found. Listen to this:

"Shadow people - also known as Shadow beings or Shades - are a rare supernatural phenomenon. The earliest reports date back to ancient Sumerian descriptions of certain demons. Most accounts describe the shadow beings as black humanoid silhouettes with red or yellow eyes. They are usually vaporous or distorted."

"Holy shit!" Marisol practically shouted. "That's exactly what we saw. Why didn't Todd pay more attention to this?"

"Because of the other part of the description," Cory said. "Shadow beings are believed to be result of the intense negative psychic energy created in areas where traumatic or evil events have occurred, such as mass murders or battlefields. The shadow beings are the mutated souls of the dead, who thrive on fear or other negative emotions."

Cory put the paper down. "We thought it was something we did. But we didn't know the history of the town. We didn't create the Shadows, we just woke them up again."

Freddy nodded. "If ever there was a place filled with negative energy, it is that area between the cemetery and Wood Hill Sanitarium."

"What else does it say?" Marisol asked.

"Let's see. Individually, Shadows or Shades, are incapable of doing anything more than frightening people. But when there are several of them in a concentrated area, they will be more powerful, and can gain the ability to possess a human body by force. Their very presence can create conditions that are favorable for the creation of more Shadows through any type of violent death."

"They multiply like bacteria," Freddy said. "Each time they kill someone, they add to their own numbers."

"There's more." Cory continued reading. "Certain places are believed to be more hospitable to the formation of Shades, whether because of magnetic energies or something we don't yet know about. That's why certain murder scenes and buildings have the reputation for being haunted, while others don't."

"That would explain much." Freddy picked at his fingernails as he spoke. "Each time members of our family fought the Shadows it diminished their numbers enough so that the remaining ones lost the power to possess people and went into hiding. They stayed harmless until another event occurred..."

"Another event like a fire, or a scientist experimenting on people," Cory finished.

"All those bodies," Marisol said. "The ones they buried beneath the sanitarium. That would be a concentrated dose of negative energy for sure."

Cory tossed the paper onto the table. "It wasn't us who triggered the Shadows this time, it was what happened at Wood Hill."

"We need to tell Todd and John about this."

"Wait." Freddy held up a hand. "Do your notes say anything about how to stop them?"

Cory smiled. For the first time in days, he felt as if Fate was finally lending them a hand. Or at least removing some of the roadblocks in their path. "Yes. Holy water and Eucharistic wafers can be used to bless a room or home and even destroy the Shades. Blessed wine works too. And you can prevent one from possessing you by letting go of fear and thinking positive thoughts. Visualize a holy light around you, a light that denies access to your person by evil beings."

"We've seen how Holy water kills them," Marisol said. "At least the Shadow forms."

"Let's go to the hospital." Cory stuffed the paper in his pocket. "This might be just the answer we've been looking for."

"Cory. Marisol."

They paused and looked at Freddy. He was tapping his watch. "It's not even nine o'clock yet. You both look like *mierda*. Get some sleep. Eat something. Then go to the hospital. After you speak with Mr. Randolph, call me."

Marisol started to object but Cory stopped her.

"He's right. We're exhausted. John needs his rest. And Todd needs to be with his mother right now. A few hours isn't going to make a difference, except to help us think clearer."

As they walked Freddy to the door and said goodbye, they had no idea that Cory was both right and wrong.

Terribly wrong.

Chapter 4

By the time Cory and Marisol arrived at the hospital it was close to three in the afternoon. Cory had set his phone alarm for eleven but they'd both slept through it; had, in fact, only woken up when Marisol's neighbor had started up a hedge trimmer right outside their bedroom window.

"Who do we see first?" Marisol asked as they entered the welcome coolness of the hospital's main entrance. Outside, the temperature was a scorching ninety-five with close to a hundred percent humidity. According to the weather report the heat wave showed no signs of breaking for the next few days.

Cory wiped sweat from his forehead. Despite the heat, he'd dressed business casual - tan pants, Italian loafers, a short-sleeve button-down - in case they had to handle any red tape. Marisol wore a reasonably conservative skirt and blouse, neither of which did anything to hide her curves but at the same time didn't draw undue attention to her assets.

"Let's check on Todd. Then maybe he'll come with us to see John."

A stop at the reception desk revealed that Todd's mother had been moved to a semi-private room in Critical Care, one step down from ICU. The woman behind the desk didn't want to let them up, since they weren't relatives, but she acquiesced when Cory informed her he was the Randolph's lawyer, leaving Cory thankful he hadn't worn the shorts and t-shirt he'd originally intended.

The poorly-hidden aroma of sickness and death tainted the air of the Critical Care ward, an odor all the pine and lemon-scented cleaning agents in the world couldn't eliminate. Cory found himself grimacing as he pushed the red button that swung the large doors open. He'd hated hospitals ever since his parents' accident. His father had died instantly in the crash but his mother had hung on for a day in ICU before perishing.

Although he hadn't spent much time in the hospital with her, it had been more than enough to leave an indelible sensory memory in his brain, one that had led him to avoid hospitals as much as possible ever since.

And now here I am for the third time in less than two days. I hope this doesn't become habitual.

When they arrived at Todd's mother's room the door was open. Marisol peeked in first. They'd already decided that if Todd was asleep or the other occupant had visitors, they'd postpone their visit.

"The other bed is empty," Marisol whispered to Cory. "Todd's reading a book."

Cory nodded. He knocked on the door and stepped into the room. "Todd? Is it okay if we come in?"

Todd glanced up from his book, which Cory noticed was a Bible. His face was haggard and pale, with dark half-moons under his eyes. He looked as if he hadn't slept in days. When he spoke, his voice was as tired as his face.

"Sure. Come in. Thank you for stopping by."

Marisol placed a small bouquet of flowers on the nightstand. "How is she doing?"

Todd shook his head. "No change. They say she could stay this way for weeks or go in hours. It's up to her now."

There was a moment of silence following Todd's statement. Marisol chewed at a fingernail, obviously remembering how he'd been so brusque at her last attempt to comfort him. For his part, Cory didn't know what to say that would do any good. *Gee, that sucks. I'm sorry to hear your mother's dying.*

Finally, Marisol broke the quiet just as it got too uncomfortable. "Todd, is there anything we can do?"

He turned away from them, took his mother's limp hand in his. "You can leave us alone. I don't blame you for this, regardless of what I said last night. I blame myself. For getting so caught up I forgot about the one person who always loved me. For starting all this shit back in high school. For not being the person my father wanted me to be."

"Todd, it's not--"

"Think about it Cory," Todd said, still not looking at them. "If I'd followed my father's footsteps, believed in God instead of rebelling against the Church, I'd have never been hanging out in that crypt, never brought any of you to it, never decided to try that damned game. None of this, not high school, not now, would have ever happened."

"Actually, that's not true." Cory hoped his words would somehow sink in. "We found out what those things are, why they're here. It's this town and all the bad things that have happened. Our families...somehow, it's always been our families that pushed the evil back underground. If we hadn't played with that Ouija board, something else would have woken the Shades up sooner or later. And they're back now because of what happened at Wood Hill, not because of us."

Todd slowly turned his head. "Did you say Shades? I remember reading something about them."

"You found the answer," Marisol said. "It was in your notes but none of us caught it. Freddy Alou filled in the missing pieces for us."

"That's why we need you now." Cory took a step closer to the bed. "Your research had the answers for how to stop the Shades. Kill them forever. But we can't do it alone. There are too many of them. We need you. We need your faith."

Todd stared at him for so long Cory thought he might actually give in and rejoin them. Eventually though, he turned his gaze back to his mother's motionless body.

"I'm sorry, I can't. I wasn't there when she needed me. I won't make that mistake again. I'm not leaving her side until...until she either wakes up or passes on."

"Todd..." Marisol began, but he cut her off.

"I said no. Now, please leave."

For a moment the only sounds in the room were the mechanical inhalations and exhalations of the equipment keeping Todd's mother alive. Then Cory allowed himself a long sigh.

"All right. We understand. Just know this: it's not your fault. None of it. Not the town, not your mother. And if you need anything you know we're here for you."

Without waiting for a goodbye, he took Marisol's hand and led her to the door.

"Let's hope we have better luck with John," Cory said while they waited for the elevator.

As it turned out, they didn't. Although more than willing to help, John was still not cleared to leave the hospital.

"One more night," he told them, after showing them the angry red line of stitches just to the left of his naval. "The doctors want to make sure there's no infection. Can you hold off for another couple of days?"

"We'll have to," Cory said. "There's no way Marisol and I can do this alone, even if Freddy helps us...we're still way outnumbered."

"Can you talk to Travers?" John asked. "He knows the truth now. That would make five of us."

"I'll sure as hell try." Cory gave John's shoulder a soft squeeze. "Get some rest. We'll be back tomorrow to get you."

Marisol gave John a quick kiss on the cheek and they left him with a pile of magazines and newspapers.

"Now what?" she asked.

"Now I talk to Chief Travers."

"And then?"

He shrugged. "And then we start making plans."

Although it wasn't what she wanted to hear or what he wanted to say, it was the best he could do.

Chapter 5

For the first time in all his years as Police Chief, Nick Travers had spent an entire workday without stepping foot in the police station. Between the missing police officers and the out-of-control crime in Rocky Point, he'd been forced to ask for assistance from the Sheriff's department to cover shifts. Unfortunately, there was only so much money in the budget for 'special circumstances,' so he'd had to take on field duties in an effort to minimize costs. Which meant, of course, that he'd be working more nights trying to catch up with paperwork.

All of which made Nick Travers an angry man as he did yet another pass through the Lowlands.

The radio crackled to life. "Chief?"

"What now?"

"Got that lawyer friend of yours, Miles, in here. He's asking to speak with you. Says it's important."

An involuntary shudder ran through Travers. He'd done his best to avoid thinking about what had happened under the cemetery. There was no explanation for what he'd seen, although his mind was trying to steer him towards druggies and hallucinogenic chemicals as it attempted to rationalize the events of the previous night.

And now Miles wanted to talk to him, no doubt to convey some supernatural enlightenment.

He'll just have to wait 'til I'm ready to listen.

"Tell him he's out of luck. I'm in the field for the foreseeable future and can't help him."

Gasses from rotting corpses. That's what made me hallucinate.

The more he thought about it, the more it made sense. The druggies had been using the tunnel below the crypt as their hangout. Who knew what chemicals or toxins they'd been exposed to down there. Well, he'd certainly rained on their parade last night! Doubtful they'd be using that place again; problem was, that meant finding their new drug den.

Shouldn't be too hard, he thought with a grimace. *Just wait until one of them commits a crime tonight and then follow them.*

In the meantime he'd posted the few men he could spare in the tunnel to run forensics and bring up the bodies. He'd cruise the streets and let the citizens of Rocky Point know the police were still on the job until then.

Before the Desk Sergeant even put down the phone, Cory knew what the answer would be. He could see it in the man's smug expression.

"Chief says he's all tied up the rest of the day, and prob'ly tomorrow too." The Sergeant didn't try to hide his smile. "Guess you're out of luck, Mister Miles."

"I'm not the only one," Cory said. He turned and headed for the exit. As he walked to his car, he briefly considered driving around town until he found Travers, but then he tossed the idea aside. Antagonizing the Police Chief wouldn't do any good, especially since they might need his help later.

"Well?" asked Marisol, as he got into the car. "Anything good to report?"

He shook his head. "Let's just say it's a good thing we're not going to Vegas anytime soon. We'd lose our life savings."

Marisol sighed and put her feet up on the dashboard. Cory momentarily cringed inside - he'd never even eaten in the car, let alone soiled the dash - but he kept his mouth shut. A dirty dashboard was the least of their worries. If they survived the next few days, he could complain then.

"So, what now? John's out of commission, Todd's quit the team and Travers won't acknowledge the problem."

"Now?" Cory put the car in gear. "Now we go home, eat something, get some sleep and hope your friend Freddy can help us. Otherwise we're in big trouble."

* * *

In Rocky Point, the setting of the summer sun no longer meant ice cream at Millie's Café or romantic walks through Riverside Park. It no longer meant sitting on the porch with a beer or an iced tea listening to the Mets or Yankees on the radio. It no longer meant heading down to the River Club or Wharf Rats to have a drink at the Tiki Bar while a half-decent cover band played classic rock hits.

No, sunset meant staying inside with the windows and doors locked, no matter how hot the night air. It meant closing up shop and getting home before dark. It meant making sure the kids were in before the streetlights came on.

And it meant praying you'd still be alive in the morning.

The residents of Rocky Point knew what the Mayor, the Town Board and the police refused to admit. They knew their town was under siege, at the mercy of an unknown force that was out for blood. Even the local papers weren't reporting the whole truth; partly because the Board wasn't giving it to them, and partly because the reporters didn't believe half the stories they were hearing. Ghosts in the night? Alien abductions? Zombies walking the streets? You didn't dare suggest that kind of story to the Senior Editor. Not unless you wanted your next job to be writing for the high school newsletter. Better to go along with the official story of 'a new drug on the streets' and 'a suspected leak of hallucinogenic fumes into the air, most likely from a meth lab or similar manufacturing site for illicit drugs.'

Sure, it smelled of cover up, but at least it didn't sound insane.

Unlike many of his friends and neighbors, Tanner Wilson had no concerns for his safety after dark. A veteran of the first Gulf War, he'd used his time in the military to become something of an expert in weaponry of all kinds, from basic survival knives to rocket launchers. He'd also mastered several forms of hand-to-hand combat and self-defense. After completing two tours of duty he'd taken out a veteran's loan and opened a personal security company. In the years since, he'd built a large customer base of high net worth individuals and medium-sized businesses.

So when four hollow-eyed, disheveled men entered Off-the-Hook Fish & Chips while he waited for his order, he felt no fear. His body immediately went into defense mode, his brain assessing the men as obvious derelicts, probably stoned out of their minds. The reek of their unwashed bodies quickly overpowered the delicious odors of batter-fried fish and hush puppies, which annoyed Tanner more than anything. He'd had a hard day and all he wanted was a greasy meal and a large soda.

One of the men grunted and the four of them spread out slightly, a strategy Tanner instantly recognized as a move to surround him. He glanced back at the counter, saw that the young girl who'd taken his order had already fled into the kitchen.

Smart kid. This is going to get messy.

"All right fellows. I'll give you one chance. Turn around and take your smelly asses out of here and there won't be any trouble."

The druggie directly in front of him made a phlegmy, gurgling kind of sound. The others continued to stare at him with blank expressions. Without warning they charged him all at once.

Tanner sent the first attacker flying through the air with a roundhouse kick. He let his follow-through bring him within arm's length of the next one, a wiry teenager with long, greasy hair. Before the kid could make a move, Tanner struck him in the nose with the bottom of his palm and then followed the blow with two quick punches to the midsection. He'd already started his turn towards the other two assailants when it registered in his mind that druggie number two hadn't gone down.

Shit. They must be fucked up on PCP or something. Feeling no pain.

Incredibly strong arms wrapped around his chest. The man's stench was powerful enough to start Tanner's eyes watering but he ignored the foul air and raked his heel down the man's shin while simultaneously whipping his head back in a vicious blow. Bone broke with a loud crunch and wet liquids streamed down his neck.

The arms didn't let go.

It came to him then that he might be in more trouble than he'd thought.

"Call nine one one!" he shouted, hoping there was still someone in the back of the restaurant.

One of the other attackers grabbed his arms, held them tight. Tanner struggled but couldn't get loose. The man leaned forward and Tanner suddenly knew why they were feeling no pain.

Death stared at him from blind, cloudy eyes.

Strong hands pushed him to the floor and pried his mouth open. There was a moment when he feared they were going to pour some kind of drug into him.

Then the creature appeared above him.

The police were still two minutes away when the thing that used to be Tanner Wilson followed the other four men as they climbed over the counter and went into the kitchen.

By the time Nick Travers arrived at Off-the-Hook, it was too late. The first officer on the scene, a rookie Deputy Sheriff only a few weeks out of the academy, lay in pieces on the kitchen floor. He'd apparently arrived as the unknown assailants - four of them, according to the 911 call - were attacking the counter girl, a nineteen-year-old college student named Jennifer Waits. Apparently was the operative term because the officers who'd come after had found spent shell casings on the floor. No sign of the perps, and it was too soon to tell if any of the copious amounts of blood in the kitchen belonged to them.

Jennifer's half-eaten body had been stuffed into a freezer.

"What about other employees?" Travers asked the room in general. Another Deputy Sheriff spoke up.

"Owner wasn't on duty. He's on his way here now. The night shift manager and cook are missing."

The officer closed his notepad with more force than necessary and shoved it into his pocket. Travers didn't say anything. He knew the man's anger stemmed from losing one of their own.

I remember that anger, he thought. Of course, that was back before death and disappearances had become the norm in Rocky Point. Now all he felt was a cold, depressing numbness.

His radio crackled, indicating an incoming call.

"All units, 10-54 on Maple Avenue in front of elementary school. Repeat, 10-54. Ambulance needed."

Travers couldn't keep his groan to himself. *10-54. Possible dead body.*

That's it.

He turned and left the restaurant without saying anything. Someone called his name but he ignored them, continued walking to his car. Got inside. Turned off both radios. Started the engine and pulled away from the crime scene.

Heading down Main Street, he saw a woman dart out from between two cars. Two men tackled her in the other lane. One of them looked up, his face highlighted by Travers' headlights just long enough for Travers to recognize him as Officer Mack Harris, one of the department's missing officers. Harris's shirt was torn and bloody.

Harris smiled and then bent down and bit the woman's face.

Travers steered his car around the carnage and kept driving. When he arrived at his house, he went inside and woke his family.

"Pack up your clothes," he told them. "You're leaving at first light."

* * *

At the same time Chief Travers was stuffing his daughters' shoes into a suitcase, the ringing of the bedroom phone woke Cory and Marisol from a deep, troubled, sleep.

"Hello?" Marisol tried focusing on the caller ID but it remained fuzzy.

"Something's happening at the hospital. I think you'd better get down here, fast."

The line went dead.

"Who was that?" Cory asked, as Marisol sat up.

"John. Trouble at the hospital. He said we should hurry."

"Damn. All right. Bring the Holy water."

Five minutes later they were driving through the deserted streets. Although they didn't see any zombies, signs of their presence were everywhere: broken windows and doors, empty cars in the middle of roads with their engines running, dark stains on the sidewalks.

The hospital was a madhouse when they arrived, with three police cars blocking the main entrance, their lights still flashing. People were running in all directions. Inside, the lobby looked like something out of a disaster movie. Chairs and end tables had been overturned, magazines were scattered across the tiled floor and a large potted palm lay crushed and broken, its dirt spread out around it like granular blood.

Marisol headed for the elevators but Cory pulled her away.

"No enclosed places," he said. "Let's take the stairs."

John's room was on the fourth floor and they made it there without encountering anyone.

It was a different story when they exited the stairwell.

Two zombies were in the process of climbing over the nurse's station. A middle-aged nurse - who'd already been bitten at least once, judging from the blood stains on her white uniform - cowered behind her chair, calling for help. A man and a woman stood near the elevators with twin boys who looked about six years old. The wife was furiously pressing the elevator buttons while her husband shouted at her to get the doors open. Down the corridor in the other direction, screams came from several of the patient rooms.

"Which way to John?" Cory asked, hating himself for not going to the nurse's aid but knowing they had to get to John.

"That way." Marisol pointed to their left.

They started down the hallway, Cory holding a baseball bat while Marisol did her best imitation of an action hero, holding a water rifle in each hand.

A zombie sprang out from a doorway in front of them. "Mine!" it yelled, nearly startling the bat out of Cory's hands. It was the first time he'd heard any of the dead speak. Cory swung the bat just as the zombie grabbed him. There was a sound like ice cracking and the creature's left arm suddenly had an extra joint between the elbow and wrist.

It showed no sign of pain.

Before the thing could grab for him again, Cory swung a second time, this one a perfectly-aimed blow that split the monster's head open, revealing pink flesh and white bone. A third strike with the bat shattered the skull and sent pieces of bone and brain across the hall.

Only then did the walking corpse go down.

"Hurry!" he told Marisol. John's room was still three doors away. More screams came from behind them and he risked a glance back as they ran. The elevator doors had finally opened, releasing five more zombies who immediately attacked the family standing there. Cory caught a glimpse of a dark, shadowy shape attached to the face of one of the children.

That would have been us if we'd taken the elevator.

Cory couldn't believe how many times they'd managed to escape death in the past few days. How long could their streak continue, especially with the enemy growing in numbers every night?

"Cory!"

He stopped at Marisol's shout, realized he'd run past John's room.

Keep zoning out and you will *get killed,* he chided himself.

"John?" Cory's heart sank. The bed was empty and one of the chairs overturned. Were they too late?

The bathroom door opened and Cory raised his bat. A figure stepped out, emitting a startled exclamation when Marisol shot it with her squirt gun.

"Hey! It's me." John had one hand in the air and the other pressed against his stomach. "I was hiding."

"John! You're all right!" Marisol ran to him, would have hugged him but he put his hand out to stop her.

"Stitches, remember? I hope you guys have a plan to get us out of here."

"Stairs," Cory said. "They were empty on the way up and hopefully they'll be that way on the way down. But we have a stop to make......."

"Todd?" John asked.

"Yeah. He's in CCU with his mother. Second floor."

"Let's go."

To Cory's relief, the stairwell was still empty. The second floor was as well. No one moved in the hallways or rooms, which looked like a war zone. Beds and chairs were turned over, papers littered the floor and bloody body parts were scattered everywhere.

They found no sign of Todd or his mother.

"Oh God." Marisol put her head on Cory's shoulder. He placed his arm around her, felt her trembling. Warm tears dampened his neck.

"Dammit." John's lips tightened, as if blocking his sorrow from escaping. Cory wondered if the man could only express fear and anger, if he kept everything else bottled up inside. Or had all his other emotions been drowned by his years of drinking?

The sound of gunfire on one of the floors above them made them all jump.

"C'mon." Cory indicated the door. "We can't stick around. We'll head back to Marisol's and figure things out later, when we're safe."

"Safe?" John let out a bitter laugh. "There's no place left that's safe. Don't you get it?"

"Get what?" Marisol asked.

"This is the end of Rocky Point."

Chapter 6

Jack Smith paced back and forth in the Mayor's private office, well aware it was getting on the nerves of Mayor Dawes and his secretary-cum-current squeeze, the well-endowed and willing Betty Smyrna. They'd been holed up since just after six p.m., going on close to nine hours. The attack had occurred as they'd sat down with the Town Council to discuss emergency procedures. Dawes wanted to continue keeping a lid on things. Jack wanted to bring in the big guns and restore order fast.

When the Mayor had objected, saying the bad press would ruin them, Jack had countered with "But think of the good press you'll garner by putting an end to the crime wave. We can put a good spin on it. Say you're not afraid to do what it takes when the town is in trouble. That you're not a typical politician, worrying more about his reputation than his constituency."

Unfortunately, Dawes had remained un-swayed. Had it been any other type of problem other than a crime wave, Jack would have been more than happy to let Dawes stay the course and screw things up even more, thereby opening the door to Jack's ascension to Mayor in the next election. But in this instance it would be guilt by association for the entire town government, which would not only mean losing any chance of re-election, but probably financial devastation as well. After all, who would do business with someone they considered responsible for needless death and property destruction?

Things had been going nicely, with several of the Councilmen jumping on board with Jack's proposal, when the sound of breaking glass had disrupted the meeting.

Two minutes later, they'd learned that something far worse than drugs and gangs had invaded Rocky Point.

It was only due to sheer luck that the three of them had made it out of the conference room alive. The room had two sets of doors and the things had entered through the set nearest where Dawes traditionally sat - except he'd been standing next to Betty, reading a file over her shoulder. The other end of the long table, where Jack traditionally sat, just happened to be right by the second set of doors.

The moment Jack saw one of the intruders bite into Councilman

Gilbert's throat, he'd run for the exit, Dawes and Betty a few steps behind him. The closest hiding place had been the Mayor's office. They'd barricaded the door with Dawes's heavy mahogany desk and then called the police station for help. No one had picked up. Jack had tried the Chief's cell phone, had gotten only voice mail. Dawes had even tried calling the fire department and the morgue.

No one had answered.

It was then Jack realized they were well and truly fucked, that even he had underestimated the problem.

"We should see if they're gone," Dawes said for the dozenth time. "We haven't heard anything in hours."

Jack didn't bother answering. He wished he had a gun to shoot the Mayor right in his brainless head. True, there hadn't been noises for quite a while, but the ones they'd heard earlier - pounding, moaning, screaming - had been so awful he wasn't sure he'd ever sleep again without nightmares.

What can be going on that the police don't have time to rescue their own town leaders? It had to be bad. Very bad. Which meant their best bet was staying right where they were.

"But what if--"

"Wait!" Betty Smyrna held up her hand, cutting off the Mayor's question. "I hear something."

Jack crossed the room, joining the other two near the door. Sure enough, there was a faint noise. *Thump. Thump.*

Except it wasn't in the hall. It was above them.

"Someone's in the ceiling," Jack whispered, motioning them to be quiet.

The others looked up at more thumping and scuffling from above the acoustic tiles. Jack backed away from underneath, then paused. Where could they go? Their best bet was to stay silent and hope the things kept moving.

A light fixture rattled and Betty let out a short cry. She covered her mouth but the damage was done.

Jack added her to his mental list of idiots to shoot.

"They know we're here!" The Mayor stood up and grabbed one end of the desk and started pushing. Betty Smyrna did the same on the other end.

"No!" Jack cried, but it was too late. The door flew open so hard it knocked Dawes to the ground. The Medical Examiner and several of his staff stormed in, stinking like summer road kill, their faces the same marbled white as the corpses they worked on every day. Two more dropped from the ceiling in a snowstorm of broken tiles. One of them grabbed Betty Smyrna and tore into her with its mouth and nails, spraying blood in all directions.

Dawes screamed, his voice higher and louder than his secretary's, as the monsters fell on him like hungry dogs.

Jack jumped onto the desk, intending to leap over Betty and her attackers and out the door. For one brief moment he actually thought it might work. Then Corish grabbed him in mid-air and slammed him to the floor so hard all the air left Jack's lungs in a single breath.

Corish pinned him down. Through a haze of sparkling lights, Jack saw something long and dark reaching for him. Before he could react, a fat, icy python entered his throat, choking him. The colored lights grew brighter as he fought for oxygen.

A thousand voices spoke inside Jack's head.

The thousand became one.

The Horde opened Jack's mind and peeled away the layers as if they were nothing more than tissue paper. When it reached the memories of Marisol and Cory, it paused.

"Those. Them. They must be stopped."

In his last moments as an independent living being, Jack smiled.

It will be my pleasure.

Then Jack Smith was washed away.

* * *

John grimaced and clenched his teeth as Marisol wrapped an Ace bandage around his midsection. She'd already re-dressed his wound with fresh gauze pads and several layers of cloth bandaging.

"That's too tight," John said.

"It needs to be tight," Marisol countered, using strips of white medical tape to hold everything in place. "Otherwise it will come loose while you're being an idiot."

John made no comment about that, something Cory was grateful for. They'd already argued enough since arriving at Marisol's house. Despite their protests, John insisted on accompanying them.

When they'd disagreed, saying his injuries would be a potential hindrance, he'd reminded them that Marisol was hurt too, and she was going.

In the end they'd given in. It was impossible to deny the fact that they needed him; the numbers were already stacked against them. Plus, it seemed important somehow that as many members of the Cemetery Club as possible should be there.

Superstition? Cory wondered, as he made coffee and breakfast. *Or perhaps intuition?*

But if that was the case, did it mean Todd's absence would make their job that much harder?

Or even impossible?

Cory tried not to think too much about that possibility. Freddy Alou was on his way over. Maybe his presence would make up for Todd's. The plan was for them to hit the zombies and Shades at their source - the burial ground under the old hospital.

The doorbell rang. "That's Freddy," Marisol said. "I'll get it."

A moment later she led Freddy to the kitchen table, just as Cory set down a steaming bowl of scrambled eggs and a plate of whole wheat toast.

"Eat up," Cory said, after greeting Freddy. "It's gonna be a long day."

Freddy accepted a cup of coffee and looked around the table. "I assume that means you've made up your minds."

"Yes." Marisol passed the eggs to him. "We talked it over and it seems that our best--"

"Only," John interrupted.

"--chance," Marisol continued, "is to find their daytime hiding place and kill as many of them as we can. Todd was able to take them on by himself the last time and it kept them under control until now."

"If we can diminish their numbers enough," Cory took up the explanation, "then we'll have months or years to find a permanent solution. But at least the town will be safe in the meantime."

"Maybe there's a better way." Freddy paused to swallow some food.

"Like what?"

"Bury the *diablos* under the ground for good."

Cory nearly choked. "What? How?"

Freddy smiled. "I can get us enough explosives to bring the roof down on them. That should be safer than trying to fight them with squirt guns and baseball bats, eh *chica*?" He gave Marisol a nudge with his elbow.

"You can get explosives?" Cory asked.

"Yes. My cousin owns a small demolition company in Manhattan. Sometimes, we go into the woods and we blow something up. Great fun. Not too often. Explosives are controlled by the government and he has to account for them. But if a tiny bit goes missing, it's usually not a problem."

"How soon can you get it?" John asked.

Freddy made a show of considering the question, furrowing his brow in an exaggerated look of heavy contemplation. Then his grin returned. "Perhaps, three hours? I took the liberty of calling my cousin yesterday. He is meeting me at my house later this morning."

"Oh my God!" Marisol threw her arms around him and gave him a kiss on the cheek. "Freddy, you're the best!"

"I am *chica*. I am." He stood up. "Where will we meet?"

"Here," Cory said. "We're going to Todd's house to get the rest of the Holy water. We'll meet back here. Then we'll go right to the source."

Freddy nodded and looked at his watch. "It is almost nine now. I'll be back at noon."

"Freddy?"

"Yes?"

"Please be careful. I don't need you blowing yourself up."

"Okay *chica*. I agree. That would be a bad thing." With a laugh, he waved goodbye.

"We should get going too," John said.

Cory and Marisol nodded but no one moved. It was as if John's statement had sucked all the good feelings out of the room, and Cory knew exactly why. Going to Todd's house meant accepting his death. Or worse, that he'd become one of the things they were trying to kill. The downcast expression on John's face showed he knew the effect of his words, had, in fact, known it before he said them.

And yet he said it anyhow. In a way he was the strongest of them all. He accepted his place as the voice of gloom and doom, the person for whom the glass was always half empty. He embraced it, even to the point of voicing bad news first so the rest of them don't have to.

"You guys get ready. I'll clean up." As Cory walked past John he made it a point to give his shoulder a quick squeeze. "Thanks, man."

He didn't expect a smile in return, but John's startled look of understanding was enough to let him know he'd done the right thing. Everyone needed acknowledgement, even if they didn't want to admit it to themselves.

Standing in front of Todd's house turned out to be rather anticlimactic for Cory. In his mind he knew it had only been two days since they'd last been there but emotionally it felt as if it had been ages, as if there should have been piles of newspapers and mail outside the door and cobwebs and vines covering the entrance.

They entered through the back door and were already halfway across the kitchen before it struck Cory that something was wrong.

A radio was playing.

Marisol heard it at the same time. "I don't think zombies listen to music," she whispered.

"Follow me."

Cory led the way upstairs. He paused at the top, trying to locate the source. It seemed to originate from Todd's mother's room. He pointed at the doorway, then motioned the others to stay behind him.

Cory crept down the hall, ears and eyes alert for any sudden attacks coming from one of the other rooms. Five steps from his goal, he stopped again. From where he stood he had a clear look into the room.

Todd sat next to his mother's bed, holding her hand while the radio droned on.

Although Cory didn't make a sound, something alerted Todd to their presence and he glanced up, his frightened expression quickly changing to resigned depression.

"Oh, it's you." Todd turned back to his mother. "I suppose you've come for the Holy water. It's downstairs. Take it and anything else you need."

"Todd..." Cory's voice trailed off. He had no idea what to say.

"You're wondering how I got here. I guess insomnia has its benefits. I was staring out the window and saw the first zombies approaching the hospital. I knew we had to get away. I rolled her to the transport elevator and then we left through the ambulance bay. I was parked close to there."

"We went looking for you. John called us. He's safe at Marisol's. But we thought you..."

"We thought you were dead and eaten. Or worse." Marisol's voice held no joy at seeing Todd, only anger for his selfish actions. "You could have called. Or answered your damn phone."

"Sorry." Todd's tone indicated he wasn't. "But you know how I feel. I want nothing more to do with any of it. We just want to be left alone."

"We're going into the tunnels today," Cory said. "With explosives. Gonna bury the fuckers and then take care of any that weren't down there."

"Good luck." This time he sounded sincere. "Come see me after, if you can."

"We will." Marisol nodded to him, her face still devoid of expression. She turned and walked down the hall.

"For what it's worth, I'm sorry," Cory said. He hoped Todd understood he meant for everything, going all the way back to high school.

Todd shrugged and Cory decided it was a lost cause. He said goodbye and followed Marisol to the car.

"It's nearly eleven." Marisol pointed at the dashboard clock. "Let's get home. I don't feel safe on the streets."

Cory didn't say anything. There was no need. The destruction they'd seen on the way to Todd's was more than enough evidence that the whole town was about to collapse.

God help us if this doesn't work.

Chapter 7

Todd listened to Cory's car pull away and then put his old friends out of his mind. He looked at his mother and sighed.

"I wish I knew if you could hear me. There's so much I want to say to you, so many things I never had the chance to tell you."

He knew he could say them anyway, tell her how it was her love that had gotten him through the dark days at Wood Hill, long after he'd written his father off. How he'd hoped to repay her by taking care of her in her old age. But it seemed like a wasted effort, talking to someone who was unconscious and never going to wake up.

Todd leaned back, let his body slide down a bit in the chair. God, he was so tired. Between what had happened in the cave and then finding his mother, and then the hospital - he'd barely slept at all in the last forty-eight hours.

Can't sleep, he told himself. *Time enough for that later. I need to be here when--*

"When what Todd?"

He sprang up at the unexpected voice. Heart pounding, he glanced around the room to see who'd spoken.

They were alone.

"Todd, it's me. Your mother."

His heart went into overdrive. It was unbelievable but true. Her eyes were open and there was a smile on her dry, cracked lips.

"M...Ma? How...?" *A miracle!* There was no other way to explain it. She'd woken from her coma with no brain damage at all.

"Todd, listen to me. We need to talk." Her face grew serious.

"I know. There's so much I want to--"

"Hush. I'm well aware of how you feel about me and how you wish things had been different. You've always been a good son. Your father and I never forgot that."

"Father?" Todd frowned. "But...but I thought he hated me. He never visited. Never wrote."

Mrs. Randolph nodded. "And it wasn't for lack of trying on my part. But your father was hard man Todd. A good man - like you - but a hard one. When you had your troubles, he buried his feelings down deep so they wouldn't cripple him. He'd have been a wreck otherwise. But he read all your letters and he sat next to me when I wrote to you. Always said to give you his love."

Todd brushed away a stray tear. "I thought...I figured you just said that to make me feel better. I never believed it."

"Well, now you know. He knew you were innocent of what they accused you of. We both did."

"We did something bad," Todd said. "We brought something back that should have stayed buried."

"The Shadows. Your father's family had a long history of dealing with them. That's why I'm talking to you now. It's the last time I'm gonna be able to, so I need you to listen close."

"Last time? What do you--"

"Darn it Todd! I said listen. You've got important things to do. Your friends, they mean well but they're going about it all wrong. There's only one way to get rid of those things for good. You got to go into the old church. Your father's office. Behind the desk, inside the wall. You'll find everything you need."

"No!" Todd surprised himself with his vehemence. "I'm not leaving you. Not now, not when you just came back."

She placed a hand on his arm. Her skin was colder than human flesh should be, cold as winter ice in the river.

"Todd, my time here is done. I'm off to a better place. Your father is waiting." She leaned forward, placed a soft, frigid kiss on his cheek. "I'll tell him you said hello. He'll be so proud."

With a smile, she closed her eyes and lay back against her pillow.

"Ma!" Tears blurred Todd's vision. When he wiped them away, she was still as stone, as if she'd never woken up.

Had she? Todd looked at his watch. Only a few minutes had passed since Cory left. Had he fallen asleep? Dreamed it all? Had he failed her again, not been there when she left the world of the living?

He felt ready to cry and then he noticed something. On his arm, the one she'd touched with her cold fingers, were four perfect ovals of white.

They matched her fingertips exactly.

Lord help me, it was a miracle, just not the kind I'd thought. Asleep or not, God had let his mother deliver a final message to him.

And this time he wouldn't let her down.

He placed a final kiss on her forehead and headed for the church.

* * *

"It may not look like much but it's more than enough to do the trick."

The four of them - Marisol, Cory, John and Freddy - were at Marisol's kitchen table, looking at the package Freddy had brought over. The two red-colored sticks, hardly larger than the emergency road flares in Cory's trunk, didn't seem capable of the type of destruction they were looking for.

"Trust me," Freddy continued, seeing their skeptical looks. "this is gonna blow them to hell. There won't be nothing left but zombie fertilizer."

Cory stared at the two unimposing sticks another moment and then snapped his fingers as a dormant memory returned. "Explosives! Todd had that M80 with him in the tunnel. He dipped it in Holy water, said it was his holy hand grenade. That must have been the explosion we heard, the one that caused the cave in."

"So we know burying them will stop them, at least temporarily," John said.

"Do you know how to find the burial ground?" Freddy asked. He was sprinkling Holy water on the dynamite as he spoke.

"Sort of. We'll go in through the main doors and then head down to the basement. From there, we find the tunnel that leads to the old building."

On the table, flashlights and squirt rifles were stacked in piles. As Cory started to divvy them up, a loud thumping noise, followed by an equally loud crash, came from the front porch.

"What the hell's that?" John asked.

Marisol moved towards the door, but Cory stopped her. "Hold it." He picked up one of the squirt guns and grabbed a long knife from the rack. "Wait here."

Cory slowly made his way to the door. When there were no

further sounds, he opened it just enough so he could see out.

The porch was empty. But something had knocked over one of Marisol's flower pots.

Turning back towards the others, Cory said, "There's nothing--"

Five figures came crashing through the sliding doors in Marisol's kitchen. Glass flew in all directions as the intruders immediately attacked. For a split second, Cory froze, unable to believe his eyes.

Is that the Mayor? And Marisol's ex-husband? What the hell are they doing?

Then he caught sight of their dead eyes and pale skin and understood all too well what had happened.

Jack Smith separated himself from the tangle of bodies and grabbed Marisol. She screamed and kicked but he didn't let go. That was enough to get Cory moving again. He charged forward with the knife, slammed the blade right into the Deputy Mayor's chest.

Smith didn't flinch.

Before Cory could do anything else, one of the other zombies hit him from the side, knocking him into a set of cabinets. His head struck one of the brass knobs and the room exploded into a myriad of colored lights. When his vision cleared, the zombies were gone and so was Marisol.

"Marisol!" Cory got up, fought through a dizzy spell, and then ran to the back doors. There was no sign of the attackers. Returning to the kitchen, he helped John to his feet.

"You okay?"

"Yeah." John had a bruise forming on his cheek but otherwise seemed fine. "All they did was knock me down. I thought one of them was gonna bite me but then it ran away."

"Same with me. But they took Marisol with them."

"Did you see who it was?" John asked. From his tone, he'd recognized the assailants as well.

"Yeah. Jack fucking Smith. Maybe fresh zombies still retain memories of their old selves and he wanted revenge."

John put a hand on Cory's shoulder. "We know where they probably took her. Let's stick to the plan. Is Freddy hurt?"

"I don't know."

They found the Town Clerk on the other side of the counter, lying in a pool of blood, his neck torn open.

"Dammit." Cory slammed his palm on the counter. "That just leaves the two of us."

Before John could say anything, the phone rang. Although he had no intention of answering it, Cory's hand was already moving towards the phone. When he saw the number on the caller ID, he clicked the talk button.

"Todd?"

"I've found the answer Cory! I know how to stop the Shades for good!"

"The zombies have Marisol. They just took her." The words were out of Cory's mouth before he even knew what he was going to say. It struck him that Marisol's abduction had left him in a kind of shock.

Todd paused before speaking again. "I'm sorry. But if you want to stop them, and maybe get Marisol back, get over to my father's church as fast as you can."

"Screw that. We're gonna blow the fuckers up."

"That won't work. But I know what will. Hurry!"

The line went dead.

"That was Todd?" John asked.

Cory nodded. "He said he's discovered how to get rid of the Shades for good."

"He doesn't think the explosives will work."

From his statement, Cory couldn't tell if John had overheard or just guessed.

"That's what he says. But I don't have time to waste. I've got to find Marisol."

"Cory." John looked like he'd swallowed rotten meat. "We don't know if she's alive or not. Or one of those things. But our best bet for saving her is to use our brains and not just rush into things. What if Todd really does have the answer?"

Cory felt like he was being torn apart. He knew what he wanted to do but also what made more sense.

"I don't know..."

"I trust Todd. Do you?"

Although John didn't say he was planning on going to Todd's, Cory understood it. Understood it meant if he wanted to go after Marisol, he'd be doing it alone.

Goddammit!

There was no avoiding it. "All right. We'll go to the church. But we can't dick around all day. We need to move fast, before it's too late."

On the way to the car, Cory said a quick prayer.

Hang in there Marisol. We're coming.

Please don't be dead.

When they arrived at the church, Todd was waiting at the front door. The day was turning out to be one of the hottest in weeks and Todd's sweating face, combined with his pale skin and the dark circles under his eyes, made him look feverishly ill.

They followed him into his father's office. The old desk had been pushed to one side and a section of mildewed wall paneling pried off, revealing what appeared to be a hidden storage area. All the papers and books that had previously been on the desk were now on the floor, replaced by new stacks of books and papers that looked just as old and rotten.

"What the hell is all this?" Cory asked. "How did you find it?"

"My--" Todd paused, grimaced, then continued. "I fell asleep earlier. After my mother...passed. And I had a dream."

"Jesus, Todd. I'm sorry. Is there--"

"No." Todd cut Cory off. "I'll take care of things later. It's the dream that's important. I remembered something in it, something my mother once said about my father having a special hiding place in his office."

Although it wasn't obvious, there was something about Todd - his expression, his body language - that told Cory he was lying. A veteran of many court rooms, Cory trusted his instincts but couldn't figure out what part of Todd's story wasn't true. Not that it mattered. What did matter was what he'd found.

"What is this stuff?"

"My father knew how to get rid the Shades. Apparently, my family has a long history of dealing with them."

"All our families do," John said. He quickly filled Todd in on what Freddy Alou had told them.

"Interesting."

"Forget interesting." Cory felt like shaking them both. "How do we kill them?"

Todd shook his head. "We don't. There are far too many of them."

"You said you had the answer!" Cory practically shouted.

"I do. Right here." Todd picked up one of the books from the desk. "We don't kill them. We send them on to where they need to be."

Cory thought his head might explode. Some of his frustration must have shown on his face, because Todd took a step back and John placed a hand on his arm. "Easy. Let him explain."

"We don't have time for explanations. They've got Marisol. Every minute we stand here talking is a minute wasted."

John started to say something else but Todd stopped him.

"It's all right. I can explain while we walk."

"Walk where?"

"To the old burial ground. You had the right idea but the wrong tools. Luckily, my father left us everything we need." Todd lifted up a canvas bag from next to the desk.

"Let's go."

"The information you found in our research held part of the answer but not everything." Todd was speaking rapidly as they walked through the woods to Wood Hill Sanitarium. "Killing the zombies just releases the Shade inhabiting it, enabling it to possess someone else. Using Holy water on a Shade destroys it but there are probably hundreds of them by now, far too many for us to handle. What we need to do is cleanse the ground where the Shades have been living."

"Freddy said that burying them would trap them, just like you did the last time."

"He was wrong," Todd said to John. "I got lucky. The Holy water in the firecracker...it acted like a shotgun. Killed a lot of them. But there weren't as many back then. They're too strong now. We have to rid the area of all corruptive energy once and for all. A total cleansing."

"Can we do it?"

"My father believed so."

"So how come no one ever tried it before?"

Todd shrugged. "They thought what they'd done had worked. My father had intended to do this but after I...well, things went back to normal after what I did, so he waited to see if they returned. Then he died."

"And that's all there is to it?" Cory asked. "Just bless the ground?"

"No. We'll have to kill some of them. And we'll need to remain positive in our thinking, trust in ourselves. That's just as important as

Holy water or blessings. The idea is to counter-act the negative energies, not let our fear get the better of us."

"Easier said than done," John muttered. His words put a frightening thought in Cory's mind.

John's already the most negative person we know. Does that mean he'll be the first of us to get taken over? And what about Marisol? She was normally pretty positive about life but she had to be terrified. Would that make her more susceptible to being possessed?

On the heels of that came another thought, one he'd been avoiding ever since the attack at Marisol's house.

Will I be strong enough to kill her if she's already one of them?

Chapter 8

Marisol woke to the sound of her ex-husband's voice.

"You...look...good enough...to eat."

Opening her eyes, she fought to control the scream that wanted to burst from her mouth. In the pale light coming from an unknown source, she saw her ex-husband's slack, dead face leering down at her.

Oh god. The attack in the kitchen. It was real. She remembered some of it, right up to the point where something very hard had hit the back of her head. But she'd been sure she'd hallucinated seeing Jack and Mayor Dawes bursting through the glass doors.

"Not...eat...wife."

He knows who I am. But there was something wrong with Jack's voice. The way he was speaking. As if...

As if his brain was dying more slowly than his body. Was that how it happened? Was that why some could talk and others couldn't?

Jack leaned closer, bringing the foul stench of death to her nose. His cold, lifeless hand gripped her jaw. She tried to resist but he stuck fingers in her mouth. She bit down and the rancid taste of blood and rotten meat washed over her tongue, making her gag. That allowed him to slip his whole hand in and pry her jaw open.

Something moved in the darkness next to him and she realized what was happening.

He wanted to make her into one of *them.*

This time, the scream burst out with the force of a runaway train. Long and loud, it didn't stop until she ran out of air.

By then the entity was moving towards her, a twisting ribbon of charcoal gray that radiated arctic cold.

Marisol did the only thing she could think of.

She closed her mouth as hard as she could, her teeth cutting through flesh and bone. At the same time, she kicked out with both feet, catching Jack in the groin.

Although he made no sound, Jack tumbled to the side from the force of her kick. Marisol spat out the two fingers she'd bitten off and got to her feet just as Jack sat up. She kicked him again, catching him right under the jaw.

There was a loud *crack!* and he fell over.

With his head hanging at an unnatural angle.

Marisol turned and started running. She had no idea where she was but it didn't matter. She just had to get away. She'd only taken six or seven steps when more zombies emerged from another room.

Marisol cried out and swung her fists as the walking corpses grabbed her. She tried kicking them. None of it did any good. Then, in the midst of her terror, she remembered what Cory had said about the Shades.

"Let go of fear and think positive thoughts. Visualize a holy light around you, a light that denies access to your person by evil beings."

Could she do it? Everything in her said *fight.* Except her fear would only make the monsters stronger. It came down to trust. She had to trust Cory. He had believed those words he'd read.

She closed her eyes and tried to think of positive things, good things. Cory's face appeared, and she pictured him holding her, his arms protecting her from all dangers. She imagined a circle of light around them, like a force field from a science fiction story. In her mind, Cory was telling her how much he loved her and she laughed and said she loved him too. He stroked a finger across her chin and kissed her. Inside their circle, everything was perfect.

Safe.

In the real world, cold, dead hands gripped her jaw.

Even though the lights were off and the corridors filled with abandoned furniture and papers, Wood Hill was still as familiar to Todd as the hallways of his own house.

The stagnant air smelled of mildew and dust but beneath that Todd still caught whiffs of more familiar odors. Pine-scented cleaner. The heavy cologne the Haitian orderlies had favored. The scent of baking cookies emanating from the kitchen. Or maybe those were just memories, so strong they'd taken physical form.

They'd arrived prepared to break into the building, either through a door or window, only to find the back entrance already open. A way for the zombies to get in and out? Vandals looking for drugs? Either way, it put them on guard to possible danger. Todd still wasn't sure what to do if that danger actually presented itself. They were armed for both supernatural and physical threats - Holy water for the Shades and tire irons for the zombies - but the whole concept of fighting went against the strategy of not emitting any negative energy.

Yet they couldn't stand motionless and let themselves get possessed or eaten.

We'll work it out if and when it becomes necessary, Todd had thought, as he stepped through the door.

So far, it hadn't been necessary.

They'd gone half the length of the building without seeing or hearing anything. By the time they reached the staircase that would bring them to the sub-basement, Todd was beginning to feel some confidence returning. The open door had most likely been from vandals. They might even actually make it all the way to the burial pit without problems.

"Are you sure this is the right staircase?" Cory asked, his whispered words unnaturally loud in the silence of the empty building. Below them, the staircase wound down into total blackness.

"Yes. It's three floors down to the engineering level. From there we'll have to search for the tunnels but they shouldn't be hard to find. I imagine all the police tape is still up."

"Okay. Are we ready?" Cory looked at Todd and John.

A woman's scream answered them from somewhere down in the darkness.

* * *

Cory's cry of "Marisol!" was still echoing in the stairwell as he pushed past John and Todd and bounded down the stairs. Shouting for him to wait, they followed, the pounding of their shoes on the stairs combining with his to create artificial thunder so loud it hurt his ears. The stairs vibrated underneath their feet and the jerking, strobe-like beams of their flashlights turned the staircase into a surprise carnival ride.

Cory knew he was letting his emotions overrule good sense but he didn't slow down. Although he'd desperately wanted to find Marisol alive, he'd also had his doubts. Why would the zombies or Shades treat her different from all the other people they'd killed? In his mind, he'd half-accepted it was too late.

But when he'd heard her scream, it meant that not only was she still alive, she was in trouble. You didn't scream like that unless things were desperate.

He took the stairs two at a time, bouncing off the walls and railing, barely in control of his descent. At the bottom, he hit the metal door with his hip and shoulder and burst into another dark cavern.

Only then did he stop.

"Todd, which way?" he shouted, as the other two joined him.

"Hang on." They cast their flashlights around, exposing glimpses of green and silver-colored pipes, giant-sized machinery and control panels covered in dust and grime. The room extended as far as their lights could penetrate in both directions, with no hint of how much further they went.

Todd pulled a compass out of his pocket and shined his light on it. "That way." He pointed to their left.

"Are you sure?"

"Yes. The old building lays to the west. It--"

Cory didn't wait to hear the rest. He took off at a fast walk, the best he could do with the only the flashlight to see by. As much as he wanted to sprint down the corridor, hitting his head on a pipe or falling into an unseen hole wasn't going to help him rescue Marisol. Random images stuck in his mind as he kept an eye on his footing. Rusty pipes as big around as his waist running parallel and vertical in the wide expanse. Sluice grates on the floor, indicating the presence of sewer drains beneath them. Chains hung in a seemingly random fashion, the action of his light giving them the illusion of movement.

Wait, they really are moving--

The zombie barreled into him like a runaway bulldozer, its shoulder striking him in the ribs and knocking him to the cement. His breath exploded from his lungs and his flashlight and crowbar went skidding across the floor. Doubled over and fighting to breathe, Cory tried to roll away from his attacker. Hands gripped him and he prepared himself for the bite that was sure to follow. Then lights appeared and someone shouted. A second later, John and Todd joined the fight, driving the zombie away with their weapons.

Cory got to his knees, sucking in air and trying to clear his head. In the strobing flickers from the flashlights, he saw more zombies emerging from the darkness.

"Look out!" he wheezed, using the little breath he'd regained. Forcing himself to his feet, he staggered forward, gaining strength and balance with each step. He paused just long enough to grab his flashlight and then smashed it into the face of a zombie that was about to bite Todd's neck. The blow forced it back a step, allowing Todd to slip away. The monster staggered towards Cory, who removed a long knife from his backpack and stabbed the corpse in the neck. The triangular blade slid through skin and muscle like it was cutting bread. Using a sawing motion, Cory worked the blade to the side, parting flesh and tendons until the head fell back, half-separated from the neck.

The zombie fell to the floor and Cory turned his attention to the macabre scene surrounding him. Bodies turned and twisted, caught in random flashes of light. Voices shouted, letting him know John and Todd were still fighting, but he had no way of discerning between his friends and their dead attackers.

Suddenly a blinding beam filled the room, causing Cory to cover his eyes. The light moved closer and then past him, revealing a single man carrying two industrial-sized lamps, like the ones often mounted on police cars.

"Chief Travers?" Cory asked, recognizing the man's silhouette.

"Thought you might need some help. Been keeping my eye on you, followed you down here." Travers handed Cory a pistol. "Can you use that?"

"With pleasure." He turned towards the fight. "John! Todd! Hit the deck!"

Two figures abruptly fell to the floor and Cory aimed at one of the standing shapes. He pulled the trigger and the figure's head jerked to one side, its shape no longer oval but something more like a broken egg.

Next to him, Travers fired and another zombie went down. Then they were both shooting as fast as they could aim, the reports of the two pistols creating a deafening thunder that echoed back and forth off cement and steel until Cory thought his head might explode. Smoke and dust formed three-dimensional shapes in the beams of light, twisting and intertwining.

It took Cory several moments to realize he'd emptied the gun but was still pulling the trigger. He turned to Chief Travers, saw the man's mouth move but couldn't hear him. He shrugged, tapped his ear. Travers nodded and pointed at the ground, and Cory understood they needed to see if Todd and John were okay.

They went to their knees and crawled forward. The fallen bodies of the zombies were extra pale in the spotlights and Cory kept thinking he saw movements. Without warning, a hand lunged at him, grabbed his arm. Cory screamed and slapped it away. A second hand joined it and he took the empty gun and slammed it down, smashing the grip onto the attacking digits. A muffled cry of pain reached him just as he was about to swing the gun again.

"John?" Cory shoved the gun in his pocket and gripped the his friend below the wrists. Pulling with all his might while pushing backwards with his feet, he slid John's body out from under the two dead zombies that had covered it.

"Are you okay?"

John nodded. "Yeah. Felt like I was gonna suffocate for a minute.

Where's Todd?"

"Over here." Travers waved to them. "I'll have him free in a second."

Once Todd was standing and had reassured them he wasn't injured, Cory turned to Travers.

"We have to keep going. They've got Marisol down here, we heard her a little while ago."

Travers nodded. "Here." He handed Cory another clip for the pistol. "Lead the way. I'll take the rear."

They didn't have to go far. Two minutes of walking brought them to an area where the machinery was spaced out more than in the previous sections. In the center of the space two zombies held a struggling Marisol on the ground. Deputy Mayor Jack Smith knelt on her chest, his head at a weird angle. A black, stringy shape hovered in front of her face, smoky tendrils poking at her nose and mouth.

"No!" Cory raised the gun, took aim at Smith's head. Marisol turned and looked at him, tried to scream. Cory saw some of the tendrils slide between her lips.

He pulled the trigger.

Jack's body flew backwards, a large chunk of its skull missing. At the same time, Todd rushed forward and sprayed Holy water on the Shade that was violating Marisol. As soon as the liquid hit it, it exploded into white flames. The other two zombies - one of them Mayor Dawes - stood up and Cory put a bullet into each of their heads.

"Marisol!" He grabbed her by the shoulders. Her face was ashen gray, her eyes closed. He put two fingers against her neck, afraid of what he might find. Or not find.

A pulse! Rapid but strong.

"She's alive," he called to the others but his words were drowned out by the sound of Travers's gun firing.

"Dammit, it's a trap!" Travers moved closer to them, handed them the portable spotlights. "Keep moving. I'll hold them off."

"Cory, can you carry her and shoot a gun at the same time?" John asked.

"I can walk." Marisol's words were barely more than a whisper but Cory heard them.

"Jesus! Thank God you're all right." He leaned down to kiss her but she pushed him away.

"No time for that now. We've got to get out of here."

"Are you sure you're okay?" Todd asked. Cory mirrored his words. Some of her color had come back but she still looked more ready for a hospital bed than a long walk.

"Help me up." She held out her arms and Todd and Cory each grabbed one, hauled her to her feet. Her skin felt clammy and cold, and Cory was about to renew his objections when Travers shouted to them.

"Let's get a move on. There's more of those things coming."

"You heard the man." Marisol attempted a smile.

"Fine. But hang on to me. I don't want you passing out again down here."

She nodded and placed a frigid hand on Cory's arm, the one not aiming a gun. Together they followed John and Todd further into the building.

At one point the corridor narrowed as large banks of machines closed in from both sides, forcing them to slow their pace and allowing Travers to catch up.

"Don't stop now. They're still coming. Almost like they're--"

"Herding us into a trap?" Todd asked, as he emerged from the narrow space.

Up ahead, the basement came to an end in a cement wall.

A cement wall with a roughly man-sized opening.

"That must be the tunnel to the burial pits." John's words came out in gasps and Cory felt a momentary pang of guilt. In all the excitement, he'd forgotten John's injuries.

No matter. Plenty of time to rest and heal later. If we survive.

"How far?" Cory asked.

"I don't know." Todd sounded apologetic. "A hundred yards, maybe? It depends where under the old buildings the pit is."

"Okay. This is it then. Todd, any last advice?"

"Think positive. According to my father's notes, you can actually prevent a Shade from entering you. He called it using God's love as a shield."

"I tried that," Marisol said. "I think it's the only reason I was able to hold them off until you found me."

"I'd rather have a real shield," John said. "The only thing I'm positive of is that we're idiots for being here."

Cory was about to chide John for his pessimism when it hit him that for all of John's complaining, he'd never once backed down from any dangers.

He's got his own shields but down deep he believes we're doing the right thing. He considered calling John on it, then decided to let the man maintain his pretenses.

Whatever gets you through the night...

For Cory, that meant keeping a picture of Marisol in his mind as he took the lead and stepped into the tunnel. He had to keep believing they were going to make it back alive. He'd never realized how lonely his life had been until he found out what he'd been missing.

Sure, there'd been women before her, but nothing serious; almost as if Fate had intended for he and Marisol to reunite someday. He refused to believe Fate would be so cruel as to take her away a second time.

They'd only gone a few hundred feet when the tunnel widened into a large, open space. At the same time, a horrible odor struck them, a stink so bad Cory had to hold his arm over his nose.

"This is it," Todd said, just as Cory caught sight of the pit in front of them.

They passed their lights over it, exposing a shallow hole that looked to be roughly fifteen feet in diameter and six feet deep. The vile stench emanated from the body parts and skeletal remains piled at the bottom. Too fresh and odorous to be any of the pit's original victims, Cory figured they must be townspeople who'd been dragged down here and eaten by the zombie things.

"Over there," John whispered, gesturing with his flashlight. Cory followed the beam, saw another tunnel on the other side of the pit.

"That must lead up to the old hospital," Todd said.

As he said the words, Cory caught a glimpse of movement in the other tunnel. Movement that quickly resolved into distinct shapes.

"Zombies," John said.

"And more behind us," added Travers, joining them. "We need to move away from this tunnel."

"And go where?" John asked.

"Partway around the pit," Cory said. "Travers and I can each take a side and keep them away with the guns while you and Todd bless the pit. Maybe that will send them on to wherever they go."

"Or leave us in the middle of a monster sandwich." John motioned with his hand. "After you."

Cory tugged at Marisol's sleeve. She seemed out of it again, her eyes glassy and sweat beading up on her forehead. In any other situation, he'd have focused all his attention on her. Right now though, they didn't have time. As long as she could stand and walk, all he could do was make sure she didn't get separated from them.

"C'mon, stay close," he said. She looked at him and for a moment he was afraid she didn't even recognize him. Then she nodded and took a step.

Not great but good enough.

Cory led them to an area roughly halfway around the pit. The path around the bodies and bones was twice as wide as an ordinary sidewalk, giving them plenty of room to walk without falling in. As a potential battleground against an army of the undead though, it left a lot to be desired. Roots and rocks stuck up from the soft earth and uneven wall negated some of the width. Add to that the darkness and the abominable stench that made breathing a hardship, and it left Cory feeling they'd have been better off in the basement.

They took up positions with Cory facing the zombies emerging from the second tunnel and Travers facing back the way they'd come. Between them, Todd already had his Holy water and Bible ready. John held a Super Soaker filled with Holy water, prepared to take on any Shades that might appear.

Marisol had sunk to her knees, her hands over her eyes.

"Get ready," Travers said. Cory didn't respond; he already had his pistol aimed at the nearest zombie of the several dozen he could see, a middle-aged man dressed in the remains of a business suit.

"In the name of the Father, the Son and the Holy Spirit, I bless this ground." Todd sprayed Holy water into the pit and then tossed down a handful of Communion wafers. "In the name of the Father, the Son and the Holy--"

The roar of Travers' gun drowned out the rest of Todd's words. At the same time, Marisol screamed.

The barrage of sounds was like a signal to the zombies. They charged forward, running towards Cory three abreast. Behind the leaders the others fought for position, several of them tripping or getting pushed into the pit, where they crashed into the skeletons of their own depraved meals. Many of the approaching bodies were silent but enough of them moaned or growled to fill the cavern with noise.

Cory pulled the trigger and the office worker went down. The others took no notice. He fired again and again, choosing his targets carefully. Bodies fell, creating obstacles for the others. For a brief moment, Cory thought things might finally be going their way.

Then the gun clicked empty.

"Travers! I need more bullets!"

"--bless this ground...In the name of the Father--" Todd continued his recital.

"Here!" The Police Chief tossed something backhand without looking. The object hit the dirt near Todd's feet.

Shit! Cory backed away and went down on his hands and knees, never taking his eyes off the approaching zombies. With one hand, he felt around on the dirt behind him.

Just then John screamed and Cory felt something wet spray across the back of his neck. He risked a quick glance to the side and then wished he hadn't.

Rising from the pit were several Shades. John was furiously pumping the squirt rifle and firing at them. The Holy water kept falling just short and Todd interrupted his ongoing blessing to shout at John to wait until they got closer. Cory located the clips, three of them, and grabbed them all. Slamming one into the gun, he turned his attention back to the zombies, several of which were almost within arm's length. He raised the pistol and prepared to shoot.

And the whole world exploded around him.

Blinding bright light burned away the darkness from one end of the cavern to the other. There was no sound but the ground vibrated underneath their feet.

The light disappeared, leaving Cory's eyes filled with purple after-images. He backed up again, afraid one of the zombies would reach him before his vision cleared. He blinked away tears and when he opened his eyes again, he was able to see.

The zombies were still the same distance away as before the flash of light.

"Whatever you did, do it again!" shouted Travers. "It stopped them in their tracks."

John let loose another stream of Holy water, catching three of the Shades and turning them into balls of white light that illuminated the entire chamber.

"Take that, you bastards!" he shouted.

Seeing the effect of the Holy water, Cory didn't waste any time. He shoved the pistol into his belt and pulled his own squirt gun, a slightly smaller model, out of his back pack. Stepping right to the edge of the pit, where dozens of Shades hovered over the dead, rotting bodies, he blasted one of the Shades into white fire. Nearby, Todd took out his water gun and began squirting as well.

"Mine doesn't reach."

"So let's charge the mother fuckers!" Cory put action to words, stepping off the lip and into the pit, flashlight in one hand and squirt gun in the other. His feet slid and slipped as he waded through the rotten flesh but he kept his eyes on the Shades, aiming and shooting any time he got close to one. John joined him, waving his more powerful toy gun back and forth like a flamethrower. The Shades exploded and emitted light so frequently that flashlights were useless. Todd began his cleansing prayer again as he waded through, spraying Holy water and tossing Communion wafers onto the bodies and ground in an ever-widening circle.

Cory's eyes burned from the constant bursts of light. He struggled to see through the colored spots that clouded his vision but he kept pulling the trigger. The sound of Travers' gun - the shots less frequent, more spaced out - told him the Chief was still picking off zombies. At one point the sound changed and Cory wondered if his hearing was screwed up from all the loud noise or if Travers had switched guns.

Something dark appeared from Cory's right side and he tried to bring his squirt rifle around but it was too late. Icy cold tendrils slithered over his arms and neck, freezing him in place.

Think positive thoughts! He tried but it was impossible with the alien visage of the Shade right in front of him. The lava-red eyes grew larger as the thing's face drew closer. He clamped his lips shut and tried to turn his head but his neck refused to obey.

Then a supernova exploded in his brain. Everything turned pure white, a light so intense it actually sent arrows of pain through his skull, worse than any hangover he'd ever had. At the same time, the cold disappeared, replaced by a feeling of pure joy, a moment where he *knew* something better existed beyond this life.

The elation ended as quickly as it had come but it left Cory with a renewed sense of purpose. Blinking away tears, he opened his eyes and found himself on his back in the fetid remains of the dead bodies. Saw John standing next to him, still firing his squirt gun like a madman.

This ends now.

He climbed to his feet and stomped through the grisly graveyard towards the nearest Shades.

"I'm not afraid of you anymore!" he shouted. "You need to leave this place. You don't belong here." With each sentence, he sent more Holy water flying, aiming carefully each time. Then an idea came to him. He started repeating Todd's prayer as he fired on the shadowy creatures.

"In the name of the Father, the Son and the Holy Spirit, I bless this ground. In the name of the Father, the Son and the Holy Spirit, I--"

"Bless this ground!" John, a manic smile on his face, joined in. Together, they marched further into the pit, Shades exploding so often the cavern took on the appearance of a silent fireworks display. Travers' random gunfire added thunder to the light show.

By the time they reached the other side, they were covered in gore and their voices were hoarse from shouting.

Not a single Shade remained.

"We did it!" Cory cried, gripping John's shoulder.

"Not yet," Todd said, coming up from behind them. "There might be other caverns to bless. We have to go all the way through to the old hospital to make sure."

"Um, guys? Problem." John pointed at the remaining zombies, who had started moving forward again.

"Not anymore. Watch our backs." Cory moved back towards the center of the pit, raised his pistol, and shot one of the zombies in the head. Up on the ledge, Travers was shooting again as well, this time with a chrome-plated revolver.

Unlike before, the undead people no longer moved in unison or with any sign of intelligence in their actions. Cory found it almost too easy to pick them off one by one, and by the time his second clip ran out, there were no more on his side left standing.

"Are we ready to get this over and done with?" John lifted his squirt rifle and gestured towards the far tunnel.

"Wait. There's something I need to do first." Cory carefully made his way back to the edge of the pit, where Travers was taking aim at the last handful of zombies standing near the first tunnel's entrance.

"Travers."

"I heard. Go do what you have to do."

"Can you get Marisol out of here?"

The Police Chief nodded. "As soon as I blow these fuckers to Hell, I'll bring her to Town Hall. We'll be waiting for you there."

"Thank you." Cory still didn't like the man, was pretty sure Travers didn't like him either, but he also knew they owed the Chief a debt they could never repay. Without him, they'd have ended up zombie food or worse. He hoped the Chief understood his gratitude was for more than just helping Marisol.

John tugged at his sleeve. "Let's go. She'll be fine."

Cory wasn't so sure. Marisol was curled up in the fetal position. She was either gasping for air or sobbing, he couldn't tell. But he couldn't stay. They had to put an end to the Shades or none of them would ever be fine.

As much as he hated doing it, Cory followed John and Todd across the pit to the other tunnel. He kept his pistol at the ready as they neared the entrance but no more zombies were waiting for them.

Then they were in darkness again, leaving Travers his lights and Marisol at the mercy of the creatures.

He prayed they were doing the right thing.

Chapter 9

Pain! The Horde felt itself breaking apart, each destruction a separate agony that all of them experienced.

Run! Attack! Hide! what do we do what do we do What do.... We go where? Attack which ones?

The confusion of thoughts jumped among them. With numbers too few to retain cohesiveness, the Horde devolved into individuals again, many of whom let go of their anger and pain and finally allowed themselves to leave the darkness behind and move on. The others retreated back to where they'd been born, the places of the Dead and Tortured. Those inhabiting human shells tried to attack the human holding the gun but without the ability to think as One they found themselves unable to carry out any focused actions. Instead, bullets put an end to the semi-living bodies, releasing more of the Horde - which quickly joined their brethren in one form of escape or another.

All except one and that one made sure to keep itself hidden from the humans.

* * *

It took Cory, John and Todd less than two hours to make their way through the tunnel and the basement of the old hospital. Along the way, they stopped to consecrate two more mass graves.

Although they killed several handfuls of Shades, they saw no more zombies.

When they returned to the first cavern, Marisol and Travers were gone and all the zombies dead. They hurried back through the asylum's basement and then headed to Gates of Heaven Cemetery, where Todd proceeded to cleanse and bless Grover Lillian's crypt and the smaller mass grave beneath it.

"That should be the end of it," Todd said, as the others helped him out of the tunnel. "God, I think I'll go to bed and sleep for a week."

For a moment none of them said anything, just stood and looked at each other. Cory wondered if the others were feeling the same mix of exhaustion, relief and sense of accomplishment as he was. They'd been through Hell together and they looked it. Dirt, spoiled body fluids and corpse slime covered them, mixing in with their own sweat to create a horrible mess. Their clothes were torn. Stinking pieces of flesh stuck to their hair and bodies. Eyes peered out from grime-covered faces, making the three of them look like coal miners emerging from a collapsed shaft.

Although he couldn't tell because of the putrid odors still wafting up from the tunnel, Cory imagined they all smelled as bad - if not worse - than they looked.

Mirroring his thoughts, John said, "I need a shower. Followed by another shower."

"Me too," Cory said. "But first I have to find Marisol. She might need to go to the hospital."

"We'll go with you." Todd bent down and picked up his pack.

"You don't have to," Cory said.

"No, we stick together. You were both there for us when we were in trouble, now we'll be there for Marisol."

Cory thanked them. Even though he felt a bit guilty about their postponing their much-needed showers and sleep, he was grateful for their presence. In truth, he was so exhausted he wasn't sure he could drive into town without falling asleep behind the wheel.

They emerged from the crypt to find only seven hours had passed since they entered the hospital, which surprised Cory. It seemed like a lifetime. He climbed into his car without a second thought for the upholstery, even though he knew no amount of detailing would ever get the smell out. He figured a ruined car was a small price to pay for their having survived.

When they arrived at Town Hall the lights were on and the front door hung half off the hinges. Cory let out a startled gasp as he pulled over but Todd cautioned him not to over-react.

"Don't forget Jack and the Mayor. This might be where they were attacked. It doesn't mean Marisol's not safe."

Cory nodded but he still took his pistol from his belt. He noticed Todd and John had their water rifles out as well. They went up the steps slowly, alert for any dangers.

Movement caught Cory's eye and he turned, already bringing the pistol up as the figure spoke.

"Miles? Is that you?" Travers's voice. The shadowy figure moved again, raising its arms into a shooting position.

"It's us Chief. We're okay. And I think the...the problem is over."

"Jesus, I hope so." Travers lowered his gun and stepped into the light. "After you left that cave, all the...all those *things* suddenly stopped moving. Just stood there as I shot them. When I was done, I got your girl up and walking and we went back to my car. Drove here. I put her on the couch in the waiting room and I've been watching her ever since."

"She's okay?" Cory tried to see around him.

"Yeah. Asleep or passed out, I can't tell. C'mon. And then I want some answers."

"We've got answers but you might not believe them," John said. said "I'm still not sure I do."

Marisol lay on a well-worn, fake-leather office sofa that screamed Ikea. She had her head down and her arms wrapped around herself, even though the temperature in the office had to be in the eighties, thanks to the broken door.

Cory knelt down beside her and placed a hand on her shoulder.

"Marisol? Hey, honey, you awake?"

Faster than he imagined possible, she sprang up and slammed both hands into Cory's chest, sending him hard into a coffee table. Magazines flew into the air and both the table and Cory slid across the floor until they crashed against the opposite wall.

Without pausing, Marisol leaped from the couch onto Chief Travers and sank her teeth into the side of his neck. Blood sprayed out in two distinct arcs, one splattering across Todd's face and chest and the other decorating the door to the County Clerk's office.

Travers let out a scream that turned into a bubbling whistle as Marisol pulled her head away, taking a huge piece of his neck with it. Inside the gaping hole, Travers' shredded windpipe emitted frothy red bubbles with each breath he tried to take.

Marisol let go of his body and it fell to the floor, where it twitched and jerked as his brain struggled for oxygen.

With an animal growl, Marisol ran past John and Todd and into the main hallway.

"Hurry!" Cory fought his way free from the magazines and stood up. "We can't let her get away."

"What about...?" Todd pointed at Chief Travers, who'd stopped moving.

"It's too late. But we can stop her from hurting anyone else."

Cory ran down the hall and out the front door, his mind awhirl from everything that had happened. *What was wrong with Marisol? She couldn't be possessed; people always died when a Shade entered them. Or did they? Maybe death didn't happen instantly. Maybe that's why she'd been sick and weak. It wasn't shock, it was the Shade taking her over.*

He remembered the tendrils poking at her mouth and nose when they'd found her. Had it infected her? He'd thought they'd destroyed it in time. Was she a full zombie now, or on her way to becoming one?

Will I have to kill her?

Did he have it in him to do it? If she was possessed, it seemed unavoidable. His stomach churned at the thought, even as he took the Town Hall steps two at a time.

He never saw her come around from behind the side of the cement-and-brick staircase.

Marisol's shoulder hit him right in the ribs, sending him hard onto the sidewalk. His gun flew from his hand, went spinning across the concrete path. Fire filled his chest as he fought to breathe. She appeared over him, her face deathly gray in the glow of the streetlights. The same lights turned the arcing waters of the Fireman's Memorial Fountain into a silver sculpture behind her.

Footsteps pounded down the cement and Marisol looked up and away for a moment. Taking advantage of her distraction, Cory rolled away, each movement sending fresh agony through his right side, along with a grinding feeling that let him know he'd cracked or broken at least one rib.

He got to his knees just as Todd and John reached them.

"What do we do?" Todd asked.

Cory was about to say he had no idea, when cool moisture drifted across the back of his neck.

And he had a sudden, desperate idea.

"Todd! The fountain. Bless the water!"

Without hesitation, Todd ran to the fountain and dipped his hand into it.

"O Lord, hear my prayer, and pour forth your blessing. May this water be endowed with your grace and serve to cast out demons and banish disease. May everything that this water touches be delivered from all that is unclean and hurtful; through your Holy name. Amen."

As he finished the prayer, Todd pulled a Communion wafer from his pocket and dropped it into the water.

Although he felt weaker than he ever had in his adult life, Cory summoned his last bit of strength and charged Marisol, who was making her way towards Todd. He hit her right in the back and landed on top of her, unable to hold back a scream as something else snapped inside him.

"Help!" he shouted, and then John was right there, grabbing his arm.

"Not..me. Marisol. Into the fountain," Cory gasped. He took one of Marisol's arms and started to pull her up. John did the same on her other side. She kicked and growled and whipped her body back and forth but they hung on and dragged her towards the water. Todd joined them, grabbing one of her legs and holding it off the ground.

At the edge of the fountain they didn't hesitate. As one, they swung her forward and into the water, so the top half of her was submerged. Cory immediately climbed in and pinned her head below the surface.

"You're killing her!" John cried.

"I have to." Cory put all his weight into it, fighting against her struggles and the slimy cement of the fountain's bottom. After a minute, her thrashing slowed and then stopped.

Still he held her under.

Then it came - flashes of white light burst from her eyes and mouth as the thing inside her succumbed to the Holy water.

Praying it wasn't too late, Cory lifted her from the fountain and laid her on the sidewalk.

"Breathe dammit!" he said, giving her chest a strong push. He repeated the motion several more times and then paused just long enough to draw a lungful of air and exhale it into her mouth. Then he resumed CPR compressions.

"It's not working," Todd said.

It has to work. C'mon, Marisol, breathe!

On the fifth cycle, just when Cory thought he might pass out from his exertions, Marisol's body jerked under his.

Cory tilted her head to one side.

There was a pause - the longest pause of his life.

Then she gasped and coughed out a mouthful of water.

Chapter 10

Cory looked at his watch and stood up.

"Sorry fellas, I have to get going."

Across the table, Todd gave him a big grin and nodded, and John's lips twitched in his version of a smile.

"We're still on for Friday, right?" Todd asked.

"Eight o'clock sharp at the bowling alley. I'll see you then." Cory grabbed his jacket and headed out to his car.

On the ride home, he was surprised to see a few of the leaves were already starting to change.

Fall's coming early this year. Wonder if it's because of the extra-hot summer we had.

As he opened the front door, he was greeted by the enticing combination of Marisol's soft lips and the intoxicating odors of garlic bread, baked chicken and fresh string beans.

"Mmm, now that's the kind of greeting a man likes when he comes home from work."

"Work?" Marisol gave a sarcastic laugh. "You call bullshitting with Todd and John work?"

"Hey, that's not all we did! I also finalized all the bank transfers for Todd. His mother's estate is officially settled."

"Well, as long as it was work..." she gave him a wink. "Why don't you grab a glass of wine and relax. Dinner'll be ready in about fifteen."

"Sounds good." As he headed into the dining room, he heard her say 'Pour me one too.'

Opening the bottle of wine as he savored the lingering feel of her lips on his, Cory smiled to himself. Two months of living together and things were still wonderful. After everything they'd been through over the summer, it was like being in heaven. John and Todd had found work, he'd set up his practice in town, and Marisol had her job back. They'd even begun discussing marriage.

How could life get any better?

Wine glass in hand, he went into the living room and turned on the TV. Time enough to catch the last inning of the Mets.

Maybe things can get better. Maybe they'll win for once.

In the kitchen, Marisol was stirring the sauce when movement by the back door caught her eye. She pulled the curtain aside, revealing a dark gray shape with fiery red eyes.

With a welcoming smile, she opened the door.

The End

Printed in Australia
AUOC02n0732140314
260235AU00001B/3/P